FIRST TASTE OF LOVE

Cayenne hesitated, afraid of the way Maverick looked down at her as if he wanted her, wanted her bad. *You've got to say whatever it will take,* she thought. *Papa Joe and the kids need you.*

Her desperation made her more bold than she could ever have imagined. "I need to get home, Maverick." She paused. "Suppose I offered to pay you with my . . . body?"

The big cowboy threw his head back and laughed.

Cayenne was enraged. "You don't think I've got anything to offer?!" Before the startled trail boss could move, she flung her arms around his neck, kissing him awkwardly.

For a moment he stiffened, then his arms went around her. "No, Cee Cee," he said softly. "Here's the way it's done."

Then he lifted her off her feet, kissing her expertly and thoroughly in a way that both excited her and scared her. Her toes were off the ground so she could only cling to him, breathless at the way his mouth dominated hers, the hot, sweet taste of his lips. She gasped and closed her eyes, dizzy with the sensation. His wide chest was hard against her flesh and she could feel the heat of his lean body all the way down her legs through her thin dress. . . .

COMANCHE COWBOY

Georgina Gentry

Zebra Books
Kensington Publishing Corp.

http://www.zebrabooks.com

ZEBRA BOOKS are published by

Kensington Publishing Corp.
850 Third Avenue
New York, NY 10022

Copyright © 1988 by Georgina Gentry

Zebra and the Z logo Reg. U.S. Pat. & TM Off.

First Printing: September, 1988
10 9 8 7 6 5 4 3 2

Printed in the United States of America

Dedicated with deep love and affection to: Uncle Sam and Auntie Mama; mi madre de criaza, (the mother who brought me up)

Oh, dear Auntie Mama! To think you will never read my dedication! I ache as I think of all the many chances I passed up to say words of love and appreciation to you. But I intended to say words of love and appreciation to you. But I intended to do something very grand and impressive like a book dedication so I waited. We both ran out of time. You died so suddenly and unexpectedly just before this book went to press. For the words unsaid and dedication unread, it is my personal agony that it is now forever too late. . . .

Prologue

It would go down in history as the Red River Indian Uprising of 1874–75. But it was really a final battle between encroaching white civilization and the way of life of the Southern Plains tribes.

This war spread across the prairie like a great out-of-control range fire, bringing terror to isolated settlers, cavalry, and luckless travelers. In many a lonesome place, only the coyotes heard those screams of the tortured and dying that drifted on relentless winds.

Most Cheyenne, Comanche, some Arapaho, and eventually the Kiowa would take up arms during the late spring of 1874 against white hunters slaughtering the great herds of buffalo. Only the Kiowa-Apache declined to ride the war trail. Others smeared themselves with scarlet paint, danced the scalp dances, and fanned out across the plains to leave death and destruction in their wake.

The Red River Uprising would ultimately become the biggest campaign in our young country's history when President Grant ordered the army to move against thousands of the best and bravest of the warriors. For the space of twelve months, Kansas, the Indian Territory, and western Texas echoed the solemn prophecy: "There is no Sunday west of St. Louis—no God west of Fort Smith."

Yet today almost no one remembers either this great, bloody outbreak or the names of the battles and the battlegrounds: Adobe Walls, Buffalo Wallow, Lost Valley, Palo Duro Canyon.

But the names of the combatants will live in western mythology forever: Bat Masterson, Colonel Ranald Mackenzie, greatest Indian fighter of them all, and Quanah Parker, the young half-breed leader of the uprising. Quanah's mother was a captive white girl who became a Texas legend. But Quanah, last chief of the Comanche, chose his Indian heritage as the path that he would walk. As part of his destiny he would cross the trail of another half-breed Comanche who hated his Indian blood and had elected to follow the path of the whites—Maverick Durango.

The Civil War had ended and the North was hungry for Texas beef. So to the east of the Indian trouble, Lone Star cowboys drove cattle up the Chisholm Trail to railheads in Kansas. The cow towns were notorious: Abilene, Newton, Ellsworth, Wichita. Soon Dodge City would write its own tale of blood and bullets.

Now in the early summer of the year of the Red River Uprising, a big herd came up from the Texas Hill Country. That tough trail boss of the giant Triple D ranch, Maverick Durango, was glad to have made it through the Indian Territory without crossing any war party's path.

A "Maverick" is an orphaned calf that carries no man's brand; it was even more descriptive considering that the half-breed ramrod had chosen the name himself. He was a handsome *hombre*, with tragic eyes gray as the gun barrel of the Colt strapped low on his hip. A white knife scar down his dark cheek added to

8

his menacing appearance, making other men greatly fear his wrath. But women yearned for his caress and sought to reach his lonely heart.

No one could say they knew him well, not even old Don Durango who had adopted him or Trace himself who had taught Maverick to handle a gun. Nevertheless, it was whispered about Maverick that he never forgot a friend . . . nor forgave an enemy. His hatred of the Comanche was legendary, although none knew why or dared to ask. Still, there was a white man he hated even more. Wherever he went, Maverick searched for this *hombre*. Cowboys said that whatever the man had done to deserve such hostility, it was connected somehow to Maverick's mysterious past. All agreed a quick death was the most merciful thing the poor devil might hope for if the half-breed ever caught up with him.

Texans prefer their women the way they like their Mexican food—hot and spicy. So they favored a hot little pepper called Cayenne. If Maverick's name was descriptive of his personality, it was more so for the fiery girl. No wonder sparks flew when the troubled trail boss tangled with the flame-haired, green-eyed Cayenne. Maverick only wanted to bed her, tame her . . . until he discovered he could use her, too, for his revenge. How was he to know she was desperate enough to use her innocence, her beauty, to lure him?

When cowboys tell the legend, they say it was *her trouble* and *his past* that started them on a journey right through the heart of the bloody plains war. As it has been told around the campfires ever since, the scorching summer of '74 turned into an adventure of love, loyalty, passion, vengeance, and bloodshed. . . .

Chapter One

Wichita, Kansas. Late June, 1874

This called for drastic action. Cayenne paused in the middle of the dusty street to study the scrawling handwriting of the letter she'd just opened.

Wrinkling her freckled nose unconsciously, she re-read the plea, thinking tenderly about Papa. It wasn't fair that she always had to shoulder every family crisis and problem just because she was the oldest. *But if not her, who? And if she went back, just what could she do about it?*

Cayenne stroked a wisp of red hair out of her eyes, squinted, and looked up and down the deserted street. In the late afternoon heat, only a sleepy hound ambled by. Even the horses tied to the hitching rail in front of the Red Garter Saloon across the river bridge seemed to doze, while inside their owners gambled and cleared their throats of trail dust.

Curious, she looked up at the second-story windows above the saloon. One of the lace curtains moved slightly. *Was it only the breeze? Or was someone watching her?* The prying of some dancing girl was the least of her worries right now. Cayenne stuffed the letter into the pocket of the green cotton dress and

11

tried to decide how to proceed.

My stars, Cayenne, she thought a little desperately as she looked around, *you can't handle this alone. Just what are you going to do?*

Old Mr. Winston limped out of his general store, stirring the dust up on the wooden sidewalk with a ragged broom. "Afternoon, ma'am," he nodded. "Sorry the job only lasted three months, but we did tell you it was only temporary 'til our schoolmaster got back from seein' about his sick Ma. . . ."

"I couldn't have stayed anyway." She ran her tongue across the dust on her lips. "Something's come up, a . . . family problem. I've got to get back to west Texas soon as I can."

Maybe Mr. Winston could suggest someone. She squared her small shoulders, lifted her hem to keep it out of the dust, and strode over to face him. Off-key music from the saloons across the Arkansas drifted on the sweltering air. "Now that Aunt Ella's died, I've got no reason to be in Kansas anyhow." Cayenne felt the crumpled letter in her pocket. "Mr. Winston, I— I'm in need of a special man, a man who can handle himself with his fists or in a gunfight." She hesitated at the look of shock and curiosity on his wrinkled face. "Now where do you suppose I'd find a man like that?"

"A gunfighter?" He paused, leaning on his broom. "I suppose you're funnin' me, ain't you, miss? A lady like you shouldn't be gettin' mixed up with trash and saddle tramps."

"Now that's for me to decide, isn't it?" She fixed him with a calm green gaze. "Would you know someone like that?"

"Lord, no! Hope I never do!" His rheumy eyes were wide with curiosity. "If you're in some kind of trouble, ma'am, the sheriff'll be back in town in a

12

couple of days. . . ."

"But he wouldn't have any jurisdiction anyway down in Texas and this is a . . . private matter." *Now just why hadn't Papa Joe called in the law himself? There was more to this than met the eye.*

A woman's raucous laughter floated through the batwing doors of the Red Garter. The shopkeeper frowned and gestured with his broom. "That's where the trail herds come in, where the gamblers and such hang out. That why we keep that street of iniquity across the river, away from decent folks! And that Red Garter is the worst!"

She turned, looking up again at the distant upstairs windows, unable to shake the feeling that she was being watched.

Maverick Durango looked out at the pretty fiery-haired girl through the lace curtain in Goodtime Molly's room. Without thinking, he whistled low.

The pretty whore sitting on the bed laughed as she paused in unbuttoning her yellow satin dress. "That whistle of appreciation for me, cowboy?" she laughed. "I know you been a long time on the trail, but just hold your horses 'til I get my clothes off! I'll fix you a drink. Bourbon and branch, same as always?"

He turned to accept the smudged glass and sipped the raw, cheap whiskey. Up until he'd looked out the window, Goodtime Molly had seemed exciting and desirable. Now he frowned at her with eyes as gray as the barrel of the Colt strapped low on his hip. The whore was not as pretty as she'd once been, even though she had magnificent hair. But her hair was dark, not red.

Maverick peered out at the girl in the street. The hot breeze brought him a light scent he couldn't quite identify. *Sugar cookies? No, not quite that either.* Whatever it was, he liked it. He took a deep breath as he leaned against the window and sipped the whiskey and water.

"Molly, come take a look," he muttered. "Who's that girl standing just across the bridge?"

The smile faded on her painted mouth as she sauntered over to the window, looked out, and snorted with derision. "Me and the new little schoolmarm don't exactly travel in the same social circles. Her name's Cayenne, never heard no last name. That's all I know about her." Molly's tone sounded cold, jealous. "You can get your sights off that one, you big Injun. I doubt she's even been kissed, much less—"

"Don't call me *Injun*, you hear me?" His dark-skinned hand reached out, grabbed her throat.

"Sure, Maverick, sure." Her painted eyes widened with fear as she shook his hand off her dirty neck. "Forgot how touchy you was about that Comanche blood. . . ."

"Sorry I was rough. I got no respect for any *hombre* who'd hurt a woman." He leaned against the window frame, looking down, studying the creamy-skinned girl standing in the middle of the dusty street. Her hair reflected the light like a prairie fire.

"Cayenne?" His Texas drawl turned it into *Kii' anne*. He thought about the cayenne peppers used in the fiery Mexican food around San Antone. "Wonder if her disposition matches her hair?"

Molly frowned down at the girl and back at him, her stained dress half open, revealing her dirty chemise. "That one couldn't satisfy you, Maverick honey. She probably ain't never had a man between her legs, wouldn't know what to do with one if she did!"

He took a good look at Molly. The whore must be

pushing forty and looked every day of it. The urge he'd had all these long weeks on the trail faded. As she leaned toward him, that mysterious scent on the breeze was overpowered by Molly's strong perfume. But even then he smelled the reek of men on her skin, wondered suddenly how many had already taken Molly today. He turned away from her and back to the window.

Probably ain't never had a man between her legs. He had a sudden vision of the redhead's long, silken legs wrapped around his dark, hard-driving hips. He imagined her warm and yielding in his arms, the soft mouth opening to his probing tongue. *I'd like to be the one to teach her. That one wouldn't take on a man for money. No, not that one.* He hadn't known many women like that.

Absently he ran his finger down the white knife scar on his high-boned cheek while he admired the pert girl in the green dress in the street. She turned and looked at him, her flame-colored hair cascading around her small face. "Now there's a real lady," he nodded. "A *real* lady!"

The pretty whore swore under her breath. "By God, you want me or not, cowboy?" She pulled her dirty chemise down and thrust her big breasts at him provocatively. "I figured after all those weeks on the trail, you needed what I got to offer." Molly scowled. "Or you gonna keep lookin' out the window at Miss Purity?"

His calloused hand reached out and cupped the whore's sweating breast, wondering how many men's mouths had tasted those nipples. The noise of laughter, music, and whirling roulette wheels drifted through the closed door. All these weeks on the cattle drive from Texas, his body aching for the relief of a woman, and now . . .

15

"Here, Molly." He reached in his vest, took out two silver dollars, and stuffed them in the front of her soiled lace underwear, smiling at the way she started at the touch of the cold metal. "I've just changed my mind, but I wouldn't want you telling everyone the trail boss of the Triple D didn't pay for taking up your time."

She put her hands on her hips and looked over his tall frame. "Aw, come on, Maverick, don't disappoint me! I ain't had such a stud since you was in town last year." She reached up and put her arms around his neck.

But he turned his face away from her smeared painted mouth, recoiling from the rank scent of dirt and men's seed on her sweating body in spite of the strong perfume. "Maybe next time, Molly. The crew's waitin' for me to get back. I've made the deal, just waiting for the bank to finish the paperwork."

She rubbed her breasts against his wide chest. "Come on, you sweet half-breed," she purred. "You know how to make a woman like it! Every trail drive I look forward to you gettin' here. Tell you what, I'll even give you your money back. Quick and free, how's that?"

"Sorry, Molly," he laughed easily as he picked up his hat and brushed back his straight black hair. The boys'll be wonderin' what happened to me. Shouldn't even have stopped for a quick drink."

The ache in his groin intensified and he was tempted to take Molly up on her offer. He wouldn't even undress for a quick one. With his eyes shut, could he imagine the cheap whore was that small redhead?

Never even been kissed. He felt abruptly annoyed and angry with the sassy girl for disrupting his thoughts. Molly had looked as tasty as sugar candy

16

when he'd first entered her room. Damn that little schoolteacher anyhow!

But the whore came back to the window, looking down through the torn lace curtain. "Miss Innocent keeps lookin' over here like she's seen us, like she might be thinking of coming in the saloon."

He shook his head, set his glass down, and began rebuttoning the shirt he'd been taking off at the moment he'd seen the flame-haired beauty from the window. "Naw. That kind don't come in saloons."

He watched the girl march over to the old storekeeper. "Feisty as a fox terrier," he muttered, liking the way her fiery hair bounced on her neck as she walked. The slim teacher paused again, looked his direction. *Her eyes were probably green like her dress. No, green like new spring pasture, like shimmering dragonfly wings . . .*

Molly said something and he started. He had forgotten she was even in the room. But one thing was certain: He'd completely lost his appetite for the pretty whore.

Molly sauntered over to her mirror, checking her dark hair as she always did. "Do I look older to you, Maverick?" She searched, found one gray hair, and pulled it.

"No, Molly," he said automatically, because he knew what she wanted to hear although he knew she lied about her age. She did have a magnificent mane of ebony hair, he thought. But truth was, her mileage was starting to show. In another five years her wrinkles would deepen until her face looked like a rutted country road. "You're pretty, just like always. Quit lookin' for gray hairs."

"You didn't say nothin' about my new combs." She preened before the cracked mirror, readjusting the pearl combs in her dark locks. "I got an admirer

17

who's sweet on me, wants to marry me. He had these sent all the way from St. Joe."

"Uh huh." He wasn't really listening or looking at her. *Feisty as a fox terrier.* The redhead walked through his mind. "I think I better get back to my crew." Maverick buttoned most of his shirt before his hand reached for reassurance to his holster and the loop of rawhide hung on his gun belt. "Keep the money," he said. "There's other men downstairs waitin' for you to show 'em a good time."

"Well, I got to make a livin'," she huffed, rearranging her dress and buttoning it. "There's only been one other man besides you I'd have left this life for, but that was almost twenty-five years ago when I was as young and innocent as that redhead. . . ." Her voice trailed off, and then she glared at him. "But the fact I'm loco over you don't mean nothin' to you. No woman means nothin' to you. Someday, Maverick, some woman's gonna cause you heartache. I hope I live to see it."

"Don't bet on it," he snapped. *Some woman already had. But not in the way Molly thought.* Maverick frowned and shook his head, the old guilt coming back. It never quite left him, really, always burning like a slow fire in his soul.

She adjusted her corset and looked at him thoughtfully. "I wish I knew what makes you tick, handsome. What the key is to your dark, brooding heart."

He winked at her, laughing a little too lightly. "They say I never forget a friend and I never, never forgive an enemy."

The whore shook her head. "It's the Injun in you, I reckon. Jesus! I hope you never get a grudge against me! I bet if you was after a man, you'd keep lookin' no matter what." She brushed wisps of hair back and caught them up with the fine combs.

How had she stumbled on that bit of truth?

"You'll never know how right you are, Molly," he muttered, thinking about Joe McBride. *More than ten years. But he'd keep looking if it took a lifetime.*

A frown crossed his rugged, dark face. Someday he would find that man. Maverick intended to kill him slowly, painfully. Very slowly and painfully as only a man raised by the Comanche knew how. The Kentuckian would beg for the mercy of death before the trail boss finished with him.

Molly gave him a long look. "You're a hard man, Maverick Durango. I almost feel sorry for the poor devil, whoever he is."

"Don't," he shrugged, reaching for the doorknob. "He was mean, low-down—"

"Naw, I knew the meanest, rottenest man in the world—Bill Slade."

Maverick frowned. "But if you knew what this bastard did—"

"Must have been over a woman." She sauntered over to the bureau, picked up her drink, and sipped it.

He kept his face a cold, hard mask. "What makes you think so?"

Molly smiled knowingly. "No man hates another that passionately over money or cattle. Naw, it had to be a woman. Was she pretty?"

Only when she smiled, he thought, and winced at the memory of Annie's delicate features. *Only when she smiled.*

Downstairs, the off-key piano tinkled out a new song and the melody drifted up the rickety stairs: . . . *Maxwell's braes are bonnie, where early falls the dew, and that's where Annie Laurie gave me her promise true. . . .*

The old anguish hit Maverick, twisting his gut in real pain. His dark hand turned white as he gripped the doorknob.

"What's the matter, half-breed? You hurt?" Her voice sounded half curious, half sympathetic.

"No, I—I'm all right," he muttered, straightening his broad shoulders. He opened the door.

She sneered, her jealous laughter carrying across the plaintive notes floating up the rickety stairs. "I hope some pretty thing does hurt you, you big stud! You think I don't know why you changed your mind just now?" She stood, arms akimbo. "But if you think you'll get a chance to play the stallion to that little sorrel filly, you'd best forget it! I hear she has some reason to hate Comanches. . . ."

"Not as much as I do," Maverick muttered, his hand going unconsciously to the jagged knife scar on his rugged cheek. "Not half as much as I do!"

Cayenne looked again at the window and turned back to the old shopkeeper. "I guess I'll just have to try the Red Garter." She took a deep breath, lifted her green skirts, and marched down the dusty street, across the wooden bridge with her bustle swaying and her red hair bouncing.

"But, ma'am, a lady can't go in there!" Mr. Winston's voice wailed in indignation.

"You just watch me!" she flung back over her shoulder. "Don't ever tell a Texan gal what she can or can't do!"

But in spite of her brave words, she paused by the hitching rail, listening to the loud laughter and plaintive music from inside the saloon. Never in her nineteen years had she entered a place like that. There were only two kinds of women on the western frontier and her kind stayed in their own territory of homes, schools, and church.

A big gray stallion at the hitching rail whinnied and

she reached out to pat its velvet nose, glancing at the brand on its hip. *The Triple D*, she thought, *that big ranching empire in the Texas Hill country of Austin and San Antone, a long way east of her father's Lazy M spread.*

"Nice boy," she patted the silky muzzle, staring curiously at the unusual bridle. It really wasn't a bridle at all, just a rawhide thong twisted around its lower jaw, Indian style. *My stars, what is that hairy thing hanging from the bridle? No, it couldn't be. . . . Or could it?*

She looked back at the shopkeeper. He frowned in obvious disapproval. A man sang drunkenly from inside the saloon. One of the horses tied to the rail stamped its feet, stirring up dust and a buzzing fly.

Cayenne licked her lips nervously as she paused at the saloon doors, listening.

. . . and that's where Annie Laurie gave me her promise true. Gave me her promise true, that ne'er forgot will be . . .

She smiled, thinking fondly of her father. The thought of him steeled her wavering resolve. She had to go in even though she had no idea what one paid a gunfighter. All she'd managed to save from her salary was eighteen dollars and twenty-five cents. Could she hire the kind of man she needed for that? No man would risk his life for that amount of money. What else did she have to offer?

Cayenne quavered before the saloon doors, whistling the old folk tune softly under her breath. Mr. Winston was probably right. The kind of cutthroats and trail trash inside this place couldn't be trusted. Eighteen dollars and twenty-five cents. Not nearly enough. She did have one thing she could trade for help, she thought reluctantly, one thing that might tempt some rough, virile man.

21

Oh, Lord, she couldn't do it. She half turned away, not liking the images that came to mind of some tough, dirty gunfighter running his hands over her skin, his hot, wet mouth covering hers.

Maybe the governor . . . No, don't you remember you thought of that first? she chided herself. *Your family supported the South. You can't expect any help from a damned Yankee carpetbagger government. Besides, if what you suspect is true . . .*

It wasn't fair that the oldest child always seemed to be the one to deal with all the problems. *But life wasn't always fair,* she reminded herself. Her four little sisters couldn't do anything, and Papa seemed to have reason not to. That left it all up to Cayenne. With a trembling hand, she pushed open the swinging doors and entered.

Gave me her promise true, that ne'er forgot will be . . .

It was dark and smoky inside and smelled of stale beer. For a long moment, as her eyes adjusted to the dimness of the interior, Cayenne paused. Painted, brash women sat familiarly on chair arms, rubbing against cardplayers. Tough, trail-weary men leaned on the bar, one foot on the brass rail.

. . . And for darlin' Annie Laurie, I'd lay me doon and dee . . .

The music stopped abruptly as the short player seemed to see her for the first time. The laughter and talk trailed off as curious people turned to look.

Cayenne smiled to hide her nervousness. "H—hello," she stammered.

A bald man came around from behind the bar. "Ma'am, I'm sorry, but I don't 'low no collecting for school bazaars and such. . . ."

"That's not why I'm here." She twisted her hands together, looking into the sea of curious faces. A

22

movement on the stairs caught her eye. A dark man, his shirt partially unbuttoned, had come halfway down, followed by a heavily painted woman. Cayenne blushed as she realized suddenly what they had been doing upstairs, that they might have been the eyes staring out at her.

The tall cowboy on the stairs looked at her a long moment. He might have been in his middle twenties, but his weathered features made it hard to tell. His eyes were as gray as a summer storm and a white knife scar marred his high cheekbone. "Ma'am," he drawled, and she recognized the accent of a fellow Texan, "you shouldn't be in a place like this." His low, authoritative voice sounded as if he were about to order her out of the Red Garter.

Cayenne stiffened, bringing her chin up stubbornly. "I expect I'll decide that," she snapped. "You see, I'm looking for a man."

A couple of the men nodded understandingly and the bald man wiped his hands on his grimy apron. "Oh, I see. Now, little lady, you tell us what your daddy looks like and if he's here havin' a drink. . . ."

"No," she flared, reluctantly taking her gaze off the dark cowboy and the leering woman behind him on the stairs. "I came looking for a man." The words tumbled out.

A drunken buffalo hunter at the bar gestured the bartender away. "Well, honey, will I do?" He swaggered over and put his hand on her shoulder while the others laughed. He was bearded and so filthy that he stank. Even his bright red shirt was stiff with grime and encrusted blood from his kills. Dark sweat stained beneath the arms of the Turkey-red cotton. Around his dirty neck he wore a beaded Indian necklace.

"Let go of me." Cayenne tried to pull away. "I

23

meant I'm trying to hire a man."

The bald man looked at the two of them uncertainly. "Now, Buck," he said, "you shouldn't—"

"Go to hell!" The giant hunter swayed a little, looking down at her. When he spoke again, she could smell stale whiskey on his sour breath. "Honey, I'm for hire. In fact, I'd gladly go with you for nothin'!"

The crowd laughed again as Cayenne tried to pull away.

"Get your hands off her!" The voice rang out like a pistol shot. The others stopped laughing, looking uncertainly at the virile man on the stairs, then at each other.

The bartender wiped sweat from his shiny head. "Buck, you better do like he says. I'd be afraid to cross Maverick if I was you. . . ."

"No Injun's gonna tell me what to do!" The drunk patted his holstered pistol, then pulled Cayenne into his embrace. "You wanted a man, honey. You got more man than you can handle right here!"

She slapped him hard as she struggled to keep his wet mouth off hers. Past his shoulder, she caught a blur of movement as the big half-breed moved as fast and silent as any warrior.

"I told you to get your hands off her! Don't you comprende, amigo?" Maverick grabbed the man by the shoulder, spinning him around. Cayenne stumbled backward.

The drunk went for his gun, and in that split second Maverick's dark hand reached for the strip of rawhide on his gunbelt, looping it over the man's head. As Cayenne watched helplessly, Maverick caught the man across the kidneys with a hard chop of his hand.

With a scream of pain, the buffalo hunter doubled up, went to his knees, and the Indian tightened the loop around the sunburned neck.

"By damn, I told you not to touch her, you piece of trash! That's a lady! Don't you know how to treat a lady? Then I'll show you!"

Cayenne put her hands over her mouth to keep from screaming. No man attempted to interfere or even moved except for the sobbing, struggling drunk and the half-breed tightening the rawhide around his neck.

"My stars!" she screamed. "You'll choke him to death! Don't kill him! Don't kill him!"

But she could see the bottled rage behind the gray eyes as he tightened the loop until it cut into the drunk's flesh. "Apologize to the lady," Maverick snarled between clenched teeth. "Apologize, or I'll kill you!"

Cayenne looked around in desperation. "Won't anyone help?"

The bartender shrugged helplessly. "Lady, you started all this!"

A gambler leaned over to the short piano player. "I'll give you odds he'll twist his head completely off!"

"What kind of animals are you all?" Cayenne scolded, and she ran over, pounding Maverick on the chest. "Don't kill him! You hear, don't kill him! He's just a drunk!"

Maverick's eyes widened at her spirited onslaught but he didn't turn loose, fending her off with one arm. The drunk gasped, trying vainly to get his fingers under the thong. "Lady," Maverick said, "it's you I was protecting! He'll apologize or I'll kill him!"

The drunk rolled his eyes at Cayenne as he struggled for breath.

"Dearie," the woman on the stairs laughed as Cayenne flew into the half-breed again, "if you was a

25

man, Maverick'd kill you for that!'"

But Cayenne was mad now, fighting mad. "Let him go! You hear me? Let him go!'"

Maverick held her off with one big hand. "By damn! I was tryin' to help you, ma'am!'"

He loosened the noose a little and the drunk gasped for air. "Sorry," he croaked, "didn't know she belonged to you. . . ."

Maverick jerked the thong off suddenly, putting it back on his belt. The drunk fell sobbing on his face.

Cayenne pulled free of Maverick's hand and readjusted her dress. "My stars! You were going to kill him. . . ."

"You started this, miss," Maverick growled, pushing his hat back as he looked down at her. "A girl like you has no business coming into a saloon! Now get out of here before some other stud decides to paw you!'"

Cayenne put her hands on her hips and looked up at him. "Now just who do you think you are, bossing me around like that? I came in here to hire a man. . . ."

Maverick took her arm and propelled her toward the swinging doors in spite of her resistance. "By damn, you are a peppery little thing, aren't you?'"

She stopped struggling as he dragged her outside into the sunlight because it suddenly occurred to her that she'd found just the kind of man she needed for this job.

"You'll do." She sized him up and down as he let go her arm. "But I've only got eighteen dollars and twenty-five cents."

He scowled at her and she realized suddenly why men seemed afraid of him. The scar down his left cheek gave him a menacing appearance and the way he wore his gun told her he knew how to use it.

"What? I don't know what you're talking about, miss," He patted the big stallion's nose affectionately and it whinnied softly.

She stared at the horse, the hairy object swinging from the bridle. "Is that . . . what I think it is?"

He looked at her with such a cold expression that she shivered despite the June heat. "What do you think it is?" he challenged.

Somehow she knew. *Oh, God, what kind of a man was this who'd kill a man to protect the honor of a woman he didn't even know? What kind of an uncivilized savage had a scalp tied to his bridle? The kind of man she needed for this dangerous task*, she thought desperately. "Never mind. What I'm trying to tell you is I came looking for a man to hire, a man like you."

He shrugged, patting the horse. "Whoa, Dust Devil. Take it easy, boy." To her he said, "Sorry, miss, old Don Durango needs me and I'm beholden to him."

"I'd pay more if I could," she said, "but that's all I've got."

He tipped his hat back, his expression a mixture of exasperation and amusement. "I told you I'm not for hire. Now you'll just have to find another handy man, errand boy, or whatever. By this time tomorrow, I expect to be headed back down to the Triple D if I don't end up in jail for havin' fun tonight." He took a deep breath. "Sugar cookies," he said. "No"—he leaned closer to her—"not quite sugar cookies, it's—"

"Vanilla," she flushed. "Papa says only hussies wear strong scent."

"Vanilla! I heard little country girls used it for perfume." He leaned closer, sniffed again. "Umm. I like that."

For a moment she thought he would put his face

right down into her hair, but then he seemed to remember and straightened up.

"I saw the way you handled yourself in there." Cayenne caught his arm, realizing how big and powerful he really was. He could have killed her with one hard blow when she foolishly attacked him in the Red Garter. "You're just the man I need for this job."

"No. N—ooo." He shook her hand off his arm. "No *comprende, Senorita?* What is this job you're tryin' to fill anyhow?"

He wouldn't ask if he weren't curious, if he weren't weakening. She was desperate enough to use her charm as a weapon. Cayenne looked up at him, lips slightly parted. "My papa's sick," she lied, "so I got to get back to our ranch right away."

He took a deep breath and smiled slightly. "So?"

The words came in a rush so that he couldn't stop her. "I need someone to escort me down across western Indian Territory to the Texas Panhandle and south from there."

He threw his head back and laughed. "Are you loco? Do I look like a complete fool? Everyone knows there's an Indian war just startin'! Ma'am, you're talking about a trip of hundreds of miles across dry, hostile country and dodgin' Indians all the way!"

"I'd heard there was a little trouble with the Southern Plains tribes. . . ."

"A little trouble!" He laughed again, reaching into his shirt for a small sack of tobacco and a paper. "Lady, there's thousands of Cheyenne, Arapaho, and Comanche on the warpath right where you're wantin' to ride through. It's touch and go whether the Kiowa will join up with them."

"But you just came from Texas. . . ."

"I came up the Chisholm Trail to the east of all the trouble. Even then, I was as nervous as a long-tailed cat in a room full of rocking chairs." He rolled a cigarette expertly with one hand.

"But I need to get home." She felt the crumpled letter in her pocket again for courage.

He stuck the cigarette in his mouth, striking a match with his thumbnail. "The army's launching the biggest campaign in history startin' soon. Besides, the country itself is dangerous, hostile, even if it weren't crawling with war parties."

"But you seemed so gallant. . . ."

"Gallant, but not loco." He took a deep puff, staring off into the little heat waves rising in the Kansas dust. "You know what Comanches would do with a pretty white girl like you?"

"How would you know? You're just trying to scare me!" she snapped.

He frowned and his gray eyes turned tragic, haunted. When he finally answered, it was a whisper of regret. "I know, that's all. They might not even kill you before they took that red hair to decorate a scalp shirt. And that's the least of it. . . ."

She leaned forward, listening. But he said no more. The only sound was the piano tinkling again inside the saloon, the stallion stamping its hooves.

Maverick took a deep drag, exhaling smoke as he looked down the line of weathered buildings. "I've got to go to the bank, then I'm headed back out to my trail herd just outside town."

He strode down the wooden sidewalk toward the bridge, spurs jingling. If nothing else, she was stubborn. She almost ran to keep up with him. "Look, I'm willing to chance it if you are. If you won't do it for money, would you do it just because you're a Texas gentleman?"

He stopped and took a deep drag, looking amused. "You just beat this gallant Texan on the chest for helping you before. I'm going back to the Triple D, miss, and stay there until this is over. I reckon you ought to stay right here in Wichita where it's safe 'til the cavalry gets the tribes back on the reservations."

Could she appeal to his patriotism?

"Would you do it for a fellow Confederate?" she asked desperately, "In memory of old Jeff Davis?"

"Why, you little Rebel!" he snorted with laughter as he inhaled smoke. "The Triple D supported Sam Houston when he tried to keep Texas in the Union!"

Her mouth dropped open, unbelieving. "A Yankee! A damned Yankee! You're an admirer of that rum-soaked old despot?"

"So much so, I intend to name my first son for that grand old gentleman!" He tossed away the cigarette and tipped his hat to her. "I think I'd better move on, miss, before this discussion goes any further. *Buenos dias.*"

"No, wait!" Cayenne was desperate enough for his help to even beg from a damned Yankee sympathizer. She had one last card to play, and if it didn't work, she didn't know what she would do. Very hesitantly, she put her hand on his arm, felt it tense, knew she affected him deeply. "If you won't do it for money, or because you're a Texan, or even for old Jeff Davis, just what could I offer to get you to escort me through the Uprising country?"

"What do you mean?" He half turned, looking down into her eyes. His smoldering expression betrayed how she affected him, even though she was innocent of men and their passions.

Cayenne hesitated, afraid of the way he looked down at her as if he wanted her, wanted her bad. *You've got to say whatever it will take*, she thought. *You've got to get home as fast as you can. Papa Joe and the kids need you.*

30

She cleared her throat, looking up at him. "Maverick, can I interest you in something else?"

She opened her lips and pressed herself against his arm so that he could feel the heat of her ripe body.

"Stop it!" he said softly. "You don't know how to play this kind of game."

His voice had an edge to it as if he'd been a long time without a woman, as if he were warning her. But his arm tensed in her grip.

"You think I don't know why you were upstairs with that girl?" she challenged. "You think I couldn't do that, too?"

"I think you're as innocent as a Sunday school." He tried to pull away from her but she held onto his arm.

Her desperation made her more bold than she could ever have imagined. "I need to get home, Maverick. Suppose I offered you something else to escort me across the Indian Territory? Suppose I offered to pay you with my . . . body?"

Chapter Two

She looked up at him expectantly, waiting for his reaction as his gray eyes widened.

The big cowboy threw back his head and laughed. "If you don't beat all! Rebel, you might ride safely through hostile country after all! Indians won't harm crazy people; they think the Great Spirit protects them!"

"You mean you're turning me down? After the way you looked at me?" She had never felt so crestfallen, so humiliated.

Maverick reached with his free hand to break her grip on his arm. "I'm sorry about your daddy, Rebel. . . ."

"Stop calling me that!" she almost screamed at him. "My name's Cayenne! Cayenne Carol! My little sisters call me Cee Cee!"

He hooked his thumbs in his gun belt. "All right, Cee Cee. I said I was sorry your old man's ailin', but you getting killed gettin' to his bedside won't help him none. When the cavalry corrals the tribes, you can get home then."

"You don't think I'm woman enough, is that it?" she flared. "You don't think I've got anything to offer! Or maybe you thought I was funnin' you!"

Before the startled cowboy could move, she threw her arms around his neck, kissing him awkwardly.

For a moment he stiffened, then his arms went around her. "No, Cee Cee," he said softly. "Here's the way it's done."

Then he lifted her off her feet, kissing her expertly and thoroughly in a way that both excited and scared her. Her toes were off the ground so she could only cling to him, breathless at the way his mouth dominated hers, the hot, whiskey taste of his lips. His wide chest was hard against her flesh and she could feel the heat of his lean body all the way down her legs through the thin dress. She gasped and closed her eyes, dizzy with the sensation. He smelled like salt and trail dust and sun-kissed prairies.

Then he plopped her back down on her feet, taking a deep, shuddering breath. "That'll teach you not to make a fool of yourself, miss."

Even though she tried to hold them back, tears started and made crooked trails down her face. "I guess I do look like a fool," she gulped, "but I needed your help bad enough to try."

He reached out with one calloused hand and caught the tear on her freckled cheek. "Reb, you're askin' for *mucho* trouble. Don't do that again. The next *hombre* might do more than kiss you."

She felt her face flame and shrugged his hand off. "Probably not. Obviously I don't make a tempting offer."

He gave her a long look and ran his finger along his mouth as if remembering. "It was tempting," he admitted very softly. "Very tempting." Maverick paused and sighed regretfully as if he were thinking it over, then shook his head. "Sorry, Cee Cee, I can't help you."

"You mean *won't*."

33

He gave her an easy smile, the smile of a man used to charming the ladies. "Okay, have it your way. Now I got a few minutes business at the bank and then I'll be leavin'. Good luck to you and maybe we'll meet again some time. *Adios.*"

With that, he strode off down the sidewalk, spurs jangling.

Cayenne stared after him, her fingers reaching for the crumpled letter in her pocket. He walked with an easy, graceful stride for such a big, wide-shouldered man. If there were anyone in Kansas who might get her safely through hostile country, she was convinced Maverick was that man. And he'd just turned her down. But he'd admitted he'd been tempted by her offer. If he'd taken her up on it, she wasn't sure what she would have done; tried to talk her way out of it once they were on the road, maybe.

Well, Papa Joe always said she was tenacious and stubborn. Once she got hold of an idea, Cayenne hung onto it like a bulldog pup sinking its teeth into a bone.

She'd follow the half-breed, that's what she'd do, plead with him some more. Maybe she could wear him down. After all, she couldn't see any other alternative. Cayenne fairly flew back to Aunt Ella's small rented house. The new renters were moving in next week and Cayenne had sold the cranky old lady's things to pay the funeral bill. All Cayenne had was a small satchel of personal belongings and her aunt's very second-rate horse.

Quickly she gathered up her things, changing into a boy's shirt and pants she usually wore riding at the Lazy M. Papa was a Kentuckian with old-fashioned Southern ideas about how ladies should dress. But ever since Mama had died, Cayenne had both taken her place and helped with the ranch chores, too. Very carefully she put her hair up on her head and pulled a western hat low over her green eyes.

Good. The gray stallion still stood tied to the hitching post in front of the saloon. She rode into the alley near the Red Garter and peeked around the corner to watch. She didn't have long to wait. Within a few minutes, she heard spurs jingling and the dark half-breed strode down the sidewalk. As she watched in disbelief, he untied the gray and stepped into the stirrup from the right side, Indian style. Cayenne tensed, waiting for Dust Devil to buck as Maverick swung up into the saddle. Everyone knew that only Indian ponies were accustomed to being mounted from the "off" side. But the stallion merely snorted a welcome and trotted off down the dusty street.

Cayenne watched the rider loping south until he was only a tiny dot on the flat horizon. Certainly she didn't want that bullheaded Yankee-lover to know he was being trailed until he was far enough out of town not to force her to return. With just a little more time to talk to him, surely she could wear him down.

Now she mounted up and followed at a brisk trot. The scorching sun sent little heat waves rising off the flat, sunbaked prairie. The afternoon was so hot that little trickles of perspiration ran down between her breasts. Cayenne saw a sudden image of Maverick's mouth, moving slowly down the cleft, his hot tongue licking, tasting the silky sheen of her skin. . . .

My stars, Cayenne! she started in sudden embarrassment. *Whatever made you think of that?* She ran the tip of her tongue across her lips, wondering if his dark skin would taste salty?

She was thirsty, that's all it was. Cayenne reached for the canteen hanging on the cantle. The water had a warm, stale taste to it.

Away ahead of her, the rider disappeared as he followed the slight dip of the landscape, reappearing as a tiny dot. Somewhere up there, he'd stop and then she'd catch up with him, plead her case again.

Cayenne looped the canteen back over the saddle horn and wiped her hand across her mouth, remembering the slight taste of whiskey, the heat of his mouth when he'd kissed her. *Her first kiss.*

On the far horizon, thunderheads built and piled atop each other like great gray piles of cotton. Cayenne sniffed the air, hoping for the promise of rain on the dry land. The breeze smelled of prairie grass, sunflowers. But the drought had shriveled the vegetation so that the grass rustled dryly. Then the wind shifted and she gasped at the stench. Dead buffalo. She smelled them even before she rode near the pile of rotting carcasses. Flies swarmed up from them as she passed and she tried not to look at the carnage. But she could only hold her breath so long.

The sweetish, decaying scent almost choked her when she had to take a breath. Dead buffalo, dozens of them. No, more likely hundreds. People coming in from the southwest areas the last few months had said there were so many that you could probably step from one of the dead beasts to the next, clear down into the Texas Panhandle without touching the ground once. As if anyone would want to.

Cayenne turned her face away from the carnage, the waste. All that the hunters were taking was the hides, leaving the meat to rot. And with the East in the throes of a depression, any man who'd learned to handle a rifle in the Civil War had bought himself a Sharps "Big Fifty" and headed for the Plains. There was good money in buffalo hides now that factories had found ways to process the tough leather.

Grimacing, she reined her horse around yet another

dead buffalo. Such a tragedy. If the hunters kept killing like they'd done the past several years, some folks said the big, stupid brutes would soon be wiped out. Cayenne shook her head skeptically, keeping her face turned away from the hapless bodies. Not likely. There was forty or fifty million of the buffalo roaming the prairie. The hunters surely couldn't kill them all.

But the Indians must believe it. That's why this plains war had broken out late in the spring. The hunters were even trespassing into Indian Territory while the government looked the other way. After all, buffalo hunters were citizens and taxpayers. Who cared about the Medicine Lodge Treaty of '67 that promised the land below the Arkansas to the tribal hunters? Besides, the Indians would never go meekly to reservations and stop their raiding until the buffalo were wiped out. Even though she had good reason to hate the Comanche, Cayenne sympathized with the Indians in their plight.

A pair of eagles drifted in circles above her, riding the wind currents. Their black shadows shaded her suddenly, and she put her hand up to shield her eyes, looking up admiringly. Eagles. Wild and free and fierce. The big male cried out sharply and his mate answered, wheeling toward him. The pair glided on the hot air, casting giant dark shadows on the dried grass and across her as she watched them. For a long moment, she envied the eagle and his mate. No, they must have problems, too, and Cayenne would just have to stay tied to the ground by gravity and learn to cope with whatever happened.

But, oh, to fly! It was such an impossible dream for mankind in spite of the hot air balloons inventors now pinned their hopes on.

Maverick. What had happened to Maverick? Frantically Cayenne stood up in her stirrups, scanning the horizon. In her disgust over the dead buffalo, her interest in the eagles still circling and shrieking above her, Cayenne had lost track of the man she followed.

Cayenne's muscles strained as she shaded her eyes with her hand, looking every direction. Nothing. She'd lost him. A few hundred yards up ahead was a creek; she could tell by the crooked line of willows and cottonwoods. That was the reason she couldn't see him. He'd ridden on past that as he traveled south, and the straggly trees blocked her view. Yes, that was it.

Standing in her stirrups, she looked in a complete circle. Nothing. Nothing but dead buffalo, buzzing flies, and the pair of eagles riding the air current above her. Never had she felt so suddenly alone, so frightened.

My stars! What had she done? She'd ridden out in haste without telling anyone where she was headed. Even the cowboy she trailed was unaware of her presence. If Indians got her this far from town, no one would hear her, help her. Worse than that, she'd heard of people lost on the vast and trackless prairie, people who were never seen again. And sometimes the lost ones they did find were blinded from the sun and crazed.

Loco. That's what the half-breed had said. *Gallant but not loco. She could go back. . . . No, she wasn't going to do that.* The man she needed was somewhere up ahead and she'd simply lost track of him. If she'd keep riding, pretty soon she'd spot him on the horizon again. *Or would she?*

The blistering wind seemed to howl at her now like the lonely lobo wolves that would come out when the sun went down. She must not think of that. The big cowboy was somewhere up ahead. She just had to find him, that's all. To bolster her own courage, she began to whistle Papa's favorite song very softly as she urged the bay forward: . . . *Maxwell's braes are bonnie, where early falls the dew* . . .

The sound of her own voice cheered her a little and she whistled more loudly as she rode. Everyone said she whistled as well as any man. Of course, like wearing pants, it wasn't a ladylike thing to do.

. . . *Gave me her promise true, that ne'er forgot will be* . . .

The grove was just up ahead now, she thought, whistling desperately to keep up her spirits while she dug her nails into her sweating palms. Just past that creek she'd see the silhouette of that tall, broad-shouldered man again.

. . . *And for bonnie Annie Laurie* . . .

She rode under the trees, squinting to see on past the creek, looking vainly for the comforting outline of the man she sought. *He wasn't out there! She didn't see him any place! Maybe he was just over the next rise. Maybe* . . .

That's when something dropped out of the tree above her, took her from her saddle as he fell with her to the ground, knocking her breathless.

Cayenne screamed in terror, struggling for her life as her face pressed into the dry sand. *Indians! Indians!*

As she fought her hat came off, tumbling her red hair down around her shoulders, and her attacker abruptly paused, chuckling softly. "Well, I'll be damned!"

He rolled her over, still sitting astraddle her slim waist. It was Maverick.

She sighed with abrupt relief, sure he could feel her heart still thudding against his thigh. "Oh, Lord, you scared me! I thought I was about to lose my scalp!"

But he made no attempt to move, still sitting astride

39

her small body. He tipped his hat back. "Cee Cee, you're lucky to be alive! I almost picked you off with my rifle before it occurred to me if there was a war party anywhere close, I didn't want to give away my position. You whistle like a man!"

She struggled a little, getting more annoyed by the minute. "Well, I'm not, as you can plainly see! How long ago did you spot me?"

He made no attempt to move, looking down at her in amusement. "The minute I left Wichita. Don't ever try to sneak up on a Comanche, Rebel."

Cayenne frowned with anger and distaste, remembering that she hated them. "Comanche! You're Comanche?"

For a moment, she thought he would deny it. The look that crossed his rugged features betrayed that he hated them as much as she did. *Did he have as much reason to?*

But instead of answering her question, he said, "I thought you were a drygulching *hombre* plannin' to rob me, not knowing I left the herd money with the bank."

She struggled again, his weight getting heavier by the minute. His thighs were warm, gripping her slim body so that they pressed into the sides of her breasts. "My stars! Do I look like a man?"

She didn't realize her shirt was partially opened until she followed his gaze, knowing he looked down at the soft curve of her breasts. She felt his manhood swell and grow hard against her body.

"No, Cee Cee, you sure don't. But from a distance and in men's clothes . . ." He took a deep breath, grinning. "Vanilla. If I hadn't been upwind from you, I'd have known you by your perfume."

Now that she wasn't frightened, she felt hot, tired, and angry. "Get off."

40

"What?"

He made no move to obey her, his gaze still on the open neck of her shirt. As she struggled, she gasped for breath, and he smiled as her breasts moved when she breathed.

"Dammit!" Cayenne lost her temper completely now. "You're supposed to be a gallant Texas gentleman! Get up!"

Now it was his turn to look annoyed, but he made no attempt to move. "Just what is it gonna take, miss, to get you to stop trailing after me like a lost calf?"

"I resent that!" She tried to pound on his thighs with her fists but his knees pinned her arms.

"Resent all you want!" He shrugged but he didn't move. "I've behaved like a gentleman almost as much as I can, Cee Cee. I'm just a man after all and you keep throwing yourself at me. . . ."

"Throwing myself?" She almost shouted, "Throwing myself! You just knocked me from my saddle, crawl all over me, and you say I was 'throwing myself'?"

The amusement left his face, and when he frowned, she realized suddenly how menacing that scar made him look. "I can't decide whether to pull your breeches down and spank you until there's red prints all over that nice little behind or show you what a man can do when he loses control."

"You wouldn't dare!" She was a little frightened now and not sure what he might do. After all, she had tried his patience and they were a long way from town.

"Don't push me, Reb," he whispered. "Don't ever push me!" His hand came down very slowly. One finger stroked along the open neck of her shirt.

"Stop that." She was both frightened and excited at the feel of his fingers stroking her bare skin. She was helpless, she realized suddenly. He could do whatever

41

he wanted to her and she wasn't big enough to stop him.

His fingers stroked the rise of her breasts. Did she want to stop him? Cayenne wouldn't even admit to herself how good it felt, that she had to fight her body to keep from arching up against the tips of his fingers.

"Maybe if I scared you enough, you'd stay in Wichita where you belong!"

His words snapped her out of the thrill that had gradually enveloped her emotions, and her temper got away from her. "They didn't name me Cayenne for nothing!" she said, and before he realized what she was up to, she turned her head and sank her teeth in his thigh right at the knee.

"By damn!" He jumped up, rubbing at his leg, looking down at her. "What're you tryin' to do? You bite like a coyote bitch!"

Cayenne scrambled to her feet. "It's all a damned Yankee sympathizer deserves," she sniffed, pushing the tumble of hair out of her eyes.

He attempted to pull his pants leg up to see the bite but the pants were too narrow.

Had she really hurt him? She felt sudden concern. "Here, let me look."

He brushed her away. "No, you've done enough damage. I swear, I knew it was gonna be a rotten day when I first got out of my bedroll. If you were a man—"

"I know, that saloon girl said you would have killed me already." Her curiosity got the best of her. "Is that girl good at what she does?"

"What?" He stopped and looked at her. "That's no question for a lady."

Cayenne came over, looking up at him with frank interest. "I'd still like to hire you."

"Haven't we been over this before just a couple of

hours ago back in town?"

She could tell by his expression that he was looking right down into the open neck of her shirt. She wore nothing beneath it. "I've offered eighteen dollars and twenty-five cents. That's almost a month's pay for a trail hand."

His expression changed to one of desire. His eyes turned smoky gray like campfire ashes shielding banked coals. She felt the color rise to her cheeks but she made no move to button her shirt.

"Lady," he murmured, "I'm the trail boss. I come higher than that."

Cayenne couldn't stop looking at his lips, remembering the taste of them, remembering the embrace of his powerful arms. Behind him thunderheads built on the horizon, the pair of eagles whirling and screaming above them in a sky the color of faded denim.

He looked up at them and his expression changed, as if he were remembering some other time, some other place. He whispered something she didn't understand.

"What?"

"Eagle's Flight," he said softly in English, still watching the majestic birds wheeling in lazy circles overhead. Then he shook his head abruptly, as if chasing away some memory that hurt too much, and looked back at her. "Just what in the world am I supposed to do with you now, Cayenne?"

Kiss me. The words came to her mind unbidden as she stood looking up at him. But she said, "I—I don't know. We're a long way from town. Maybe I could ride along with you and we'll talk about it?"

Kiss me, her heart said again, and he looked at her as if he'd heard it. The blood pounded so hard through her veins she wondered if she heard that, too. He moved close enough for her to feel the virile heat

43

radiated by his muscular body.

"Maverick," she whispered, her hand going up to cover her heaving breasts. "Maverick, I—"

She went into his arms then without realizing it, just because they opened for her, and her lips turned up to his as his mouth covered hers, demanding, dominating.

His tongue probed hotly between her lips as her head tilted backward, and his big hands burned through the thin fabric of her clothes as he pulled her hard against him.

Cayenne ran her hands around his neck into the open throat of his shirt. She couldn't stop herself from pressing against him all the way down their bodies, and she felt his hard manhood pulsating against her. She was both afraid and excited, and suddenly she trembled violently.

He held her out from him at arm's length, breathing heavily. "I—I must be loco! To even think about tumbling you in the grass like some cheap whore!"

She felt the blood rush to her face at her own unchecked, innocent passion. "Well, if we're going to be married anyhow—"

"What?" He looked at her blankly.

She gestured. "You know. Aren't you accepting my offer?"

"Now wait just a minute. No one said anything about marriage. . . ."

"My stars! I did, too!" She felt both humiliation and anger. No, maybe it was disappointment at the way he was backing off like a skittish wild mustang. "My papa doesn't have any sons, only five girls. He could use a son-in-law to take over and run the ranch."

Maverick looked bewildered and backed off. "Whoa now! You mean what you said back in

Wichita, you meant marriage?"

He sounded incredulous, which puzzled her. Of course she had meant marriage. She had a sudden vision of Papa's little country church all decorated with Blue Bonnets, scarlet Indian Blanket and Indian Paintbrush blooms.

She smiled at him, imagining him all dressed up, reaching out to her as she came down the aisle in white. "I come with a dowry," she said hopefully. "The Lazy M's a nice spread. Like I said, I've got four little sisters and no brothers to inherit it."

"I think we're back where we started," Maverick said wryly, reaching into his vest for cigarette "makins." "I don't need a ranch, Cayenne. Maybe you didn't understand. I'm the old Don's adopted son. I come in for a share of the Triple D."

The giant Triple D empire that spread across two counties, and she'd been trying to buy him with eighteen dollars or the dowry of her papa's modest ranch!

"I feel like a fool." She brushed her hair back and gestured helplessly. "I. . . . don't know what to say. You could have told me your last name was Durango."

He rolled a cigarette expertly one-handed. "Last names never seemed to have come up today, Miss—? Miss—?"

"McBride," she answered haughtily. "Cayenne Carol McBride. And I suppose now that you've let me completely humiliate myself, I'll just get my horse, ride back to Wichita, and try to find someone else. . . ."

"McBride," he said softly, the cigarette halfway to his lips. "McBride. A common-enough name, I reckon."

"I reckon," she agreed, leaning over to pick up her hat off the ground. "Why, do you know a McBride?"

45

His hand seemed to tremble as he stuck the cigarette between his lips. "No. I never met a man by that name." His tone seemed suddenly hostile, guarded. "The family's from Texas?"

She reached for the bay's reins. "You should know from my politics that we're not just Texans, we're Southerners."

He lit a match with his thumbnail and studied her with a searching look that made her uneasy. "Couldn't be," he murmured so softly, and she was not quite sure she caught the words.

"What did you say?" Cayenne watched him smoke and study her, as if really seeing her for the very first time. The storm clouds built even higher behind him, all silver gray and lavender. Above, the eagles flew up into the sun until they were only tiny black dots against the golden light.

"I guess I'll be heading back to town," she sighed regretfully when he didn't answer but just stared at her. She patted the bay's nose. "Papa Joe's going to be awfully disappointed when I don't get there."

"Say that again?" There was something about his expression that scared her. It was a mixture of shock—no, something worse; something dark and ugly.

He was only weary and put out with her, that was all. She supposed he couldn't be blamed for that. Cayenne had created problems for him. "I said Papa Joe would be disappointed—"

"Cayenne," he said very slowly, deliberately, "just where is your family from?"

She checked her stirrup, made ready to mount. "Kentucky. I told you Papa was a Southerner."

Maverick had gone loco from the heat. At least that was her first thought from the look on his face. She was even more startled by the way he threw his head back and laughed long and loud. "Well, I'll be damned!" he said. "I'll be damned! All these years lookin' and to think we almost passed and went our ways without knowing—"

"I don't understand," she shrugged. "Have you met my papa?"

She couldn't read his expression. "No," Maverick said, and he hesitated. "But maybe we had a mutual acquaintance once a long time ago."

"Oh?" Cayenne brightened. "Well, that's almost the same as knowing him! Isn't it a small world after all?"

He blew smoke like an angry dragon. "It's probably not even the same Joe McBride."

Cayenne felt sudden hope. "Maybe it is," she said, smiling. "Did your friend say Joe was a preacher? He's met a lot of men that way."

A look of regret crossed Maverick's dark face as he smoked. "My friend thought very highly of Joe McBride." Then her words seemed to sink in and the half-breed shook his head in apparent amazement. "Preacher? Your old man's a preacher?"

"Just when the circuit rider doesn't get there." She tied her horse to a bush and came over to Maverick.

"A preacher," he said to himself. "A preacher!" And then he laughed and laughed. "I never would have thought to look in a church!"

Cayenne reddened. "Don't you laugh at my papa! He's brave and good! Why, when the Comanche—"

No, she'd better not tell that. Maverick's relatives might have been involved that terrible time eight months ago.

He tossed away the cigarette with a deliberate gesture and came over to her. "Does your offer still hold?"

She blinked in confusion. "You mean, the eighteen

47

dollars and—"

"No," he said very coldly, "your body!"

"That's a crude way to put it, but if you're asking if I'd marry you to get escort home, why—"

"No, baby, that's not what you said, that's not what you offered me." Before she could say anything else, he grabbed her, pulling her into his embrace, and his hot mouth came down to cover hers.

For only a moment, she went stiff in his arms as he kissed her, as his hands ran up and down her back. Of course he was putting it badly; he meant marriage. After all, he'd been so gallant before and he and Papa shared a mutual friend.

But all she could think of was the taste of his mouth burning into hers as he caught her small face between his two big hands, holding her so she couldn't move. His tongue flicked along her lips, teasing, tantalizing.

Swinging her up in his arms, Maverick's gaze burned into hers with fire lust that left no doubt what he was thinking.

"Not—not here," she protested weakly. His chest heaved as he breathed deeply, looking down at her with an expression that confused her. *Was it passion? Anger? Hate?* But she'd done nothing to make him hate her with the cold steel glint she saw in his eyes.

"You made me a deal, remember? I want payment in advance!"

She hadn't expected this treatment from the gallant cowboy. Something had happened to change him. Cayenne felt his heart thudding against her breast as she swung there in his arms. His face moved lower, his breath warm against her bare skin as he moved to nuzzle her shirt open.

"Maverick, I—I don't know—"

"Don't tell me no," he commanded, carrying her with masterful strides to the grass in the shade of the trees. "Baby, don't tell me no! Not as bad as I want you!"

As big as he was, could she stop him if she tried? The eagles screamed again and her eyes flickered open, looked up. Maverick looked up, too.

The smaller eagle whirled so that her golden breast turned upward to the sky. As she plummeted toward the earth, the great male caught her claws in his, locked with her.

Cayenne watched the birds locked together, plummeting toward the earth. "What's happened?" She sat up in alarm. "They'll fall! They'll die!"

"No, they won't." He smiled mysteriously at her, and past his shoulder she saw the eagles suddenly part, flying up into the sun again. "Eagles mate in midair, in flight."

She looked from the majestic birds to his face, knowing what was coming even before he enveloped her in his arms and fumbled with the buttons of her shirt. And as his hot mouth came down to cover her breast, she gasped, arching up against the heat of his tongue on her nipple. "Oh, Maverick, Maverick! You shouldn't!"

But though her mind protested, her body pressed up against his heat, against his stroking hands.

"Love me, baby," he commanded. "Love me!"

"I don't know how!" She ran her hand inside his shirt, along his ropy muscles, hating herself for her ignorance. "I never—"

"Just relax and let it happen," he whispered against her ear. "Let it happen, baby, it was meant to be."

His tongue probed the innermost recesses of her ear, sending shivers of delight through her, and she moaned aloud.

"You like that? Beg me! Beg me for it!" His eyes were wild, angry, and she had a sudden feeling that he was being cruel, humiliating her. For a split second it almost seemed as if he hated her. *Why should he hate her?*

"I—I can't," she whispered, shamefaced as she turned her head. But he caught her face and turned her to look into his eyes.

"I'll make you want me that bad," he promised, "just like I want you!"

She felt him slip out of his pants, reaching to pull hers off and jerking her shirt open. Automatically, she tried to cover herself with her hands but he slapped them away. "You're beautiful! God, you're beautiful! You know that? Let me look at you before I take you!"

She tried to twist away but he caught her wrists, pinning them above her head so that her breasts arched up to his lips. Cayenne couldn't stop herself from moaning aloud as he sucked her nipples into erect pinkness.

Without thinking, she managed to free her hands and reached out to embrace him, clawing at his muscular back in her frenzy.

His hand went down to stroke between her thighs and she shuddered at the feel of his probing fingers. "Oh, baby, I never wanted a woman this bad before! You want me, I know you do! Say it!"

If she said it, would he end this need that was consuming her like a roaring fire? "Maverick, please!" she gasped. "I never felt like this before! I—I want you!"

"Then touch me," he commanded. Half frightened, she slid her hand down to hold the hot, throbbing maleness of him. Then drew back.

"Touch me, baby," he commanded, "as I touch you."

She touched him, sighing and spreading her thighs

farther, tilting herself up for the stroke of his fingers.

"You're so big, Maverick, I'm afraid—"

"Don't be," he said urgently, "don't be."

He moved between her thighs, probing with his searing maleness for her velvet place. "It may hurt a little the first time, baby, but don't fight me. Don't fight me. . . ."

Her urgent need was greater than her fear, and she tilted her hips up, digging her nails into his wide shoulders.

She felt him slip inside her, pushing against the thin silk of her virginity. She had a sudden vision of eagles locked in midair, and it was magnificent and passionate and beautiful.

She spread her thighs wide. "Take me," she gasped, "Oh, please!"

And then Maverick seemed to put all the power of his virile body into one hard stroke. His mouth came down to cover hers, his tongue plunging deep into her mouth as his maleness plunged into her depths. She cried out against his lips, but she was locked in his embrace, powerless as they meshed.

For a long moment, she felt she was being impaled by a fiery, throbbing sword against the ground. She struggled against the pain, which only seemed to excite him more.

"You're mine!" His lips kissed her face over and over in a strange fever of desire and fury. "You're mine now, baby! God! I never dreamed I could want a woman so much!"

And he began to ride her. There was no more pain, only desire. She felt her body answering his stroke, felt her hips tilting up to take him still deeper. In a frenzy, she dug her nails into his hips, trying to pull his throbbing blade into the very depth of her being. What it was she wanted she was too innocent to know, but she knew there was even more than this.

Any reluctance, any hesitance she'd felt was lost in her own hungry need. But a small portion of her brain warned her as she arched against him. The aura of civilization had faded and he was as primitive, as savage as his Comanche ancestors. Traveling with Maverick Durango could bring only regret, only trouble to her.

She wouldn't think of that now. She thought only of this moment, taking him deep within her, capturing this feeling that moved toward a crashing crescendo. Nothing mattered but eagles plummeting toward their destiny, locked in a dizzying fall!

Chapter Three

Maverick looked at the girl in his arms. Never had he felt such an urge for fulfillment. Any moment he would cry out with his driving need. "Wrap your legs around me, baby," he commanded fiercely as he kissed her.

She did so uncertainly, hesitantly. He felt his maleness pulsating deep within her warm body. He ought to love her gently, control his own wild desire. But she was Joe McBride's daughter, and for that, the flame-haired beauty must pay!

He began to ride her hard, relentlessly. She flinched away from him even as she dug her nails into his muscular back, whimpering in protest against his mouth. "Maverick," she gasped, "you're hurting me. . . ."

Vengeance made him cold, uncaring. *How often had he stood by and heard Annie whimper and cry out while he was helpless to stop the braves?*

The girl in his arms felt soft, sensual. Her creamy skin brushed like satin against his dark-bronzed length. He took a deep breath of the slight scent of vanilla. Never had a woman affected him so totally, made him want her so much. The virginal Cayenne had become part of his revenge. He would strike out

53

at his enemy by deflowering McBride's innocent daughter!

She gasped beneath him and Maverick felt fire consume him all the way down. He couldn't get deep enough into her warmth to satisfy his primitive urge, couldn't drive hard enough.

His intensity mounted as he rode her harder, deeper, faster. Beneath his big body, he felt her protesting, fighting, but she was powerless in his muscular arms. Somewhere on high, he dimly heard the eagles scream again. The man who had been the boy the Comanche called Eagle's Flight reached that summit of emotion and drove hard into the girl's velvet softness one last time. She arched herself against him and cried out. But his searing mouth muffled her sobs as his body shuddered and gave up its seed.

It seemed a long time that he drifted on the wind currents, spiraling and falling through emptiness like the great eagles mating in midair. When he gradually regained consciousness, he tasted the salt of the tears running down Cayenne's face.

He was almost contrite, apologetic. Then he remembered that Annie had cried, too, many times, while Pine da poi and the other warriors raped her. How often had the boy called Eagle's Flight wept and pounded his fists against the ground in helpless rage and frustration because he could not help her?

The vengeance had come full circle. And a circle to Plains Indians was a magic, mystical thing. Would Joe McBride's guts twist and would he swear in anguish when he heard that an Indian had despoiled his beloved daughter? *Not just any Indian; one particular half-breed Comanche.*

A preacher. What a joke; a preacher. But wasn't the safest hiding place for a wolf a flock of innocent lambs, all wrapped in a lambskin?

But now the girl beneath him clawed at him in fury. Maverick caught her hands to stop her from scratching bloody trails down his rugged face. "You rotten—! How could you?"

He had never raped a woman before, never hurt one. His memories had turned him into an avenging fury. "I—I'm sorry, Reb," he murmured, kissing the tears off her cheeks. "I hadn't had a woman in weeks, couldn't stop myself. I didn't mean to hurt you."

"I hate you!" She pushed at him furiously. "I'm going back to Wichita!"

Maverick slid off her, sat up. The telltale sign of her virginity smeared him. It had been a first for both of them—her first mating, his first virgin. All his women had been saloon whores. "I'm sorry I got rough," he said again. "Believe me, I never meant to."

Cayenne scrambled to her feet. "I never pictured my first time happening like this." She sounded saddened, regretful as she tried to cleanse herself and get dressed.

He watched her as he reached for his clothes. *No,* he thought, *for a girl like you it shouldn't have happened this way. There should have been a dress of antique lace and a preacher. Then a soft bed with white, perfumed sheets.* Maverick had destroyed that wedding night forever for her, along with her innocence, and for a moment he had never regretted anything so much. But he thought of Annie and hardened his heart. "By damn! I said I was sorry! I can't do anything about it now!"

She glared at him and her green eyes turned as hard, as cold as emeralds. "You bastard! I was feeling something very special for you and you treated me just like you'd treat one of the girls at the Red Garter!"

He grabbed her arm. "Cayenne—"

"Let go of me!" She jerked away from him and flounced over to her horse. "Believe me, I never threw myself at a man like this before, but I was so desperate to get home. . . ."

"Oh, is that all it is? You'd use that pretty body as a bribe! Well, baby, you'll get home!" Maverick caught her reins, holding his hands out to help her mount as any Texas cowboy would. "In some ways, you're no better than the girls at the Garter. At least I know what they'll charge! None of them ever accused Maverick Durango of not paying what she asked for her services! But that's a pretty high price, riding through Indian Territory!"

The girl ignored his hands and swung up on the bay unaided. But he saw hope flicker across her features. "I—I don't know. After the way you've treated me, I think I'll find someone else to escort me back to Texas!"

He couldn't let that happen. He needed her to lead him to Joe, so he swallowed his pride. "Cee Cee, I'm sorry about that. It just happened, that's all. You're too beautiful, too desirable." He had enough experience with women to know what she wanted to hear. Maverick looked up at her and unconsciously ran his finger down the jagged white scar on his high cheekbone.

That long-ago night, the boy called Eagle's Flight had dipped his fingers in Annie's scarlet blood, mingling it with his own that ran from the deep knife cut on his cheek. In anguish, he had made his terrible vow on Annie's still-warm body. He would get everyone who had hurt her, yes, get them all. He had sworn he would search forever if need be. When the halfbreed finally found Joe McBride, he would torture and slowly kill him as only a Comanche could. An eye for an eye and a tooth for a tooth.

Her face reflected her confusion, her uncertainty. "I don't know . . . maybe it was partly my fault. Expecting to be able to stop things after they got started is, I reckon, like stopping a snowball once it starts rolling downhill, gathering speed. . . ."

Maverick gave her his most contrite smile. "You're the most beautiful, desirable girl I've ever met." *Dammit*, he thought with annoyance, *it was true.*

He glanced up at the building thunderheads. "We'd better get out to the herd before that storm blows in."

Saying that, he caught Dust Devil's bridle, glancing at the scalp tied to it. *Pine da poi. Whip Owner.* In his memory, he saw the cruel, hatchet-faced Comanche raping Annie. He smiled as he remembered the frozen horror of that same face years later as Maverick garroted him slowly, deliberately. *Pine da poi. His own uncle.*

Maverick swung up on the stallion's right side, Indian fashion. Cayenne's expression showed uncertainty, hurt, anger. Not only might she not lead him home, what would he do if she went back to Wichita and got the sheriff? A jury of cowboys would go hard on a man who had forced himself on an innocent woman.

"Reb, believe me, I'm sorry." He gave her his most charming expression. *He'd gotten all four of the Comanche; now there was only Joe McBride.*

"I—I don't know." The girl seemed to be turning things over in her mind, and he had a sudden feeling that she was being driven by her own reasons, her own secrets. "All right," she said finally, "but from here on out, if you touch me again, I'll—I'll kill you!"

Maverick shrugged. "Fair enough, baby. I've got my pride, too. You'll have to make the first move next time!"

She snorted with contempt, shaking back her tou-

57

sled hair, and they loped out of the grove toward the herd grazing only a few miles farther south.

They rode a long time in silence. The sky looked like great folds of deep purple and black velvet spreading slowly across the sky. Thunder rumbled and echoed on the horizon.

Cayenne glanced over at him. "When I was little and afraid, Papa used to rock me when it thundered. He said someone he once knew said thunder was only God clearing his throat."

God clearing his throat. When he was a small boy, how often had his mother held him close in the middle of a storm, comforted him with those same words? He looked over at the flame-haired beauty. Somehow he had never imagined Joe McBride as a loving father, rocking a small daughter to sleep.

Maverick gritted his teeth, remembering. While the Texan rocked his little girl in the warmth of a comfortable ranch house, Annie and the child called Eagle's Flight had clung together through the rain. She dreamed of the day Joe McBride would ransom her from the Indians. Surely he would take the little half-breed boy, too, and raise him as his own son. But Joe never came. Never. He wondered suddenly what Cayenne's mother had been like, that second wife? Funny how things turned out. If Annie had never been carried off by the Comanche, taken to wife by a warrior named Blood Arrow, Maverick might have been Cayenne's brother instead of her lover.

Cayenne looked over at him. "What you thinking about? You're so quiet."

"About what you said about thunder," he lied. "The Indians believe the thunderbird brings the rain, its giant wings flapping makes the noise. But once I knew a white captive who said it was only God clear-

58

ing his throat."

She looked over at him as they rode along, her eyes alive with interest. "It's a common-enough tale, I reckon. Tell me about the captive."

If he looked at her, the anguish in his soul would surely show in his eyes. Maverick kept his gaze on the dusty trail ahead. "She waited for more than fourteen years for her husband to ransom her from the Comanche."

"And he never came? Never sent the ransom?"

Was it raining already? Then why had his vision suddenly blurred? "No, the rotten bastard never came. Probably didn't want a woman who'd been raped by half the braves in camp."

Blood Arrow had been killed in battle before his son was ever born, and his brother, Pine da poi, had inherited his captive woman. It was a Comanche custom for a brave to share his woman with his younger brothers. Sometimes when Pine da poi had been drinking, he'd share Annie with any man in camp who offered whiskey.

"That's the most terrible thing I ever heard," Cayenne frowned at him angrily. "Why didn't you help her escape?"

Maverick squeezed his eyes shut tight for a long moment, blinking away the horrible images. "I helped her escape," he muttered. "I helped her escape."

He felt rather than saw her piercing stare as he kept his gaze on the trail. "You loved her, didn't you?" she asked softly.

Only enough that I would have given my life to save hers and in the end . . . no, he wouldn't think about that. The memory hurt too much.

"*Si*, I loved her." He struggled to keep his voice flat, devoid of emotion. "I hate the *gringo* bastard who

59

cared so little for her. But she loved him; never gave up hope that someday he'd come. I hate him for all those days she wept and waited. And someday I'll find that man, kill him in the most painful way I can imagine!"

Her face paled and her mouth dropped open. "You don't mean that. Maverick, you're talking murder!"

"No, justice." He gritted his teeth, sorry he had opened up to her, told her too much.

Her expression told him that she didn't really believe him. The innocent girl could not comprehend such a crime. "But you helped her escape, so maybe you shouldn't hate him too much." Her voice was soft, sympathetic. "Papa says the Good Book says: 'Vengeance is mine, says the Lord, and we should forgive our enemies.'"

Maverick laughed softly, bitterly.

"It is hard to do, isn't it?" she admitted, a little shamefaced as he looked over at her. "I can't keep myself from hating Comanches because of—"

"Including half-breeds?" What reason did she have to hate Indians?

But she seemed lost in thought as she rode along, the thunder echoing occasionally. "I can't imagine that man abandoning a white woman to the savages. It's just too cruel, too horrible. Maybe he was dead and couldn't come."

He would have to be careful not to give himself away. Still, he couldn't let her words go unchallenged. "I don't think so. I think the rotten skunk had married again, maybe some rich woman."

"Oh, God, no man could be that cruel and cold-blooded!" she protested. "He'd better make peace with God or he'll roast in hell!"

That was exactly where he intended to send Joe McBride, Maverick thought with grim satisfaction.

60

Lightning crackled across the far horizon, lighting the shadowy lavender dusk. The thunder boomed again like phantom drums of long-dead warriors, echoing and reechoing across the purple clouds, the greenish twilight sky.

Cayenne looked over at him as they loped across the prairie. "I hope we make it before the sky opens!"

He only nodded, worried now about the great, restless herd of cattle back at camp.

A shadowy, unnatural darkness fell across them as they rode into the camp in silence. Foreboding gray clouds built into a great sky mountain.

"We made it, but there'll be a storm," he said uneasily. "Hope we can keep that herd quiet."

His *caudillo*, old Sanchez, rode out to meet them. Maverick smiled warmly at his second in command as the Mexican waved his hat with a crippled hand. *"Dios!* Boss! We thought maybe the Injuns got our *caporal!"*

Maverick glanced from the gray-haired, mustached rider over to the girl. "I was . . . detained," he said, reining up. "But I've made the sale. Don Durango will be pleased. And the cattle needed the rest and a chance to graze anyhow."

The gentle old Mexican nodded and looked at Cayenne, curiosity on his wrinkled face. *"Si*, that's right, *hombre*. And Trace said you'd make him proud."

Trace, the old Don's son, had been like an older brother, teaching Maverick to handle a pistol with the best of them. "Sanchez," he smiled, "this is Miss Cayenne Carol McBride."

"Buenos noches, Senorita." The old *vaquero* touched his battered hat with his disfigured right hand that was missing two fingers. Cowboys, particu-

61

larly ropers, often carried this mark of the trade, one of the hazards of getting their fingers caught in the lariat as the steer tightened it.

Cayenne smiled. *"Buenos noches to you, Senor."*

Maverick watched her, reminding himself that he intended to use her as part of his revenge. He must not think about how pretty she looked when she smiled, how her hair looked like the mane of a wild sorrel filly, how soft and yielding she'd been in his arms. . . .

He frowned at the curiosity in the old man's gaze. "Just as well we didn't try to move the herd this afternoon," Maverick snapped. "We wouldn't want to be strung out along the trail with a storm moving in."

"Si, boss. Looks like it'll be a bad 'un."

Maverick hooked his thumbs in his belt, watching the big herd moving restlessly in the distance. *Two thousand steers. If they ever panicked and started running . . .*

"Maybe it won't be as bad as it looks, Sanchez. But we won't take any chances. Have half the boys riding nighthawk while the others gets some rest. At dawn we'll take them on into the holding pens at Wichita."

The old Mexican pulled at his gray mustache, shaking his head as he looked up at the ominous sky. Behind him, the big herd of longhorns moved restlessly, sniffing the rain-scented air. "Don't like it, boss. If there's much lightning and thunder—"

"Let's not buy trouble," Maverick said sharply. "And we'd better get a bite to eat. It may be a long night!"

The hands were already gathered around the campfire for their evening meal and they stood up, smiling and doffing their hats gallantly as Maverick and the girl joined them.

"Amigos," Maverick said, "this is Cayenne. She's riding into Wichita with us in the morning."

"Howdy do, miss?"

"Glad to make your acquaintance, ma'am."

Somehow it annoyed Maverick the way the men fell over each other to find the girl a blanket to sit on, almost fighting with each other for the chance to bring her a plate of spicy beef stew from the fire. Cayenne smiled at them one and all and made charming conversation. *She looks like a queen with her court,* he thought with annoyance as he went over and got himself some stew, sourdough biscuits, and a cup of strong "Rio" coffee.

For a moment, as he watched his crew making fools of themselves, vying for her attention, he felt a pang of unaccustomed emotion. He'd once heard a cowboy describe that unpleasant feeling as "jealousy".

No, it couldn't be that, he shook his head, wolfing down the peppery beef and potatoes. He only wanted to use Cayenne to hurt Joe McBride; use her, break her heart, crush her spirit even as Annie had been hurt.

"You *hombres* better hit the blankets early," he drawled, reaching for his sack of tobacco. "I think it's going to be one hell of a night!"

A handsome cowboy protested. "Heck, Maverick, we've hardly gotten a chance to visit with the lady!"

Maverick rolled a cigarette with one hand. "Tom, there'll be plenty of ladies in Wichita tomorrow night to visit with once we get this herd in."

Besides, he thought as he lit the match with his thumbnail, *this one's mine and you'll never bed her.*

Hell, why should he care? He shook out the Lucifer, tossing it aside as he watched the men rise reluctantly and move away from the camp fire. If some hot-blooded young *hombre* managed to get in her blankets tonight, why should Maverick care?

He inhaled and watched her get up, come toward

63

him. The firelight reflected on her hair as she moved, and he remembered the warm scent of its silken strands entangled in his fingers.

He frowned as he stood. "Rebel, you'd better spread your blankets close to mine. . . ."

"I will not!" she flared, hands on hips. "I wouldn't dream of sleeping close to you, you damned Yankee sympathizer!"

"Suit yourself," he shrugged, watching her as he smoked. "Just remember, none of these men have had a woman in two months." *Except me*, he thought with grim satisfaction, looking her over, remembering the slight scent of vanilla, the taste of her pink nipples.

Her face reddened suddenly, as if she read his thoughts, because her hand went protectively to the front of her shirt. "I suppose you're right," she answered reluctantly. When she got her blankets, she came over and spread them only a few feet from his.

He watched her a long moment, then with a sigh went out to check with the nighthawks, with old Sanchez. "Everything okay, *compadre?*"

"*Sí.*" The Mexican pulled thoughtfully at his mustache. "I'll see to things before I take to my blanket for a few hours."

Maverick grunted, rolled a cigarette, and gave it to his old friend. "None of us will get much sleep, but we'd better try." He looked off into the lightning patchwork of the sky, sniffing the air as he rolled a "quirley" for himself. "Rain. It's gonna be a long night for tired cowboys."

The old man smiled with affection and cupped his hand to protect the flame as Maverick struck the match. They both lit up and smoked a long moment, feeling no need for conversation. Sanchez had been his very good friend since Maverick had almost gotten himself hanged for butchering a steer in Don Durango's pasture after he had run away from the Comanches forever.

"*Hombre*," he said softly, "how long we known each other?"

Sanchez shrugged. "Maybe ten years." He smiled as if he remembered that day, too.

Maverick watched the lightning cut across the black sky like broken shards of crystal, then the thunder roared and rumbled. "Are we good friends?"

The Mexican smiled gently as he smoked. "The best. You know that, Maverick. 'Long as I got a biscuit, you got half."

Maverick grinned at the compliment. Among the people of the great southwest, no one could pay another a higher compliment. Offering to share a last biscuit was an even deeper commitment than offering to give someone the shirt off your back.

He'd thought to confess his plot to the old man, now decided against it. He cared too much for the old Mexican to involve him in anything that might bring him trouble. "We'd better catch a little shuteye," he grumbled, sniffing the rain-ladened wind. "Unless this blows north of us, we'll be up soon enough."

They ground out their cigarettes and went back over to the campfire. Most of the cowboys were already asleep. Maverick looked over at the girl, then lay down with his head on his saddle, pulling his slicker over him. Half the crew was riding nighthawk, the other half sprawled around the fire in their blankets. Lightning flashed across the turbulent sky, and seconds later, thunder rolled and echoed.

He heard a nighthawk singing softly to the nervous cattle that stamped and bellowed, shifted and shoved. The sweet scent of rain came to him, along with the scent of drought-dried grass, steers. He took another breath. Vanilla. He tried not to smile to himself as he looked at her.

Cayenne lay wrapped in her blanket. Her breasts rose and fell gently as she breathed. Maverick studied the small form. What he'd really like to do would be slip over under her cover, hold her close, make love to her again.

By damn, she's got you thinking as loco as the crew, Maverick! With an angry gesture, he tipped his hat over his eyes and yawned. If any *hombres* got an idea about crawling in with her tonight . . . No, they'd gotten the message. She might as well have his initials burnt right across that sweet little bottom. He'd marked her with his seed, slipping into her warmth like a hot, hard branding iron. Maybe she'd turn up pregnant.

Maverick smiled to himself as he dozed. Somehow he liked the idea of her flat little belly swelling with his child. *Si*, it would add to his revenge. Just before he tortured Joe McBride, Maverick would tell him his daughter was disgraced, carrying the child of a half-breed Comanche. It would be a grim justice. But as he floated off to sleep, he saw Annie's big gray eyes in his mind and she smiled at him and shook her head. What was the gentle memory trying to tell him?

The loud crack of lightning brought him out of his blankets with a start. Even as he scrambled to his feet, he heard the thunder rumble and shake the night like the vibrations of a dozen giant thunderbirds swooping past.

"Hit leather, boys!" Maverick shouted. "I don't think the nighthawks can hold 'em!"

Men came up out of their blankets, grabbing for their hats as the big herd moved restlessly, milling, while little darts of fire played off the longhorns.

Cayenne ran over to him. "I can help! At home, Papa depends on me—"

"Hell, no!" He brushed her hand off as he turned toward the hobbled *remuda* of horses. "I got enough trouble without worrying about a girl getting caught in that herd!"

Even as he saddled the big gray, he saw the girl running with a bridle. By damn! When she got hold of an idea, she hung onto it as stubborn as a snapping turtle!

"No," he shouted at her. "Don't, Cayenne! The men can handle this!"

And then the fast-moving storm made a liar out of him. Even as he started to swing up into the saddle, lightning lit the blackness bright as Judgment Day. He smelled acrid sulphur, and thunder rolled and shook the ground as the startled longhorns bawled in terror and milled frantically.

"Get those saddles on, boy!" Maverick shouted, forgetting about the girl in the excitement. "If we can keep them milling—"

It was already too late for that. When the orange lightning fired the sky again, he saw the nighthawks on the outskirts, struggling to keep the steers milling. But in spite of all they could do, the cattle moved and stamped like a great, living wave. And then they began to run.

Maverick swore loudly as he dug spurs into the great gray. But Dust Devil, named for the small tornados that swirled often across the dusty prairie, needed no urging. The giant horse, pale as fog, lunged forward to race along the outer edge of the galloping herd.

"Stampede!" Maverick shouted over the roar of running cattle. "Stampede!"

There were only three words that made a Texan's

heart pound in terror, he thought grimly as he leaned over the big stallion's neck, urging him into a gallop. *Comanche. Prairie fire. Stampede.*

A man who had dealt with any of those three was not ashamed to admit his terror. "Stampede!" Maverick shouted again. He saw the crew strung out along the cattle's path, galloping into the darkness to overtake the running herd.

The rain came down hard suddenly, driving like needles against his face. He couldn't see but still he leaned forward, urging the gray on. Someone had to overtake the leaders, get them milling in a circle. And longhorns had a peculiar habit: They always milled to the right, Maverick remembered, the rain cold and wet on his sweating face. Since all cowboys knew that, they might use it to their advantage, pushing the herd toward confused milling. But the driving rain only terrified the galloping cattle more and they charged blindly onward.

The cattle might run for miles and go over those rock ledges along that little creek where he and Cayenne had stopped this afternoon, he thought with sudden alarm. He'd seen that happen before—cattle running blindly off a ledge, the leaders crushed and bellowing under the onrushing stampede. They had to stop the herd, get it milling!

Prairie dogs. The thought came to him as he galloped through the darkness, but he concentrated on the running herd and didn't look toward the ground, trying to push the thought from his mind. If there were prairie dog holes anywhere in his dark path, the gray might step in one, stumble, and go down with a broken leg. Maverick shuddered at the thought. He'd seen what was left of a cowboy whose horse had fallen before a maddened cattle herd. Thousands of sharp hooves and tons of running beef had crushed both man and gelding into one shapeless, indistinguishable mass.

He was out in front of the herd now, galloping along, firing his pistol, trying to turn the leaders.

He saw old Sanchez moving in from the other direction, firing his Colt, too. They weren't going to be able to stop them!

Lightning rent the sky and he saw Tom caught in the herd to one side, his paint horse carried along by the momentum. And Cayenne! Dammit! What was she doing out here? The light reflected off her fiery hair and he realized she was trying to work her way through the herd to reach Tom. Then Tom's paint stumbled and went down.

Maverick saw the cowboy's startled, terrified face in the flashing light, then horse and rider went under a brown wave of moving cattle. Without thinking, he said a prayer to his spirit animal, the eagle, although he knew it was too late for Tom. But they had the herd milling now!

It seemed a scene right out of hell, hooves flashing, the roaring thunder of cattle galloping, slowing, stumbling. He smelt the heat and stink of the herd, felt the cold rain driving against his face. The cattle slowed and began milling to the right the way longhorns always did. The night was as black as the devil's heart and Maverick might as well have been blind.

Cayenne! Where was Cayenne? He reined in sharply, causing the big gray to rear. The lightning cut a jagged path across the sky and he saw her caught now among the milling cattle, her frightened bay horse staggering and stumbling to stay on its feet.

He saw her pale lips form the word "Maverick," but if she cried out, he couldn't hear her over the thundering, milling cattle. The rain plastered her long hair against her as it did her shirt, outlining those small, proud breasts.

He would be risking death to fight his way through all those tons of beef. *His enemy's daughter.* His own shirt plastered wetly to his back as he urged his gallant mount forward. "Hang on, baby, I'm coming!"

The bay stumbled again and Cayenne grabbed the cantle to keep from falling. She turned her face toward him and her eyes reflected the terror she must feel as the cattle jostled and pushed.

Using his quirt, Maverick slashed a path through the longhorns toward her. "Hang on, Reb, I'm coming for you!"

He rode close enough to hear her call his name now. "Maverick! Hurry! I—I can't keep the bay on his feet!"

Even as she said it, the tons of beef shifted again and her horse struggled to keep its balance as Maverick reached her. Leaning from his saddle, he lifted her even as the bay went down beneath the bellowing, stamping cattle. Maverick held her against him while the gray whinnied and reared.

Could Dust Devil keep his feet? Maverick felt the big horse stagger beneath him, and he moved expertly to shift his weight, helping the giant horse retain its footing. He had a better chance if he'd turn loose of the dead weight of the girl. But even as the thought crossed his mind, he pulled her tightly against his chest. Her heart pounded against him through their wet clothes and she clung to him. "Maverick! Oh, Maverick!"

We're all three going down together, he thought as the stallion struggled against the longhorns pushing from all directions. Maybe he could shield her with his body as they fell. Maybe if he did, the cowboys could save her at least. He felt the tons of sweating

70

beef push against his legs, bruising them in the crush. Maverick swore as only a Texan can swear, great oaths of fear and fury.

Then Dust Devil caught his balance and pushed for the edge of the giant herd. On the outskirts of it, he saw Sanchez and the others with their quirts, trying to clear a path through to him.

He held her very close against him, aware of the way her heart pounded, aware of her warm breasts pressing against his chest through their wet, clinging clothing. "It's okay, baby," he murmured without thinking, pressing her face protectively against his wide chest. "It's okay, we'll make it!"

He still wasn't sure they would. It seemed like a million miles through the milling cattle to the safety of the perimeter, but the big gray pushed forward valiantly as Sanchez quirted a path clear for him.

Sanchez crossed himself anxiously as Maverick fought through the cattle. "*Dios*, boss! I think the saints watch out for you tonight!"

"No, the devil!" Maverick shouted over the noise. He couldn't die yet; he still had that oath to fulfill. That's why he'd saved her, Maverick told himself grimly as he held her against him, protecting her from the hard-driving rain. He didn't know the whereabouts of the Lazy M Ranch. He needed Cayenne to lead him to her father. Of course that was why he'd risked his neck to save her.

Clear of the herd, he swung down, holding his arms up for the girl. She slid off the horse and collapsed, trembling against his chest. "Maverick! Maverick! I was so scared!"

"I know, I know," he said gently, handing his reins to Sanchez. "That was a brave thing you did, trying to help Tom. It almost cost you your life!"

She looked up at him, lips trembling, and he gently

71

brushed a wet wisp of hair out of the green eyes. "That poor man! I—I tried—"

"Hush, Cee Cee, I know." She staggered and he caught her, swinging her up in his arms. "You'll be all right in a minute with a little coffee and dry clothes."

With long strides, he carried her under a rock ledge above the creek as the rain turned into a fine mist. "Stay here," he commanded. "I'll have one of the boys bring you some blankets, build you a fire."

"But Maverick—"

"Cee Cee, I'm the ramrod here, and I'm used to people doing what I tell them! Stay here," he commanded. "I'll be back when I'm sure the herd is settled for the night, after we find Tom and . . . well, you know."

He left her sitting wet and forlorn under the dry safety of the rock ledge. After he had Cookie take her some blankets, see to a fire and some coffee for her, he turned his attention back to the cattle, the crew.

It was hours before things settled down, before they found all that was left of Tom. And to think only that evening he'd spoke harshly to the young cowboy for flirting with Maverick's woman. *Maverick's woman.* The thought came to him naturally and unquestioned, and yet, he told himself, he'd only saved her to complete his oath. He thought of the girl as he dealt with the weary cattle, got them quieted, saw to the comfort of his exhausted crew.

The rain stopped. There hand't been much on the parched prairie anyway. But it was the middle of the night, and Maverick was wet and weary before all his duties were taken care of. He went back out to check on the girl.

She sat wrapped in a blanket before a small fire and looked up, smiling as he came over. "I saved you some coffee," she said, holding out a cup.

"Thanks." He squatted by the fire, taking the cup from her hand. Every muscle ached with weariness, and even in the summer heat, the wind made him shiver a little as it touched his soaked clothes.

"You ought to get out of those wet things," she scolded gently.

"Later," he sighed. "I'm too tired to move, to think. We lost about a hundred head, your horse, and of course—" He didn't finish, not wanting to remember the blood and bones that had been Tom and his paint gelding.

He heard her swallow hard. "Can I do a little service for him in the morning?"

"If it makes you feel better," he shrugged. He looked at her wrapped in her blanket. Her hair had dried and hung around her shoulders like silken flames. From here he could smell the slight scent of vanilla and the smoky scent of the campfire on her skin. "You need anything?"

She shook her head, and reluctantly he stood up, stretching. "Then I'll go back over to my bed for a couple of hours." He turned to walk away.

"Maverick," she hesitated, and he turned to look down at her. "Aren't your blankets wet?"

He shrugged. "I can sleep standing up if I have to; I'm tired enough."

"Do I have the last dry blankets in camp?"

He paused. There was no use making her feel guilty about the damned blankets. Of course he'd given her the only dry ones. "You got a lot of guts for a woman, Cee Cee," he said grudgingly, "I mean about your tryin' to help Tom. Only one other woman ever showed me that kind of courage."

In his mind's eye, he saw Annie's plain little face, the large gray eyes. *Was she pretty? Only when she smiled,* he remembered, *only when she smiled. God*

73

damn you, Joe McBride, he thought in sudden pain and fury. *God damn you for marrying Cayenne's mother and leaving mine to the Comanche!*

" 'Night," he said, and turned away.

"Maverick, don't go." He looked back at her hunched in her blankets as she held out a hand to him. "You saved my life. I'm beholden—"

"I owed you something for what I did to you this afternoon." He couldn't look at her, remembering he really hadn't meant to hurt her.

"Maverick, look at me," she commanded in a whisper, and when he did, very slowly she opened her blanket.

As she did so, he realized in sudden wonder that she was naked under the blankets, naked and warm and holding out her arms to him. *His enemy's child.*

With his emotions stormy as the night, Maverick crossed the ground to her in three giant strides.

Chapter Four

Cayenne held her arms out to him without even realizing she did so, without thinking of the right or wrong of it. In three strides, he crossed the distance between them and took her in his arms.

"Maverick, you're wet!" She flinched from the contact of his soaked clothes against her skin. "Here, let me warm you."

He sat there obediently, looking down at her as she worked with the buttons of his shirt, unbuckled his belt. Then his bronzed skin was on hers, damp and cool. Maverick acted almost hesitant, not forceful and dominating as before.

She should hate him for robbing her of her virginity, treating her so roughly. But he had just saved her life. She was grateful, she told herself, that's why she felt the urge to take him in her arms, pull his shivering body against her own warm one under the blanket there by the small fire. He turned her so that her back lay against his chest and belly, her head on his arm while he buried his face in the tumble of hair on the back of her neck.

"God, your little body's hot," he murmured, snuggling closer against her as they both lay looking into the flickering flames. "I feel like I'm embracing coals!"

His lips caressed the nape of her neck, pulled her hair up, kissed her there. *I should hate him because of what his tribe did to Papa six months ago.* Yet she knew she could not pull away from his Comanche caress.

His muscular arm went around her waist as he leaned on his other elbow. She sighed and tipped her head forward to give him more expanse of neck to nuzzle. Cayenne was abruptly weary and saddened by the night's events, and somehow, the feel of his body close to hers communicated that he felt the same.

"Oh, Maverick, it was so terrible!"

"I know, baby," he whispered, and his hand came up from her waist to stroke her breasts. "I know. Don't think about it. Things like that just happen."

Cayenne felt the warmth of his breath on her ear as he whispered and she knew he felt even worse about it than she did. She rolled over to face him, reaching up to touch the jagged scar on his face. "You're a strange man, Maverick Durango," she said, stroking his face. "So angry, so full of fury one moment; so tender the next."

He tried to laugh it off, catching her hand and kissing the tips of her fingers. "Now you sound like the old Don and Trace."

She leaned on her elbow, wrapped in the blankets, and looked up into his face, conscious of the feel of his naked body touching hers. "You think the world of that pair, don't you?"

Maverick hesitated, seeming to search for words, looking as if he were afraid to admit how much he might care for another human being, as if it were a weakness. "They're all I've got, the Durangos," he said finally. " 'Long as I got a biscuit, they got half."

She nodded in understanding. No cowboy could offer any more than to share his very last biscuit with a friend. She felt the heat of his big body against hers as his skin dried and radiated warmth from hers. Her gaze went again to the scar. "How'd you come by that?"

He reached to brush a lock of hair from her eyes. "A long time ago, a Comanche brave tried to kill me because I fought him after he'd tortured that white captive. . . ." His voice trailed off and his gray eyes became tortured, tragic as he looked past her shoulder.

She felt a sudden need to comfort him, this man who had raped her brutally, then saved her life. With her fingertips, she turned his chin down so she could look into his eyes. Then she reached up and kissed him very gently on the lips.

For a long moment, he stiffened and she felt his body tighten as his hand on her waist held her close. "You're askin' for trouble, Cee Cee." But he made no move.

"No, I'm not," she whispered, and her arm went up around his neck. She kissed him thoroughly while she pressed her full breasts against the hard muscles of his chest. "You just told me this afternoon I didn't know anything about kissing a man. Besides, you said I'd have to beg you—"

"Cee Cee, I'm warning you—"

"Warning me about what?" She was almost flippant about it as she rubbed her body against his, kissing him again.

He swore softly. "You know about what!"

"I'm not worried." Even though his skin felt hot as a Texas summer against hers all the way down their legs, even though she could feel his manhood erect and throbbing, she wasn't afraid. After this afternoon, she had a definite feeling that he wouldn't force himself on her again, that she would have to be the aggressor. She was dizzy, heady with the power she suddenly felt over this big, rugged man as his breath quickened.

"Oh, Cayenne! Damn you!" He rolled over on his back suddenly, pulling her on top of him.

In the flickering firelight, she put one hand on each side of him, palms on the ground, and looked down at him. Her long hair fell around them both. She lay on top of him and felt his hard maleness pushing against her, his pulse beating in his flat belly. And abruptly she was weary, in need of comfort herself, tired of playing games. Cayenne leaned over, ran her tongue deeply between his lips, felt him gasp before his hands came up to grasp her slim waist like steel bands.

"Cayenne," he said huskily, "I don't want a repeat of this afternoon. I—I never meant to hurt you. . . ."

And she cut off his words by nipping at his lips with her sharp teeth, straddling him with her legs. "I think I love you, Maverick," she murmured. She saw herself coming down the aisle with an armful of flowers to his waiting arms, and later, a baby boy named Jefferson Davis Durango.

But he caught her shoulders, holding her up off his wide chest. "Don't, Cee Cee," he said. "Don't. A woman never forgets the first man who takes her, but I'll bring you trouble. You don't know—"

"I know all I want to know," she protested huskily, and slipped her tongue deep into his mouth, probing its warm recesses as her hands went down to stroke his nipples.

Maverick moaned against her lips, arching himself up against her, pulling her body up so that her breasts hung over his face. "Can't get enough of these, of you," he gasped, and his mouth reached up for her nipples.

His tongue moved wetly across her breasts as he held her above him, imprisoned in his embrace. Cayenne trembled with delight as his teeth traced the edge of the pink rosettes and he sucked at her nipples. She couldn't stop herself from moaning aloud.

"That's right, baby, let me know you like it! Tell me!" He pulled her down, opening his mouth wide to take much of her breast in his mouth, sucking hard.

She couldn't keep herself from digging her nails into his shoulders. "Don't stop!" she whimpered. "Oh, Maverick, don't stop!"

His big hands cupped her small bottom as she crouched over him, legs astraddle. And as he kissed her nipples, his fingers stroked around the back and inner parts of her thighs.

She had a sudden feeling of power, as if she rode and controlled a great stallion, could do with him as she wished. Although in his frenzy, the cowboy arched up off the blanket against her.

"Ride me, Cayenne," he commanded. "Ride me! It won't hurt this time, I promise!"

She hesitated, arching back as his mouth again sucked her taut nipples. Would it hurt? This afternoon was a confused memory of ecstasy and pain. Then she felt her body moisten as he stroked her, felt her body almost hurt from wanting him.

"Please, baby." His hands on her waist were hot and shaking. "Oh, Cayenne!"

Very slowly, she raised up, sliding backward on her knees until she felt his hard manhood pulsating against her inner thigh. She leaned over, biting his nipple, and he gasped and shuddered. "You little hussy! If I don't get some relief—"

He never finished, because she spread her thighs and came down on him very slowly while he writhed and cursed under her. And she arched backward as she took him to the hilt, so deeply that she could almost feel him throbbing up under her navel. And he was right. It didn't hurt.

Cayenne rode him expertly, instinctively, rhythmically. He grasped her waist, trying to pull her down on his manhood, to grind himself against her. But she controlled this mating and she was giddy with the power she held, the way the man writhed and begged under her.

She lay down on him as she rode him harder, wrapping her arms around him. His tongue explored feverishly between her lips.

"Baby, I—I'm not going to be able to hold it, stop it. Come with me!"

Puzzled, she looked down at his tortured face, unsure what he was talking about, although she could feel him pulsating within her, could hear him gasping for breath as the coupling grew more frenzied. His hands caught her breasts, squeezing them as his thumbs caressed her nipples.

Then suddenly he gasped and cried out, his face contorted as he locked her in an embrace so hard she could scarcely breathe.

Then she felt his body shudder, felt his manhood give up its seed deep within her. The idea of his seed flowing deep in her waiting vessel excited her and her own body trembled with expectation. Cayenne had a sudden vision of two great eagles mating as they fell toward the earth locked together. And then she fell, too, fell into an endless blackness of ecstasy, her body locking onto his as if reluctant to ever give him up or let him go.

It was sort of like dreaming: strange, crazy images of eagles falling, the rugged face of Maverick Durango, the feel of his powerful arms holding her so tightly she couldn't breathe. She was falling . . . falling. *They say if you hit the ground before you wake up, you die,* she thought, but she didn't want to come out of the exhilarating plunge. If this were death, so be it.

"Cayenne?"

For a moment, she didn't know where she was but she felt lips gently kissing her face. "Baby, are you all right?"

She blinked, opening her eyes. Had she been unconscious or asleep? Her muscles were relaxed, weary. All she wanted to do was sleep. The big cowboy disengaged himself, rolled her over on her side, and pulled her up against the protection of his muscular chest.

"Maverick, I never felt like that before. . . ."

"I know, I know." He stroked her, pulling her against the warmth of him, pushing her tangled curls out of her eyes while his lips caressed her face. "Oh, God!" He sounded angry. "Why do you have to be who you are? Why do you have to be—?"

"What?" She looked at him sleepily, snuggling even closer against him. She was so sleepy and she was safe in his arms; she knew it somehow. Safe.

"Never mind," he whispered. "Go to sleep. It's not long 'til dawn."

She felt him lay his face against her hair. As she dozed off, she heard the even rhythm of his breathing.

In the morning, the pair was up and dressed before the others, and after breakfast, Cayenne insisted on a proper service for poor Tom. She said a few words for which the cowboys seemed grateful. And then as they all stood there in the coming light of dawn, she sang the hymn that had become her father's favorite:

Lead, kindly light amid the'n circling gloom, lead

Thou me on. The night is dark, and I am far from home. Lead Thou me on. Keep Thou my feet. I do not ask to see the distant scene, one step enough for me. . . .

Many of the men had wet eyes when she finished. Several took out bandanas and wiped their eyes. The dawn came, pink and orange over the scene. Even Maverick looked shaken, troubled.

But he only said, "Thanks, Cayenne. The men appreciated that. It's hard enough to leave one of our own so far from Texas soil, and nobody usually knows enough Scripture to have a proper service."

Cayenne wiped her own eyes, and turned away from the simple grave. "It was the least I could do. I wish I could have done more."

Old Sanchez came over to her, twisting his battered hat between his calloused, mangled fingers. "The men asked me to tell you, Senorita McBride, how much they appreciated your singing."

She patted his arm. "Tell the men I'm only sorry my papa wasn't here to preach a real service, but I did the best I could."

She looked at Maverick and saw troubled doubt there.

"Cee Cee, I'll catch up a Triple D horse for you and we'll go on to Wichita."

Such a strange, tortured man, she thought as she watched him stride away. She had never met anyone quite like him, so sensitive, so brutal. His tragic gray eyes seemed to be hiding something, something terrible that drove him relentlessly. Well, maybe someday he would finally unlock his heart and soul to her. Maybe then she could help him against whatever inner demons possessed him.

He caught up a fine roan mare. "This is Strawberry," he smiled, handing her the reins. "She's 'lady broke.' "

Cayenne frowned as she mounted. "I'll have you know I ride well enough that you don't have to find me a 'lady broke' horse like some eastern dude!' "

"Then let's just say Strawberry's a pretty filly and her red tail and mane reminded me of your hair!"

Cayenne felt the blood rush hotly to her face, remembering last night, and she glanced quickly around to see if the crew was listening. But the cowboys were busy stringing the herd out along the trail.

"Ride point with me," Maverick gestured, and she fell in alongside him as he led out on the trail. From the corner of her eye, she saw the "swing" riders lope out along the sides of the herd, keeping the stragglers in line as the weary longhorns bawled and pushed each other. She felt sorry for the "drag" riders bringing up the rear, eating the others' dust, but someone had to do it.

In spite of last night's terrible events, she enjoyed herself riding alongside the half-breed on his big gray. The morning sun felt warm like a lover's kiss on her face, and she remembered Maverick's mouth on hers, his hands cupping her breasts. She sighed audibly.

He glanced over at her. "What're you thinking about?"

She wasn't about to tell him. In a flurry of embarrassment, she asked, "Why'd you leave the herd so far out of Wichita?"

"You remember the summer drive of '71?"

She shifted her weight in the saddle, enjoying the smell of leather, the bawl and lowing of the big longhorns walking behind her. "No, I've only been in Kansas three months."

"It was a terrible drive year." Maverick shook his head. "All these thousands of cattle coming into Kansas, more than could be sold."

83

She looked over at him, appreciating the outline of his wide-shouldered frame. "So what'd you do with them if you couldn't sell them? Drive them back to Texas?"

"Take coals to Newcastle?" He laughed.

When his big gray eyes crinkled with laughter, it transformed his face, made him so much more handsome.

He said, "All the trail crews kept them grazing around town, hoping the market would pick up, but it didn't."

"My stars! What happened?"

Maverick tipped his hat back. "There were fifty thousand unsold cattle grazing up all the grass around town and we couldn't sell them. Then when the grass ran out, the blizzards moved in."

"And the cattle starved and died." She suddenly remembered her neighboring ranchers talking about that year.

"That's right," Maverick nodded grimly. "Poor devils could have survived the winter, maybe, if there'd been enough grass. Fifty thousand dead cattle. Now it's Durango policy to keep the herd far enough out that we could graze them a long time on the open range if we don't sell them."

"I guess the drives will go on as long as there's open range, maybe forever."

"No, Cayenne," he shook his head regretfully. "Somehow I feel the days of these cattle drives are numbered, that someone's going to invent some kind of cheap fencing—"

"Cheap fencing?" she scoffed, shaking her hair back, enjoying the creak of the saddle, the pleasant smell of the sweating horse. "There's no such thing! The range will always be open because of the cost of stones and rails."

He looked over at her. "Don't count on it, Cee Cee. Someone will figure out a cheap way to fence off fields, keep the cattle in, the buffalo out. Then if they can find a way to get water to their fields, the homesteaders will move in with their plows and start farming."

"Maybe the cattle drive is doomed anyway," she admitted, "with trains beginning to lay track everywhere. Sooner or later, it'll be cheaper to ship the cattle by train out of Texas rather than walk them all the way to Kansas."

"The Indians must know that, too," he said softly. "With trains bringing in settlers, fields fenced, and hunters killing off the buffalo, no wonder they're fighting, determined to save their civilization."

She saw the sympathy in the gray eyes. "I thought you hated Indians."

"I hate Comanche," he said, and his eyes turned as cold and hard as gray granite. "Because of what happened to Annie." He started, as if he'd said something he'd never meant to say, never meant to share with her. "Nice day, isn't it?"

She wanted to ask but saw the hostility, the closed expression of his rugged face. Someday she would get inside his shell, get him to open up and share his pain with her. Until then she could only guess at his past, some wall between them. What secrets did he hide? It was a long way to the Lazy M Ranch. She'd know Maverick inside out in the weeks it took to ride there.

In Wichita, Maverick reined up, shouting at her over the bawling cattle. "I've got to get this beef to the railroad pens so they can be shipped east. Then I'll go over to the Red Garter, have one last drink with the crew."

She nodded, shouting back, "That's fine. I want to

85

go see some of the children from my school, tell them good-bye. When and where shall we meet?"

He hesitated, reining in his snorting horse. "Cayenne, are you sure you want to do this? With all the Indian trouble, maybe you should rethink—"

"My stars! Must we cover that ground again? I'm going home, Maverick. Now if you've changed your mind, I'll find some other cowboy to take me."

He scowled blackly at her. "You're still innocent as a Sunday school! You'd pick some *hombre* who'd get you just far enough out of town to tear your clothes off—"

"As I recall, that's just what did happen," she snapped acidly. "But if you bow out, my future's no concern of yours, now, is it?"

"By damn!" he swore. "If I ever met a girl who needed her bottom blistered for being so headstrong—"

"When you get ready to spank me, cowboy, you'd better bring your dinner, because it may take a while!" She smiled back in smug satisfaction.

He shrugged. "Okay, have it your way. Meet me out in front of the general store." He glanced up at the sun. "Let's say about eleven."

Cayenne nodded, waved to old Sanchez, and rode away. First she visited some of her favorite little children and told them good-bye. At one of the homes, she took a bath in a tin washtub, put on a clean blue gingham dress, brushed her hair, and dabbed a little vanilla behind each ear before eyeing herself critically in a cracked mirror.

She wasn't sure whether she should hate that Yankee sympathizer or love him. But she wanted him to think her pretty, desirable. Otherwise, he might back out on accompanying her on this dangerous trip. Cayenne frowned. There might be even more danger for him at the end of it.

But she must not think about that, she told her troubled conscience. After all, Papa and the kids were more important to her than that trail boss. Weren't they?

She should let her family know she'd gotten the letter and was on her way home. She'd go down to the telegraph office and . . . No, she'd better not do it that way. Cayenne shook her head, remembering the unpleasant little telegrapher gossiping peoples' business all over Wichita. Besides, it would cost more than a letter and she had so little money.

She found a piece of paper and pencil stub. How could she word it so as not to arouse suspicion if the mail should fall into the wrong hands? Maybe if she addressed it to her nine-year-old sister, the gunslingers wouldn't think it was important if they managed to get the mail first. After a moment, she wrote: *Dear Lynnie: You'll be glad to hear I've found the man who can help us.*

No, that wouldn't do. Slade might get curious and open it. It had to sound very innocent.

She erased part of the sentence and began rewriting. Finally Cayenne paused, her tongue in the corner of her mouth. Had she given enough double meanings so that serious, smart Lynnie would understand big sister was bringing help? Did it sound casual, trivial enough?

Cayenne hesitated again. If anyone else picked up the mail, opened it, would they think she meant wedding plans? She must not let on she'd gotten a warning letter. What she really should do was contact the army or the Texas Rangers.

She shook her head. The new governor, Coke, was trying to deal with the Yankee carpetbaggers who'd taken over the state at war's end. But since she'd been

87

gone, she didn't know whether he'd been successful or not. And the Yankees had disbanded the Rangers, feeling the Texans were a threat to their regime.

She'd done the best she could do. With a little prayer for luck, she put it in an envelope, addressing it to her sister in care of the general store where the Lazy M picked up its mail. Cayenne paused before she wrote the name of the tiny town, beaming proudly. Up until Papa's heroic deed eight months ago, it had been a nameless community of gentle, religious folk. But the settlers were as proud of Papa as Cayenne had been. Underneath *Billing's General Store*, she wrote the town and state: *McBride, Texas*.

She mailed the letter at the small post office and rode over to the general store. The unpleasant little telegraph operator came by, heading to his post.

"Good day, Miss Cayenne." He tipped his green eyeshade at her and she nodded politely as he passed, wishing she could like Wilbur. Nobody in town seemed to think much of the scrawny, humpbacked little man. She decided it was because of Wilbur's habit of never looking you in the eye when he talked to you. And he did have the most annoying habit of gossiping about all the messages that came through his hands. Probably it made him feel important.

Judging by the hot June sun, it must be at least eleven. Over across the bridge at the Red Garter's hitching post, more than a dozen Triple D horses stood dozing. The big gray was one of them. Strawberry whinnied in greeting to the stallion.

Cayenne smiled to herself. Even the dainty mare had an eye for a good-looking male.

She waited. And waited. And waited. The sun overhead told her it must be at least high noon. Mr. Winston came out of his store. "Is something the matter, Miss McBride?"

She tried not to seem as hot and furious as she felt. "Do you happen to have a watch, sir?"

He nodded, pulling out a big pocket watch. "12:15," he announced importantly. "I'm going home for dinner."

Now just what was keeping that cowboy? 12:15. She watched the old storekeeper amble down the sidewalk, listened to the laughter and singing echoing from the Red Garter. Well, she'd just have to go in and get him!

Upstairs in Molly's room, Maverick leaned back in the tin washtub. He sighed with pleasure at the girl in the scarlet dress. "Thanks, Molly, for loaning me your bathtub. I was filthy and the hotel is full up—"

"Think nothin' of it, handsome," she smirked at him as she poured liquor from the decanter on the dresser. "Bourbon and branch, right?"

He nodded agreeably, soaping his muscular chest. "I could use some more hot water."

"I told the maid when she came to bring your clean clothes." Molly came over, handed him the drink. "She'll be right up with more water." The whore looked down at him. "And after you get out of that tub, maybe you got time for me."

He laughed easily. "Sorry, no can do. Got to meet someone. What time is it, anyway?"

"Oh, early yet," she said, coming over to the tub. "Can I wash your back?"

He nodded and she knelt behind him. "I think I let time get away from me downstairs. You know how it is when men get to drinkin' and gamblin'."

"I know how it is." He heard her pick up a washcloth and he sighed with pleasure as she scrubbed his back. "Damn! You got the best-lookin' body of any man I ever met, Maverick. How long we known each other, anyway?"

89

He sighed, sipping the whiskey and enjoying the feel of her scrubbing his sore muscles. "Hell, I don't know, Molly. Who remembers something like that?"

"I remember," she said almost wistfully. "Maybe because it meant something to me. It was just ten years ago this coming September at a birthday party for the old Don on the patio of the Triple D ranch house. It was just before the big Indian Outbreak."

Maverick laughed gently. "I was just a half-grown boy. I don't remember you. . . ."

"I was one of Miss Fancy's girls then, you know, in San Antone, and everyone in the county was invited. I remember thinking then someday when you was a grown man, women would be loco over you. Never dreamed it'd be me."

He felt suddenly sorry for her, even though he couldn't love her. He handed her his empty glass. "Aw, Molly, you don't mean that. All you want is fun, a good time. You wouldn't leave this life just to scrub clothes, raise kids."

"I do like a good time," she admitted. She put the glass down and rubbed the soapy rag across his shoulders. "That's why I ran off with a worthless tinhorn named Slade when I was only fifteen. He had a partner I would have given it all up for just like I'd give it up for you now, handsome."

Maverick laughed. "Sorry, Molly. I got other plans and I'm runnin' late, got to hurry. Scrub a little to the left. Ah . . . that's it."

Downstairs, Cayenne marched through the swinging doors of the Red Garter. Immediately, the music stopped in mid-note. All the cowboys hushed talking, the painted women quit laughing. The crowd stared at her.

She looked around the saloon. No Maverick. "All

right! Where is he?"

The bald bartender groaned. "Oh, no, not again! Look, miss, I just got that buffalo hunter, Buck, on his feet and back out with his partners late last night, and now you come in here again ready to get another fight started."

Old Sanchez fumbled with his hat. *Dios! Senorita*, you don't belong in a place like this! Go back outside and wait. I'll find him and send him out."

"No, I've waited for that Yankee-lovin' saddle bum long enough!" She was furious, hands on hips. "Now just where is he?"

Nobody answered but she saw their eyes turn toward the stairway. She was speechless with anger, hurt, and shock. After making love with her, Maverick was upstairs with that dark-haired girl? That pretty older one with the fancy pearl combs?

"Never mind!" she said through gritted teeth. "I'll just go up and get him myself!" Before anyone could move to stop her, she marched toward the stairs, red hair bouncing on her neck.

"Miss, you can't go up there!" The bartender twisted his hands in his grimy apron. "It ain't a fit place for a lady! You can't go up there!"

"You just watch me!" And she marched up the stairs, glancing back to see the horrified expressions of the openmouthed men below.

Upstairs, she wasn't sure which door. Then she heard that pretty dark-haired whore laugh somewhere down the hall.

A black girl brushed past her carrying a bucket of steaming water.

Cayenne grabbed her arm. "Where's that cowboy called Maverick?"

The girl hesitated, obviously as shocked as the cowboys to see a lady on the second floor. She gestured. "He's in Miss Molly's room takin' a bath, dat's whare he be. But you can't go in there, Missus!"

"Just watch me!" Cayenne said again. "That water for his bath?"

The girl only nodded dumbly, and Cayenne took the bucket away from her, marched to the door the maid had indicated, and rapped sharply.

"Bring it on in, LuLu," said a woman's voice.

Cayenne swung the door wide. There he sat in a tub of sudsy water, the pretty brunette scrubbing his back. "Well!" Cayenne said. "No wonder you couldn't meet me!"

The two stared at her in openmouthed horror.

Maverick half rose from the tub. "What the hell you doin' here? This is no place for a lady!"

"But it is a place for a two-timing cowboy! I don't suppose you were expecting me," Cayenne snapped, "but I thought I'd help your friend there with your bath!" Before either of them could make another move, she marched across the room and threw the bucket of warm water all over the two of them.

They both shouted in surprise and Molly gestured wildly. "My new red dress! She's ruined my dress! Why, I ought to wipe up the floor with you, you little—!"

"I hope you've got some help," Cayenne smiled a little too sweetly, setting the pail down. "Because, honey, you're gonna need it!"

Maverick scrambled out of the tub, dripping across the floor as he grabbed for a towel to wrap around his lean body. "Cayenne's right, Molly, I'd think twice about layin' into her if I was you. Texas gals are tough—"

"So are gals from Missouri!" Molly faced Cayenne in the wet scarlet dress, looking like a slightly bedraggled and enraged Rhode Island red hen.

92

Maverick pushed between them. "Here! Here! Stop this! Now let's try to talk this out sensibly. . . ."

Cayenne glared at him with eyes as cold as green emeralds. "You're fired!" she snapped. "I'll go to Texas by myself!"

"Texas?" Molly wailed. "Handsome, you was going to Texas with her after I loaned you my bathtub? You was cleaning up for her?"

Cayenne pulled out of Maverick's grasp and confronted her. "Honey, you can have him! If I ever see him again, that's one day too soon!"

And with that, she spun on her heel, marching out of the room and down the stairs. The men didn't meet her glare as she stormed out of the Red Garter like the Texans taking San Jacinto!

As she marched over to her horse, Maverick leaned out of the upstairs window. "By damn, baby, you can't cross Texas alone! Wait 'til I get my clothes. . . ."

"You just watch me!" she snapped in a fury, swinging up in the saddle. It was hard to straddle the mare with a dress on but she didn't care if her legs did show. She'd meant to get a sidesaddle or change into boy's pants before they started their journey. She felt too angry to care as she urged the startled mare into a lope, leaving Wichita behind. She had a little compass in her saddlebags, which would be of some help, and she had a rifle and some food. But most of the gear would be on a packhorse Maverick would have brought along.

She headed southwest at a walk, and the farther she got from town, the more she regretted her peppery temper.

"My stars! He deserved more than just a sloshing," she said aloud to quiet her fears, her doubts. But that didn't alter the facts that now she was out here on

93

these endless plains all alone with nothing but the wind and dozens of dead, reeking buffalo carcasses around her.

Buck. That big buffalo hunter was out here some place, too, she thought with sudden alarm. But of course the southern plains were endless. The chance she'd cross his trail was small. Still . . .

She reined up. Maybe she should go back to town, try to hire someone else to help her get through hostile territory. Cayenne bit her lip, wiping at the perspiration on her freckled face as the midday sun beat down on her. Somehow she didn't have any confidence in any other *hombre* but that damned half-breed. He was all man, supremely confident in his ability to handle anything he came up against.

The hot wind smelled like dry dust, like the drought that had shriveled the Southern Plains for months now. A drop of perspiration ran down her breast and she blotted it with the blue gingham of her dress, remembering Maverick's mouth hot and moist on her nipples. She thought of him with both longing and regret. The strange, tortured cowboy had been her very first man and she would never, never forget him. But to him she'd been only another conquest.

Strawberry craned her head around and whinnied. Frightened, Cayenne turned in her saddle to look behind her. Way off toward Wichita, small dots moved on the horizon. Who could it be? That filthy buffalo hunter? An Indian? Strawberry nickered again as the rider came on fast, leading a loaded packhorse behind him.

Cayenne felt a surge of both fury and relief. The expert way he rode, the size of the man, and the big gray stallion identified him long before the man galloped close enough for her to recognize his dark face. Maverick Durango.

"By damn, if it isn't the little horse thief," he sneered as he galloped up beside her.

She blinked. "Horse thief?"

Maverick nodded toward the brand on Strawberry's rump. "I believe that is a Triple D mark, isn't it?"

Cayenne gasped. Horse stealing was a hanging offense anywhere in the West. "You're bluffin'!"

He grinned slowly. "Am I?"

Chapter Five

She watched the big half-breed, her emotions a mixture of relief and anger. He looked so stern, so forbidding riding that stallion that reminded her of a ghost, a spectre. She just kept riding.

Then she remembered him sitting in the soapy water, that whore with the long black hair running her hands familiarly over his broad back. *How dare he follow her?* Cayenne slapped the mare with the reins, loping off to the southwest.

"Cayenne!" He took in after her, the big gray slowly gaining on her. "Cayenne!"

She didn't look at him even when she heard him overtake her.

"By damn, baby, look at me when I talk to you!"

She lifted her head high and kept riding.

He rode along beside her. "I believe when you set a course for yourself, you're as stubborn as a snapping turtle!"

"Then you should remember," she answered coldly without looking over at him. "It's an old Texas legend that snapping turtles don't let go 'til they hear it thunder."

"I ought to paddle your butt!" he said.

"Don't be crude," she said, chin high, not looking

96

at him. She couldn't remember ever being this angry before. "You loaned me this horse, remember? Go back to Wichita! I'll find someone else along the way to ride with me!"

"What you'll find is some war party, some gang of filthy buffalo hunters, Reb! Either one would keep you as a playpretty—"

"That doesn't concern you now, does it?" Her anger had given way to a sense of relief that he rode by her side. But she was too proud to let him know how frightened, how uncertain she'd been.

"Cayenne, I've never had to answer to any woman and I'm not about to start now!"

"I didn't ask for an explanation," she said frostily. "After all, I was raised on a ranch; I know a stallion will mount any eager mare that sidles up to him."

"Dammit, I just took a bath in her tub."

She didn't answer, keeping her eyes on the flat prairie ahead of her.

"Are we going to ride clear to Texas with you not speaking to me?"

"You don't have to ride to Texas. I didn't ask you to come along. You're sticking to me like a burr in a pony's mane."

"And I intend to," he answered grimly. "I told you I'd get you home. After all, it cost you enough!"

She felt the blood rise to her face. "No gentleman would bring that up."

"No lady would seduce a man in exchange for his accompanying her."

"Seduce? Seduce?" She looked at him, unable to keep the anger from her voice. "I'd call it *rape*, you— you—!" She tried to think of some terrible insult. "You Yankee, you!"

"I think it's going to be a long trip," he said coldly, and he didn't smile.

Cayenne felt too much fury to say anything else. She had a feeling if it went much further, she would take her quirt to the stony-faced man, and if she did, there'd be hell to pay. And yet, she felt relief that he'd shown up. She glanced over at him, his strong hands on the reins, the big Colt he wore. They rode southwest through the heat for at least two hours, neither saying anything.

It was Maverick who finally broke the silence. "Haven't you got a hat?" he snapped. "With that sheer fabric, those short sleeves, you're gonna get sunburned."

"That's hardly your concern, cowboy."

They rode for another hour in silence.

Finally Maverick asked peevishly, "Are we going all the way to Texas without your saying a word to me?"

"Probably," she answered coolly.

"Well then, you ornery little vixen, I can be as stubborn as you are!" His voice trailed off in sullen silence.

That's what you think, she thought, but she said nothing.

So they rode through the hot afternoon. Except for an occasional rabbit and the buzzards swooping down to feast off the rank buffalo carcasses, they saw no movement. But once when they stopped to rest the horses, Maverick examined the ground, looking at tracks.

"Unshod ponies," he muttered, and said no more.

Cayenne wet her handkerchief from her canteen, dabbing her face and her pony's muzzle. The damp cloth felt cold against her sunburned face and she winced.

"Here, baby, take my hat." He held it out to her. She wasn't going to give him the satisfaction of realizing how sunburned she was. "No thanks. I'm just fine, really."

"Suit yourself, Cee Cee," he shrugged. "Remember, I offered—"

"Don't put yourself out on my account," she snapped. Had he always seemed so arrogant, so confident? And to think she'd been stupid enough to let this Yankee-lovin' range bum charm her out of her virginity. She gritted her teeth with grim satisfaction. She didn't even feel guilty that Bill Slade and his men would gun Maverick down when he finally reached the Lazy M.

She glared at him as they mounted up. "If the Rangers hadn't been broken up, I'd have asked them for help instead of you."

Maverick grinned. "Oh, hasn't someone told you? In the last several months, Governor Coke has managed to throw out the carpetbagger government. First thing he did in April was reactivate the Texas Rangers."

She'd outwitted herself. "How was I to know that? I've been in Kansas since late March."

"What kind of help?"

She stuttered, unused to lying. "Why—why, help getting home, that's all." *She hadn't needed the half-breed in her plans after all,* Cayenne thought grimly as they struck out southwest again. She could have called on the Rangers to help. No, she couldn't either, she remembered. If it had been that simple, the letter wouldn't have come to her. Papa could have called in the Rangers himself. Just what hold did Slade have on the gentle preacher? It was too bad the tiny community of McBride didn't even have a sheriff. The quiet, religious people had never needed one before. But the letter hinted something might be going to happen, maybe in a few weeks. What were Slade and his men up to and why was Papa so hesitant to call in the authorities?

Cayenne looked over at the grim half-breed riding beside her. How ironic it was she'd had to ask a Comanche for help when it was the Comanche who'd tortured her gentle papa. Joe McBride was not only a hero but much loved in the community for what had happened eight months ago.

Damned Comanche! She swallowed hard, looking over at the man who rode beside her. If he and Papa weren't a contrast! Maverick believed in "an eye for an eye" while her kindly, religious father preached "vengeance is mine says the Lord" and about turning the other cheek. Papa had been the man brave enough to carry the ransom out to that war party when they took some of the women and children hostage at a church picnic. They'd turned the captives loose but kept Papa to torture. Only the arrival of that chief, Quanah Parker, at the last minute had kept the war party from killing him.

Maverick held up his hand to halt. "There's something on the horizon ahead, not sure what."

Cayenne stood in her stirrups, shielding her eyes from the late afternoon sun. "Where? I don't see anything. You must have eyes like a hawk."

He smiled wryly. "Among the Comanche, if you don't keep all your senses alert, you don't live to grow up. I'll ride out, see what it is. Stay here, Cee Cee."

She started to protest that he was not the ramrod here, that she would not be ordered around by him, but then decided against it. Maverick seemed as much at home on these hostile plains as any big lobo wolf. He rode forward until he was only a small figure on the great, barren horizon with the sun setting orange and gold behind him. She almost seemed to see a silver-gray lobo loping silently through the tall

100

grass. *A lobo mates for life.* The fact came to her and she was annoyed with herself for the thought.

The wind picked up, whining a little, and she remembered how many times she'd heard the lonely call of a solitary lobo. Suppose he rode off and left her? Cayenne felt both isolated and alone, with only the sound of the constant wind ruffling the dry grass as she watched him disappear over the horizon.

She almost called out to him, then remembered how keen an Indian's senses were, how her call might carry on the wind if there were a war party anywhere nearby. Cayenne ran the tip of her tongue over her dusty lips, feeling the sting of perspiration on her sunburned face. The wind shifted and she smelled the stink of dead buffalo, hundreds of them. No wonder the plains tribes had taken the warpath. She almost cried out with relief when she saw Maverick suddenly reappear on the horizon, waving her forward.

Cayenne loped the mare through the grass to where Maverick sat his mount, staring up at some kind of crude platform built into the air. A dead paint horse lay beneath the platform, crude symbols and red handprints painted on its shoulders and flanks.

She frowned, staring upward. "What in God's name is that? What happened to that horse?"

Dust Devil whinnied, stamping his feet, ears forward inquiringly. Maverick patted the gray's neck. "Whoa, boy, take it easy." He looked up at the platform, over at Cayenne. "It's a Cheyenne burial—a chief, judging from the finery and the quality of the horse. I saw unshod tracks early this afternoon."

There was something eerie about the scene, she thought, although she didn't believe in ghosts, in spirits. But still there was something about the black silhouette against the orange and pink sunset that made her nervous. "How do you know he's Cheyenne?"

Maverick dismounted, pointing to the arrow embedded in the dead pony. "See the striped feathers? Cheyenne favor those. Some say that's why the Cheyenne are called the 'striped people' in sign language." Maverick made a gesture of drawing his right forefinger across his left. "Besides, Comanche and Kiowa bury their dead in the ground."

"Why would they kill a fine horse like that?" she asked. "It doesn't make any sense."

"It does to an Indian," Maverick said flatly, his dark face betraying no emotion. "I'd say the warrior died in battle, needed his best pony to carry him up the Milky Way, the road to heaven the Cheyenne call *Ekutsihimmiyo*, the Hanging Road to the Sky."

"What battle?" None of this made any sense to her and she was exhausted and hungry.

Maverick looked off at the horizon and it was a long time before he answered. "I think somewhere out there, we're gonna find the ruins of a ranch and whatever's left of the poor devils who lived there. God help them!"

The grim images his words brought to mind made her shiver a little, remembering what the Indians had done to Papa. "How do you know that?" she demanded, shifting her weight in the saddle. "Maybe the settlers whipped the Indians, ran them off."

Maverick shook his head, remounting. "If they'd lost, if they were being chased, the war party wouldn't have taken the time to go clear to the nearest creek for tree limbs to build this platform, do this elaborate ceremony. They would have just left him where he fell. The Cheyenne think it no shame to leave a fallen man where he's died in battle."

Something about the scorn of his tone, the way his lip curled, made her ask without thinking, "The

102

Comanche don't leave their dead?"

"No," Maverick said. "I've seen Comanche warriors killed trying to go back to retrieve the bodies of the fallen."

Her curiosity got the better of her and she almost asked, but the hardness of his eyes, the grim set of his jaw discouraged her.

"Remember that, Reb," he said softly as they rode toward the sunset. "If you're ever attacked by Comanches, it's to your advantage to try to pick them off when they come riding back in for their dead."

His life among the Indians must hold terrible memories, she thought, still angry with him yet sympathetic to the sadness of his face. He reached up to touch the jagged white scar on his cheek and she wondered about it, about him. *Such a strange, tortured man*, she thought, watching his face, wondering what bedeviled him. Maverick Durango might have been adopted, raised by the Durangos, but he was little more than a savage himself. No white man would hang a trophy scalp from his bridle or mount a horse from the right side like an Indian.

Dusk fell all lavender and purple, golden around the edges. Somewhere a quail called: *Bob white! Bob, bob, white!* Soon the sun would set and the wild life would come out in the cool of the darkness.

Maverick glanced over at her. "We need to find a place to bed down."

She thought about the war party. "Will the Indians be roaming around after dark, maybe find us?"

He shook his head. "Most Indians don't raid at night, don't like the idea of fighting in the darkness—except the Comanche. They love raiding beneath a full moon."

She remembered then. In Texas, a full moon wasn't called a "harvest" moon, it was known as a "Coman-

103

che moon" because that tribe so often spread death
and destruction on moonlit nights.

It was dark before they saw the ranch with its few
outbuildings, the house built of cut sod. They reined
up at a distance.

"Stay here," Maverick ordered. "I'll ride in alone."

"I don't want to stay out here by myself," she
protested.

He tipped his hat back and she saw the grimness of
his face in the light of the rising moon. "Do as I tell
you, Cayenne," he commanded, and she knew why he
was the leader of the trail drive. His confident, mascu-
line tone indicated a capable man; a man who expected to lead a herd while the more docile followed.
A stallion, she thought suddenly. *He's not a lobo, he's
a stallion.*

He gestured toward the ranch. "If it's okay, I'll
signal. If you don't hear me whistle in a few minutes,
get the hell out of here and ride as hard and as fast as
you can. Forget the packhorse."

"And leave you behind?" she protested.

Maverick hesitated. "Baby," he said finally, "if I'm
riding into an ambush, there's not anything you could
do to help me anyway."

"I could, too," she protested, gesturing toward her
saddle gun. "My papa's the best rifle shot in west
Texas and he taught me!"

"Do as I tell you!" he said sharply. "You got a
pistol?"

"No," she shook her head. "Papa said handguns
were for murder, not for hunting meat."

Maverick reached back and got a Colt from his
saddlebags. "Here's my extra." He leaned over to put
it in her hands.

She looked down at it, puzzled. "I could pick off

104

more of them with a rifle. . . ."

"Cayenne," he hesitated. "The pistol's for you, in case—" His voice trailed off and she suddenly realized with horror what he hinted at.

"You don't mean—?"

"Baby," he said, and his voice was as grim as his face, "if I don't get back, don't let them take you alive. You hear me? If you'd ever seen the results of Indian torture—"

"I've seen," she closed her eyes, thinking of Papa's scars, his poor hands and feet.

"Stay alert," he whispered, "and, baby, if I don't get back—" He hesitated, and for a split second she thought he would reach across to touch her face with his uplifted hand. Then he frowned, made a gesture of dismissal, and turned to ride into the ranch yard at a walk.

He disappeared into the darkness like the shadow of a ghostly pale horse. He was swallowed up by the black night like a spectre, a phantom.

She waited obediently, the pistol cold and heavy in her hand. Could she use it on herself if there were no escape? She remembered Papa's ordeal by fire and winced. Yes, she would rather do so than endure that agony. She wasn't as brave, as religious as Joe McBride.

Each slow second was ticked off by the pounding of her heart as she waited, tense and ready to flee. Clouds drifted across the moon and the flat, shadowy landscape seemed suddenly as black as the path to hell. Perspiration gathered in little beads on her palms and the roof of her mouth went so dry she couldn't swallow. For a long moment, she thought she smelled blood on the wind blowing from the dark shadows of the buildings.

Taking a deep breath, she wondered if fear and

105

terror had their own smells? *Of course they did*, she thought. *They smelled like cold sweat and warm blood.*

How long was she supposed to stay out here before she made a decision about what to do? He hadn't told her that, not knowing what might be lying in wait for him in the sinister shadows of the ranch. Should she turn and ride back to Wichita? Cayenne imagined him dead or dying somewhere among the outbuildings of the ranch, savages even now sneaking up on her. The pack pony stamped his feet and she jumped at the sound.

What should she do? Maybe he'd just forgotten to signal her or found something so terrible he'd forgotten all about her.

He'd told her to wait but she couldn't sit out here forever. She had to know what was happening. Cayenne urged the red roan forward, leading the packhorse. She rode at a walk into the ranch house yard. She thought she heard a sound and froze like a frightened baby deer, too afraid to move or even run. Another thought came to her. Suppose the warriors had grabbed him, killed him, or were holding a knife to his throat at this very moment while they watched her ride into the ranch?

What should she do?

The whistle floated on the still air like a ghostly refrain, very soft and low:

. . . *Maxwell's braes are bonnie, where early falls the dew* . . .

She whistled back, almost faint with relief.

. . . *and that's where Annie Laurie gave me her promise true* . . .

Maverick stepped around the corner of the barn, gesturing in the moonlight. Never had she been so glad to see anyone. She forgot about her anger, forgot everything but how big and strong and protective he looked.

Quickly she slid from the roan and ran into his arms. "Oh, I'm glad to see you! They haven't been here after all?"

He held her very close, brushed the hair out of her eyes. "They've been here," his voice was flat, devoid of emotion. "Don't ask, baby," he said. "Don't ask."

A thousand questions came to her mind, but for the moment she was content to obey him, to seek the safety of his powerful embrace.

"Cee Cee," he said against her hair, "I've checked things out. It was that Cheyenne war party, all right. We'd better stay right here, go to ground like quail do when there's danger. If we ride blindly into the dark, we might stumble right into their camp. See if you can rustle up some grub for us but don't light a fire or any lamps." He held her out at arm's length.

"What are you going to do?" She peered anxiously up at the outline of his rugged face.

"Feed three tired horses if the warriors didn't take the grain or burn it, put them out of sight in the barn."

"Are you sure we wouldn't be better off to keep riding under cover of darkness?"

He shook his head. "We're both tired and the horses are, too. Besides, at daylight we've got to bury—"

She waited for him to go on but he didn't. Tears came to her eyes. "Oh, Maverick, how awful! Are there children?"

"No, just a couple of cowhands. Probably two immigrants hoping to make a new life for themselves in the west, then go back east for wives." His voice sounded angry. "Poor devils probably never shot a single buffalo, but because of the hunters, these two

107

will never see another sunrise."

She looked up at him. "I used to think it was so simple, so black and white. I hated the Indians for their raiding and killing. . . ."

"The Indians are just fighting to stay alive," Maverick said grimly. "But that doesn't keep me from hating the Comanche. . . ."

"Why, Maverick? Why should you hate your own people? I hate them, too, but I've got good reason. They tortured my poor papa when he went into their camp as a hostage to free the women and children they'd taken. . . ."

"Joe McBride did that?" She saw the look of surprise on his face.

"Yes, and I hate them for it!" she said with deep feeling, remembering the terrible things they'd done to him. "But Papa says I shouldn't, that vengeance belongs to the Lord and He'll repay."

Maverick snorted and she saw the disdain on his hard features. "Some of us haven't the patience to wait for the Lord to get around to it!" He made a gesture of dismissal. "Let's not stand out here all night," he snapped. "Get some 'airtights' out of the packs; see what else you can find in the house while I put the horses away."

The inside of the small sod shack smelled like dirt and old smoke from the little fireplace. There was only one window with the moon shining in and she stumbled over a chair. Cayenne found the stub of a candle. Before she lit it, she carefully hung a burlap feed bag over the window.

The inside of the place was a wreck, things strewn about. The war party had taken any food supplies. *The Indians were hungry, too,* she thought, remembering the hundreds of buffalo skeletons and rotting

108

carcasses she'd ridden past that day. And because of that slaughter, two innocent settlers would be laid to rest in Kansas's red soil.

She found a pan of cold cornbread that the Indians had overlooked and a small jar of sand plum preserves. Whatever else they ate would have to come from their packhorse.

Maverick came in later and sat down to "airtights," canned peaches, and tomatoes. They ate in the flickering light of the one candle in silence.

Finally, he rolled a cigarette with a sigh and sat down on the cornshuck bed. "I'm so tired my body thinks I've died and forgot to lie down."

She started tidying up the dishes as he pulled his boots off and lay down on the bed.

"You don't have to bother," he said. "After all, who'll ever know whether you straightened up or not?"

She felt suddenly foolish. "I suppose you're right," she said. "It's just a habit from being the oldest child, looking after the others. Mama died when the little one, Angel, was born three years ago. I stepped in and took over."

"How many little sisters you got?"

"Four, all younger. Lynnie, she's nine. She's the smart one. Then there's Steve and Gracious. . . ."

"I thought you said you only had sisters?"

Cayenne grinned in spite of herself. "I do. But Papa named her Steve anyway. He wanted a boy; never got one." She watched the big half-breed smoke. "Papa always said he guessed he'd have to settle for a son-in-law to keep the ranch running."

A troubled look crossed his face. "Then if something happens to your old man, if he got killed, there'd be little kids left orphaned? Who's running the house now?"

"Old Rosita, the Mexican cook and housekeeper. I had to go off to Wichita to see after Mama's sister Ella who was dying."

"Tough," Maverick murmured. "Tough to be without a mama."

The sad way he said it told her somehow that Maverick's mother was dead. Cayenne pictured a gentle Comanche girl with beautiful dark hair and skin. Had his father been a "squaw man," a gray-eyed *gringo* who'd taken an Indian girl to warm his blankets for a while, then deserted her when her belly swelled with child?

She looked around. There was only the one bed. "Where am I supposed to sleep?" Surely he would do the gentlemanly thing—give her the bed, take a blanket himself, and sleep on the packed dirt floor.

He crossed his legs at the ankles and grinned at her, propping his head up on a stained pillow as he took his pistol out of its holster and stuck it under the pillow. "We aren't exactly strangers."

Now she remembered that same grin as he sat in a bathtub, that dark-haired, pretty whore scrubbing his back. Her indignation returned with the memory. "Since you're not going to treat me like a gentleman should, I'll just take a blanket and sleep on the floor!"

With an angry gesture, she jerked a worn quilt out from under his feet, waiting for him to jump up in protest.

But he only shrugged and snuffed out his cigarette. "Suit yourself, baby, I'm too tired to argue. There's room for both of us here, and believe me, you're safe as a church tonight."

She wasn't sure she trusted him. He'd hurt her feelings badly by being in that whore's room. Her own stubborn anger made her spread the blanket on the hard dirt. She blew out the candle.

Just as she lay down on the quilt, he said, "Don't be too nervous if a scorpion or centipede crawls across the dirt. If you brush them off gently, they shouldn't sting you."

"My stars! You had to say that, didn't you?" She jumped up in a fury, sitting down on a rickety chair. Then she wrapped herself in the blanket and pulled her knees up under her chin.

No answer. She waited. Any second now he'd relent and offer her the bed. Every muscle ached from sitting hunched up in the chair. "Maverick?"

In the darkness, she heard his gentle breathing and it dawned on her that he was asleep. Now what was she going to do? She resisted the urge to stride to the bed and attack him with both fists for his lack of gentlemanly concern. He'd threatened to whip her bottom several times already.

She thought about the butchered cowboys lying outside, waiting for burial. Maverick was right. She was childish to make such a big thing over who slept where. Gingerly she crept through the darkness, getting in on the far side of the bed. The rope springs creaked and groaned beneath her, and she held her breath but he didn't awaken. She clung to her edge of the cornshuck mattress, dropping off into a fitful sleep. Sometime in the night, she thought she heard something and it scared her enough to move closer to the protective warmth of his big body.

When she woke up just before dawn, she found herself in his arms with her face on his chest. Her eyes flickered open as she realized where she was, and she started. That slight movement awakened him and he came up grabbing for his pistol.

"It's okay," she pushed her hair out of her eyes.

111

"Do you suppose I dare make coffee?"

He stood up, stretching. "Let me look around outside." He reached for his boots, put them on, and went outside. In a moment, he returned. "There's not a breath of wind to carry the scent of smoke. Make some coffee but don't build a fire any bigger than your hand."

"You like your coffee the way all Texans like it?"

"Just like I like my women"—he winked at her—"hot and sweet."

"I meant strong and dark!" she blushed.

"That's the way Texan women like it, isn't it? Just like they like their men!"

Why had she ever thought there was anything salvageable in this savage? She got out a hunk of the stale corn bread and fried some bacon. And when she served up his coffee, she dumped four heaping spoons of sugar in it.

He made a wry face when he tasted it. "You have to be the orneriest little Scots-Irish bitch it's ever been my misfortune to run up against."

"It's the Rebel in me," she said coldly as she ate. "Of course a damned Yankee sympathizer couldn't appreciate that."

He drank the coffee, obviously determined not to lose the round. When he finished eating, he said, "I'm going out and bury those two men."

"I can help." She stood up.

"No, Cayenne," he answered sternly. "There's some things women shouldn't have to see. I'll take care of it."

She winced at the thought and turned away. Poor devils. She'd say prayers over the graves before they moved on.

* * *

112

Finally they were ready to ride out. She'd tucked the foolish blue gingham dress in her saddlebags, putting on the boy's shirt and pants she'd brought from Wichita.

Maverick handed her a straw hat. "Found it in the barn; guess it belonged to the younger man. It'll keep the sun off that fair skin. You're so sunburned your nose is starting to peel."

At least he hadn't said, "I told you so." She accepted the hat and put it on. "I feel funny about taking things that don't belong to me."

Maverick shrugged. "One thing's for certain, those *hombres* don't need anything anymore. The Cheyenne saw to that."

She looked at him curiously. "Are you sure it was Cheyenne?"

He nodded. "Kinda far north mostly for Comanche and Kiowa and too far south for Sioux, although the Sioux'll be the next to take the war path. Hear Custer's taking an expedition looking for gold through the Black Hills this summer. And that's Sioux hunting grounds."

Only a savage himself could know so very much about the tribes. Without thinking, she asked, "How long did you live with them, Maverick?"

" 'Til I was almost fourteen." His tone betrayed nothing.

"Why did you leave? Come back to the whites?"

"Baby, you ask too many questions," he snapped, and his hand seemed to go automatically to the jagged scar on his face as he dug his spurs in the gray. "Let's get out of here. By the way, I found a little jar of butter cooling in the well that the braves overlooked."

Butter. It seemed almost comical to be thinking about butter with the country swarming with Indians and with two fresh graves in the yard behind them.

113

She followed him and the packhorse away from the ranch.

She had more and more misgivings as they rode out to the southwest. Up ahead of them somewhere lay the Cherokee Outlet of the Territory and even more Indians.

"Maybe we should go back to Wichita and wait this out like you said."

He turned in his saddle, frowning at her. "A little late to decide that now. That war party may be combing the area between us and Wichita for buffalo hunters, any poor traveler, or wagon train they can raid."

"But what about the soldiers at Fort Dodge and the other forts? Why don't they do something?"

"What would you suggest?" He raised one eyebrow sardonically. "There's a thousand miles of wide-open country and the army can't be everywhere."

It must have been about noon when they crossed the dry stream and found the shade of the wild sand plum bushes. They ate their fill of the ripening fruit and rested. Maverick dug down in the dry sand until he'd formed a little well that gradually filled full of water. He filled their spare canteens before leading the eager, thirsty horses over to drink.

"You're a wonder," she said respectfully. "I feel more and more confident traveling with you."

He laughed and sat down next to her in the shade. "You'll think confident if we cross the trail of a war party."

She watched the horses drink. "Maverick, what do war parties do for water in a dry place?"

He hesitated as if he didn't want to relive that part of his life. "They say when a white man gives up on a

114

horse, a Mexican can get on him and ride him a few more miles, and when the Mexican can't get anything else out of him, a Comanche can get on it, make it go a few more miles. When the horse finally stumbles and dies, a Comanche'll take the horse's guts, fill them with muddy water, wrap them around his body for the extra supply, and keep riding."

She shuddered. "What terrible memories you must have."

He looked at her and the gray eyes softened. "They are, except for Annie Laurie. . . ."

She waited curiously for him to go on, wondering if the emotion that took hold of her was jealousy. She suddenly remembered his talking of a white captive. Had she been his woman? No, he'd only been fourteen when he left them.

Maverick stared into her face, abruptly frowning as he reached out to touch the tip of her nose. "By damn, baby, you're sunburned all down your neck, your arms."

Was he going to say, "I told you so"? "It's not bad," she insisted.

He got up, went over to the grazing packhorse, took out a little tin, and came back.

"I was planning on using this to make that stale hardtack worth eatin'," he said, "but I think you need it worse."

Her face felt as if it were on fire, but she'd never give him the satisfaction of knowing that. *The first day of July,* she thought wearily, watching him dip his fingers in the melted butter, *and oh, the weather was so hot; she was so weary.*

He rubbed the butter on her face with hands so gentle, a touch so sensitive, it surprised her. But she knew she must protest. "I can do that myself."

"I know that. But I'm going to." His tone told her

he expected no argument. She closed her eyes, enjoying his stroking the butter all over her burned face.

Maverick made a little sound of disapproval. "Reb, you're burned worse than I thought. I think we'll stay here and rest 'til this evening, travel after dark."

"You don't have to baby me," she bristled, not opening her eyes, enjoying the touch of his fingers on her face, "I'm perfectly capable of going on!"

"Then let's just say I'm tired," he chuckled as his fingers spread the butter down her throat. "I have to say your name suits you, Cayenne. You've got more fire and pepper to you than most women."

She caught the hint of admiration in his voice and was pleased, although she reminded herself that he was faithless, that she meant nothing to him. "Well, okay, if you're tired," she said, leaning back against the grass with a sigh. "But, remember, I offered to go on."

"Sure, baby, sure." She felt his fingers rub the warm butter into her throat, work their way down into the neck of her shirt. "By damn," he muttered, "you're burned worse than I thought. Next time, do like I tell you."

"Stop bossing me like I belonged to you."

His voice was almost a caress as his fingers fumbled with the top button of her shirt. "Don't you?"

She started to argue with him, to protest his unbuttoning that top button. But now his fingers moved still lower, lightly stroking her lower throat with the warm, rich butter. Cayenne sighed. She hadn't realized it would feel so good on her sunburned skin.

"You'll stain my shirt."

"I need to doctor that sunburn."

She let her eyes flicker open, look at him. She hesitated a long moment before she unbuttoned the second button, pulling the shirt off her shoulders so

116

he could stroke there. It felt so good, his fingers caressing her skin as he smeared hot butter on them.

"I need to get your arms." His gaze on hers was intense as he stroked her shoulders.

She shuddered all over at the gentle stroking of his hands on her skin. Then, without opening her eyes, she reached to unbutton the shirt all the way to the waist and jerked it open. She couldn't keep from arching up for the touch of his hands as they came down on her breasts.

Chapter Six

She closed her eyes, leaning back and relaxing as he rubbed the warm butter into her sunburned breasts.

"Roll over," he ordered. "Let me do your back."

Obediently she rolled over, shivering at the feel of his fingers massaging the hot, melted liquid into her shoulders, along her spine. Without thinking, she made a sound of animal pleasure.

"Your skin's so dry it's chapping from this hot wind," he complained. "I'd better oil you down all over. Unbutton your pants."

"I don't know—"

"I've seen everything you've got," he snorted. "Unbutton 'em."

Lying on her belly, she reached under herself and unbuttoned them. She felt Maverick jerk her boots off, then her pants. Before she could protest, he pulled off her lace drawers.

If she'd felt embarrassment, she forgot it as his hands crept lower down her waist, massaging the warm butter into her hips.

"Kid, you've got the best-lookin' bottom I've ever seen on a woman."

She stiffened, unsure whether to be insulted or complimented. "And I'll bet you've seen a lot of them!"

He popped her smartly on the rear. "Relax! I've seen my share," he admitted, "none so fine as yours."

She tried to remember she was angry with him, but it was hard to do with his strong hands gently massaging the butter the length of her back, caressing her hips. "Better than that saloon girl's?"

He laughed. "You still het up over her? I swear I haven't touched another woman since the first time I saw you, wanted you."

His hands were kneading the back of her thighs now, working their sure way down her calves. *He was flattering her,* she thought. "When was the first time you saw me?"

"From the upstairs window at the Red Garter." His fingers caressed the back of her calves, sending little shivers of pleasure all over her. "I'd gone up there with Molly, but once I saw you standing down there in the street, I couldn't take her. All I wanted was you."

His hard, sure hands rubbed the butter into her feet, between her toes.

She rolled over and looked up at him. "Are you lying to me to get me over my mad?"

He shrugged and began rubbing her throat, working his way down toward her breasts. "Cee Cee, I don't care whether you believe me or not. I'm just tellin' you how it is."

She looked into the gray eyes and they were soft, warm for once, like a gray kitten she'd once owned. Somehow she knew he spoke the truth. *She was taking him back to face three gunfighters who were probably going to kill him.* Cayenne felt such shame she couldn't look at him. "Rub me all over," she sighed, closing her eyes.

She heard him dip his hand in the butter again, and

119

then his calloused hands cupped her breasts, massaging the hot butter into the skin, into her nipples. She took a deep breath and felt her nipples harden into erect pink buds as he caressed them, moved down to her belly.

"Umm, baby," he murmured as he stroked her, "with that vanilla scent and all this butter, you're good enough to eat!" She felt him lean over and his tongue licked the butter from the hollow of her navel. That sent sensations of pleasure tingling through her very being.

Her eyes flickered open, looked up at him, and saw the slight redness of his own nose. "You're burnt, too," she whispered and reached over, dipping her fingertips in the butter, rubbing it on his face, across the jagged scar.

He hesitated, as if unsure how to react while her fingers rubbed the oil across his high cheekbones and down into the open neck of his shirt.

"Take it off," she whispered.

His eyes never left hers as he hesistated. "Baby, you'd better think twice—"

"I said take it off."

With a shrug, he unbuttoned the shirt, pulling it off.

Cayenne looked at his big chest critically. "I thought you'd have Sun Dance scars."

He laughed. "Comanches don't sun dance. I've got scars, though." He pointed to a long one on his ribs. "Here's where a bear almost got me before I got him." He touched one on his arm. "Here's where a Ute missed my heart, caught my arm with that lance; cost him his life."

She reached out, running her finger over the jagged scar on his cheek. "What about that one?"

He hesitated. "A Comanche named Pine da poi,

Whip Owner, gave me that."

Something about his hesitance, the forbidding look on his face, warned her off, but her curiosity got the better of her. "And did you kill him, too?"

He smiled in grim satisfaction. "Not that night. But a few months later I got him; got him in a way Comanches fear most. I strangled him."

She winced at the satisfaction in his dark face. "You—you did what?

He nodded toward the loop of rawhide lying by his gunbelt. "Comanches fear to die that way. They think a man's soul escapes up his throat, out his mouth as he dies. If he's strangled or hanged, his soul can't escape; it's trapped in his dead body forever. I'm only sorry I didn't have time to torture him. My uncle's death was too easy."

He looked toward the scalp hanging on the gray's bridle and smiled slowly.

"Your own uncle?" Cayenne stared at him with helpless horror. Maverick was a strange, savage animal and yet she was attracted to him like a moth to a deadly fire. She knew she should be repulsed by his primitive cruelty, and yet when his hand reached out to touch her face, he was both gentle and hesitant.

Cayenne dipped her hand in the butter, rubbing it on his wide shoulders, down the powerful chest. His bronzed skin, like most Indians, was almost hairless. She hesitated only a moment, then worked her hand down the big chest, stroking his dark nipples.

He took a deep, shuddering breath and caught her hand. "You'd better stop while you can, Reb," he warned. "You're about to build a fire you can't put out."

She looked at him, her small hand completely enclosed by his big one, and she wanted him. "I know

121

how to put it out," she said.

He laughed uneasily, not letting go of her hand. "You're mad at me, remember?"

He was a damned Yankee sympathizer, a Comanche, and a rough, arrogant cowboy who had tumbled her in the grass on a creek bank, taking her virginity. And yet, that was all outweighed by the ecstasy she had found in his arms, the way her body even now cried out for him. "Lie down," she said. "I'll cover you with butter."

"My skin's too dark to sunburn."

"I'll do it anyway."

He chuckled. "Suit yourself, baby." He unbuckled his gun belt and lay down on his belly.

Cayenne straddled his waist with her naked body as she rubbed the hot oil into his ropy back muscles. Never had she seen such a virile, powerful build. *A stallion,* she thought, *a stallion of a man.* "Roll over."

He rolled over and she dipped her hand in the butter again, rubbing it on his wide chest and into his dark nipples, feeling them go taut beneath her fingers.

His eyes were as dark and deep as gray mountain pools. "Baby, you're about to get into serious trouble."

"Am I?" She leaned over then, kissed him.

With a groan, his hands came up, catching her face, and he kissed her deeply, thoroughly.

Straddling his body, she felt his manhood go rigid, throbbing against her hips. She pulled back, reaching down to unbuckle his belt. "Make love to me, Maverick."

He breathed hard but didn't move. "Uh uh, baby," he shook his head. "You'll never accuse me of rape again."

She bent, running her tongue over his nipple. "Aren't you planning to marry me when we get to

Texas?" *If he lived*, she thought with a pang of conscience.

"No fair!" he gasped, arching up against her tongue. "No man's responsible for what he says when a woman does that to him!"

"I come with a dowry of a nice ranch," she whispered, and rubbed the edge of the dark circle hard with her tongue.

He swore under his breath, caught her shoulders, and pulled her mouth down on his nipple. "Baby, at this moment I don't give a damn about a ranch!"

She moved off him, running her hand down his skin under his pants. His manhood throbbed hotly against her hand. And her body needed him as she had never realized she could need a man. "Make love to me, Maverick," she whispered again.

With a low groan, he reached down, took his pants off, and pulled her to him in a crushing embrace. "Baby, you really know how to make a man want you!"

She dipped her hand in the butter, rubbing it into his lean, dark body, and they clung together, both covered with oil, both kissing each other's skin.

He pulled her hard up against him, kissing her lips feverishly. "I'm going to put my baby in your belly!" he said.

"Then do it!" she challenged.

He grabbed her, turned her on her back; took her hard and fast and deep. Cayenne dug her nails into his dark, powerful shoulders, tilting herself up so he could go into her very core while she wrapped her long legs around his hard-driving hips.

She arched herself to nip his nipples with her sharp little teeth, sending spasms of pleasure through him. "Ride me!" she whispered. "Ride me deep and good!"

And he obliged with a savage frenzy, like some wild

mustang stallion taking a mare. She didn't care any-more whether this was right or wrong. He was her man, had been since the first fumbling innocent kiss on the boardwalk in Wichita. He was her man and she wanted no other.

Afterwards they lay naked and spent in each other's arms, sleeping the hot afternoon away while the horses grazed. Toward dusk he awakened her by kissing her skin gently, running his tongue across her breasts. "Maybe that wasn't such a waste of the butter," he grinned down at her. "We'll have to do this again sometime."

She smiled contentedly at him, ruffling his black hair with her hand. For once, the troubled, closed expression he usually wore seemed replaced by a gentle peace. "I love you, Maverick Durango," she whispered, "and you'll like it on our ranch. It's the Lazy M; now that can stand for Maverick and McBride."

His expression changed suddenly, as if a disturbing thought had crossed his mind. He sat up and looked down at her. "Sometimes things don't work out hap-pily, Cee Cee, even when we wish they could."

What was he driving at? Then she remembered his words about the man he sought vengeance against. "You're still determined to go after that man?"

He nodded, turning away as if he didn't want her to look into his troubled eyes, see his troubled soul.

"Why, Maverick? Why do you feel you must?"

"I—I made a vow I'd get him. I made it in blood."

Whose blood? she thought with shock and horror, trying to imagine that scene. "Can't you forget it? It happened so very long ago. Do you hate the man so much?"

What she saw in his face was brutal and ugly. When

124

he finally spoke, his voice shook with a terrible anger. "I hate him so much, if he were on fire, I wouldn't spit on him to put it out!"

"This revenge, this hate is liable to consume you!"

He ran his hand through his black hair. "I don't care about that as long as I get him. I owe it to Annie Laurie."

She imagined the white girl with a pang of jealousy. *Wasn't it an unusual coincidence that it was her father's favorite song?* Maybe not; it was a common old Scots folk tune. "Would Annie herself approve?"

Maverick looked at her and she saw real agony there. "No, she'd try to stop me. Annie loved the bastard right up 'til the end. But I intend to kill him for the hurt she suffered. And I won't kill him fast; I'll kill him Comanche style, very slowly and painfully!"

She felt a loss then, a deep hurting loss. "Then there can be no future for us if you're going to spend your life looking for this man. You're a tortured soul, Maverick."

"My friends say I never forget a friend nor forgive an enemy."

He was diametrically opposite in every way to the manner in which she'd been raised, what Joe McBride stood for. "I feel sorry for you," she whispered, but she felt sorrier for herself, "What a horrible way to spend the rest of your life!"

He looked away. "I think I know where he is now. When I've done what I intend to do, would you still want me?"

"With blood on your hands?" She cringed away from him in dismay. "Maverick, do you think a preacher's daughter could marry a man she knew had cold-bloodedly tracked a man down and killed him the way ranchers do coyotes?"

125

His face turned remote, the eyes cold and hard as gray steel. "To my way of thinking, he's no better than a coyote."

She reached out, put her hand on his shoulder. "Give it up, Maverick. For your own sake, stop this vengeance quest!"

He shook her hand off, standing up, and she thought he was after all only a magnificent, uncivilized savage. Maybe it was just as well that things had come to this. She had been about to tell him about the three men who had ridden into the ranch a couple of weeks ago and holed up there. And now it was her job to do something about them because Papa couldn't—or maybe wouldn't. Well, if Maverick survived the confrontation with Slade, he could ride on to his vengeance. If he didn't maybe she wouldn't have to feel so guilty, knowing that she had saved some unsuspecting man's life. Maverick Durango had no more heart, no more conscience than the Comanches who had tortured her father and had changed the McBride family's lives forever.

The distance between them was too far, the chasms too deep for them to ever cross, Cayenne thought sadly as she looked at his cold, remote features. She stood up and began to dress. "I guess this is where we leave it, then."

He reached for his shirt. "I should have realized you'd do this," he said coldly. "Try to use your body to stop me. I suppose I'd do the same thing in your place."

She stared at him in puzzlement. "My stars! What on earth are you talking about?"

He grabbed up the rest of his clothes, smiling without mirth. "By damn, you know what I'm talking about!"

126

She started to argue that she hadn't the faintest idea what he was driving at but decided by his hostile expression that he wouldn't believe her, whatever she said.

They traveled for several days only in the darkness until they were deep into the Cherokee Outlet of the Indian Territory. They kept a remote politeness between them as they rode, and each spread his own blanket for sleeping. He made no more moves to touch her, and sometimes when she lay watching him sleep, she longed for his embrace, his caress. But she knew nothing would come of it, that their worlds were too far apart, so she did not reach out to him.

I'm going to put my baby in your belly. She wondered curiously if he'd made good that promise, thrilled with the emotion of carrying the big half-breed's child, then realized it was an impossible dream. Even if he survived the showdown with the trio back home, the two of them could never have any kind of a life together—not unless he finally forgot his vengeance and stopped this restless search for that mysterious man he'd vowed to kill.

Sometimes as they rode across the flat, hot prairie, she wondered about that doomed man—who he was, what had ever happened to him. It had been a long time. He might not be on the frontier anymore. He might even be dead. But when she thought about it, she, like Maverick, felt a surge of contempt and hatred for the man who had left his wife to the Indians. She wondered idly why Maverick's "squawman" father had not helped her? Then she recalled he'd said something that indicated to her his father had died when he was quite small, leaving him at the mercy of the others. Well, no doubt they hated him because of his white blood. Had they mistreated his Indian mother, too? But she was dead also; he'd said that.

Once as they rode along, she absentmindedly whistled the old folk tune! . . . *Maxwell's braes are bonnie, where early falls the dew . . .*

Maverick looked over at her and she broke off. "I'm sorry," she blurted. "I'd forgotten what the song meant to you."

"It's all right," he shrugged. "Somehow, when it comes from you, it doesn't hurt. It just brings back the good memories. Go ahead and whistle."

Had Annie been his woman or only his unfulfilled love? Even though he'd left the Comanche at fourteen, she'd heard the Indians mated early. *Annie Laurie.* Cayenne felt helpless against this ghost. Annie would always come between them until the day that Maverick was willing to let go of her, let her fade away in peace. Jealousy bedeviled Cayenne because she couldn't bear to think of any woman in his arms but herself.

So they rode across the Cherokee Outlet. Once Maverick spotted signs of a war party—a broken blade of brass, an almost invisible hoofprint of an unshod horse. But they kept riding. And everywhere were dead buffalo. Flies and buzzards flew up from the stinking carcasses as the pair rode past.

Maverick shook his head and muttered, "Used to be the hunters at least stayed above the 'Dead line' that marks the Territory because there were plenty of buffalo still on the Kansas plains and the hunters were terrified of the tribes catching them on Indian lands. But they're getting bolder and greedier as the buffalo thin out."

Cayenne tried to keep track of the days as they rode but it was hard to do. She figured it must have been late in the evening of the last week of June when the pair came upon the three supply wagons camped on the prairie a few miles above the Cimarron River.

"Hello the camp!" Maverick shouted from a distance, not wanting to risk getting shot at by nervous teamsters.

Four white men armed with rifles stood up, inspected the pair at a distance, and waved them on in.

Cayenne felt relief at finally seeing other civilized people. They rode into the camp and dismounted. There were four giant freighter wagons loaded with goods. Teams of big mules grazed contentedly on the sparse buffalo grass among the red Indian Blanket blooms that Cayenne knew as "Firewheel."

The big bearded leader waved the pair in by the campfire. "Howdy, folks, get down and set a spell; I'm Pat Hennessy."

Cayenne smiled gratefully. "It was getting mighty lonely out here; glad to see some human faces. I'm Cayenne McBride and this is Maverick Durango."

Maverick touched the brim of his hat with two fingers and dismounted. He started toward her but one of the young drivers rushed over and helped her dismount. The half-breed frowned but said nothing as he knelt by the fire, and it came to her suddenly that his displeasure was created by the other man's hands on her waist. *Why, he thinks he owns me!* she thought defiantly.

The good-natured leader introduced the other three drivers. "This is Rand, Byrd, and Fleming." He handed Cayenne a cup of steaming coffee and she sipped it gratefully.

"Thanks," she sighed.

"You two are sure taking a chance," Hennessy said. "We are too, I reckon. They warned us not to try to come from Fort Supply, but we got food that's got to be delivered down to the Kiowa at their reservation near Fort Sill."

Maverick shrugged and sipped his coffee. "I told the lady the Territory was workin' alive with war parties, but she's stubborn."

Hennessy pulled at his beard and smiled. "A mite headstrong, is she?"

Maverick favored her with a slight smile. "You might say that."

Rand, the driver who had helped Cayenne dismount, winked at her. "The best women are like good mustangs—a little wild and headstrong until broken by the right cowboy."

Silence fell over the group. Maverick looked at the flippant driver with an expression that made Cayenne shiver. "Don't ever try to break a filly out of another man's string."

Cayenne felt the tenseness in the air as the two men eyed each other like fighting dogs.

Rand was a little too handsome, a little too sure of his charm. He smiled at Cayenne and looked at her left hand. "I don't see no man's brand on her."

Maverick put one hand on his thigh, within easy reach of his pistol. "That don't mean she'll be willin' to wear yours," he said so softly. Cayenne barely heard him but there was no mistaking the cold threat in his gray eyes.

"My," she said, a little too brightly to break the awkward silence, "aren't we glad we stumbled onto you all! We're headed to the Texas Panhandle, south of Palo Duro Canyon. Where'd you say you're headed, Mr. Hennessy?"

The big man nodded toward the wagons. "We hope to make it into the Darlington Indian Agency

130

by July 4."

Rand rolled a cigarette. "There'll be a big Independence Day celebration there probably, dancing and all." His eyes looked Cayenne over, desire evident. "You two got no business out here traveling alone. You should go along with us to the agency."

Maverick sipped his coffee, glowering at the man. *Why, he's jealous*, Cayenne thought, and heady with her suddenly discovered power, she couldn't resist flirting a little.

"Why, Rand, that sounds like fun. I'll bet you two-step beautifully."

Maverick glared at her but she ignored him.

Hennessy cleared his throat. "We may not be there long enough to party, Rand. If we don't get this food to those starving Kiowa down in the Wichita Mountains, they've sworn to join the Uprising."

Maverick sighed. "You can hardly blame them for that. The plains tribes are all starving because of the damned buffalo hunters."

"Let 'em starve," Rand sneered. "The sooner we get the buffalo killed off, the sooner we can corral all those damned savages, pen 'em up like the animals they are."

For a moment, Maverick's face darkened and she wondered if there would be a fight, knowing there was an unspoken rivalry here for her favors. She had never been one to keep her mouth shut when she disagreed. "You should be ashamed," she said to Rand. "I got good reason to hate the Comanche myself, but I can't really blame the warriors for putting on war paint. Any man'd do the same if his family was starving."

Rand colored and ducked his head at her scolding.

Maverick smiled thinly. "Like the mustang, she's got spirit," he chided his rival.

The tension in the air was too heavy to bear. Cayenne

131

jumped up. "How about me cooking up some supper for all of us? How'd that be?"

The freighters nodded eagerly.

Hennessy said, "I shot a half-dozen quail an hour ago. Could you fry them?"

"Sure," Cayenne nodded. "And if one of you will pick some of those wild sand plums off those bushes over there, I'll make some fried pies."

Byrd and Fleming rushed to pick the plums while the good-natured freighter boss cleaned the quail. Maverick and Rand both sat by the fire, smoking and glaring at each other while she got out flour to dip the quail in and mixed up some corn dodger batter.

"You two aren't doing anything," she scolded. "I needed more fuel for my fire; go find me some prairie coal." Both men rose reluctantly, going to search the treeless plains and coming back with dried buffalo chips for the fire.

Then she watched with satisfaction as she handed out the tin plates, watched the men gobble the succulent golden brown quail, the hot corn dodgers. But Maverick bit into the fried quail hesitantly.

Rand sneered, his mouth full of food. "What's the matter, Injun? The lady's cookin' don't suit you?"

Maverick looked at the meat in distaste. "Comanche don't eat birds or fish; it's taboo."

Arrogantly, Rand reached over as if to grab the quail off Maverick's plate. "In that case, I'll—"

Maverick's hand caught his wrist in a steel grip, twisting until Rand screamed with pain. "A little dog doesn't grab a big dog's bone!"

Hennessy stood up. "Here! Here, boys! Rand, you're out of line! You been looking for a fight ever since this pair rode in and I think you'd better back off! If it's 'fight' you want, you may get it 'afore we get

132

where we're going!'"

Rand pulled away, nursing his injured arm. "Plain's workin' alive with redskins wantin' to scalp folks and we got to feed one at our campfire!'"

Cayenne paused in eating the juicy, crisp quail. "Mr. Hennessy invited us to eat."

Hennessy nodded, glaring at Rand. "I beg your pardon for his bad manners, ma'am. We're all a little edgy over all this Uprisin' talk. You see any Injun sign?"

Maverick ate the quail reluctantly. "We buried a pair of cow hands up above the Territory border. Found a burial platform; seen a lot of unshod pony tracks."

Hennessy frowned, wiping his greasy hands on his pants. "Cheyenne?"

Maverick nodded.

"How'd you know it was Cheyenne?" Rand challenged. "How you know it wasn't, say, Kiowa?"

Maverick smiled grimly. "When the Kiowa take a scalp, they also take one of the ears as a trophy. Those poor devils had no hair left but they had both ears."

The men looked at each other in stunned silence and Cayenne saw fear in their eyes.

Hennessy sighed. "We was warned not to make this trip; the cavalry says they can't patrol the whole frontier. But if we can get all this food down to the Kiowa, maybe they won't join the war parties."

Rand looked at Cayenne. "You heard that, miss? Injuns everywhere! You'd be a lot safer traveling with us than with him."

Maverick frowned at him. "No woman'd be safe with you, cowboy."

"Boys, stop that!" Cayenne scolded sharply. "I—I'll think about your offer, Rand. I know we're riding right into a hornet's nest but I need to get home. My—my papa's sick," she lied.

Paunchy little Fleming tilted his head to one side. "McBride? I don't suppose that might be Joe McBride?"

"You know my papa?" she smiled warmly.

The man grinned, shaking his head. "Just heard of him. He the one they call 'the shootin' preacher'? Heard he gave the cash prize to charity but kept the fancy rifle he won as first prize."

Maverick looked at her. "What rifle?"

Cayenne stood up, brushing grass off her pants. "I told you Papa was the best rifle shot in west Texas." *Or used to be,* she thought.

Fleming shook his head. "Man! Man! What I wouldn't give for a fancy rifle like that! Guess that's why so many tried to win it. Your papa must be some shot! A gun like that'd be a real treasure to give to a son."

Cayenne shook her head sadly. "Papa has no sons."

Rand wiped up the last of his gravy with the corn bread. "If you're in the market, ma'am, I'm not married and I'd be right proud—"

"She's not in the market," Maverick said flatly.

Rand looked at Cayenne. "That right?"

Her temper flared as she resented Maverick's arrogant assumption. "No, that's not right! You know, Rand, maybe I ought to ride along with you all to the Darlington Agency; it wouldn't be much out of the way since it's south of here. Suppose it would be a whole lot safer."

Rand's face lit up. "From there, I could escort you the rest of the way home, ma'am. I'd be interested in talkin' to your pa about courtin' you."

"I don't know. . . ." She looked over at Maverick. His eyes were as cold as a Texas norther.

Hennessy scratched his head. "Well, you don't have to decide right this here minute, Miss McBride. Let's all bed down for the night, talk about it at dawn."

Maverick glared at her in sullen silence as he went over, got her blankets, and tossed them to her. "Just keep it up!" he said. "You're too innocent to know what you do to men. You had him prancin' around as eager as some stud horse!"

"Rand's a perfect gentleman!" She colored at his words, tossed her head in defiance, and went back to the camp circle.

In minutes, the fire was banked, the small group asleep on the ground.

It was the middle of the night when Cayenne felt an urge to relieve herself, quietly got up, and crept out of the circle of sleeping men. She tiptoed out to the grove of wild plum bushes. Cayenne was on her way back through the thicket when she heard a twig crackle and she started.

Rand stepped out of the bushes ahead of her. "Evening, ma'am," he said softly. "Sorry if I scared you. I heard you leave, got worried something might happen to you out here unescorted. Decided I'd better come see about you."

She was touched by his chivalrous concern. "Why, thanks, Rand, it was kind of you."

"Miss McBride"—he moved closer—"about this evenin', I really meant that. I'd be proud to accompany you back to Texas, proud to court you, give you a chance to get to know me. I'd be interested in marryin' up with you."

"I—I don't know what to say except I'm flattered, Rand." He was handsome, she thought, and polite. She couldn't stop her mind from picturing him naked.

Would he have hard, sinewy muscles like the half-breed? Would he take her with the savage frenzy of Maverick Durango?

The cowboy must have taken her hesitation for encouragement because he reached out and put his hands on her shoulders. "Stop actin' so innocent!" His tone dripped arrogance. "You built a fire in me, honey, flirting with me like you done. I know what you want; why you came out to the bushes, hopin' I'd follow you!"

Before she realized his intent, he pulled her to him, kissing her thoroughly while she froze in shock. One of his arms held her tightly to him while he tried to force his knee between her thighs. Her arms were pinned to her sides by his embrace, and when she tried to cry out, his tongue went into her mouth, hot and demanding. She struggled against his strength but he held her easily, his free hand coming up to stroke her breasts.

She saw the dark shadow past his shoulder as she struggled in his arms. Before she could move, a hand came out of the darkness, caught Rand's shoulder, and spun him around.

Maverick's white teeth shone in the darkness as he snarled. "You snake!" He hit Rand then, a solid blow that caught the man in the chin with a thud, sending him stumbling backward.

Over by the campfire, the others came out of their blankets. "Fight! Fight!" one of them yelled.

As the others came running, Cayenne watched the two square off, snarling with fury. There might be a killing here tonight and whoever won figured her body would be the prize!

Chapter Seven

All Cayenne could do was watch as the two men fought. Hennessy and the others came running, but when paunchy Fleming moved as if to stop them, the bearded leader gestured him away. "These two been snarlin' and circlin' each other all evenin' over that girl! We might as well let them get it outa their blood!"

The moon came out, lighting up the shadowy ground as the two men meshed in combat.

Maverick hit Rand hard, sending him falling into a plum bush. "You dirty sonovabitch! I'll teach you how to treat a woman!"

Rand came up, blood dripping down his chin. "She can't be much, travelin' with a filthy Injun!" He swung, catching Maverick on the jaw, the half-breed went down.

Cayenne looked on helplessly as the fight moved out onto the grassy prairie. She gestured toward the others. "Aren't you gonna stop them! They'll kill each other!"

Hennessy shrugged. "I can only do so much, miss. Are you going with the winner?"

Maverick hit Rand again and they clenched, rolling over and over.

Of course not, she thought. *I never had any interest in Rand. I'm going with Maverick.* And with that decision, she grabbed up a plum bush branch, running over to attack Rand who had Maverick down choking him.

She flayed him about the head and shoulders until he

137

was forced to let go, trying to fend her off. "You little bitch!" he howled.

"Don't call her that!" Maverick roared, stumbling to his feet. Cayenne backed off as Maverick hit him again. This time when the driver went down, and the half-breed looped the rawhide thong around his neck and pulled both ends.

Cayenne saw the fury on Maverick's face as he garroted Rand, and she knew the savage half-breed intended to kill him.

She ran over and caught Maverick's hands. "Stop!" she shrieked. "Maverick! Don't kill him! He isn't worth it!"

For a split second she thought he would strike her as she struggled to pull his hands away. Then reason seemed to return to the cold gray eyes, and he loosened the thong and stood up. "You're right," he muttered. "He isn't worth it."

Rand stumbled to his feet, clutching at his reddened throat and gasping, "He was going to kill me! Damned Injun!"

Hennessy shrugged. "You brought it on yourself, boy, messin' with his woman! No real man'd do any less! Now maybe you'll behave yourself 'til we get to Darlington!"

Maverick came over to Cayenne and caught her shoulders in his strong hands. "Are you all right, Reb?" His voice still shook with uncontrolled fury. "If he's hurt you, I'll—"

"I'm all right," she nodded quickly. "Don't kill him!"

Maverick's grip relaxed and he let go of her shoulders almost reluctantly.

So uncivilized, so savage, she thought, studying his hard features. She remembered the gentle way his hands had stroked her when they made love, but those same

138

hands had almost taken a man's life because of her. Maverick Durango was clearly no one to be messed with!

Maverick glanced up at the moon. "We need to move out anyway, see how far we can get before the heat of day."

Hennessy stroked his beard and looked over at the choking, stumbling Rand. "You two are ridin' into the heart of the Uprising country! You'd be a lot safer going to the Darlington agency with us, then on down to Fort Sill."

Maverick ran his hand through his tousled black hair. "No. Rand might decide to paw Cayenne again and I'd kill him next time for sure!"

Hennessy laughed. "And I reckon you're surely the man who could do it, Maverick!"

Rand didn't say anything as he brushed past them, limping back to camp.

So the pair saddled up, loaded their packhorse, and headed southwest again. They rode until late afternoon, stopping only to make a cold camp and eat a little dried beef jerky and stale cornbread.

Maverick smiled at her. "Now I wish I'd saved the butter."

She felt a flush of embarrassment at her wild, abandoned behavior. There was something about this man that heated her blood, made her react in ways she'd never dreamed possible. "I didn't ask you to waste it on my sunburn," she replied coldly.

He grinned and her heart melted. *Was he really all that handsome? Only when he smiled,* she thought suddenly, watching the big gray eyes soften, *only when he smiled.* She imagined a son with those big gray eyes. Would he be dark like Maverick, too? Jefferson Davis Durango. Then she remembered that he would never settle down to a peaceful, married life, would always roam and search until his thirst for vengeance was sated.

"What are you thinking about?" he asked, standing feet wide apart, thumbs hooked in his gun belt.

She glanced at the scalp dangling from the big gray's bridle. No, he was too much of an uncivilized savage to ever be tamed, even if he survived the showdown in Texas.

"Nothing," she lied. "Nothing."

They spread their blankets, resting through the heat of the afternoon in what little shade they found under a lone cottonwood, while the horses grazed peacefully. He made no moves toward her and quickly dropped off to sleep on his blanket, his pistol ever ready under his hand. As he slept, his face smoothed out, the worry and emotion leaving it. She realized then he wasn't nearly as old as he'd seemed before, surely not more than his middle twenties. A troubled frown crossed his face and she heard him whisper, "Annie, I'm sorry . . . I couldn't stop him. . . ."

She listened jealously, straining to hear his words, but he only moaned softly, as if remembering something too horrible to face, and thrashed around.

Cayenne reached over and put a comforting hand on his shoulder. "Maverick, wake up. Are you all right?"

He jerked upright suddenly, startling her. "What happened?"

"Nothing. You were having a nightmare, that's all."

He frowned, running his hand down the scar on his cheek. "Sometimes it's so bad, I'm afraid to go to bed, afraid I'll dream. . . ."

She waited expectantly but he only sighed, running his hand through his tousled black hair.

"Maverick," she said softly, "if you'd let go of her memory, you wouldn't have those dreams."

His eyes shone with unshed tears and his hand trembled as he reached for his tobacco. "Not until I get him." His voice shook with anger and she didn't need to ask what he meant. "When I get him, then she can rest in peace."

Could she give this tortured soul any comfort at all? "Papa used to pace the floor at night. I can remember hearing him walking up and down when I was little."

Maverick rolled a cigarette. "Lots of men have regrets, guilt they can't deal with," he said acidly.

"Who? Papa?" she almost scoffed. She couldn't imagine her beloved papa doing anything wrong. But then she knew nothing about his past except that he'd been a poor immigrant who'd come with a wagon train many years ago from Kentucky. His drawling accent still betrayed his southern past.

"Then why'd he pace the floor?" He stuck the "quirley" between his lips.

Cayenne shrugged. "I—I don't know, really. It started when some boy came to the ranch with some kind of message. That was maybe a little over ten years ago. After that, until Mama died three years ago, he paced nearly every night. I used to lie in my little bed wondering what worried him and how I could help."

"Ten years," Maverick seemed to speak without thinking. "Twenty-five is what it should be."

"What?" she eyed him curiously.

"Nothing, nothing," he muttered, and seemed flustered as he lit a match with his thumbnail. "What'd the young man say?"

Cayenne shook her head. "Don't know, really. Papa and Mama took him into the parlor, closed the door, sent me out to swing. But things were never the same after that day. There was tension between my parents; I could feel it. Mama always acted as if she was jealous of me." The old hurt came back as she reluctantly relived those years. She'd never discussed it with anyone before.

"You're the most beautiful woman I ever met, Cayenne," he said simply, shaking out the match. "Was your mother pretty?"

She blushed at the compliment, ducking her head. "No, Mama was plump and plain. But she'd inherited a big ranch. Sometimes when I was little, I used to wonder why a handsome redheaded man like Joe McBride would marry a homely, sour woman like Hannah Adams."

Maverick snorted as he smoked. "It wouldn't be the first time a man married a lonely spinster for her dowry."

Cayenne frowned. "Well, he sure doesn't have anything now. He mortgaged it all to raise the ransom for the Comanche hostages eight months ago."

"Any of those hostages related to him?"

"No. My papa is a kind man, a heroic man. That's why he mortgaged our place to stingy banker Ogle to raise the money; went into that camp when everyone else was afraid to." She swallowed hard, remembering that terrible day. "I tried to keep him from going, told him it wasn't his responsibility. He said the welfare of other people was his responsibility, and besides, he owed a debt to someone he'd never paid. This was his way of evening things up."

Maverick appeared visibly shaken. His hand trembled as it brought the cigarette to his lips. "Joe McBride said that?"

She nodded, wondering what memories her discussion of Comanches had brought back from his own past. "I wondered what he meant but he never mentioned it again, even after what the Indians did. . . ." Her voice trailed off as she thought about the way they'd tortured him. Some of those braves might be Maverick's relatives. But Papa hadn't been bitter about it. "Papa turned his life around, became very religious after Mama died."

142

Maverick smoked and studied her. "She died havin' your youngest sister?"

Cayenne nodded and tasted salt as the tears came to her eyes. "When Mama was dying, I bent over her bed and she whispered, 'We was wrong, wrong. He did it to protect you, Cee Cee, but I did it to hold onto him. Joe always loved you more than me. I hated you for it.' " Cayenne wiped the crooked tear streaks on her sleeve. "I've always wondered what she meant but I never asked Papa. He had so much to bear already with five motherless kids."

Maverick cleared his throat several times and turned his head so she could not see his face. "It's—it's tough to be alone in the world, no parents," he said finally.

She watched him smoke in silence, wondering about his bereft, lonely expression. *Had any woman ever held his love besides Annie Laurie?* "After Mama died, Papa found peace in religion, stopped pacing the floor at night."

"Peace!" Maverick sneered. "Even the dead have no peace! And there's sure none for those of us left behind!" Maverick ground out his cigarette. He looked up at the sky. "It'll be dusk soon. The Cimarron's up ahead of us some place. If we can find it, it'd be a good place to camp."

Cayenne watched him, thinking of the dead, mysterious girl whose love goaded Maverick incessantly toward revenge. *He would only find peace with a new love*, she thought, *when he let go of that other ghost, let the dead rest in the haziness of memory.*

A distant boom rumbled, interrupting her thoughts. It was followed by another echoing boom. "Is that thunder? The sky's too clear for rain. . . ."

" 'Big Fifty' buffalo guns," Maverick said grimly as he stood up and stuck his thumbs in his gun belt. "They seem to be off to the west a way, we'll avoid that area."

She nodded, picking up her hat.

Maverick hesitated. "Cee Cee, until we clear this area, I'd think it wise for you to put your hair up under your hat, wear one of my shirts so your curves don't show."

"I don't understand—"

"Buffalo hunters," he nodded toward the sound again. "Just in case we run onto them, I'd just as soon they'd think you were a boy."

She realized what he intimated and the thought scared her a little. She did as he told her, and soon they were mounted up, riding toward the Cimarron River while the big buffalo guns boomed off to their right. Without even thinking about it, she rode closer to Maverick so that their stirrups were almost brushing, then realizing what she did, Cayenne laughed to herself a little, knowing how much she had come to depend on him.

Maverick glanced over at her. "We'll try to stay far enough away. They won't see us, although a man can see for miles on this flat prairie. If we should cross their trail, you keep your mouth shut, let me do the talking."

She nodded and they rode on toward the river. And as they rode, they began to pass dead buffalo, freshly skinned.

Maverick swore under his breath at the carnage, the waste. "Taking nothing but the hides, with Indian women and children starving!"

Cayenne winced away from the sight of the slaughter. "I think you're not as tough and mean as you'd have me believe," she said to him, "otherwise, you wouldn't be worried about starving Indians."

"I only hate Comanche," he muttered, his eyes hard. "And even then, I hate to see their kids starve!"

It was almost dusk, and the Cimarron River was in sight when Cayenne heard the roar in the distance.

"What's that?" She turned in her saddle curiously.

Maverick shook his head, puzzlement on his rugged face as the roar grew louder. "Never heard that before; isn't buffalo running."

Across the lavender sky to the north, a black cloud moved toward them as the roaring buzz increased.

Cayenne looked up at the gigantic cloud moving toward them and the roar grew so loud that she had to shout. "A cyclone!" she shouted. "A tornado!"

Maverick seemed hypnotized as he stared at the black cloud moving closer and closer. The horses seemed to sense something because they snorted, pulling at their bridles and whinnying nervously.

Maverick shook his head. "I don't know what it is," he shouted at her, "but it's not a tornado! Maybe we'd better seek shelter, maybe—"

She couldn't hear him now as the roar heightened as the boiling cloud drew nearer, dipped, and moved.

Strawberry whinnied and reared while Cayenne fought to control her. Maverick shouted but she couldn't hear him, couldn't understand over the roar. Then the dark cloud descended and she was covered and surrounded by crawling things.

Rocky Mountain locust! Grasshoppers! Millions of them in a gigantic cloud whirling down around her. Cayenne screamed in terror as they flew in her face, down her shirt, clung to her clothes. She was covered with the crawling, flying things.

She glanced over at Maverick as she shuddered and clawed at herself, trying to get the insects off her. He, too, slapped at his face, trying to shake them from his clothes while the three horses neighed and plunged in confusion and terror.

Cayenne screamed again as she struggled to rein in the terrified horse. The grasshoppers were everywhere now, crawling on her clothes, down the neck of her shirt, hopping across the grass. The ground seethed and writhed with them as the insects landed, and in moments, they were as deep as the horses' fetlocks. The grass turned black under the millions of crawling grasshoppers. The buzz of their wings, of the chewing jaws attacking the vegetation, drowned out any shouts.

It was worse than her most horrible nightmare to have the grasshoppers covering her, crawling down her shirt, her arms. She shuddered, raking at them wildly while her horse neighed and stamped. The sky turned black as another cloud of them moved in. The ground seemed a wiggling, living thing as the insects spread across the prairie for miles, chewing greedily at the grass.

She couldn't stand any more! She had to escape! Maverick shouted to her, gesturing, but her fright overwhelmed her thinking. She had to get away from these millions of winged, crawling monsters! *The river! If she could ride her horse down into the water!*

She gestured that direction and Maverick shook his head, shouting something. Cayenne was too terrified to think clearly. She had to escape! Unmindful of the packhorse tied to her mare, she took off at a dead gallop toward the Cimarron. Behind her she heard Maverick shout, start after her. *Good! He'd understood her plan, was coming along!*

In blind panic, she galloped toward the river in the pale pink dusk. Grasshoppers crawled over her clothes and the grass teemed with them. Strawberry crushed them under her hooves as she loped. Cayenne heard them pop beneath the mare's hooves, smelled the scent of the crushed, mangled insects. All she could think of was reaching the water that seemed so far up ahead. If she could ride down into the river, she'd be safe, wash them off. Leading the packhorse, she galloped onto the river bank sand.

She saw the sign, read the words, but their meaning

146

didn't register as she plunged the mare across the crusted sand toward the tepid water. And when the words registered, it was already too late.

"WATCH OUT!! 125 MILES TO FT. SILL!! 3 FEET TO HELL!!" the weather-beaten sign read, but the other words were too dim and she was too terrified to care. All she could think of was riding even deeper, leading the packhorse behind her. Maverick yelled a warning behind her. "No! Cayenne! Cayenne! No! Stop!"

But she ignored him, feeling only relief that the grasshoppers were washing away, swimming for their lives as she rode the mare deeper into the waters of the Cimarron. She reined up, turning back to gesture Maverick into the water.

Why was his face so anguished? Why did he reach for his lariat? "Cayenne! My God! I'll get you out!"

Out? She didn't want out. She wanted to ride even deeper so that the muddy water washed the creeping insects from her skin. But his agonized expression made her start back toward the shore. Was it her imagination that the sand ahead of her shook like jelly? Why on earth was he screaming at her? And then the mare hesitated, stumbled, and began to sink. Only as the mare foundered and the packhorse behind her in the water whinnied in terror did she understand the sign, the horror on Maverick's face.

"Quicksand!" she shrieked. "Oh, God! Quicksand!"

Even the grasshoppers held no more fright for her now as she felt the sand give way beneath the strawberry roan.

"Maverick! Help!"

"Hang on, baby!"

He brushed the grasshoppers off his shirt, moving gingerly onto the sand shore and eyeing it carefully. "I'll

147

try to rope you, Reb! Let that packhorse go!"

"No!" she shouted back, hanging onto the lead rope grimly. "No! We need the supplies! We need—"

"Remind me to spank your butt later for arguing with me!" he shouted as he roped her mare, but she heard the tension in his voice, knew he was scared for her.

Strawberry whinnied and foundered as Maverick tightened the rope.

"Hang on, horse!" he yelled. "Dust Devil'll do the best he can! Cayenne, let go of that packhorse! You'll have to let it drown!"

The packhorse foundered, sinking deeper into the sand and rolling its eyes in panic.

"No," Cayenne screamed. "I won't leave the poor thing!"

He looked exasperated but said no more as he tightened the rope on the mare's neck, reining the big stallion backward.

Strawberry sank slowly and whinnied in terror as Maverick backed his horse, tightening the lariat.

Cayenne thought suddenly. "She'd have a better chance without my weight!" And she slid off even as Maverick protested.

"No, Cayenne! By damn! Stay with her! The current'll get you!"

She wasn't going to let two horses drown because of her poor judgment, she thought stubbornly, working her way through the water back to the foundering, terrified packhorse.

"Cayenne! Dammit! Hang onto the mare's tail! I'll save the packhorse!"

She was afraid now, more afraid than she'd ever been in her life as the quicksand sucked at her feet and legs, pulling her and the horses still deeper. Images flashed through her mind of every horrible story she'd ever heard about people and animals dragged under, slowly

148

drowned in quicksand.

"Here, baby, free that rope from the horse and put it around your waist! You'll have to let the horses go!"

"No! I won't let them drown! Save Strawberry!"

Maverick swore terrible oaths and his hands shook as he reined the big gray backward. "Hang onto her tail," he ordered again. "I'll get her out, then go for the packhorse myself!"

Cayenne needed no further urging, so great was her terror. Strawberry was almost chest-deep in the sand now as she struggled and only went deeper. Behind them, the packhorse plunged frantically, trying to get a footing in the bottomless ooze as it sank slowly.

Cayenne hung onto the mare's tail as Maverick backed Dust Devil, tightening the rope. The tepid current pulled at her and she got a mouthful of muddy water as she gasped and fought to hang onto Strawberry's tail. Drowned grasshoppers floated on the river's brown surface while the others on the prairie chewed their way through every bit of vegetation.

"Oh, Maverick, hurry!"

He backed the stallion and the rope tightened on the mare's neck. She clung to Strawberry's tail and watched him. *Suppose the rope snapped? Suppose he broke the mare's neck trying to get her out?* But there was no other answer.

The big gray horse backed up slowly, expertly as any cow pony used to working cattle would. Maverick talked to the stud, encouraged him. "That's it, boy! Keep backing! Steady now!"

Strawberry whinnied as if she knew the pair was trying to help her. Behind them the packhorse foundered still deeper. The current and the sand pulled at Cayenne's legs as if determined to take her under, suffocate her slowly in the quicksand. Was there a more horrible, slow death than that? Cayenne couldn't think

149

of one as she put her faith in the half-breed and his gray stallion. She even prayed a little as Maverick backed his horse.

For a long moment, the lariat stretched so tautly she was certain it would break and knew he had only one. If it broke, she and the horses would surely drown, but she pushed that possibility from her mind. She smelled the brown water washing past her face and it smelled like mud and sudden death. Cayenne's head went under as the mare thrashed, and she choked and coughed on the dirty water. And then Maverick backed up another step and the line went so taunt, it vibrated.

"Cayenne, it's no use!" he yelled. "I can't budge her! I'm gonna let her go, toss the rope to you!"

Even in her terror, she was adamant. "My stars! You'd better not! Don't you dare let my horse drown!"

He shrugged, muttering something about "stubborn Rebel," and backed the stallion one more step while the mare choked and gasped.

For a long, heart-stopping minute, Cayenne thought the rope might break or he'd strangle the roan. But just as she'd almost despaired, the mare seemed to move a little, thrashing wildly.

Maverick warned, "Watch out for her feet; she'll kick you from here to Sunday!"

Cayenne nodded, sliding around to the mare's side as Maverick urged his stallion back. Then with a mighty lunge and a great sucking sound, the quicksand let go its greedy grasp of the mare and Maverick pulled her to safety and Cayenne along with her.

The mare stood dripping water as Maverick dismounted, ran over, and caught Cayenne as she fell.

She threw her arms around his neck, unmindful that her wet body soaked his clothes. "I was such a fool!"

"It's okay, baby." He held her tightly against the haven of his virile chest as he brushed a wet curl from her eyes. "It's okay now!"

The grasshoppers had consumed every bit of vegetation. Now they gathered in a great cloud and flew off, leaving thousands of dead, crushed insects behind.

Cayenne turned back toward the river where the packhorse struggled. "Maverick—"

"Okay, dammit, okay!" He loosed the rope from the mare's neck and led his stallion closer to the water's edge, carefully choosing his footing. Expertly he roped the struggling gelding as it sank still deeper.

He studied the situation and turned to Cayenne. "Baby, to save that horse, I'm gonna have to cut the packs loose. . . ."

"Maverick, no!" She ran over and grabbed his arm. "Don't go in that water! Suppose something went wrong! You might drown! Can't you just pull it out like you did Strawberry?"

Maverick shook her hand off reluctantly. "I'll never get it out with those packs weighing it down. I've got to swim out there and cut them loose!"

She looked from him to the struggling horse. He was right, there was no alternative. But once he was in the water, it would be her responsibility to back the stallion and try to pull Maverick and the packhorse out. "What do you want me to do?" she asked coolly.

"That's my girl!" he patted her cheek. "Can you back a horse? Have you ever worked cattle?"

"Of course, I was raised on a ranch! I've had to do a lot of the work around the place in the past eight months. . . ."

"Then I'm counting on you, Reb." He gave her a disarming grin. "Just remember, Dust Devil mounts from the right, Injun style!"

She swung up in the saddle as Maverick picked his way across the sand gingerly. The rivers of the Indian Territory were notorious for treacherous quicksand, she

151

remembered too late as she watched him pick his footing. He'd remembered and had been trying to warn her when she plunged into the water in blind panic. Here and there, the sandy crust trembled like jelly and he avoided those areas as he moved toward the struggling horse.

Her heart pounded in her throat as she watched Maverick hip-deep in the brown water, moving toward the sinking horse. He turned to shout over his shoulder, "I'll cut the packs loose. . . ."

"What'll we do for food without them?" she shouted.

"We'll worry about that later! I've got to try to get it on its side. Spread out on a larger surface area, it'll sink slower."

She sat the stallion, wet, miserable, and scared for Maverick's safety as she watched him moving around the quicksand to the struggling horse. He cut the packs loose and they bobbed only an instant in the water before the deadly sand sucked them under forever. The horse seemed to know the humans were trying to help because he nickered frantically.

"Whoa boy! I'll save you!" Maverick kept up a soothing patter as he took his knife and dug sand from under the gelding until he got it off its feet, sprawled on its side in heaving exhaustion.

"Okay, baby," he shouted as he moved around behind the prone horse. "It's all up to you and Dust Devil now! Back up and see if you can free him!"

Very slowly Cayenne urged the stallion back. Dust Devil seemed to know his master's life depended on him. He backed carefully, tightening the lariat.

The packhorse whinnied and struggled, but it was too weak from exertion to free itself. Maverick moved around behind it, trying to free its rear legs.

"Maverick, be careful!" she shouted in alarm. "You'll get kicked!"

152

"Keep backing, Cee Cee!"

The rope tightened, trembling as Dust Devil took up the slack. Nothing happened. Cayenne despaired, fearing for Maverick out in the water. Her fingers clenched on the reins as she urged the gray. She had a sudden image of Maverick and the packhorse sinking forever into the bottomless quagmire.

Well, she wouldn't let him die, she told herself as she tried backing the stallion again. And it wasn't because he meant anything to her personally. No, of course not. It was the humane thing; it was what Papa would have done.

Desperately, she pulled back on the reins, arching the stallion's neck as she urged him to retreat, to put even more tension on the lariat. If it broke, there'd be nothing she could do but watch helplessly as Maverick and the luckless gelding sank forever in the deadly sand.

"Oh, Maverick, I—I'm so afraid it'll break!"

"Don't go soft on me now, Rebel," he scolded, waving her backward. "That's the chance I've got to take!"

It was the chance she had to take, too, she realized, admitting to herself how very much this man meant to her.

She tightened the lariat even more and the giant stallion put all his strength into pulling. "Back up, boy," she urged, every muscle tense as she watched the drama before her. "Oh, Dust Devil! You've got to do it!"

Then the big gray seemed to realize that the life of the man he loved, whom he'd served faithfully since his young colt days, was about to be forfeited. The horse snorted, and shook his head, and leaned almost down on his haunches as he pulled.

Even as she watched, the gelding's trapped hooves seemed to flail and kick free. "Watch out!" Cayenne screamed, but her warning came too late. She saw a trickle of blood on Maverick's forehead as one of the flailing hooves caught his head.

Was he even still conscious? She couldn't let up the tension on the rope to find out. "Hang on, Maverick," she shouted. "Hang onto its tail! Do you hear me? Hang on! Oh, Maverick!" She couldn't hold back the sobs now as the gelding kicked wildly, freeing its hooves, and the mighty gray dragged it toward the safety of firm ground. She wasn't sure that Maverick heard her because he seemed unconscious. But one of his hands tangled in the gelding's mane, locked there. He hung limp as death while Dust Devil dragged the pair toward firm sand.

Once there, Cayenne eased the tension and jumped down to run to them. The gelding scrambled to its feet and stood with head hanging weakly. "Maverick! Maverick, dearest! Are you hurt bad?"

She knelt, gathering him into her arms. His eyes flickered open and his skin looked pale under the smear of blood. "Cayenne? What—what happened?"

She hugged him to her, kissing his face. "I was so scared for you! How do you feel?"

He tried to get up. "Like I been dragged through a knot hole backward!"

She caught him as he stumbled, as he collapsed against her. "Oh, my God!" she wept. "What do I do now?" She cradled him against her breasts, kissing his face.

"Baby," he whispered, "I—I don't know if I'm bad hurt or if I'm just dizzy. If I don't get better after a while, leave me. You hear me? Don't stay here and die with me! If you ride back east, you could cross Hennessy's trail, ride safely into Darlington. . . ."

"My stars, no!" she exploded. "I'm not about leave you!"

He tried to grin but flinched in pain. "You little firecracker! Don't you ever do what you're told?"

She winked, trying to keep her voice light so he wouldn't know how worried she was about him. "They don't call me Cayenne for nothin'!'"

Just what was she going to do? They had no food and it might be hours before she could decide how badly he was injured. Somewhere in the distance, the big Sharps rifles boomed again over and over.

She looked down at him questioningly.

He frowned, lying with his face against her breasts. "Twilight," he mumbled. "They're picking off the buffalo as they come down for a drink at the river."

She jumped up, laying him down gently. Very carefully, she picked her way across the sand to the river. Cayenne tore a scrap of her shirttail off and dipped it in the water. When she returned, she washed his bruised face.

He winced and smiled. "That feels good, baby. I'm feeling a mite better. Maybe I'm not hurt bad after all."

Anxiously she turned her head toward the sound of the echoing guns further down the river. "Maverick, they'll have food, supplies."

"Hell, no!" He struggled to sit up. "You know what a bunch of hunters would do to you? They probably haven't seen a woman for weeks!"

She was going to get food and help for Maverick if she had to sleep with every one of the hunters to get it for him. She gagged at the thought, remembering that filthy beast, Buck, who had grabbed her, mauled her in the Red Garter Saloon. But she wasn't going to let Maverick die out here if she could buy help for him with her body.

He seemed to read her thoughts because he sat up, looking at her a long moment. "No, baby, you're not gonna do it. By damn, you're not whoring to help me!"

She swallowed hard, afraid to trust her voice.

Then his rugged face softened. "I didn't realize you cared that much about me." He took a deep, shuddering

155

breath and seemed to reach a decision. "Baby, there's something I ought to tell you. . . ."

"Of course I'm not doing it for you; I'm doing it for myself." She kept her voice cold, flippant, knowing he'd never allow her to sacrifice her body to help him. No gallant Texas cowboy would.

"What?" He sounded crushed.

She turned her face away, not wanting him to see the tears running down her cheeks in the growing dusk. "Of course I'm not doing it for you," she snapped again. "I'm hungry and those hunters'll have food. Maybe they'll be willing to help me make it back to civilization."

"Oh, I see." Was that disappointment, anger on his dark, bruised face? "I guess I should have expected that." He sounded bitter. "After all, there's no reason you should care anything about me."

"None at all." She stood up, trying to keep her voice brittle. "Any more'n you care about me."

He felt his forehead gingerly and sighed. "I guess I'm loco to think you might have cared. . . ." He stood up very slowly. "Okay, Reb, I'm feeling better now. Let's ride into their camp, see if we can talk them out of food and supplies. All we got right now are my pistols, a couple of saddle guns, a few cartridges."

"We've got a change of clothes in our saddlebags," she reminded him. He'd been about to tell her something a while ago, something deep and revealing. "Maverick," she said as she helped him to his horse, "what'd you start to say about something you ought to tell me?"

He smiled wryly. "Was I about to say something? I don't remember; kinda out of my head. Probably wasn't important anyway. Let's put on dry clothes. Don't want them to realize we're desperate, although they probably will anyhow when they see no supplies on the pack-horse."

They changed clothes, mounted up, and Maverick

managed to sit the stallion even though he swayed a little. In the growing darkness, his face looked pale. "Cayenne, some of these hunters aren't bad fellows, just hungry and needin' to make a livin' with this depression still on. Put your hair back up under your hat and let me do the talking."

"Why?"

Maverick shrugged, urging the stallion forward toward the sound of the guns. "In the darkness, in boy's clothes, maybe they'll never know you're a woman."

She realized the logic in this and nodded as she followed him out along the trail. Maybe Maverick was right. Some of these hunters were bound to be decent men, just desperate and hungry. With any luck, they might get a few supplies and supper, and ride out without any trouble at all.

It took them the better part of an hour, riding at a walk to find the hunter's camp. Maverick seemed to be doing a little better but still swayed in his saddle. The guns had ceased as the hunters gathered in their camp at the end of the day.

Maverick took a deep breath. "I smell coffee, bacon up ahead."

She sniffed the air, hungry and eager. "I don't smell anything."

Maverick chuckled, swaying in his saddle. "You aren't a Comanche."

She didn't comment, watching his outline sway a little as he rode ahead of her. If she had to, she'd trade her body to those men to get food and medicine for Maverick. She told herself she was just grateful, that she owed him for what he'd done just now. But maybe this bunch would turn out to be decent human beings.

Maverick reined up just a few hundred feet from where she saw half a dozen men hunkered down around a campfire. "Hello, the camp!" he called.

The hunters grabbed for their guns, but Maverick yelled quickly. "It's okay, we're friends! Can you spare some food?"

"Mister, you scared the pee-diddly out of us!" a giant bearded man in a Turkey-red shirt scolded as he waved them on in.

Cayenne searched her memory. *Why did that voice sound so familiar?*

The pair rode into the circle and dismounted. Cayenne turned with a smile as the man approached her. Then the smile froze on her face in terror as she got a good look, remembered. Maybe she was mistaken. She blinked again, staring at him as the big frame loomed closer. There was no mistake. It was Buck.

Chapter Eight

Cayenne took a deep breath as she recognized the filthy buffalo hunter who had pawed and handled her only a few days ago in the Red Garter. He still wore the dirty Turkey-red shirt and the little beaded Indian necklace.

She glanced over at Maverick, who stiffened and gave her the slightest shake of his head while the other man greeted them. "What in the name a' hell you two doin' out here?" Buck smiled affably, motioning them on in by the fire.

Maverick hesitated, his hands hovering near his gun belt.

Buck waved him in. "Come on. We got plenty of buffalo meat." He stared at Maverick's swollen forehead. "What happened to you?"

Did Buck not recognize them? She stood in confusion, watching the scene.

Maverick's hand went to his forehead and he stammered, "Fell off my horse."

Buck guffawed. "Some cowhand! Come on and set a spell. Clint, give these two fellers a plate full!"

Clint wore yellow satin sleeve garters, which reflected the firelight as he dished up boiled meat. "Buck had a bump that bad a few days ago when he got through celebratin' in Wichita."

"Tell the truth, I don't remember much about it," Buck nodded ruefully. "I was drunker'n a polecat. Suppose it was over a woman. Wish I could remember whether she was worth it!"

The others roared with laughter and one of them told a ribald joke.

Cayenne heaved a sigh of relief. Buck had been too drunk to remember, to recognize them now.

Buck studied Maverick's horse. "Stranger, do my eyes deceive me or did I see you dismount off that gray's right side?"

Maverick stiffened. "I . . . stole him from the Indians," he said, "and never had time to rebreak him."

Buck looked at the scalp dangling from the lead rope. "Looks like you took somebody's hair doin' it!"

Maverick stuck his thumbs in his gun belt and laughed. "Hell! He didn't need it anymore! Damned redskins!"

They all laughed and nodded in agreement.

Cayenne looked at Maverick and saw him visibly relax. "If you boys don't mind," he said, "I'll just ground tie these two good ponies, unsaddle them later." Maverick led Strawberry and Dust Devil a few yards out and dropped the reins. Like any well-trained cow ponies, the pair grazed peacefully, dragging their reins in a small circle. In the southwest, where there was seldom anything to tie a horse to or when a man had to dismount in a hurry to deal with a steer, his life might depend on a good horse that would stand in one spot without hightailing it off.

Cayenne approached the men cautiously, trying to keep her face in the shadows as she took the tin plate and nodded her thanks. The buffalo meat was lean and sweeter than beef. But she was hungry enough to eat a rattlesnake.

160

Maverick came over to the fire and accepted a plate from Clint. "Much obliged. I'm Ma—rvin, this is Ca—Kyle."

Buck looked over at Cayenne then back at Maverick, who sat down next to her on a blanket. "Your little pard don't say much, do he?"

Maverick gobbled the food and reached for a tin cup of coffee. "Nope, he don't. But then it's better than listenin' to someone run off at the mouth all the time who has nothin' to say."

The filthy hunters whooped with laughter, nodding in agreement. "You're right about that, *hombre.*"

Buck's face looked puzzled and he combed his tangled beard with his fingers, wiping his filthy hand on the faded Turkey-red shirt. "Have we met before, *amigo?*" he asked Maverick.

Maverick shook his head.

"Gil," Buck asked the one with no teeth, "do you recall meeting this man?"

Gil shook his head, wiping up gravy with his bread and poking it into his toothless mouth.

"Clint," Buck said to the one wearing the sleeve garters, "have we met this fella before? I do declare, stranger, your voice sure sounds familiar."

Clint shook his head, pulling at the satin sleeve garters. "Aw, hell, Buck, he just drawls like a Texan. All Texas cowboys sound alike."

One of the others scratched himself and Cayenne wondered suddenly if he had lice or the common buffalo mange. They all looked dirty enough to invite vermin. When the wind shifted a little, she could smell the rank scent of the bunch. Their clothes were stiff with dried blood and none of them looked like they'd washed since last Christmas—if then.

She watched Maverick as she gobbled her food, gratefully accepting a cup of coffee made the way Texans like it—strong enough to float a horseshoe. The men laughed and told dirty jokes while she and Maverick ate. The half-breed appeared to be getting stronger by the minute as he filled his belly with warm food. Her hopes rose. Maybe he wasn't hurt bad after all. She looked over the six hunters as she ate, trying not to shudder in distaste. The memory of Buck's hot, wet mouth on hers came back to her. Could she let any of these men touch her even to get the supplies they needed so badly?

Maverick must have read her mind because he gave her the slightest shake of his head, glancing over to make sure the horses still grazed close by.

She knew what he was thinking: If Buck should suddenly remember that day in the Red Garter, remember where he'd heard that voice before, Maverick wanted to be able to clear out fast. She looked at the cut on his forehead, wondering if he were physically able to deal with an emergency.

Maverick filled his plate two more times, finally cleaned it one last time, and put it on a rock. "*Amigos*, that was good. I was so hungry, my belly thought my throat had been cut!"

The men laughed, and Cayenne finished her food, too, keeping her face down so her hat shadowed it.

Gil reached into his stained vest, pulled out a twist of tobacco, tore off a chew with his gums, and offered the twist to Maverick. Maverick shook his head, reaching into his own vest for "makin's." Gil offered the twist to Cayenne and she started to speak, remembering in time and shaking her head.

Maverick rolled himself a cigarette. "My little pard never picked up the habit."

Buck laughed. "No real man turns down women, whiskey, or tobacco."

Maverick froze, then continued rolling the "quirley."

162

"Kyle's just a kid yet. How's the huntin', boys?"

The one-eyed one nodded. "Good. Damned good! 'Course we don't think we'll equal Billy Dixon's record. Ol' Billy killed seventy-five thousand around Dodge City last winter. They say there's been four million hides shipped back east the last couple of years."

Maverick frowned as he reached into the fire, picked up a burning buffalo chip, and lit his smoke. "That makes for a lot of hungry Indians."

Clint laughed. "That's what it's gonna take to finally corral them Injuns, put them on reservations eatin' government rations. As long as they can live off the land, they'll always roam free and proud."

Maverick opened his mouth to say something, evidently decided against it. His face looked hard and grim as he sat looking into the fire, smoking.

Buck spat tobacco juice into the fire and the flames hissed. "We seen a lot of Injun sign, stranger. Have you?"

"Some," Maverick answered, exhaling smoke slowly. "The army know you boys are below the 'dead line' in Indian Territory? This is theirs by treaty."

"Sure," Buck nodded, wiping the spittle off his beard and onto his sleeve. "There're a few officers'd raise old Billy Ned if they catch us where we ain't suppose to be, but most of the army is encouragin' us. Just like every other white man, they all figure the sooner the damned buffalo are all killed off, the sooner they can cage them Injuns so decent people can start farmin' these plains."

"Now, Buck, we did run acrost one loco white man last year sometime. You 'member that one who run us off his land down in west Texas? Told us we oughta be ashamed and the Injuns deserved to eat, too?"

Buck's expression turned ugly. "I remember. Who could forget that McBride fella? If I hadn't heard he was the best rifle in Texas, I'd argued with him more. Imagine a white man wantin' fair play for the Injuns! He was actually worried about us wiping out all the buffalo!"

Cayenne choked on her coffee but the others seemed too engrossed in the discussion to notice.

The one-eyed one scoffed. "Hell, Buck, we could shoot forever and not kill 'em off. There's millions of them."

Maverick looked at him. "Then why are the tribes starving, going on the war trail?"

Gil looked at him intently. "Is it gettin' worse? We don't get much news out here."

Clint's eyes widened. "Hell, sorry to hear that. Me'n Buck forgot our 'bites' and nobody's willin' to share with us."

Maverick whistled long and low. "It's bad for a hunter to get caught out by Indians without a 'bite.' I'd be scared if I were you."

The others nodded in agreement. Cayenne thought about it. She'd heard all the buffalo hunters carried a fifty-caliber shell, emptied of powder and filled with poison. If hopelessly surrounded by hostile Indians, a man could "bite the bullet"—commit suicide quickly rather than be captured alive and tortured.

Buck spat to one side. "You see anybody along the way, stranger?"

Maverick nodded as he smoked. "We saw a freighter a day or so ago. He's tryin' to get supplies down to the Kiowa before they decide to join the Comanche and Cheyenne on the warpath."

Buck looked at him with interest. "You're a 'breed. You think they won't?"

"Kiowa like to council," Maverick said. "Comanches just jump up and take action, every man for himself. Kiowas always got to talk a subject to death first."

164

Gil wiped his greasy mouth on his sleeve and looked at Maverick. "The Kiowa-Apache and the Arapaho sittin' this one out?"

"Most of them, I hear."

Buck yawned. "So where you and your pard headed?"

Maverick snuffed out his smoke. "West Texas. We could use a few supplies if you could spare 'em."

"Right down through the Uprising country?" Buck's eyes widened. "Damn, Mister, by tomorrow or the next day, painted braves'd be eatin' that food!"

"We don't intend to let them catch us," Maverick shrugged.

"Neither do we," Clint said, spitting into the fire. "Tomorrow we're headin' out of this area and splittin' up. Just don't know whether to head for Fort Sill or Fort Dodge to wait 'til the army puts them braves back on the reservations."

"Reckon you're right, reckon we should do the same, but we got to get on," Maverick said.

Buck scratched his beard, looking at Maverick closely. "I do wish I could remember where we'd met before, *amigo*. Even your little pard seems familiar. . . ."

"Maybe we had a beer together at some saloon somewhere," Maverick hedged, and Cayenne saw him glance again toward the grazing horses.

Buck stood up, running his hand across the bulge in his filthy buckskin pants. "Now that we've et and had some tobacco, I'd like a little whiskey and a woman."

Clint got up and went over to his pack. "I got some whiskey, boss. For the other, you'll have to catch yourself up a mare!"

The others laughed coarsely. Buck smiled slowly as he stroked himself. "I ain't had a really good humpin' since we caught that little Comanche gal and enjoyed

165

her last fall."

Gil frowned. "We shouldn't done that, Buck, killed her, I mean. And if I was you, I'd quit wearin' her necklace. Sooner or later, a war party'll make us pay for that. . . ."

"Hell, it was her own fault! I wouldn't have strangled her with it if she'd stopped screamin'," Buck complained, still staring at Cayenne, fingering the Indian beaded piece he wore. "A white man expects an Injun girl to be willin' to accommodate him. And after all, we was willin' to pay her with mirrors and trash like that."

Cayenne shuddered at the image that came to mind, and when she looked up, Buck was staring at her, his hand still on the bulge in his pants, his tongue running slowly over his teeth.

"Stranger," he said to Maverick, "your pard one of them kind of boys?"

She saw Maverick stiffen. "No *comprende*. I don't know what you mean."

Buck laughed easily, looking down at Cayenne. "Ah, sure you do. Is he one of them dainty, sissy boys that know how to make a man happy?"

Maverick stood up. "No, he ain't. We need to move on, Buck, if you'll just let us have a little food. . . ."

"Now that ain't hospitable, just to eat and leave sudden like," Buck whined, watching Cayenne. "And supplies comes high way out here on the plains. We bought this stuff clear over at Adobe Walls."

Cayenne didn't look up but she could feel his eyes staring down at her.

Maverick laughed, but it sounded forced. "I've got a little money. . . ."

"That ain't what I want and you know it," Buck growled.

"No," Maverick said. "Nothin' doin'. But I've got a

166

few dollars on me. . . ."

"What I'll take is a chance to mount your little boy partner there like you probably been doin'," Buck said softly. "I'll bet he's got a purty soft bottom on him as nice as any girl's!"

Gil frowned. "I don't know, Buck. I don't cotton to messin' with young boys!"

Cayenne glanced over at Maverick, saw his hand creeping toward the Colt on his hip.

Buck started unbuttoning his pants. "Gil, if you shut your eyes, I swear you won't know the difference! But if you'd rather, I'd say he's got a sweet-lookin' mouth—"

Cayenne heard a sudden movement and looked up as Maverick went for his gun. But Clint had moved around unnoticed behind Maverick. She opened her mouth to scream a warning but it was already too late. Clint caught Maverick across the kidneys with a rifle butt, and she could only gasp in horror as the half-breed groaned, doubling up in pain.

Buck nodded with satisfaction. "Keep an eye on him, Clint! We'll take turns at this prissy-lookin' boy!"

Cayenne stood up and backed slowly away. *What on earth was she going to do?* She turned to run but Buck tripped her and she fell on her face.

"Now, young fella, that ain't sociable," he scolded, and he put one big hand in the middle of her back, reaching under her to jerk open her pants. Even as she struggled and the hunters laughed, Buck jerked her pants down so that her bare bottom was exposed.

"Umm! Umm!" Buck said, and he held her down as she struggled, running his hand across her hips. "I tole you, boys. Got a rear on him like a girl's!"

In terror, she struggled against the weight of the man kneeling on the small of her back and glanced over at Maverick. His face was a fury, but he was still doubled over in pain.

167

She struggled, felt the man run his filthy hands across her rear. "There, now, young fellow. We ain't gonna hurt you! You just won't be able to set down when we get through. . . ."

Gil protested. "Buck, this ain't right!"

The one-eyed one snickered. "I ain't ever tried it before, but I musta' been out here a long time! Damned if he don't look mighty good to me!"

"You and me both!" Buck guffawed as he straddled the back of her legs, her pants halfway down. She felt his throbbing maleness trail wetly against her rear. And she could no longer contain her fright and fury. She screamed at the same time her hat fell off and her red hair cascaded down her shoulders.

There were cries of amazement. "Well, I'll be damned! It really is a girl!"

Gil laughed. "Roll her over, Buck, let's make sure!"

Cayenne fought and bit him while Clint held Maverick at bay with his "Big Fifty."

Maverick swore long and loud. "By damn! You bastards keep your hands off her or I'll—"

"You'll what?" Buck laughed easily, turning Cayenne on her back while she fought and bit. " 'Pears you're makin' a lot of noise when you can't do nothin' with Clint's gun in your belly!"

With that, he reached down, ripping Cayenne's shirt open to the waist. "My God! Look at them white tits!"

Cayenne put her hands on her breasts, protecting them from the hungry stares of the men. "Don't you touch me!" she screamed in frightened fury. "Don't you touch me!"

"Honey, I intend to do more than touch you!" Buck ran his tongue over his lips and reached down to grasp his big manhood. "I'd swear I've heard your voice somewheres before, too!"

Gil pushed forward eagerly. "You're gonna share

her, ain't you, Buck?"

He advanced on her, holding his hard manhood in his hand. " 'Course I'll share with my buddies. Now that 'breed is a selfish one, ain't he?" He nodded with a malicious grin toward Maverick, who stood shaking with anger, held off by Clint's gun. "Here he's had this cute thing all to hisself and didn't intend to let us ease ourselves when we all been without for so long!"

Clint cackled. "Shall I kill him, Buck?"

"In a minute," Buck said, looking down at Cayenne shaking on the ground. "I think he ought to get to watch the fun. Then we'll just take this sweet thang along with us and share and share alike. Them officers at the fort won't listen to her story when I tell them she's just a tramp, belonged to a 'breed. I could probably buy a lotta whiskey with what I could make off her from soldiers."

He reached down to grab her and she bit his hand. "You bitch!" He struck her savagely, and her head rang with an explosion of pain and the taste of blood. "You're gonna pay for that, bitch!" he snarled, shaking his injured hand. "I'll reckon I know how to tame you, make you whimper and beg me not to hurt you no more!"

Maverick tried to push forward but Clint held the gun in his belly. "Get your hands off her!" Maverick shouted. "That's a lady!"

Gil sneered. "Ladies don't travel with 'breeds. She's just a whore and we'll use her like one!"

A light seemed to come on in Buck's animallike face. He reached up to touch his throat, which still bore a red mark under the beaded neck piece from Maverick's rawhide thong. "I'll be damned!" First he looked angry, then he threw back his head and laughed. "No wonder you two seemed familiar even though I was drunk that afternoon! A lady! Yeah, that's what you

169

said that day, too!"

He looked from Maverick back to Cayenne, who was crouched on the ground trying to cover herself modestly with her hands. "I'm gonna take her, Injun, every way I can think of while you watch me. Then I'm gonna let my boys do anything they want to her." He grinned. "And then we'll try a little Injun torture on you; see how loud you scream when I cut your balls off 'afore I kill you slow!"

"No!" Cayenne protested, shuddering in revulsion at the reek of the man's filth. "If—if you'll let him go, I'll . . . take you all on, pleasure you like you never been pleasured!" She smiled archly and stood up, pivoting slowly, putting her shoulders back so her proud, small breasts jutted out.

"Cayenne, don't!" Maverick snarled.

But she didn't listen. If she could charm these men with her body, charm them into letting Maverick go, that's all that mattered to her.

She put her hands under her breasts, offering them up to Buck as she battered her lashes at him. "Come on, stud, let's see if you got anything besides big words!"

Buck chortled with delight and grabbed her in a hot embrace. "Now you're talkin', gal! You please me, maybe we'll let yore man go!"

She let him pull her up against his blood-incrusted vest and rub her against his male hardness. His filthy hands went around her, pulling her close. She took a deep breath and saw lice moving in his greasy hair. His mouth came down on hers and she recoiled from his foul breath but remembered not to fight him.

The others whooped and hollered. "Whooee! Buck! I believe she's one of them fancy whores after all! When do I get a turn?"

They set up a clamor like a pack of coyotes around a

170

bitch in heat and she had to force herself not to struggle while he lifted her off the ground, grabbing at her nipple with his teeth. *If it would save Maverick's life, it was worth whatever they did to her.*

All the men were holding their breaths, concentrating on Buck's mouth on her breast, even Clint who was supposed to be guarding Maverick. She realized that, and in that moment, she nodded ever so slightly to Maverick.

With an oath, Maverick wrestled the rifle from Clint's hands, swung it by the barrel, and caught him in the belly so that he went down screaming.

"What the hell—?" Buck and the others jerked around.

"You bastard!" Maverick's face twisted in fury. "You're gonna pay for roughin' up my woman!"

"Maverick, thank God!" She pulled out of Buck's hands and ran to the half-breed, struggling not to weep.

He put his arm around her shoulders, hugging her briefly, never taking his eyes off the hunters. "Cee Cee, gather up the guns, my pistol. Get the horses! I'm gonna see that this bastard never rapes another woman!"

Even as Cayenne watched, Maverick swung the big gun with all his strength and caught Buck between the legs.

The man screamed in agony, doubled up, and fell writhing to the ground. "Damn! Oh, God! He's crushed them! He's crushed them! Somebody do something!"

Maverick gestured with the "Big Fifty." "Come right on, who wants this slug?" he invited, his voice shaking with fury. "It'll only make a hole big enough to put your fist in!"

The hunters backed away slowly, showing fright at the anger written on Maverick's dark face.

171

Gil gestured helplessly. "We never touched her; it was him." He pointed to Buck still writhing and moaning on the ground.

"I oughta kill the lot of you but I'd hate to do the warriors out of the chance!" Maverick seethed, backing slowly toward the horses. "You okay, baby?"

"I'm okay, Maverick. Let's get out of here!"

She tried to pull her torn shirt closed as she mounted Strawberry and watched Maverick swing up on the gray.

Clint's head turned toward the other rifles piled up by a tent.

"Go ahead," Maverick challenged. "Let's see if you can reach them before I put a slug in you!"

He'd made a believer out of all of them. None of them moved except Buck rolling and thrashing on the ground. Cayenne and Maverick backed their mounts out of the camp into the darkness as he kept the big rifle trained on the six.

"Come on baby, let's move!"

She needed no urging to dig her heels in the red roan's sides, galloping off to the southwest through the darkness.

They rode at a steady pace for hours in case they were being pursued, although Maverick said he didn't expect that. "Buck has other things on his mind," he smiled. "Don't think he could sit a horse right now."

Finally they dismounted to cool the lathered horses.

He looked her over anxiously. "You okay, Cee Cee? When I saw him touch you, put his mouth on you, I just went loco! I shoulda killed him."

She could weep with the terror and the horror of it now that she was safe. "Oh, Maverick! It was so terrible!"

He took her in his arms, holding her tightly while he

172

kissed the top of her head. "I know, baby, I know. Try not to think about it. You're safe now. You'll always be safe in my arms."

She pressed her face into his powerful shoulder, felt his hands stroke her hair ever so gently, as gently as any woman would comfort a child. "I—I think I love you, Maverick."

He laughed softly and shrugged. "Naw, you don't. You're just grateful, that's all. I'd have done it for any woman."

"Then I'm not special?"

He hesitated, turning her small face up to his by placing his finger under her chin. "I didn't say that, Reb. I—I—If you only knew how ironic this whole thing is. Why it can never work out . . ."

"It can work out if we want it to!" She didn't know what she would do about Slade now. If she had to sacrifice Maverick to the gunslinger's deadly aim to help her family, could she do it? *No! She loved this strange, savage man too much.*

He tried to pull away from her. "Baby, I never in a million years expected to run into someone like you! Would you believe I keep picturing you with my child in your arms? Isn't that loco? Maybe it's God's idea of a cruel joke!"

She didn't understand what he meant, but it didn't matter. All she heard was that he saw her with his child in her arms. She pulled his face down to hers, kissing him.

"Oh, Cayenne! Cayenne! Baby!" He crushed her to him as if he wanted to pull her inside him, and his mouth seared hers like a smoldering branding iron.

She was breathless from his kiss, clinging to him as he embraced her, kissed her again. "Maverick, I—I've got to tell you there's some men at my father's ranch—"

But he was kissing her again, bending her backward

as one hand went around her shoulders, the other cupped her small bottom. She forgot whatever it was she was trying to tell him as she clung to the powerful, virile heat of him.

"Baby," he gasped, "I gotta warn you I'm no good for you! You don't know how bad I am! What I planned to do!"

"I don't care, dearest, I love you!" She kissed him feverishly. "I don't care how bad you've been! We can make a fresh start! Forget the past! I'd go anywhere with you without a backward glance!"

He held her at arm's length, looking into her face, and she saw the indecision, the torture in his. "You'd do that for me? Turn your back on everything and ride away with me?"

Cayenne hesitated, torn with the momentous decision. Joe McBride really needed her on the Lazy M and she loved the ranch so, she couldn't imagine ever living anywhere else. And never to see her four beloved little sisters again . . .

Maverick's face fell as she hesitated and he sighed, turning loose of her shoulders. "I reckon I got my answer."

"I didn't give you one."

"Yes, you did, Cayenne. You answered with your silence. I guess I don't mean so much to you after all. Well, that makes my other decision easier. I don't have to regret or change my original plans now." His face had a look of infinite sadness. Somehow, he looked much older, like a man who carried the weight of the world on his shoulders.

"Maverick, let me think it over. . . ."

"No need. I got my answer." He started walking along in the darkness of the prairie, leading his lathered horse.

She ran to catch up with him and they walked in

silence for a long way to cool the horses out. Several times she started to speak but seemed unable to find the right words. Maybe it was better this way. Could she live the life of a drifter's woman? She to whom roots and security meant so much? And what of her crippled father and little sisters?

It was a dark, moonless night like the soft, silky sheen of an ebony panther. The prairie wind picked up a little, carrying the slight scent of wild flowers. Once she reached out and caught his strong arm, but he shook her hand off and walked on in hostile silence.

"I don't know why I keep foolin' myself," he mused softly as they walked. "I keep forgettin' I'm a half-breed bastard. No decent woman could really want me."

"That's not true!" She kept walking doggedly forward, but she closed her eyes, running the tip of her tongue across her lips, remembering his fervent kiss.

"Even Annie," he said so softly that she had to strain to hear. "At the last, it was his name she called out. . . ."

She looked over at his grim face and there was no need to ask of whom he spoke as they walked in silence, leading the horses. The bitter hate of his expression told her. If she couldn't forget her family responsibilities, certainly he had no intentions of forgoing his revenge for her. No, not even if she asked him to. Maverick's soul had been deeply wounded, maybe too wounded to ever outlive the scars of his terrible past. In her heart, because of Maverick's pain, she hated the man, too, wished him dead and buried so that her love might be free from this memory that seemed to haunt him.

Cayenne sighed audibly. He was right, of course; there could be no future for the two of them. If he did survive the showdown, he would be so furious by her betrayal, by her trickery, he'd walk out of her life and never look back.

Caught between love and loyalty to her family and the man she loved, she remounted the roan and they loped through the night together.

They followed the Canadian river toward Adobe Walls in the Texas Panhandle because the buffalo hunter had said there were supplies there. The packhorse had been left in the hunter's camp in their escape, but it didn't matter because they had no food, only the few supplies in their saddlebags. It had been tricky enough holding those six men at bay without attempting to load a horse with their food. They might have overpowered Maverick.

She was ravenous by morning, but there was nothing to eat and they kept riding southwest toward Adobe Walls. As Maverick had said, they might as well try to make it there, turn straight south, and keep riding. It would make more of a straight shot toward her father's ranch, but it was right through the heart of the hostile country.

"Are we liable to run into Buck and the hunters again?" she asked, feeling her tummy complain and rumble.

"No, Fort Sill is straight south and Fort Dodge is north; that's where they talked of going for safety. We're going due west to the Panhandle and then turning back south. There's several hundred miles between our trails."

At dawn a covey of quail flew up unexpectedly from the tall grass ahead of them and Maverick brought down two with his pistol.

Cayenne made a small fire and cooked them crispy brown in the coals. "That was good shooting."

Maverick shrugged. "Not many men can outshoot me with a handgun."

176

Cayenne pulled one of the quail out of the coals and blew on it to cool it before sinking her teeth into the juicy meat. "My papa was always the best there is with a rifle, a shotgun. He said never let a man get close enough to use a pistol."

"But a pistol's faster if a man can work his way close in to the target." Maverick smiled, hesitating only a moment before picking up a quail and tearing meat from it.

She watched him, thinking what a son-in-law he'd make for Joe, thinking how badly her father needed a strong young cowboy like Maverick on the Lazy M. "I'll bet with that Comanche blood, you could sneak up on a man before he knew you were there."

Maverick ate. "I've done it a dozen times, why?" There was something hesitant, suspicious about his tone.

"No reason." The stealth of the Comanche was the very reason Joe had always kept that old sawed-off shotgun hanging low over the fireplace. You had to take time to aim a rifle, but even in the dark, you could blow a hole big as a coffee cup with a shotgun without aiming at all.

Maverick looked at her a long moment. "It would be interesting, wouldn't it? A duel between an expert shot with a rifle, a top gun with a pistol?"

She wiped the grease from her mouth, still thinking about what the Indians had done to Papa. He talked about "turning the other cheek," but she couldn't help hating them for it. Yet she had let a half-breed Comanche make passionate love to her. Even now she might be carrying his child. "That's not the right word," she corrected. "You don't mean *duel*, you mean *shooting match*."

He didn't seem to hear her. "The range of a rifle against a fast draw. Wonder what the outcome'd be?"

177

She wondered if he just hungered to win or lusted for the fancy One-in-a-Thousand rifle that hung above the shotgun over the fireplace she'd told him about? It was Joe's pride and joy but of course he didn't shoot it anymore. She thought about Joe's burned, twisted fingers. At least he could still do his carving.

She smiled. "You ever have a willow whistle, Maverick?"

He looked puzzled. "No."

"Papa carves them for the children in our town."

"Somehow, I didn't think he'd be that kind."

She shrugged. "What kind? Don't you think a preacher does anything but read his Bible? You should see him with all my little sisters in his lap, telling them a bedtime story."

Was that regret, sadness on his dark features? "When you were sitting safely in your daddy's lap in that nice ranch house, listening to him tell stories, play a whistle, I was eating raw liver, learning how to torture a man without killin' him so the agony would last a long, long time."

And with that he stood up, kicked sand over the little fire, and went to check the horses' hooves.

What had made him so angry? Was it her mention of a father, of a tight-knit family when he seemed so alone in the world even though he'd been adopted by the Durangos?

Such a troubled man, she thought as she took a sip from her canteen. *Why had she ever thought she might find happiness with him?*

"We'll keep following the river," Maverick interrupted her thoughts. "But it's a long way over to Adobe Walls."

"Is it a fort?"

He put his big hands on her waist and for a moment she thought he would kiss her, but he only lifted her to

178

her saddle. "No, it was a trading post the Bents set up and later abandoned. Back during the Civil War, the Indians thought they'd take advantage of the soldiers being gone. I reckon you're too young to recall the Outbreak of '64?"

"I was only nine then."

He swung up on the big gray. "I'd just been found by the Durangos and ended up right in the middle of it. Kit Carson defeated the Navahos at Adobe Walls."

She looked over at him uneasily as they rode out. "We're riding into danger, aren't we, Maverick?"

"I told you that from the front end. Now it's easier to ride forward than it is to go back. We know there's Cheyenne war parties between us and Kansas. We don't know for sure what's ahead of us."

And so they headed west for the old trading post that now supplied buffalo hunters. Maverick amazed her with his ability to provide food off the land. Afraid to use up his ammunition, he set snares for rabbits. He found all sorts of roots and berries to eat, and pointed out the fruit of the prickly pear. He was at home in the hostile, dangerous country and she felt safe, confident of his ability to look after her.

At night he made no advances toward her and they slept in their own blankets, although she longed for the reassurance of his embrace. But surviving this dangerous journey became uppermost in her mind after Maverick pointed out the almost invisible unshod pony tracks, the moccasin prints.

"Nermernuh," he said as he studied the prints.

"What's that mean?"

He studied the footprint. "In our language, it means 'the People.' That's what Comanches call themselves."

She looked down at him kneeling on the ground. "What does *Comanche* mean?"

179

"Our hated rivals, the Utes, gave us that name. It means *enemy* in their language."

"Are you sure those are Comanche footprints?"

He nodded, pointing. "Flat, broad feet. See the trail the moccasin made from dragging fringe? Comanche like a lot of decorative fringe on their moccasins."

Once they saw smoke signals miles away to the north in the rough country. Another time, they found a broken bow thrown in the tall grass.

They traveled after dark for fear of being seen, because of the heat. Her nerves grew frayed. She began to wonder if he knew where he was going, if he might be lost.

Several days passed. They had ridden all night and she was exhausted and hungry. "Aren't we ever going to get there?" She looked off to the east. "It's almost dawn. I'm tired, Maverick. Can't we find some shelter and rest?"

He didn't turn his head, staring off into the distance. "Rest is for the dead," he answered, but his eyes still stared at the far horizon.

"What do you see?" She'd grown used to the idea that his senses were all keener than hers. She stood up in her stirrups and saw the silhouette of buildings now in the coming dawn, gray against the pink-rose sky.

"Oh, Maverick!" she laughed with delight. "There's riders and they've spotted us! They're coming out to meet us!" She turned in her saddle to smile at him. "Do you suppose they've got soap? I'd love a bath and—"

"How fast can you ride, Cee Cee?" She looked over at him, startled by his grim tone. His features were drawn, pale. And he still stared at the tiny figures on horseback.

"Why?" She looked again toward the riders. She

hadn't realized there'd be dozens—no, hundreds of hunters. And then the awful implication struck her. "Oh, my God!"

Maverick leaned over and pressed his spare pistol into her nerveless fingers. "Remember, don't let them take you alive, baby. Surprise is our only chance. They'll be expecting us to turn and run, not gallop through the middle of them for the Walls."

She couldn't look at him, couldn't tear her terrified gaze from the war-painted braves moving closer. The pistol felt cold and heavy in her numb fingers. "No, Maverick, I'm afraid!"

"Reb, you got to." Now get the hell outa here!"

And before she realized his intentions, he struck her startled mare with his quirt. Cayenne hung on for dear life as Strawberry bolted, and she dropped the pistol but it was too late for that. She clenched her sweating fingers in the roan's mane and galloped right into the oncoming riders. Now she either had to outrun them or be taken alive!

Chapter Nine

Cayenne had no time to think now as she bent over the mare's neck and the roan stretched out into a gallop toward the low-lying adobe and sod buildings. Glancing back for reassurance, she saw Maverick pause for just an instant, outlined against the coming light, his face as grim as the dread Reaper's. In that split second, one of her father's sermons came to her mind: *And I looked and beheld a pale horse and his name that sat upon him was Death and Hell followed with him. . . .*

Then she had no more time to think because garishly painted warriors galloped toward her, shrieking in triumph.

She heard Maverick shout a warning but she jerked the reins too late as a brave swung a war club and her horse shied. Strawberry stumbled and went to her knees. The warrior's small, foxlike features grinned with triumph as she fell. With a shriek of victory, another big brave vaulted from his running horse and raced toward her.

Now was when she was supposed to kill herself, she thought, scrambling to her feet. *Hell, if she hadn't lost her pistol, she wouldn't kill herself, she'd shoot the Indian!*

"Maverick! Help!" Cayenne swung around as the big warrior grabbed her. She struggled with him, hearing the big gray's hooves drumming across the hard ground

182

like echoing thunder. She fought the painted Indian, too terrified to think, to do anything but claw at him. He smelled of bear grease and raw, rancid meat.

The other warriors raced toward the struggling pair, yelping with delight. The fox-faced one with the long arms led the pack after her. It seemed a toss-up as to whether Maverick would get there before the savages did.

"Run, baby, run!" the half-breed shouted, and the big brave who had been chasing her on foot whirled to face the oncoming horse.

She needed no urging as she bolted toward her heaving roan, standing trembling and lathered nearby.

The brave screamed once but Maverick was merciless. He rode him down, the sharp hooves colliding with soft flesh as the man screamed, trying to dodge away from the stallion's pounding hooves. His skull crushed like an egg under the giant stallion's hooves.

Cayenne stumbled as she looked back but kept running. Around her now, other braves closed in, but Maverick's pistol cracked three times and blood spurted from three chests as the warriors screamed and went down.

"Come to me, baby!" Maverick shouted, and he leaned out of his saddle to reach for her, never slackening his pace. The Indians seemed to surround them but she saw only Maverick's grim face, his powerful arms reaching to save her. His strong arm lifted her to the saddle before him. She slipped her arms around him, clinging to him as the big stallion galloped. Strawberry fell in beside them and galloped along, too.

She heard the shrieks around them as the Indians closed in, so she closed her eyes and buried her face against his wide chest. His left hand held the reins and pulled her to him; the right held his pistol that cracked again, and another brave screamed and fell from his galloping paint behind them.

She looked around wildly and saw the gleaming faces, so garishly painted, so arrogantly sure they'd ride them down before they made it to the cluster of huts. She looked behind them, looked up ahead as her courage faltered. So near, yet so very far!

Maverick's Colt echoed in her ears and she smelled the acrid powder, heard a Comanche shriek in agony, saw him fall and go down beneath a pack of thundering hooves. There must have been fifty of the feathered braves gaining on them.

If they didn't make it, would Maverick put that last bullet in her brain to keep her from being captured alive? In a six-shooter, a man only carried five bullets, keeping the empty chamber as a precaution in case he accidentally pulled the trigger. Oh, God, how she wished he carried six or had time to stop and reload!

She remembered her father's ordeal, all the stories of torture she'd heard. No wonder the buffalo hunters carried "bites" so they could give themselves a quick, merciful death! Cayenne felt his heart beating, smelled the sweat of the lathered horses as they galloped through the pale dawn toward the safety of the buildings. Off to one side, she saw a butte, a party of war leaders watching the small drama being played out. Behind the low buildings lay gently rolling rises of river sand.

Her mouth tasted as dry as a west Texas dust storm. The rising sun cut a searing path across her skin so that perspiration ran down between her breasts. She clung to Maverick and they crouched low over the gray's neck.

They weren't going to make it. She realized that now as she glanced back and saw the war party gaining on them. On the outlying plains, other warriors sat their ponies, watching with amusement. Clearly they, too, knew the pair would never make it to the walls. She saw the grim terror of Maverick's face as he lashed the horse with the reins.

184

And about that time, the big buffalo guns behind the walls opened up, knocking braves from their horses at incredible distances, farther than she'd realized they could shoot. "Come on, Maverick, we can make it now!"

A hunter ran to swing the corral gate open and they galloped in with the Indians whooping behind them. The hunters set off a volley of lead and the war party hesitated, retreated.

Cayenne slid from the horse and staggered forward. A handsome man, not as old as Maverick, ran up to her. He was shorter but of a stocky build, with dark hair. "Hey, boy, you've had a close call! Get inside!"

Cayenne and Maverick ran into the big soddie.

The young man asked, "Would you like some water?"

Cayenne could only nod in exhausted appreciation. "Thanks!"

He started, looking at her curiously. "What'd you say, kid?" He held out his hand. "I'm Bat Masterson."

She took his hand, shook it, and decided there was no point in trying to hide her identity anymore. Maverick frowned at her as he slid down the inside wall, sighing heavily.

She reached up and took her hat off. "Thanks for the help, Bat. I'm Cayenne McBride."

"It's a girl! Look, it's a girl!" The shocked whisper went through the crowd of grizzled men and the ones nearest her turned to look.

Bat Masterson let go of her hand grudgingly and smiled. "Well, Miss McBride, this is an unexpected pleasure! If those braves had known what a prize they were chasing, they wouldn't have given up so easily!"

Maverick took his hat off, wiping the dust and sweat from his dark face. "Don't worry, I wouldn't have let them take her! Why do you think I saved that one last cartridge?"

Looking into the hard set of his face, she realized he had almost put a bullet behind her ear when he thought they weren't going to make it.

Maverick stood now, stuck out his hand, and the other let go of hers. "Howdy, I'm Maverick Durango."

He glanced at her out of the corner of his eye and she knew suddenly that he'd offered his hand to the handsome hunter so Masterson would be forced to turn loose of hers.

Bat shook hands with Maverick. "Thought you two were goners. You're just lucky to make it within the range of our 'Big Fifties' so we could drive them off."

"Lucky!" Maverick snorted. "They're out to kill buffalo hunters and we come ridin' into a whole nest of them! Ranchers like me aren't the ones who've been killing the herds off."

Around them, the guns cracked as dozens of hunters cut down on the braves who had ridden to catch the pair and had gotten too close to the walls.

Then Maverick took Cayenne's arm, steering her away with an easy grip of ownership that she knew was meant to convey a message to the handsome young man. He rolled a cigarette one-handed while Cayenne drank gratefully from the water barrel.

"Never thought I'd be grateful to see buffalo hunters," he smirked, sticking the "quirley" between his lips, searching his pocket for matches. "How many are there holed up here?"

Cayenne shook her hair back and looked at Bat, who smiled slowly at her.

"Twenty-eight all together, and one woman." Bat said, but he was looking at her. "Missus Olds is here with her husband and six of the men over in Rath's store. She'll be happy to hear another woman has arrived."

"What building is this?" Cayenne sighed with relief and exhaustion, looking around.

186

"Hanrahan's Saloon," Bat said. "There's nine of us holed up here, including my friend Billy Dixon. All the others are in Myers's store."

Maverick lit the match with his thumbnail. "The saloon, huh? Maybe we're in luck after all. When this is over, I want a good drink of bourbon and branch."

Cayenne looked up. Bat Masterson's eyes studied her in frank admiration.

Maverick frowned. "You can quit looking her over, Masterson," he said as he smoked. "The lady's with me."

"Is she?" Bat smiled at her and Cayenne thought he had the brightest gray-blue eyes, the most charming smile she'd seen anywhere. "I didn't hear her say so."

"She rode in with me, didn't she?"

Cayenne was both annoyed and angry. "My stars, Maverick! If you want to fight, there's a thousand Indians out there!" She gestured toward the savages ringing the place outside. The Indians gradually retreated out of range, leaving their dead behind.

"Get ready," Maverick warned. "They'll come back in, try to take out their dead. We can pick off a lot of them then."

He was a natural born leader, she thought as the other men hastened to obey him. Sure enough, the Comanche charged again, and when they did, the hunters laid down a withering fire that cut the charge to pieces.

One of the hunters handed Maverick a rifle. "If we could just pick off a chief, a war leader, they might give it up all together," Maverick said. "That's what happened back in '64 during the Great Outbreak. When I killed Little Buffalo, the Comanche and Kiowa decided the battle was bad medicine, quit, and went back across the Red River. But I'm a helluva lot better with a handgun."

A smallish man studied him with interest. "I heared about that Outbreak. So you're *that* half-breed, huh?

187

Heard no one but Trace Durango could outshoot you. Except that preacher over in west Texas. I saw him handle a rifle once. My God, what an eye! He could hit a nail head at fifty yards!"

Maverick smoked his cigarette. "He can't be that good. Nobody shoots that good!"

She started to tell him that, yes, Papa was that good a shot . . . up until a few months ago. . . . *But what difference did it make anyhow?*

Bat now looked visibly impressed on finding out who Maverick was. "Me and my friend, Wyatt Earp, sat down at a poker table one time with a gunslinger that was every bit as good as you're supposed to be, Durango."

"Who's Wyatt Earp?"

"He's with the law in Wichita. Wants to be a big marshal or sheriff."

Dixon laughed. "I tole old Wyatt that was a good way to get killed."

Bat snorted in disgust. "I'd say huntin' buffalo is a good way to get killed right now, Billy. As I said, Maverick, that stranger was as good with a pistol as I hear you are."

"Oh?" Maverick smoked, looking him over curiously. "Only one as good as me, the man who taught me to shoot, Trace Durango."

Bat shook his head and pulled at his chin, considering. "Nope, that wasn't his name. I remember he had eyes as expressionless as a rattlesnake. I think he could shoot a little old lady without any qualms; that kind of cold-blooded killer. He was the best and fastest I ever saw. Slade, yeah, that was the name." He thought about it. "Bill Slade."

Cayenne took a shuddering breath and splashed a little more water on her face from the barrel. She didn't want to think about the man with the cold, expressionless eyes who waited even now at her father's ranch. Could he outshoot Maverick? She didn't want to think about it. "How long you all been holed up here, anyway?"

Bat looked over at the other hunters. "I don't know; lost track of time because it seems like forever. Two, three days, maybe. I think this all started in the middle of the night on June 26. The Injuns caught the Shadler brothers outside the walls, asleep in their wagon, and killed them. Then young Tyler got shot through the lungs and died. We've killed dozens of Injuns; can't really know since they keep carrying off their dead. But so far, it's a Mexican standoff. They run all our horses off and surround us so we can't escape, but the range of our guns and the fact we got plenty of powder is holding them at bay."

Billy Dixon ran his hand through his tangled locks and looked at Bat with evident admiration. "If I got to fight, this is sure the best bunch to be with. Bat, you're a chunk of steel, and anything that strikes you is gonna draw fire!"

Bat Masterson flushed modestly and looked at Cayenne. "The only fire that takes my fancy is this lady's hair."

Cayenne looked from one hunter to the other and back at Maverick, who glowered at her. "You're quite a ladies' man, aren't you, Mr. Masterson?"

"I meant it, ma'am."

"Back off, Masterson." Maverick's voice had an edge as hard as his gray eyes.

Cayenne said hastily, "Now, boys, let's not fuss and make trouble. Looks like you all are gonna get all the trouble you can handle from outside."

Masterson picked up the sixteen-pound Sharps. "You wouldn't be any trouble, miss."

Maverick snorted and blew smoke. "I haven't had

189

anything but trouble since I met this little firebrand Rebel."

"You damned Yankee!" Cayenne turned and flounced off.

She met Mrs. Olds later during a lull. Her husband, William, ran one of two stores and she had been operating a little cafe in the back of the store for the hungry hunters.

"Glad to see another woman," she said heartily, hugging Cayenne. "Appears we may be here awhile, at least until they overrun us or get tired and ride out."

Cayenne shivered at her implication. "I guess there's too many; we can't possibly shoot them all."

The woman nodded grimly. "Near a thousand as we make out, and did you see that Quanah Parker's leading the pack?"

Curiously, Cayenne went to a rifle hole and stared out. "I've heard of him." She could see him now, proudly sitting a big gray pacer on a small rise a safe distance from the fight with his sub-chiefs. The gray-eyed half-breed was a head taller and bigger than the other Comanches. She thought how much he resembled Maverick, speculating a long moment on the quirks of Fate. One half-breed had chosen to follow his Indian heritage onto the warpath. The other hated his tribe, wanting to turn his back on it forever and live like a white man.

Cayenne helped Mrs. Olds prepare food for the men. The day stretched into long hot hours as the Indians sat their ponies just outside the range of the big guns like buzzards waiting for a wounded animal to die.

"By damn!" Maverick swore as he carried his plate of beef, hot peppers, and tortillas back over to stare out at the silent sentinels. "They're just sitting out there wait-

190

ing, knowing we can't hold out forever!'"

Bat nodded, his mouth full. "We sure ain't going any place, and the chances a cavalry patrol might be out and in the area are pretty slim. Although, as word gets out to stray parties of hunters that the Injuns are on the warpath, they might try to make it into here. Safety in numbers, you know."

Billy said, "I figure the Injuns is gettin' tired, maybe plannin' one last big rush in the morning to try to overrun us."

Maverick took a bite of the hot chili beans. "If we could just kill one of them major chiefs, they might lose heart and go away."

After dark, some of the men slept while others kept the vigil around the perimeters of the walls. Cayenne was afraid of the sudden silence, the darkness closing in as the sun set all orange and gold. She hugged herself as she came over to the isolated spot where Maverick leaned against the wall, watching out a gun port.

"It's awfully quiet," she said, sitting down on the dirt floor next to him.

Maverick shrugged, tipping his hat back. "Indians have to rest and eat, too."

She watched the strong outline of his profile in the growing dust. "You think they'll hit us full force in the morning?"

"Don't worry about it," he answered a little too easily, and his hand went up to stroke the jagged white scar.

Cayenne looked around. There was no one close by and the nearest man was over behind some barrels asleep. Once in a while, she could hear his gentle snoring. Bat had gone down to the other end of the building to check things out.

"Don't lie to me, Maverick." She leaned up against him without thinking, seeking the comfort of his shoulder. "We've come a long way together. I'm beginning to know you like the back of my hand, know when you're lying to me."

"By damn, you sound like a wife!" He gave a forced laugh, obviously determined to keep her off the subject. His big arm slipped around her and she pressed her face against his shirt, thinking what a haven of protection and strength his arms had become for her. She didn't speak for a few minutes, looking through the gun port at the rose and purple sunset.

"Maverick, this might be our last night, our last sunset together."

He hesitated, watching the sunset himself, and he didn't speak until the dusk turned into darkness. "And if it is?"

She sighed, leaning against his chest and listening to his heartbeat. "Everyone ought to know when he's going to die so he can set things right, say the things he always meant to say to people and almost never does."

Maverick laughed again, but it was a forced laugh. "Don't count us out yet, baby. Maybe we'll get lucky. Something's gotta happen at dawn; this can't go on forever!"

She could feel the cold steel of his pistol in her side. "You won't let them take me if we're overrun?"

He didn't answer for a long moment, and his hand came down to tilt her her small face up. "You know the answer to that. I've seen what they can do to a white woman when they're mad." He kissed her gently, as if she were a fragile porcelain doll.

She clung to him. "I'm afraid, Maverick! So afraid!"

"Naw! Rebels aren't afraid! Stubborn and wrong-headed, maybe, but not afraid." His voice was joking, full of forced lightness. "Now what would old Jeff Davis think of you if he heard that?"

"I'll bet even your old Sam Houston would have been

scared right now!"

He laughed and shook his head. "Old Sam Houston would have charged hell with a water bucket!" Maverick stroked her hair. "Besides, old Sam got along fine with Indians. If we'd followed his lead, we might not have had all these troubles with the tribes."

"It's going to be a very long night," she swallowed hard. "Maverick, can I—can I stay here with you so I won't have to be alone?"

She felt him nod, grunting as he pulled her closer. "I've been alone most of my life, and now that I've finally found you . . . it isn't fair," he said bitterly against her hair. "It just isn't fair!"

"Papa says life's not fair but God'll even things up someday; see to it that people get what they deserve."

He hesitated and she felt him stiffen. "Sometimes maybe God needs a little help to get justice done."

He stood diametrically opposed to what she believed in, this bitter loner, and yet . . .

She slipped her arms around his neck and he kissed her deeply. "Oh, Maverick, I—I think I love you! I'm sorry things have come to this."

He didn't answer and she sighed. He didn't care about her at all. She must sound like a fool. His big body trembled ever so slightly. In wonder, she reached up to touch his rugged face. Were those tears there? "Maverick," she whispered. "Oh, Maverick!"

He clung to her in the dark like a frightened child, and without thinking, she opened her shirt, letting him press his face against the comfort of her naked breasts.

"Cayenne, I want you one last time," he whispered, his breath warm against her nipples. Her body wanted him, too, but even in the darkened adobe building, there was no way they could undress completely and make love.

She felt her body moisten itself, eager for him to fill

193

her as his hand stroked down her breasts to her waist. She touched his maleness, felt it throb strongly as she unbuttoned his pants and reached to caress him.

His fingers fumbled with the buttons of her pants, and then his hand reached inside to touch her, to stroke her. They lay down on a pile of burlap bags behind a stack of crates. She moved so that she lay with her head in his lap, spreading her thighs so his fingers could tease and stroke her wet, velvet softness. When his fingers slipped deep inside to caress her depths, she gasped and arched against him. And then she turned her head to take his pulsating manhood between her lips.

"Cayenne, you—you don't need to do that, baby." But he didn't push her away as her tongue tasted the seed of him, tilting her head so that he could thrust deeply between her lips. He made a sighing sound of pleasure, and his fingers reached again to stroke her depths while his other hand cupped her breasts, caressed her nipples.

She was wet and ready for entry. Cayenne felt her body arching eagerly up against his probing hand. She relaxed her throat so she could take his thrusting deeper, wanting to taste the very essence of the man.

The hand that stroked her breasts came down to pull her face against his crotch, and he moaned slightly. "You're drivin' me loco, you little vixen! I—I can't imagine not having you beside me forever!"

She had a sudden vision of eagles, their mighty wings spread, their bodies locked together as they plummeted toward the earth. And in that moment, her body shuddered and convulsed, and tasting him was not enough; she had to have more of him. Greedily, she took him deep in the softness of her mouth. When he came, she clung to him. Cayenne would not stop, as he moaned and writhed against her mouth, until she had taken every virile drop he could offer.

"Cayenne! Oh, Cayenne! Baby . . ." He pulled her

up to kiss his seed from her lips. "I always wanted a woman to do that to me, never had the nerve to ask."

"I—I couldn't stop myself, Maverick, dearest," she whispered, and was finally content with the taste of him still on her lips as he kissed her again. If this were the very last time, she had wanted an indescribable ecstasy to remember, and that it had been.

Cayenne dropped off into an exhausted sleep in his arms, not caring anymore what tomorrow would bring as long as she could have this night in his embrace. Funny, she had struggled and schemed to get back to Texas because of Slade and his men, and now she wasn't going to be able to get there. Well, Papa was always praying for miracles, and that's sure what they needed to get out of this one.

Long before dawn, she helped Mrs. Olds fry up some bacon and make a big pan of biscuits.

She took a platter around to all the men guarding the walls, along with a pot of fresh, strong coffee.

Bat Masterson smiled at her as he accepted a plate. "If we get out of here, I think I've about had enough of buffalo hunting. There's bound to be a better way to make a living. I figure there's a future for me in Dodge City; maybe there's a future for you there, too."

She laughed, pleased that he was interested enough to flirt. "It'll be dawn soon, and there's still a thousand Comanches, Cheyennes, and a handful of Kiowas out there. You'll have to do something about them first."

He sipped his coffee and she thought how handsome he was. "Okay, Cayenne. But when this is over, think about what I said about going with me. I meant it."

"Sorry, I've got a man," she said softly, and realized it was true. Things had changed so much in the few days since she'd left Wichita. What was she going to do about Maverick?

195

My stars, Cayenne, she scolded herself as she went around handing out steaming tin cups of coffee, *you've got to survive this morning before you worry about planning the rest of your life.*

She went last to Maverick and sat down beside him with a contented sigh. "I'm happy, Maverick, really happy. Would you ever consider living on the Lazy M?" Should she tell him about what the Comanche had done to Papa? No, he might consider a handicapped man too much of a burden. And he was such a loner, maybe he wouldn't want a ready-made family of all her little sisters.

Maverick sipped his coffee. "Cayenne, with what we're facing this morning, I figure I should clean the slate, tell you something. . . ."

"Will it make me unhappy?" She looked at him and he looked away, as if unable to meet her eyes. "If it will, don't tell me, Maverick. My God, if I may die in an hour, don't tell me just to clear your conscience!"

She felt crushed, betrayed. She felt sure he had started to tell her that there was another girl somewhere. Maybe he wanted to confess that he'd been too human to pass up a chance to make love to Cayenne but he didn't want any kind of lasting relationship, any burdens. "No." She put her hand over her ears. "Don't tell me."

"Okay, then I won't." He sipped the coffee, running his finger thoughtfully down the knife scar on his cheek.

Maybe he was married! Of course that was it. It was her own fault, she supposed. "I guess I threw myself at you, not realizing—"

"No, it's not that," he hesitated, then said nothing as he drank the coffee and stared out at the pale rose glow of dawn on the eastern horizon.

She peered out the gun port. Indian braves were coming from every direction now, resplendent in feathered headdresses, beads, and paint. They were going to

196

make one final charge. Almost a mile away, she saw the majestic figure of the half-breed Comanche chief, Quanah Parker, gathered with his leaders to direct the coming battle.

Maverick put his face close to hers, peered out, and cursed. "If I was only as good a shot with a rifle as I am with a pistol!"

The younger hunter, Billy Dixon, turned to look at him. "Mister, I'm one of the best with a buffalo gun and it's got a lot of range. What do you have in mind?"

She saw the sudden flicker of hope in Maverick's eyes, and he leaned over and kissed her quickly. "For luck," he said.

A bugle blew a charge and Cayenne almost cheered. "Hear that? It's the cavalry!"

Bat chuckled. "It'd be funny if it weren't so sad. Take another look ma'am. Those damned Injuns have a black soldier riding with them and he blows their charges! Must be a buffalo soldier who's deserted."

"A buffalo soldier?" She had never felt so bereft as she did now when she stared out and saw the dark man in the blue uniform riding with the Indians.

Maverick cursed. "The braves call the black troops that because of their dark, wooly hair."

Bat yelled, "They're ready to rush us! I see Quanah raising his arm, getting ready send the charge!"

Maverick grabbed Billy by the shoulder. "We'll talk after this charge, Billy. I got an idea that if we're lucky might bring this whole thing to a halt!"

"Here they come!" Bat yelled.

Cayenne looked up into Maverick's tense face. "If we don't come out of this—" She started to tell him she loved him, then realized it wasn't right if there were another woman waiting for him somewhere. Funny, up 'til now, that Annie was the only one she'd thought about, been jealous of.

"Get down, baby!" He snapped and pushed her head down as he stuck the rifle out the gun port. She looked out from her crouched position and saw the Indians gathering for a charge. She reached out and put her hand on Maverick's arm. The look he gave her told her she had his heart, no matter whether there was another woman in his life.

From her place, she saw the tall half-breed chief as he directed the placement of the warriors. What was Quanah Parker thinking this morning? That it was a fine day to die? That it was a great day for victory? She watched him, so noble and majestic on that fine gray pacer. Even though his signal would probably bring the final charge that would overrun her refuge, kill them all, she could sympathize with the Indians. She could understand because she just now realized their struggle against hunger and the buffalo hunters invading their lands, against the white civilization pushing at them from all sides. The plains tribes were doing the only thing they could—fight.

She tried to remember that she hated the Comanche but it was hard because Quanah reminded her so much of Maverick. She glanced over at Maverick. Yes, the two gray-eyed half-breeds even looked a little alike.

In that split-second, Cayenne wondered what the great chief thought as he surveyed the scene? Was he, too, thinking about life and death and a love that had come too late? She didn't want to die. But she saw the stern anger on Quanah's face in the distance, knew that this morning she surely would.

198

Chapter Ten

Quanah Parker sat the gray horse he had stolen from "Three-Fingered" Colonel Mackenzie and studied the distant, crumbling walls of the buffalo hunters' fortress in the first pink light of the coming dawn.

He glanced over at the war chiefs astride their ponies in a circle around him. All respectfully awaited his signal to begin the morning's attack. *Could he, should he waste the lives of any more of his men?*

"Isa-tai," he grunted to the *Noconi* whose vision had launched this campaign. "I think your *puha*, your magic is weak. Your visions have availed us nothing."

The man frowned, his face distorted by garish paint. Isa-tai was stripped for battle as were the others, although he had not participated in the fighting, which was his privilege as war leader. The *Noconi* Comanche wore a cap of sacred sage leaves, and both he and his pony were painted with bright yellow war paint. "When I predicted the comet, you were impressed. When the hot drought came this year as I predicted, you believed me. Now I tell you my power should protect us against the whites' guns, make their bullets bound off us. . . ."

"And yet I see my men dead and wounded everywhere!" Quanah snarled. "And we have lost even more trying to recover the bodies!"

The others muttered and nodded in agreement. So far, in the time the Comanche, Cheyenne, and Kiowa

199

had besieged this place, they had lost dozens of men. But they were no closer to overrunning the fortress than they had been the first dawn when they had caught those two hunters asleep in their wagon, and had killed and scalped them.

Lone Wolf, the Kiowa chief, pointed toward the adobe buildings. "If we cannot win here against a handful of hunters, we cannot win anywhere on the plains."

Isa-tai shook his head, shifting his weight on the magically painted pony. "It is not my fault," he answered peevishly as the pony stamped its feet. "I told you I had powerful medicine, but all know the many taboos. A warrior killed a skunk on our way to this place. That is a bad omen."

Some of the others nodded in agreement as Quanah studied them.

"It is so," grumbled another Kiowa leader, Woman's Heart. "But sometimes very young braves act without thinking."

But mature warriors should not. Quanah sighed again, surveying the desolate landscape from the butte as the first rays of dawn chased the purple shadows, turning them pale pink. The soapweed that the whites called yucca or beargrass thrust its spiky white blooms into the pale sky, accentuated by the red wild flowers he knew *Tejanos* called Firewheel. Around him, hundreds of Comanche, Kiowa, and Cheyenne warriors awaited his signal to attack again.

Should he send them against the foe now that he had lost faith in Isa-tai's vision, his medicine? After Isa-tai's other predictions, Quanah had been only too eager to believe the prophet and his urging to rise up against the invading whites. Isa-tai predicted that the "Big Fifty" rifles the Indians said "could shoot today and kill tomorrow" would not harm them. This place called Adobe Walls was a gathering place that must be destroyed; a

200

symbol of the buffalo slaughter; the stronghold of the white hunters.

And yet Quanah resented sending men to their deaths for a hopeless cause. He sat his horse straight and taller than the others, his white heritage evident in his height and strength. From his father, Chief Peta Nocona, he had inherited bravery and the cunning of the Comanche. From his white captive mother, Cynthia Ann Parker, he had his Texas forbearers' height and size, his gray eyes.

"My heart is heavy"—Quanah turned on the medicine man—"because there will already be much wailing in tepees on our return. Our people are fewer each year."

Isa-tai persisted. "I had a vision that with only one more day, we would sweep the hated killers of our buffalo before us like flood waters sweep over the river sand."

"And if we kill all these here?" Quanah argued. "You misread your vision! It is they who are the floods sweeping over the Indian! If we kill all these, there will only be more coming from the east with their big guns." He wiped at the sweat on his bronzed, naked skin, smearing the scarlet paint. Although it was only dawn, already the heat of the first day of that month whites called July breathed its hot breath on man and beast alike.

The Cheyenne leader, Stone Calf, waved his lance for emphasis. "Your white blood makes you a coward," he complained. "We must fight, must send a message to the great chief in that place called Washington that they must stop killing our buffalo. Otherwise, we die anyway from slow starvation. We cannot live on what the government agents give us."

"Yes," agreed the Comanche, Big Red Meat. "On the reservations early this year, food got so scarce we were eating our beloved ponies. The white men the government gives contracts to cheat us and give us little or nothing."

Quanah grunted in agreement. "That white chief,

Grant, sent preacher men called Quakers to try to tame us, make us learn to plow; tell us we must not fight old enemies such as the Utes, the Apache."

There was a murmur of agreement, of scornful laughter. Each knew no proud plains warrior would till the earth like the gentle tribes these leaders scorned. And if a man could not take the war trail sometimes to count coup, do great deeds of bravery to tell later around the campfire, what was he supposed to do?

"All my ears hear from you is true," Quanah admitted. He had brought his own men of the *Quahadi* band to join this great uprising that Isa-tai had predicted would sweep the hated white killers of the buffalo, yes, even all the whites from their lands so that things would be as they had been in the past.

And yet nothing could be returned to the way it had been. Trying to put the disintegrating pieces of the collapsing Indian civilization back to what it had been was like trying to restore a shattered mirror from the *Comanchero*'s trade goods.

The war ponies, all painted and decorated with feathers and scalps tied to their manes and bridles, stamped at the flies that bothered their legs. That was the only sound as the leaders awaited the decision that hung so heavy on his soul. Quanah looked around the silent circle of war chiefs, out at the hundreds of waiting warriors. His heart was heavy because early in the battle he had lost a good comrade and had ridden in right under the gun muzzles to recover the body. Quanah had been knocked from his horse by a spent bullet, had had to crouch behind a putrid, rotting buffalo carcass for a time until he could escape.

Now he surveyed the low-lying buildings from his sandy rise. They must be almost a mile away. And the rifles the whites called "Big Fifties" had been taking his men from their ponies with deadly accuracy.

"Oh, great chief," said Wild Mustang, a Comanche war leader, "we have danced the sun dance for the very first time this year; perhaps that is an omen of good luck."

"It is an omen that the *Nerm*, the Comanche have lost their way, no longer trust their own culture," Quanah answered sadly. "Never before has the dancing of the Kiowa and the Cheyenne seemed important to us. We are like frightened children who have lost their way in the dark, trusting others' customs because we no longer have confidence in our own."

It was true. The Comanche had danced their very first sun dance in the month the whites called May, but Quanah had no confidence in this new thing.

The other Comanches lapsed into embarrassed silence as if they knew he spoke true.

Quanah shook his head. "If we take this place after losing so many men, what have we gained?"

Isa-tai answered eagerly. "But if we lose it after the deaths of so many brave warriors, we are shamed. We cannot paint our faces with the black paint of victory, dance the scalp dances with our proud women."

"Besides," the war leader, Little Fox, leered, "if we take this place, we can stake the captured out on the ground for the soldiers to find when they come. When the Bluecoats see how we have tortured them, how long it took the hunters to die, word will spread and there will be much fear. The white hunters will be afraid to venture onto our plains."

Quanah shook his head. "The hunters all carry 'bites'—cartridges full of poison in case they are taken alive."

Little Fox's small, foxlike features smiled cruelly. "There is at least one woman inside those walls, a white woman."

Isa-tai nodded. "Yes, and Little Fox deserves to revenge himself on her after what white buffalo hunters did to his sister."

Quanah grimaced at the thought of what the half-crazed Little Fox would do to a captive woman. His own mother had been a captive taken from Texas in 1836. And she had loved his father so that she had fought the whites when the Texas Rangers had recaptured her in 1860, but they returned her to her white family anyway. "You won't get that woman to rape and torture as they did your sister," he said to the fox-faced one. "A white man will put a bullet in her brain or she will kill herself rather than be taken."

Little Fox's sharp features wrinkled with disdain. "You do not want me to seek vengeance on a woman because of your mother's blood. Maybe you have a white heart in a red body when we thought you were your father's son."

Quanah straightened his tall frame and glared at him with his cold, gray eyes. "Choose your words well when you speak of my mother. Word has come she has died among the whites, and my baby sister, *Topsanah*, too. I am Comanche; let none deny my father's blood. If the Indians go down to defeat in this great Uprising over who shall control the plains, I swear that I, Quanah, will be the last one to surrender, to bring my people in to be trod on by the white man's boots."

The others muttered in agreement. "None doubt your courage," White Shield said. "We know Little Fox's problems. We only await your orders."

Quanah sighed. Sometimes the weight of leadership felt like iron manacles and chains from the white man's stockade on his shoulders. "Then ready your men for the attack," he said grudgingly.

The leaders dispersed to ride with their own warriors. Even Isa-tai rode over to a nearby butte for a better view. But the minor chief, Little Fox, stayed at Quanah's side.

204

As leader of this attack, Quanah must stay out of range, out here where he could oversee everything that happened. Besides, it was very bad medicine for a chief to fall in a fight. That had happened to the Comanche, Little Buffalo, in the Great Uprising ten years ago. After he fell in battle, the fight had broken off, the Indians giving up and returning to their reservations. When a chief or a war leader fell, it was a sign of bad medicine and the Indians would usually give up the attack.

Little Fox scratched himself with his unusually long arms. "You have no stomach for today's fight?"

Quanah shook his head. "Yesterday I saw a man on a gray horse, very much like my own, who almost gave up his life to save a young boy whom we chased. I find no pleasure that we may spill that brave one's blood today."

Little Fox smiled evilly. "Yet I look forward to it!"

Quanah eyed the brave with distaste. "Besides, I have no stomach for all these hundreds of people. My warriors and I seldom mix with the other Comanche for good reason. We stay with our own *Quahadis* isolated in the area the whites called the Staked Plains and scorn to sign the white man's worthless treaties."

"Your band mixes so seldom with other Comanche, we know little about your clan and their great gray-eyed chief. Do you not have kin among the other bands?"

Quanah shook his head sadly. "I am alone now. My father, Peta Nocona, never took another wife after the Rangers forced my mother to return to her white family. He has died of an old battle wound that troubled him much. My brother, Poco, has caught one of the whites many diseases and died. Sometimes I wonder if I did the right thing, choosing to walk the Indian road instead of taking the path of my white heritage."

Little Fox snorted. "The whites would not accept you."

"They have evidently accepted that half-breed on the

205

gray stallion who got past us in the dash for the walls yesterday!"

Little Fox grinned. "But did he come by his fine horse in the brave manner you did, oh, Great Chief?"

Quanah smiled with memory. His own gray pacer had been stolen from that great chief of the whites, the one called Mackenzie. It was said that "Three-Fingered" Mackenzie had been in a fury ever since, determined to recover his prized horse. "A Comanche is skilled at stealing horses. It was not that brave a thing."

Little Fox ran his tongue over his lips. "I hunger for a white woman! If there is one inside this place, I will enjoy her, humiliate and rape her. Then I will hang her scalp from my war lance so that every time I see it blowing in the wind, I will remember my sister!"

Quanah didn't answer, watching the braves fan out for the charge on the adobe buildings. All knew that Little Fox's mind had become twisted since some moons ago when white hunters had raped and strangled his beloved younger sister with her own beaded necklace that he had given her. Only the wildest and most reckless of the braves would follow Little Fox now, because he lacked caution and judgment.

"Little Fox, you brought our people much trouble when your war party raided that white gathering in the land of the *Tejanos*."

Little Fox frowned. "Holding white captives for ransom is an old custom."

"But you broke your word and took prisoner that brave red-haired white man who brought the ransom." He felt scorn for Little Fox. Quanah had arrived at the last minute, in time to keep the warrior from killing the man, and made him set the Texan free. But Quanah hadn't arrived before Little Fox had tortured the white man most cruelly with fire. Little Fox had taken a burning stick and . . . .

206

"Why should I keep my word to whites?" Little Fox snorted, his animal-like features contorted with scorn. "Trickery is good enough for them after what they did to my sister! Every white who crosses my path will pay because she died such a cruel death!"

He could not fault the man there. To die of strangulation or hanging, so that the soul could not escape out the throat, was a death most dreaded by the Comanche. But the sharp-faced brave with the long arms had become a crazed wolf running amok on the plains, leaving trouble and death in his wake.

Sunlight reflected off the barrel of a warrior's old rifle as he gestured to Quanah, signaling that all warriors were in place. In spite of his white blood, Quanah was as Indian, as Comanche as the great chief who had sired him. Even though in his heart he felt the future had already been written, still he must make the motions of defiance. With a regretful sigh, Quanah brought his upraised arm down to signal the attack.

Cayenne watched the great chief through a gun port. As he made the downward sweep with his arm, she turned and shouted to the others, "I think they're gettin' ready to charge again!"

Maverick grabbed her shoulder, spun her around, and pushed her to the dirt at his feet. "Hang onto your pistol and stay down, Reb," he commanded as he aimed through the gun port.

"I won't stay down!" She scampered to her feet, peering out at the wave of riders gathering in a line out on the flat plains. "I want to see what's happening! Here, give me that extra rifle! I can shoot as good as you can!"

Maverick favored her with an amused grin. "By damn! You are hardheaded!" She caught the admiration in his voice.

Handsome young Bat Masterson looked over at them. "She's quite a woman! Cayenne, if we come through all this alive, I've had my fill of buffalo hunting. Me and my friend Wyatt Earp have some plans. Would you be interested in accompanying me back to Dodge?"

"No, she wouldn't," Maverick bristled as he aimed his rifle, waiting for the riders to gallop closer.

"My stars!" Cayenne snapped as she loaded the rifle. "Talk about hardheaded! Has it occurred to you I just might be interested in Bat's offer?"

"No, you're not," Maverick said. "I figure you're my responsibility and you're going with me!"

"Yankees!" Cayenne sniffed disdainfully.

Bat seemed to assess Maverick as if trying to decide whether to challenge him. "I think the lady can make up her own mind," he said coolly as he peered out the gun port.

Maverick glanced over at the younger man. "You got a lot of grit, Masterson, and maybe you'll go far. But I ought to warn you you're grazing in another man's pasture."

Bat cocked his rifle and looked at Cayenne. He had to shout over the sound of the yelping warriors galloping toward them, moving into gun range. "We'll continue this discussion later. You got a pistol, Cayenne?"

"Hell, yes!" she exploded at both of them. "Why do both of you keep asking that? If either of you think I'll blow my own brains out like some weak, snivelling—! That last cartridge is for some Comanche! I don't intend to waste it on myself!"

She felt absolute rage sweep over her at the idea she might be weak enough to kill herself when surrounded. Her terror had been replaced by anger, so much so that her hands shook as she aimed the rifle and fired.

A garishly painted brave screamed and tumbled from his running pony.

And then there was no time for anything, no terror or thought, just reloading and shooting as the painted savages shouted and circled the buildings. The sun pushed above the horizon and hung like a hard fried egg in the faded sky. Her nostrils stung with the acrid smell of powder. Cayenne was as thirsty as she had ever been in her life, but there was no time to stop for even a mouthful of water as she reloaded and fired. The barrel of her rifle grew so hot she dare not touch it, and her shoulder ached from the recoil as she pulled the trigger. Her ears rang with the echo of gunfire, curses and high-pitched screams of dying men.

She would pretend she was someplace else, she thought stubbornly as she reloaded, *remember some good time from the past*. Bits and pieces of memories came to her mind like scraps from a patterned quilt: sitting on Papa's lap while he read her a story from the few dog-eared books they owned. He'd read them so often over the years, he could still repeat the stories to her little sisters without even looking at the pages. She thought of Sunday dinner at the long oak table with all the family, lots of friends and neighbors. There was always fried chicken and chocolate cake.

She glanced over at Maverick, imagining him at one end of that long table. His gaze caught hers and he nodded encouragingly. She wasn't fooled; she could see the concern on his bronzed face. Maverick. In her mind, she saw eagles locked as they mated, plummeting from the sky, and Cayenne remembered the taste and touch and heat of the man.

Oh, Maverick Durango, I love you, she thought suddenly and realized it was true. No, no, it couldn't be. He was Comanche and damned Yankee, and he'd taken her innocence. She must remember that, remember that she had reason to hate him. That would stop her nagging conscience that said she ought to warn him about those three men who might at the least be gunfighters. They might even be outlaws! But, no, Papa was known for his character. He wouldn't be friends with outlaws.

She didn't have time to worry about that now as she aimed, taking another brave from his saddle. Neither of them might survive Adobe Walls and then she wouldn't have to worry about Slade and his partners at all.

The bugle call echoed and reechoed through the morning and the braves seemed to take courage from it, attacking with new zeal.

Bat gestured to get the hunters' attention as the black renegade crept toward the wagon where the slain buffalo hunters lay. "Billy, you got a clear shot! That bugle is getting on my nerves!"

Dixon nodded, aimed carefully, and fired. Even as Cayenne watched, the dark man in the blue cavalry jacket stumbled, falling forward on his face near the wagon.

"The loss of that bugler will put a dent in their morale," Maverick shouted. "And remember, Cheyenne will let their dead lay but Comanches are duty-bound to come back for their warriors' bodies! Make every shot count when they come in!"

And even as he said it, the braves who had retreated swept toward them in an undulating wave of running, painted war ponies, leaning over to sweep the dead up in a dazzling display of expert horsemanship.

The besieged whites laid down a withering fire from their rifles, knocking warriors from their ponies. The Indians retreated out of gun range.

Cayenne suddenly realized how exhausted, how tense she was. She leaned against the crumbling adobe and shook.

"Reb, you all right?" Maverick looked up.

For a split second, she almost ran to throw herself into the safety of his big arms but stopped herself. The last thing he needed to deal with right now was a weeping, hysterical female. "I'm fine, really," she lied, brushing a wisp of red hair out of her eyes.

Bat Masterson went over to the water barrel, came back with a dipperful, and made a sweeping bow. "Allow me, my dear. I'm sorry it's not champagne, but it's all I can offer. Someday, in some elegant place, I'll make up for it."

She accepted the dipper and drank greedily, a little amused by the jealous annoyance on Maverick's face. "That's all right," she hastened to say to the handsome Bat. "I've never tasted champagne anyway."

Bat smiled. *Had she forgotten how blue-gray his eyes were?* "Cayenne, you belong in some exciting place, dancing away the night and drinking champagne. . . ."

"She belongs in front of a ranch house fireplace on a cold winter's night, snuggled down with a husband and a couple of kids in her lap. . . ." Maverick broke off, looking away as if embarrassed. "At least, that's how I see her."

That was how she saw herself, too, she thought, and she found herself sharing that vision. Yes, children in her lap, and when the little ones were asleep and tucked in, the man would take her in his arms and carry her to the soft feather bed in the big upstairs bedroom of the Lazy M. When she closed her eyes to envision the scene, she didn't see Bat Masterson, she saw Maverick Durango and his children. *Would they be dark with her green eyes? Or would their eyes be gunmetal gray like his?*

Maverick gestured the men in close. "Listen, I've got an idea! The Indians have retreated, but there'll be another attack and another. There's hundreds of them and less than thirty of us. We need to think like Indians."

Bat sneered. "That shouldn't be hard for you, but the rest of us may have a little trouble!"

"My Gawd, you two!" Billy Dixon snapped. *The long-haired young buffalo hunter's nerves must be frayed*, Cayenne thought. "Can't you two forget your differences over that girl until we get rid of the Indians? Then you can fight over her!"

"No need," Cayenne said, glancing from one to the other. And then she said what in her heart she had already known. "If we get out of this alive, I'm going on south with Maverick."

Bat shrugged and smiled ruefully. "You're making a big mistake, Cayenne. The world hasn't seen the last of me, but a hundred years from now, who'll remember a cowboy named Maverick Durango?"

"Let's talk about Indians, shall we?" Maverick smiled thinly at him as he reached for cigarette "makin's," rolling a smoke with one hand. "We've got to do something to make the braves think their medicine is bad so they'll give up and retreat."

"Retreat, hell!" young Dixon swore. "We're surrounded by hundreds of Indians and all they got to do is outwait us! They ain't gonna retreat!"

"Listen to the half-breed," one of the other hunters said as he pushed his hat back. "He makes good sense!"

There was a murmur of assent from the others.

Maverick strode over and looked out the gun port. "The war leaders have gathered now back up on that little butte with Quanah, safe out of range. But if we could kill one of them, they'd think it was bad medicine. . . ."

"Medicine!" Bat scoffed, coming over to peer out himself. "A miracle's more like it! It must be almost a mile out to where they're palavering!"

Cayenne went over and looked out. Bat was right. It must be nearly a mile to where the little group of chiefs sat their ponies, discussing the next maneuver while the hundreds of warriors reformed their lines. No one had to tell her which one was the legendary half-breed chief, Quanah Parker. His height and regal bearing gave him away. Besides, everyone said he had gray eyes and rode a gray horse as did Maverick.

Two half Comanches, she thought. One had chosen the Indian path, the other his white heritage, and now they had come up against each other in this isolated spot in the Texas Panhandle.

She watched Quanah evidently discussing tactics, because he gestured toward the buildings. Another brave gleamed with sweat and yellow paint all over his naked body. Even his horse had been painted ochre.

She recognized a face suddenly, even at this distance, and shivered. The brave speaking to Quanah now had to be that one she remembered seeing on her dash for the walls, the one with the small, sharp foxlike features. *Hadn't Papa described the Comanche who tortured him as looking like a fox?*

Maverick ran his finger down the white jagged scar. "I've got an idea that might work. . . ."

"Might work!" Bat snorted. "You're loco, Maverick!"

Cayenne felt exhausted and discouraged, but she was also angry. "The least you men can do is listen to Maverick's idea! No one else seems to have any!"

The others looked away, embarrassed at her scolding.

Maverick grinned as he lit the match with his thumbnail. "They don't call her Cayenne for nothing. The lady has a little pepper to her!" There was a glow of frank admiration in his eyes.

"It's the Rebel in me!" she snapped back with spirit.

"Naw," Maverick grinned. "It's the Texan in you! Texas gals always have more grit to them!"

"Amen to that!" Billy Dixon leaned on his "Big Fifty."

Maverick looked at the young buffalo hunter thoughtfully, then back out toward the little group of chiefs on the far rise. "I've watched you shoot, Dixon. By damn, you're one of the best with a rifle I've seen. How far can you shoot?"

Young Billy colored modestly at the compliment and shrugged. "Don't know, stranger. I've taken buffalo at nigh on half a mile."

Maverick whistled low, taking another puff as he looked out. "Could you shoot that far?" He gestured toward the chiefs on the little rise of prairie.

Dixon peered out the gun hole. "You're funning me, ain't you? Mister, it must be nearly a mile from here to that hill!"

Maverick didn't seem to hear him as he stared at the chiefs engaged in heated conversation. "It would be very bad medicine if they lost a chief this morning; they'd quit and go home."

Bat laughed. "Which is exactly the reason they're staying out of gun range! You don't think they haven't thought of that themselves?"

Maverick smoked and stared out for a long moment. Cayenne wondered what his thoughts were. Somehow, she had confidence that if anyone could come up with a plan to save the people here, it'd be Maverick.

He blew smoke out the gun port and seemed to watch the way it drifted on the breeze. "You know," he said to Dixon, "if you could get Quanah, you might end this whole uprising here and now. After all, he's the leader."

Dixon peered out the gun port. "That's an impossible shot!"

"Maybe not," Maverick said softly and blew smoke out the gun port again, watching it drift on the breeze.

"My stars, Maverick." Cayenne was tired, hot, and a little out of patience. "That's not a plan, that calls for a miracle!"

He smiled at her. "Preacher's daughters shouldn't be

214

surprised at miracles." Then for a long moment, Maverick just smoked and stared out at the group of chiefs and war leaders ringed around Quanah Parker. "It's less than a mile," he said softly to no one in particular, "and with a little help from the wind and allowing for the peculiarities of that gun, it might just work."

He turned to face the group of expectant faces ringing him as he tossed away the cigarette. "Dixon, I'd do it myself, but I'm not tops with a rifle; the handgun was always my choice."

One of the other hunters nodded vigorously and scratched at his filthy buckskin shirt. "Billy Dixon's the best there is with a 'Big Fifty,' and that's a fact!"

Maverick tipped his hat to the back of his head. "Then he's gonna get a chance to prove it! If what I have in mind works, he can take Quanah down and the rest of them will go home. Well, even if it isn't Quanah, they'll think it's big magic if you could get any one of them."

Bat Masterson sneered. "At that distance? Are you loco?"

Cayenne glared at Bat. "Listen to him," she said. "If anyone knows about Indians, it's Maverick!"

The half-breed winked at her. "There's one vote of confidence."

The others nodded grudgingly. "We'll listen, stranger, because nobody else had any ideas."

Maverick caught young Dixon by the arm. "Get that Sharps of yours, and I'll help you figure the wind and all. With a little luck, you can hit Quanah and they'll all scatter. Now, Billy, here's my plan. . . ."

Quanah Parker looked around at his chiefs and shook with rage. "We have lost yet more good men! There will be much weeping in many tepees tonight! Even the black renegade buffalo soldier has fallen!"

Isa-tai said again, "It is not my fault! I told them that

to kill that skunk would destroy my magic!"

One of the Cheyenne chiefs could not seem to hold his temper longer. He attacked Isa-tai with his quirt, beating him about the head. "Because of this false leader, my own son lays dead before those walls!"

The prophet threw up his arm to protect himself and Quanah grunted to the Cheyenne. "Enough! The boy died bravely! It is all any man can hope for—to die with bravery and honor rather than starve to death on the reservation!"

The Cheyenne subsided, taking deep, shuddering breaths. "The great Comanche chief is right."

Quanah frowned. "So now I await another medicine sign to know whether to stay here and keep attacking until we overrun them from sheer numbers or move on to another target!"

He heard grumbling and discord around him. Quanah said, "Our scouts tell us the Bluecoats are beginning to move like hawks swooping down on their prey." He gestured with a lance. "Even now, the white soldiers come from the west, the east, the south, and yes, Fort Dodge to the north. The warring tribes will be trapped between all five of the cavalry columns that their chief, Grant, sends!"

Little Fox frowned. "But as always, we will slip through their fingers, oh, Great Leader. After we level this place, burn and torture and kill these whites, we will scatter and disappear into the night like smoke. All those Bluecoats will hunt us in vain while we reassemble in the great canyon to the south!"

"Sooner or later," Quanah predicted direly, "the Bluecoats will find that canyon called the Palo Duro. Then, instead of a refuge, the canyon will become a trap for our people!"

"Never!" Little Fox shouted. "It will always be a haven we can retreat to. The soldier leaders are too stupid to find it."

Quanah looked down at the fine gray horse he rode. "Have you forgotten 'Three Fingers' so soon from the last time we clashed with the calvary? Mackenzie is not a stupid soldier chief. He doesn't give up once he has picked up the scent like a lobo wolf relentlessly chasing a deer to ground."

Little Fox's lip curled in scorn, unconvinced. "The canyon will always be there for our retreat and the stupid soldiers will never find it! There's good grass for our ponies, plenty of water even in dry summers, and fat game for our cooking fires!"

Quanah glared at him, not liking the man. Little Fox lacked judgment. "Sooner or later, someone will tell the soldiers of it."

Little Fox shook his head. "You become like an old woman, letting caution make a coward of you. The only ones who know the canyon besides Indians are the *Comancheros* who trade guns for the booty from our raids! Soon they will send a messenger about bringing us more guns!"

To-ha-koh looked concerned, shook his head, "I like it not that any white man knows our hiding place."

Little Fox nodded to reassure him. "We have dealt with this one many years. The messenger will be the one with the blind eye and limp, the one called Pedro."

Quanah felt a little uneasy, as if his spirit animal were attempting to warn him of something. "The *Comanchero* are the weak link in our chain of supply," he grumbled, looking toward the walls. *Was that a reflection off a gun barrel he saw?* "No Comanche would betray our canyon to the south, but a *Comanchero* might."

"The *Comanchero* have never betrayed us," Big Red Meat protested.

Quanah sneered with disdain. "I trust them not. Any

of them would betray his own mother for gold."

Little Fox gestured impatiently. "You delay your decision, Quanah, while we argue uselessly about what has already happened. I cannot recall the message now. The *Comanchero*, Pedro, will meet with us at the Canyon in a few weeks to tell us about a new supply of guns. With them, we can sweep the whites from the plains."

"Little Fox is right," Stone Calf, the Cheyenne leader said. "We will discuss the *Comanchero* later. Right now, Great Leader," he addressed Quanah respectfully, "shall we continue to attack this place or shall we scatter to hit unsuspecting hunters' camps and isolated ranches?"

Little Fox's ugly face leered. "Can we not do both? Let us stay until we overrun this place! I think there is a white woman inside and I want to mount one as she begs for mercy as my sister must have done. . . ."

"Your need for vengeance clouds your judgment," Quanah interrupted, although it was considered rude for one warrior to interrupt another. Good manners dictated that each await the other to finish speaking. "What would you have us do?"

"I say we take this place no matter how many warriors it costs! We must let the white devils know that we are serious about how we intend to deal with those who slaughter our buffalo for money, leaving our women and children hungry!"

There was a murmur of agreement from the others, but Quanah only half listened. Instead, he watched the low-lying adobe buildings. There it was again, that slight flash as if the sun were reflecting off a gun barrel. Certainly the chiefs were safe at this distance. . . .

Little Fox, obviously encouraged by the murmur of agreement, went on. "After we overrun and torture the hunters to death, we'll break up into small war parties, spread out over the entire plains, catching ranchers and hunters, taking their scalps! The stage coaches still run, and they must be destroyed because they bring travelers looking for new places to settle."

The Kiowa, Lone Wolf, spoke now. "The Comanche held their very first sun dance one moon ago. But the Kiowa have yet to hold their annual ceremony. More of our warriors would be willing to take the war trail if the Kiowa had already finished the magic of our sun dance. Some fear to take any action until that happens a few suns from now in our beloved Wichita hills in that place whites call the Indian Territory."

To-ha-koh nodded. "Hai! I like Little Fox's new idea! Let us spread out, bring death and destruction to as many whites as possible for the next several weeks, then reassemble at the great canyon to meet with the *Comanchero*, get more weapons, make more plans!"

Quanah sighed. "It is agreed then. Barring some sign of bad medicine, we will keep attacking this haven of the buffalo hunters until we slaughter them all. Then we will scatter and do what damage we can before meeting thirty suns from now at the big canyon to the south. . . ."

He never finished. Quanah saw a flash of light from a rifle at the walls and jerked his horse's reins abruptly so that it reared and stumbled backward. Even as the echoing sound of the shot came to him, the warrior, To-ha-koh, screamed in shock and pain, clutching at his chest.

Scarlet blood pumped out between the man's brown fingers. "I'm . . . hit! He gasped, "Magic!" His face seemed frozen in amazement as he tried vainly to hold back the red stream that pumped between his fingers.

Now Quanah smelled the sweet, coppery scent of the warm blood. The wounded man's horse reared and neighed in confusion at the sudden scent.

"Bad medicine!" he gasped. "The spirits do not smile on us today. . . . We must scatter to the four winds, come together at the canyon. . . ."

Quanah tried to catch the warrior, but the man slumped and slipped from his horse. As he slid down its side, his wound left a scarlet trail on the pony's hair. All around Quanah raged confusion and shouting as warriors galloped out of range. *Magic. Bad medicine.* The buffalo hunters had killed one of the chiefs at the impossible range of almost a mile in white man's terms. Why was he so sure that half-breed had something to do with this? He had a sudden omen of very bad medicine. This war would amount to nothing and, yet, he could not stop it any more than he could stop the rivers when they overflowed and flooded.

"Scatter!" he commanded. "We meet at the canyon in thirty sun's time as we had planned!"

With a heavy heart and much foreboding, the great chief turned and rode away from the place called Adobe Walls.

Chapter Eleven

Cayenne stared out in disbelief. "They're leaving! The Indians are leaving!"

She felt a giddy rush of relief as she stared out the gun port and watched the warriors retreating in confusion. Even as she watched, she saw the big half-breed chief, Quanah Parker, rein his gray horse around and ride out at a gallop. The others scattered into small war parties, shouting and shrieking as they rode away.

Maverick peered out the gun port beside her. "That did it!" He nodded with satisfaction. "I told you if we could kill one of their important chiefs, they'd think it was bad medicine and give up the attack!"

The buffalo hunters in the saloon sent up a rousing cheer. "Hurrah for Maverick! Hurrah for Billy Dixon!"

Cayenne watched the warriors galloping away in the early morning heat. "Looks like they're going in all directions! What do you suppose they're up to?"

Maverick sighed and tipped his hat back on the blue-black hair. "Up to no good, I'll tell you that! A lot of poor devils, including women and children, will catch hell the next few weeks! Some settlers are too isolated out on these plains to even know there's an Indian war in progress until a war party rides into the yard!"

She leaned against the rough adobe, suddenly exhausted and emotionally drained, and studied the half-breed's profile. *Such a rugged, strong face . . . just like his hands.* Her gaze went to his big, calloused hands, remembering his gentle touch on her silken skin, remembering his mouth on hers. . . .

Bat Masterson laughed, interrupting her thoughts as he peered out the gun port. "If that don't beat all! Look at those damned birds!"

She went over and peered out, oblivious to the noisy conversation and raucous laughter of the rough men around her. "What is it, Bat?"

He hesitated. "Nothing a lady should see." He cocked his rifle. "Always wanted to kill me an eagle."

She looked out, saw a pair of giant eagles soaring in circles on the hot air currents, and watched them mesh and fall as they mated. *Could that be the same pair of eagles she had seen before?* In her memory, she was again on a creek bank, locked in the half-breed's embrace as he took her with all the heat and fire of some wild, uncivilized thing. And she became as passionate and unfettered as he was, lost in his kiss, his Comanche caress. . . .

Bat aimed at the soaring birds. But Cayenne reached out, knocking the gun aside. "No, Bat, let them go. They belong up there together, free and wild!"

"But I'd like some feathers to trim a hat," Bat complained, and again he aimed the rifle.

She heard Maverick's step, quiet and quick as a shadow although he wore cowboy boots. "Mind the lady and don't do it," he said softly, and his tone sounded almost like the warning hiss of a rattlesnake. "Eagles are special to us."

Cayenne glanced at him, seeing by his expression that Maverick remembered, too.

Bat laughed good-naturedly and leaned the rifle against the wall. "I've had enough fighting for a while, or you and me'd tangle, Maverick. But I want to please the lady, and if she don't want me to shoot them birds—"

"I don't," she said quickly. "They aren't bothering anyone." *If she had been a Comanche, might the eagle have been her spirit animal? Was it his?* She looked at Maverick's stern face but read nothing in his eyes.

A sudden gunshot echoed and reechoed from one of the other two buildings.

Cayenne started. "My stars! What do you think that was about?"

Maverick shook his head, checked his pistol. "Reckon I'd better find out!"

But just then, a hunter ran from the other building. "Olds accidentally killed hisself, just now!"

Cayenne felt stunned shock. "Oh, my God! That poor woman!" Quickly she ran over to help, to comfort the grief-stricken wife.

The plump woman sobbed uncontrollably as she gestured toward the prone form under a blanket on the floor. "He went up the ladder to watch the Injuns! When they acted like they might be gonna attack again, he yelled a warning and started back down the ladder. I guess the trigger caught on something . . . I saw it all happen! Oh, God, it was so awful!" She began to weep and Cayenne put her arm around her, looking around helplessly at the silent hunters.

One of the dirty, grizzled men scratched his beard. "That's just the way it was, too, miss! We heard him shout, and when I turned around, he was coming down the ladder. Reckon the trigger fouled on something 'cause his gun went off, caught him in the face! 'Nigh blew his head completely off!"

Cayenne felt the tears well up in her own eyes as she patted the woman's shaking shoulders. In a few more minutes, the danger would have been past, the Indians driven off thanks to Maverick's savvy about bad medicine. It was ironic that at that moment, Olds had accidently shot himself.

Maverick came in, followed by Bat Masterson and the other hunters. "What happened?"

Cayenne told him briefly. He shook his head. "Tough luck. I'm real sorry, ma'am."

The woman turned on him, spitting like a bobcat. "You! You damned Comanche! It ain't fair that you're alive and my man is dead!"

Cayenne grabbed the woman when she would have attacked Maverick with her fists. She wasn't sure what she'd expected from the half-breed, but he only shook his head, speaking gently. "I really am sorry, Missus Olds."

Billy protested. "Beggin' yore pardon, ma'am, if it hadn't been for this fella's idea, we might all be dead by now!" He held out his hand to shake. "I want to thank you, mister. You probably saved all our lives!"

But Maverick glared at him coldly and didn't shake the offered hand. "Now that it's all over, I can tell you men what bastards all buffalo hunters are! Because of your wholesale slaughter, the tribes will either starve or kill a lot of innocent people!"

Bat grinned. "Injun lover, huh?"

"Injun hater," Maverick corrected him coldly. "At least, I got plenty of reason to hate the Comanche, kill every one I see! But yet, I can sympathize even with them. Any man will pick up a weapon and do something when his woman and kids are hungry!"

"Injuns ain't the only ones with hungry kids," a grizzled hunter said. "You think some of us are just doin' this for fun? When that money panic hit back east last year, I couldn't find work and I've got six kids myself, mister! Sellin' them hides and sending the money home feeds my little ones!"

Billy Dixon rested the stock of the heavy Sharps on

the floor. "There's too many hunters," he complained. "Prices for hides is less than half what it was a couple of years ago. Besides, we're doin' the government a favor. They say they'll never be able to force the tribes onto reservations 'long as there's plenty of buffalo for them to live off of!"

Cayenne patted Mrs. Old's arm. "What do we do now? We need to get help in case the war parties return."

One of the men pushed forward. "Me'n Lem will try to make it into Fort Dodge, let them know what's happened."

Maverick spoke with a voice of authority, obviously used to taking charge. "You do that. In the meantime, the rest of us have graves to dig, make plans in case the war parties do return, and . . ." His voice trailed off as he looked out across the prairie, cursing softly under his breath. "Sometimes it's hard to tell which ones are the savages!"

Curiously, Cayenne followed his gaze. Some of the buffalo hunters had walked out on the prairie to inspect the bodies of the fallen Indians and were stealing small items from them. She winced as she saw the scalps dangling from the grinning white men's hands, saw them actually taking heads.

One of them held the black bugler's head aloft triumphantly. "We'll put these on posts all around the walls! That'll give 'em a message if they come back!"

Maverick turned away with a low curse. "I hate Comanche, but I wouldn't stoop to that!"

Cayenne turned, horror-stricken, to Bat. "You know those men; can't you stop that?"

Bat shrugged. "I'd have to fight them all, and for what?"

"You're no better than they are!" Cayenne flung at him. She looked over at Maverick's grim face, remembering that he had a scalp hanging from Dust Devil's

Indian bridle. But that was a trophy of war like a medal to a warrior. The hunters cutting off heads was shameful and disgusting to him.

She could still hear the men outside shouting with glee as they defiled the dead. She went over and put her hand on Maverick's arm. "What do we do now?"

He looked down at her. "You're not going with him?" He nodded toward Bat Masterson.

She shook her head. "I'm going with you on south to the Lazy M Ranch."

"Then let's bury the dead and clear outa this place," he muttered. "I don't like the company we're keepin'." He turned and looked at Mrs. Olds, who had regained her composure. "We'll see you get into Fort Dodge, ma'am."

The widow nodded her thanks and Maverick organized a burial detail. Once again Cayenne found herself saying scripture over yet more graves.

She couldn't read Maverick's expression as they turned away from the mounded dirt. "Your daddy teach you that?" he asked. "Is he really a preacher?"

"The only one in our sleepy little town," she said. "Everyone depends on him for comfort when they have trouble; don't know what folks would do without him."

Maverick looked troubled.

"Why do you ask?"

He hooked his thumbs in his gun belt, not meeting her eyes. "No reason."

Bat rubbed his chin thoughtfully. "I think I've had all the buffalo huntin' I want. Any of those crews get caught out now will wish for death before the Injuns finish with them."

Cayenne thought about Buck and his skinning crew. Even though those men deserved it, she wouldn't want to see them tortured to death. Buck and Clint had said they were without "bites." If trapped by Indians with no hope

226

of escape, "biting the bullet" gave a man a quick death by suicide rather than a slow agony at the hands of a war party.

She wondered if Buck's crew had gone back to the safety of Fort Dodge or one of the Kansas cow towns. It wasn't likely. As greedy as they were, that bunch was probably taking their chances, still out on the plains slaughtering buffalo.

Cayenne and Maverick stayed on for several days, helping give the dead a decent burial. Mrs. Olds was glad to have the comfort of another woman. Most of the horses, except for Strawberry and Dust Devil, had either been shot and killed during the fracas or run off by the Indians. Someone rode into Fort Dodge to bring back help and alert the cavalry to the large war parties marauding through the area.

When Cayenne and Maverick finally had time to stop and look things over, it was nothing short of a miracle that only four white men were dead, including Mr. Olds who had accidently killed himself. The "Big Fifty" rifles had held almost a thousand Indians at bay. No one would ever know how many Indians were killed or wounded because the warriors managed to retrieve so many of the bodies of the fallen for death ceremonies later.

Out of curiosity, Maverick stepped off the distance from Billy Dixon's shooting position out to where the Indian had fallen from his saddle. The distance measured an incredible 1,538 yards—eight tenths of a mile.

Maverick grunted in wonder. "A hundred years from now, men will still be talkin' about that shot; how it turned this battle."

Cayenne watched him. "It was you who suggested it, Maverick; you saved the day for all of us, but I suppose history books will give the credit to Billy, since he did the shooting. He does shoot well. As I remember the telling, he came in second to Papa last year when Papa won the fancy Winchester rifle the Cattlemen Association gave as first prize."

She thought about it a moment. "Come to think about it, that's where Papa said he met Don Durango."

Maverick's face went almost pale, then he seemed to recover and gave a slight shake of the head. "You've made a mistake, Reb. I remember the old Don coming back from that cattleman's meeting. He didn't mention anything about meeting any Joe McBride."

"Maybe he forgot or didn't think it important," Cayenne shrugged. "But I'm sure Papa said 'the owner of the Triple D.' I think they had a long talk about something; Papa never said exactly what."

Maverick took off his hat and ran his hand through his black hair. "Must be a mistake," he muttered. "The old Don would have mentioned it. . . ." His voice trailed off and he stared into space, looking puzzled.

When things were under control, the pair saddled up their horses so they could ride on.

Bat Masterson tried to convince Maverick and Cayenne to cancel their journey. "Why don't you wait here with us?" he said as they loaded supplies from the sutler's store on a spare packhorse. "We've sent a couple of men for help from Fort Dodge to the north."

Maverick shook his head, frowning as he helped Cayenne up on Strawberry. "The stink of you hide men would gag a self-respectin' coyote. We'll take our chances riding south."

Bat sneered. "You'll take a chance, all right!" He gestured toward Cayenne. "But it ain't fair to the lady!"

Cayenne whistled softly under her breath to hold her temper. "I've a little bit of a maverick heart myself, Bat, and I need to get home!"

"But suppose you cross the trail of a war party?"

"Don't worry about her, Bat." Maverick's hand went to the butt of his pistol. "I won't let them take her."

Could falling into the Indian's hands be so terrible that he'd put a bullet in her brain rather than let it happen? She shivered a little in spite of the July heat and thought again of the mysterious Annie Laurie.

Bat took off his hat and looked at her. "Cayenne, I don't mind telling you I've never been so taken by a woman. I got big plans, don't intend to be a hide man forever. You could go with me to Dodge City. . . ."

"She's going with me," Maverick said softly as if he dared anyone to deny it.

She looked from one to the other and thought about the trouble awaiting her at the ranch. Duty called. No, it wasn't duty, it was the memory of Maverick Durango's arms around her, the feel of his hot mouth on her breasts. And yet she hated him because he was both a damned Yankee sympathizer and a Comanche—and more than that, he aroused passion in her that she had never known existed until a few days ago.

"Maverick's right," she said quickly, grasping Strawberry's reins. "I'm going with him. If anyone can make it down through the Panhandle, I think it's Maverick."

They rode out, leaving the miserable hovel of adobe behind. They didn't talk much as they headed straight south down through the stark, hostile Panhandle country.

She wiped at the perspiration soaking her boy's shirt, glad she'd put her hair back up under her hat so the slight breeze could cool her neck. "I think a horny toad would have a hard time makin' it out here," she complained.

He took off his hat and wiped his dark face. "Not

much besides mesquite, sagebrush, and rattlesnakes," he agreed, patting Dust Devil's lathered neck. "You know what they say about Texas: 'It's great for men and dogs but hell on women and horses.' "

She regarded him coolly. "I believe it was one of your damned Yankee officers who complained that 'if he owned both hell and Texas, he'd rent out Texas and live in hell.' "

Maverick smiled sheepishly. "You can't expect folks from up north to deal with all this vast space and heat until they've had a chance to get used to it."

"I hope those carpetbaggers get out of Texas and let us deal with our own problems!"

Cayenne lost track of sunrises and sunsets as the pair traveled. The days became an endless glare of hot orange suns and purple shadows of evening. Sometimes Maverick seemed lost in thought, struggling with some inner conflict, and once she caught him staring at her with great passion as if he either loved her . . . or hated her.

She wasn't sure which because he said little and they rode in silence through the shimmering heat for hours without speaking. Nor did he make any advances toward her. Each slept wrapped in his own blanket at night with only a very small fire because he said he feared a passing war party might spot it. When they camped, he cautioned her about rattlesnakes that might be curled up in the cool recesses of rocks.

Then one day, Maverick saw smoke signals to the north. The next evening, to the south, they crossed the trail of unshod ponies.

Maverick leaned on his saddle horn, staring down at the faint tracks. "Masterson's right, Cee Cee," he grumbled as he studied the almost invisible marks. "I shouldn't risk trying to get a woman through this hostile country. Why don't I take you over to Fort Griffin and go on alone? If you'd give me the exact location of your family's ranch, I'd check on your daddy's health, send a message to you."

"No," she said. *Why did she have a feeling he was hiding something?* If she didn't go with him, she'd have no way of knowing whether he might give up the whole thing and ride out of the Panhandle, go back to the Triple D. After all, there was no reason for him to get to McBride, Texas, except to accompany her. She really hadn't figured out why he had come along unless he felt guilty about taking her innocence without at least trying to help her with her problem. Texas cowboys were gallant like that.

"No," she said again, shaking her head stubbornly. "You're not dumping me at the fort. I'm going along with you. After all, it's my papa who's sick," she lied.

"You hardheaded little Rebel," he swore. "With all this Indian sign, it might be smart of me to masquerade as a Comanche warrior. I did it back in '64 during the Great Outbreak down in the Hill Country."

She ran her tongue over her dry lips. "You get some clothing off one of those dead Comanche back at the Walls?"

"Other things, too," he nodded as he dismounted, digging in his saddlebags. "I took war paint, clothing from one of those dead Comanche braves," he said, pulling items from the saddlebag. "I think we have a better chance if I cross this country as a Comanche, and you can be a captive I stole from some ranch."

"My stars! What are you doing?" She was hot, tired, and annoyed as she watched him strip off his shirt and his boots. "Are you going to go around in nothing but beads and a breechcloth?"

He grinned and winked at her as he redressed as a warrior. "I sure am, Reb. I might just talk our way out of a mess if we run across a stray war party."

She watched him smear the gaudy paint on his dark face. It was amazing how in seconds he was becoming a savage before her eyes. "Suppose we run into soldiers instead?"

He paused, looking at her. "In that case, you'll have to save my bacon, baby. Tell them I'm not really an Injun kidnapping you."

"Suppose I don't?" she asked pointedly, trying not to stare at his almost naked body. Maverick really looked like an authentic savage. Without her, he'd have a time convincing any white stranger that he wasn't what he looked like—a half-naked, fierce Comanche brave bent on rape, pillage, and murder.

Maverick smiled thinly. "I guess I just have to trust that you'll protect me from the soldiers, although it's not likely we'll run across a patrol in this isolated country. It's too hot to ride through the heat of the afternoon. I see a few scattered willows off to the south; maybe we can camp and ride out again tonight."

They found the small spring and the shade of the trees, and while Maverick slept, she sneaked off to strip down and wash the dust from her perspiring skin. She enjoyed herself so much, splashing in the water, that she forgot about where they were, the danger, until she had the sudden feeling she was being watched. She almost screamed in terror as she whirled around and saw the war-painted, half-naked Comanche brave leaning against a tree watching her. Just as she started to scream, she realized the savage had gray eyes.

"Maverick! You scared me to death!" she scolded, sinking down into the little pool to cover her nakedness. "You look enough like Quanah Parker in that outfit; you could be mistaken for him!"

"If I'd been a scout for a war party, you'd been dead by now," he said grimly, but he kept staring at her, "or

232

lying spread-eagled while a half dozen of them got their fill of that white skin."

She blushed furiously at the image that came to her mind, an image of herself lying under a certain warrior and she wasn't fighting him; she was digging her nails into his broad back, clinging to him, kissing the white scar down his left cheek.

"My stars!" she said. "As you've pointed out so ungallantly before, you've seen everything I've got. Come on in."

"I intend to," he said easily, stripping off the beads and breechcloth. He stood there naked a long moment, obviously wanting her to see him.

Cayenne tried to look away but she couldn't keep her gaze off his maleness. He was a stallion of a man. Then he waded out waist-deep into the shallow pool toward her.

She ought to get out, leave him here to swim. But she didn't. The tepid water washed against her bare skin as his movements sent ripples through the small pool. He reached out, pulling her up against his naked body in the water. She could feel the hard heat off him all the way from her breasts down her thighs.

"No, Maverick," she protested.

Immediately, he let go of her, stepped back, and chastened. "Okay, baby, whatever you want. Reckon I misunderstood. If I ever touch you again, believe me, you'll have to beg for it!"

"Why, you conceited—!" She stepped away, even though in her heart, she didn't want to. Her traitor body wanted to cling to his hot, wet one, make love to him right there in the shallows. "It'll be a cold day in hell!" she vowed, striding toward shore. If only he'd overwhelmed her, taken her by sheer force where she didn't have to think, couldn't stop him . . .

She heard him laugh behind her as she grabbed up her

clothes, flounced over to the shade of a willow tree, and sat down naked on the blanket he had spread. The heat would dry her skin in minutes, and besides, she had no towel.

Maverick came out of the shallow pool and fell down beside her, lying on his back.

"You're getting the blanket wet."

"So I am." He crossed his long legs at the ankles and put his hands behind his head.

She looked away, furious with herself that her gaze kept going to his wide chest, narrow hips, and virile manhood. "Have you no shame? No modesty?"

He turned his head, raised one eyebrow at her. "You're sitting there naked as the day you were born and say that to me, Reb?"

She shook her hair back in annoyance. "Put your pants on, Maverick." Cayenne grabbed her shirt, slipped it on, and pulled it closed.

"Why? Don't like what you see?" His tone was almost defiant and he didn't move.

"Oh, you!" She sighed loudly, lay flat on her back, and pulled her shirt down primly to cover herself. "I'm scared to drop off to sleep, afraid I'll wake up with you on me!"

"Remember what I told you in the water, baby," he reminded her softly, insolently.

She turned her head and looked into the gray eyes. *Steel-gray.* They drew her like a magnet draws iron. She had to stifle an urge to reach out and run her hand through the black hair. "You don't mean that!"

"Don't push me, baby," he said coldly.

Cayenne reached out and ran her finger thoughtfully down the jagged scar on his cheek. "I don't think you ever really told me how you got that."

"You don't need to know." He caught her hand and held it in a strong grip. "Don't toy with me, Cayenne. I

234

don't like women who flirt and tease."

She pulled out of his grasp, shaking her head so that her hair fell down around her shoulders like spun fire. "That's not teasing. This is teasing." Before he seemed to realize what she was up to, she leaned over and kissed him.

He gasped and started, but he put his hands back under his head. Somehow, she had expected him to grab her in a passionate embrace, make love to her with wild abandon.

She kissed him again, very gently, touching his lips with the tip of her tongue.

He didn't move. "I told you not to tease me, Reb. I won't force myself on you."

She leaned on one elbow and looked down at him, annoyed now that he made no move toward her. "I'm not that appealing?"

She noticed his hand lying on his flat belly trembled a little. "I didn't say that. I said you'd have to beg for it."

She threw her head back and laughed. "You are an arrogant devil, aren't you? You think I'd ever want your body that bad? That I'd beg for it?"

"I didn't say that either." He closed his eyes and she realized he had long lashes. "Go to sleep, Cee Cee. We'll be leaving about sundown and you need the rest."

With his eyes closed, she could study his naked body without feeling embarrassed. The brown, ropy muscles were almost hairless, but there was a scar here and there. She had aroused him, even though he'd denied it. His erect manhood pulsated and she stared at it, remembering how it had felt inside her, wondering that her body could have accepted a sword that big.

"Like what you see?"

When she jerked around, his eyes were open and he smiled impishly at her.

"Damn you, Maverick!" She felt the blood rush to

235

her face.

"That's mighty strong language for a preacher's daughter," he admonished.

"Well, you could cover yourself!" She was furious both with him and herself.

His voice was a whisper. "Why don't you admit it, baby; you want me. Tell me you want me."

"You've got a lot of nerve! That's the furthest thing from my mind!" She felt both anger and guilt at the lie. All she'd thought of for days was how it would feel to have him take her in his arms, make love to her again. And when she'd seen him in the water naked just now and to have him lying here on the blanket in the afternoon heat . . .

"Kiss me and tell me that, Cayenne, that you don't want me like I want you," he commanded. His hand reached out, caught her chin, and turned her face so he could look into her eyes.

"You're wrong!" she said furiously, trying to avoid his gaze. "I could kiss you all day long and not want you! That doesn't affect me a bit! See?" She bent over and kissed him again, expecting his arms to come around her, pull her hard against him, overpower her with his strength and passion.

He gasped for breath but didn't embrace her as she kissed him. She would make him lose control! Cayenne slipped the tip of her tongue between his lips, caressed the roof of his mouth. His big body quivered under hers and she felt him moan low in his throat.

She'd make him want her like he never wanted a woman before! She lay against his chest as she kissed him, and both her hands came up to tease his dark nipples, which grew hard beneath her fingers. Her unbuttoned shirt came open as she pressed against him, and she could feel the heat of his dark, bare skin against her naked breasts.

A sudden wetness smeared her thighs as her body reacted eagerly, but Maverick didn't move to take her in his arms. She ran her tongue deep in his throat and her hand went down to touch his turgid manhood. And suddenly, it didn't matter anymore who did the begging; not to her. "Maverick," she gasped against his lips, "I—I want you."

"Are you asking?" He caught her face between his two hands and looked up at her as her hair fell like a halo around them both.

"I'm asking," she said softly, and her lips caressed his. "I'm asking."

His big hands came up then as he pulled her down on his chest with a groan. "You were driving me loco, baby; no woman ever drove me that crazy before!" He held her face and kissed the edges of her mouth. "Now I'll show you what it's like to be driven over the edge!"

If she had thought she knew what desire was before, he taught her a whole new dimension now. His hot mouth moved over every inch of her skin as he rolled her over on her back and opened her shirt. She arched up, wanting to feel his mouth on her nipples, but he only stroked them with a sound of awe.

"By damn, Cayenne, you have the most beautiful breasts, such white skin!" And then his mouth came down on them, sucking like a greedy baby.

She whimpered and struggled. "Take me! I can't stand any more of this!"

His tongue caressed the inner part of her ear. "I told you I'd make you beg, Reb. I don't make promises I can't keep!"

"I—I can't want you any more than I do now!" She writhed under him, trying to pull him down on top of her impatiently.

"Yes you can, baby. Yes, you can." She felt him slide down the length of her body, felt the warm, wet touch of

237

his kiss on her bare thigh as his fingers stroked and teased between her legs.

Surely he wouldn't? . . .

But even as she thought that, his big hands were spreading her thighs. "You don't know what begging is, baby," he whispered, and his breath was hot on her womanhood. "I'm going to give you the Ultimate Kiss, something I've never done to a woman before."

She felt a sense of shock at the idea but her body wanted what he was offering too badly to stop him. Very slowly, she stopped resisting, let his big hands spread her thighs and then gasped when his hot mouth kissed her there. The sensation drove her nearly wild and she caught his dark head in her hands, pressing his mouth against the forbidden place. "Oh, Maverick! Oh, please! Don't stop now! Ahhh!"

She shuddered as she felt the hot blade of his tongue probe deep within her, his hard hands grasping her thighs, pulling her against his seeking mouth. She turned her body so that her lips could kiss and caress his forbidden place, too. He was big and hard and the slight salt taste of his seed excited her as much as the musky scent of him.

With a moan, she tilted her head back, surrendering to his thrusting in the soft velvet of her mouth while his own kisses probed her womanhood.

Eagles, she thought, clinging to his hips as he clung to hers. *Eagles falling to the earth.* And with that thought, she surrendered to his lips teasing the very depths of her, sucking him deep within herself so that she might drink his seed. She couldn't get enough of him, had never wanted him so badly. And as she fell into blackness, surrendering to her desire, to the warm probing of his tongue, she drank deeply of him. She felt him surge and shudder as he gave up the very essence of his maleness to her eager mouth.

They both gave themselves to that ecstasy, and when it was over, they were both almost weeping. Then he turned and took her in his arms, kissed his seed off her lips. "Baby, baby! I don't know. . . . What am I going to do about you?"

He sounded sad and despairing as he cradled her in his arms, kissing her again. "Why, after all these years, did I have to find you, fall for you?"

She felt both guilty and puzzled. *What was he hinting at?* She thought of the possible trap she might be leading him into if her worst suspicions proved correct. She cared about him too much not to play fair with him. "There's . . . something I should tell you, Maverick," she began.

"I don't want to hear it," he shook his head stubbornly. "Let's forget about all the problems and complications just for today, imagine what it would be like to be together forever, making love like this the rest of our lives."

She was only too eager to forget about everything but him, the way she felt fulfillment in his powerful arms. They made love again very leisurely with great gentleness, and it was fulfilling in a peaceful, different sort of way. After that, they lay on the blanket locked in each other's arms and slept away the afternoon.

It was almost sundown when she finally stirred and sat up, yawning. Maverick sat on a nearby rock, smoking and watching her quietly. She couldn't read his troubled expression. "What are you doing awake?"

"Protecting you," he said simply, patting the holstered Colt in his lap. "If both of us slept that soundly, we'd be easy to sneak up on." His face was gentle, his eyes soft as he looked at her. "You've complicated the hell out of my life, Reb. Always before, I could drift, go anywhere, do anything I pleased."

She shrugged as she pulled on her jeans. "I'm not

holding you."

His face contorted as if the confession were being wrung out of him against his will. "Oh, yes you are, baby, in an invisible grip so strong, I'm not sure I can ever break free . . . or want to."

She didn't know what to say to that. *Was he proposing marriage? Did he hold her responsible for the magic they held for each other?*

When he continued to stare into space, smoking silently, she decided she might as well finish getting dressed. Cayenne looked around. *Where had she left her boots?*

She spotted them over by a rock, where she had taken them off to go into the pool, and started after them.

"Be careful poking around in those rocks," Maverick called after her. "Snakes like to bed up in cool places like that in the daytime."

"Oh, you worry too much!" She reached for the boots, her attention on them. The warning rattle came too late and she saw only the flash of the triangle-shaped head as the rattler struck.

Horrified, she looked down at the gray-green, writhing body of the big rattlesnake, staring in horror at the two fang marks on her ankle. "Oh, Lord, Maverick! He got me! I've been bit!"

Chapter Twelve

"Maverick! Help! I'm bit!" Even as she stared unbelievingly at the two drops of blood oozing from the fang marks on her angle, her mind recoiled from what her eyes told her. The big diamondback rattler slithered across the ground back toward the safety of the rocks.

Maverick ran to her side and the snake reared its head, hissing and rattling a warning.

He grabbed a stone. "Afraid to shoot it; might be a war party in the area!" He crushed the ugly triangle-shaped head, leaving the thick body writhing and twisting as the snake died.

Then he turned back to her. "Let's see, Cayenne."

Trembling, Cayenne sat down on the ground and held out one bare foot. Maverick took her trim ankle in his two hands and inspected the fang marks.

She knew by his frown it was serious. She was suddenly aware of their distance from a doctor, from any kind of help. "Maverick, what happens now?"

He glanced up and she saw the fear in his eyes.

She said, "It's bad, isn't it?"

He didn't answer for a long moment, staring at the bite. "Need to work fast," he murmured, "before that poison spreads." He took the piece of rawhide he always carried in his gun belt, looped it around her thigh over her pants, and pulled it into a tourniquet to slow the flow of blood. Then, very slowly, he took his knife from the scabbard.

She tried to remember she was a hero's daughter. "You—you're going to have to cut into it, aren't you?"

"That's what they usually do," he answered softly, not looking at her as he turned the knife over and over in his big hands.

Cayenne swallowed hard. Raised in Texas, she knew what had to be done to save a rattler's victim. Although some said a snake bite should be wrapped tight with rags soaked in coal oil, there was a better way. Someone good with a knife made crisscross cuts across the fang marks, sucking out as much of the poisoned blood as possible. Then they filled the hapless victim full of whiskey. Sometimes the person lived, sometimes not. But it was her only chance.

She took a deep breath. "I'm ready when you are."

Maverick seemed to be studying his own reflection in the shiny blade of the knife. "I—I can't," he mumbled. "I just can't cut a woman."

"What?" She sat bolt upright in surprise. "You've got to, Maverick. There's no one else and I'm no good with a knife!"

His hands were actually trembling as he stared at his own reflection in the blade. "I can't do it, Cayenne, I'm sorry . . . I just can't!"

"You mean *won't!*" she snapped, really frightened now. *What was wrong with him?* He seemed to be going to pieces before her eyes, crumbling into a helpless mass of indecision. She had never seen him like this before and she was scared, realizing how much she had come to depend on the strong, decisive Maverick Durango with whom she'd ridden out of Kansas. "Maverick, you've got to do it! Otherwise, I might die!"

Her words seemed to arouse him from his stupor and

242

he looked into her eyes and she saw fresh anguish there. "Oh, God, baby! I—I don't think I can!"

"Then give me the knife and I'll try to do it myself!" Her hand covered his, and his was cold, shaking.

"Cayenne, if you're no hand with a knife—"

"Then you do it!" She was both angry and terrified. *What would happen to her out here in the middle of nowhere, badly snake-bitten and depending on a man who seemed to be coming apart before her eyes?*

He shook his head and there was dread, terror in his eyes. "Don't ask me to cut you, baby; have your blood running over my hands. . . ."

"Maverick, I may die! Do you hear me?" She reached out and caught his dark face between her palms. "Don't you care about me?"

His gray, tortured eyes looked into hers. "I—I love you, Cee Cee."

"Maverick," she pleaded, "if you love me, do it! You're good with a knife! You won't hurt me as much as I'd hurt myself! If you love me, do it!"

He shook her hands off and the scar on his cheek looked very white on his dark cheek as she stroked it unconsciously. "That's what she said . . . exactly what she said," he mumbled. "I'll never forget how white her skin was. . . ."

Dear God, what was he muttering about? She seemed to feel the poison starting to course through her veins with every beat of her heart, spreading slowly through her body. She had never felt such helpless frustration and rage. "If you love me, help me!" she begged. "Do you want to see me die a slow, painful death?"

His eyes seemed almost glazed with shock. "No, Annie, no, don't beg me to do that. Please don't ask—"

"I'm not Annie, I'm Cayenne, remember?" She

leaned over, kissing his trembling lips as his eyes stared into some horror of the past. "I love you, Maverick Durango! Oh, dearest, I need your help so badly!"

He shook all over abruptly, as if awakening from a bad dream, and stared at her, then down at the knife in his hands, the fang marks on her ankle. Once again, he became the competent stallion of a man she had come to rely on. "Here, baby, lie back and I'll take care of this. I'm sorry, but it'll hurt a little."

"I'm not afraid," she lied, knowing in his expert hands the knife would hurt as little as possible. She bit down on her lip so she wouldn't cry out as the sharp knife poised above her white skin. For just a moment, he hesitated, and then he made two expert cuts across the wound.

She forced herself not to whimper at the pain, afraid of the effect on the man who had her blood smeared on his hands. "It's okay, Maverick, I'm okay." She sighed and swallowed hard to keep from weeping.

He bent over her slim ankle, putting his mouth, hot and wet, on the wound and sucking the poisonous blood. She felt faint now as she watched him suck the wound, her blood smeared across his mouth as he spat the poison out.

Cayenne lay back, her leg throbbing from the poison, his mouth warm and sucking on her ankle.

He reached up and loosened the tourniquet, her blood smeared across his face. "You okay, baby?"

She tried to appear perkier than she felt. "I'm fine. Really I am."

"What'd you do with that bottle of vanilla?"

She rose up on her elbows. "Why on earth do you want that at a time like this?"

"Is it in the saddlebags? We don't have any whiskey but there's alcohol in vanilla. I need to wash that wound out."

She nodded, feeling worse by the second as the poison slowly worked its way through her system with each beat of her heart. "Yes, saddlebags. Just don't make me drink it."

He got it and came back, pouring it over the wound.

She winced at the sting. "Papa always blew on it when he had to put liniment on a hurt."

Maverick looked at her thoughtfully as he put the cork back in the bottle and she wished she could read his thoughts. "You think a lot of your father, don't you?"

"Everyone does. Joe McBride is the kindliest, bravest man in all Texas."

"That's a big state." He looked away.

"Papa's a big man." Cayenne lay back on the blanket and closed her eyes. Her head throbbed dully.

"I always wanted a dad like that," Maverick said wistfully, "wondered what it would be like to sit at a real dinner table surrounded by a family rather than fighting for scraps in a teepee like a bunch of hungry wolves."

"Didn't the Durangos have a dinner table?" She supposed it would be sad to have been fathered by some "squawman" hunter and then deserted. No doubt his Indian mother wasn't well treated by the tribe after the white man left. Maverick had more scars than the one on his face.

"Yes, but it wasn't really *my* family, *my* dinner table, *my* home the way Annie described the way it should be."

Annie. Again Annie. But as the poison moved through her system, she felt too bad to be jealous, to ask curious questions. Perspiration beaded on her upper lip and her vision seemed clouded when she looked at him. "Thirsty," she whispered, "so thirsty."

"I'll get some water." She tried to watch him as he

went over, filled a canteen at the little pool, and brought it back. Objects wavered before her eyes. He came back and half lifted her, pouring a trickle of cold water between her dry lips. Cayenne drank greedily.

"In a few minutes," she whispered, "when I get to feeling a little better, we need to ride on."

He shook his head, lying her back down on the blanket. "Cee, Cee, you aren't going anywhere, not for days."

"But we need to get to Texas. . . ."

"I said you weren't going anywhere," he said sharply. "I won't lie to you, Cee Cee; you've got tough sledding ahead of you. I'll take care of you the best way I can."

She felt too weak, too sick to argue with him as she sighed and stretched out on the shaded blanket. "You bossy Yankee sympathizer . . ."

"That's right, Little Rebel, and you do what I tell you! We won, remember?" His tone sounded a little too strained, a little too light as he tried to joke.

Her head swam dizzily. "Oh, Maverick, I feel so bad! I'm scared! Can't we get help?"

"Easy, baby, easy." He sat down next to her, gathering her into his arms. "You can't ride and I sure can't leave you to go for help. . . ."

"No, don't leave me. Don't leave me." She caught his hand, suddenly terrified of waking up and finding him gone.

She felt his lips brush her forehead lightly as one does a frightened child. "I'll be here for you always, Cayenne. You hear me? I'm not leaving or going anywhere without you."

The words came faintly, as if he were vowing it to himself. As if he felt angry with himself for his feelings. She lay her face against his wide, bare chest, taking comfort in the strength and size of the man. "You'll look after me?" she whispered. "You'll look after me?"

246

He kissed her hair. "Always and forever, baby. *'Long as I got a biscuit, you got half.'*"

No Westerner could make a stronger commitment than that. She sighed and relaxed as he lay her back on the blanket, fanning her perspiring face with his hat.

The pain seemed to be inching up her swollen leg with every beat of her heart. By twisting her head, she could see the discolored ankle. She tried to keep her thoughts straight but they tangled with each other like brightly colored ribbons in a swirl.

"Maverick, what you said about Annie—"

"We won't discuss that. Not now, not ever," he said coldly and stopped fanning. "That's in the past."

She tried to straighten out the dizzying swirl of colored ribbons in her vision, wondering jealously if Annie had been beautiful, if he had loved her so very much. "But that past is never very far from your mind, is it? Why don't you tell me about her?"

"Because it hurts to have your heart torn out! Dammit, can you understand that?"

"Funny, Papa said the same thing," she whispered, remembering the grave. Somehow, the grave seemed important now. . . . She should try to tell Maverick about it if she could ever get her thoughts and her words straight. But all she managed to say was, "I—I think I'm in love with you." The ribbons swirled her around in a spin toward blackness.

"And I love you, by damn, I love you!" She felt him kiss the tips of her fingers. "That complicates the hell out of my plans!"

"Complicates mine, too," she mumbled to herself as she drifted in and out of consciousness. "I just needed a gunfighter, that's all, didn't mean to fall for you. . . ."

"What?" Maverick said. "What'd you say?"

She tried to tell him then about how Bill Slade and his partners had showed up several weeks ago to stay at

247

her papa's ranch, but the words came out in a delirious mumble. She intended now to confess her plans; to warn him not to go to McBride, Texas with her, that she'd probably only get him killed. But she couldn't connect one word with another and her head pounded and echoed like distant war drums.

She felt him lay her on the blanket, brush her damp hair from her face. "Oh, Little Reb," he choked out, "don't leave me! I've waited too long for you and now I've got a terrible decision to make! But I swore on her body! I swore!"

She barely heard him, wanted to ask him but couldn't remember how to connect words together in a question. The thoughts swirled again like bright ribbons in a dazzling light and she knew it was the sun as it moved so that she was only partially lying in the shade of the hot July day. . . .

It had been unseasonably hot that day, too, that fateful day. . . .

Because of the unseasonably warm weather, the church and ladies decided on a Saturday afternoon picnic. Most of the men had been busy with farm chores.

Cayenne twisted restlessly on the blanket and felt Maverick wipe the sweat from her face with a cold rag. "Easy, Reb," he whispered, "take it easy."

"Late," she whispered, thinking of the picnic, "going to be late."

From a long way off, she heard him chuckle softly. "Wherever it is you think you're going, baby, I'm afraid you aren't going to make it."

Of course she was going to make it. She'd packed the picnic basket full of fried chicken, her best chocolate cake, homemade pickles, and crusty fresh bread. *If she could just get her little sisters dressed!* Papa had har-

248

nessed the old mule to the buggy for her and then ridden away. He had left to comfort a dying old lady on the far side of the nameless little community recently formed near the Lazy M Ranch.

Ribbons of dazzling color whirled and tangled themselves through her mind as she writhed and sweated on the blanket. *Ribbons*, she thought. *Hair ribbons. Brightly colored sashes.*

In her mind, it was a warm Saturday afternoon in the past and she was trying to hurry her little sisters who dawdled as usual.

Lynnie, are your eyeglasses clean? The thin, serious nine-year-old looked up from her book and nodded. *Lynnie, must you read all the time? My stars! Where's your baby sister?*

Lynnie put her book down reluctantly and went up the stairs. In a minute, she called down the stairs, *Angel has wet her drawers again.*

Oh, honestly! Trying to get four younger sisters off to the picnic was almost more trouble than it was worth! *Well, Lynnie, change them and get Angel's dress on her!* she shouted up the stairs. *Steve! Steve! Where are you?*

The seven-year-old sister, the one who carried a boy's name, came in from the kitchen. *Cee Cee, I can't get my hair braided and tie the ribbons, too*, she complained.

Come here, I'll tie the ribbons. Steve's hair was more fiery even than Cayenne's own. Cayenne finished braiding the long pigtails and tied the ends with bright ribbons.

Five-year-old Gracious stuck her freckled pug nose around the corner. *Sister, I can't get my sash tied.*

Cayenne sighed heavily, praying for patience. *Aren't you ever gonna learn to tie your own sash, Gracie?*

*Come here, I'll do it! We're already late, girls. The
picnic was supposed to start at noon.* She tied the
bright ribbons of Gracious's sash around the little girl's
plump waist. *Ribbons. Brightly colored ribbons . . .*

In her mind, she looked through the lace curtains of
the parlor window and saw the old mule standing
patiently hitched to the buggy by the front porch.

"We're going to be late for the picnic," she whispered, and a hand reached through the maze of multi-
colored fragments of dreams and stroked her cheek.

"Sure, baby," a voice whispered, and soft lips
brushed her face. "Sure, baby. Take it easy."

*She must hurry her little sisters if they were to arrive
at the picnic before the sack races and the games were
over.* In her memory, Cayenne went to the foot of the
stairs. *Lynnie! Angel! My stars! What's keeping you?*

The two children sauntered down the stairs, baby
Angel sucking her thumb as usual.

Cayenne frowned. *Angel, don't suck your thumb.
You'll have crooked teeth! Do you want teeth so
crooked you could eat corn on the cob through a picket
fence?*

Angel smiled and it was hard to scold her. The
dimpled red-haired toddler had cost Cayenne's mother
her life.

Cayenne brushed flour off the front of her own simple blue calico dress. *Now, if everyone's ready, let's go
to the picnic!*

They never got to the picnic. As the five got into the
old buggy, the young Billings boy galloped into the yard
on his father's fine-blooded thoroughbred. The bay was
foaming and lathered, the half-grown boy shouting and
weeping. *Oh, Miss Cayenne! Something terrible
happened! Where's your pa? My Lord, where's your
Pa?*

250

A chill of apprehension went through her as the young man dismounted hastily. *He's not here! What's the matter, Hank?*

Injuns, he choked out. *A war party surprised the picnic . . . carried off the women and kids. . . .*

What? What did you say, Hank?

He gestured wildly. *I had gone off in the woods to—* His face colored. *Well, you know. I saw it all, Miss Cayenne, saw the Indians ride in, gather them all up. It was awful! They was all cryin' and a screamin'.*

Oh my God! Her hand went to her mouth, and she looked down at her curious little sisters. *We've got to tell the men, get help! I—I don't know what do! What kind of Indians were they, Hank? I didn't think we were having Indian troubles again.*

The lanky boy wiped his eyes with smudged hands. *I—I don't know, Miss Cayenne; Comanche, I think. The leader had funny, sharp little features like a fox and long arms. They got my ma and both my little sisters! Your pa always knows what to do and mine's clear across the county at a barn raisin'—*

Cayenne chewed her lip, thinking. *What do you suppose they want?*

That leader saw me just as they were riding out. I couldn't even move; just stared back at him, waiting to be killed. Then he said something to me in English. . . .

What, Hank? She grabbed his arm. *Tell me what he said!*

His thin face wrinkled in thought. *Something like: "White women pay for my sister. Bring ransom by sundown or we kill." Oh, Miss Cayenne, what do we do?*

But Cayenne was already in the process of unhitching the buggy so she could ride the old mule. *I'll get Papa, he'll know what to do. You get on into the settlement, alert as many men as possible. How much ransom we got to get and where do we take it?*

He named a sum and a place. Cayenne's green eyes widened in shock. *Hank, that's a lot of money! None of us has that much except banker Ogle. The Indians must gonna plan on using it to buy guns from the renegade Comancheros over in the Santa de Cristo mountains!*

He turned back to his lathered, wheezing horse. *What'll I tell everyone, Miss Cayenne?*

She considered a long moment. *Tell them to gather at the bank. Maybe we can mortgage our ranches and things to get the money.* She looked around the Lazy M, thinking it wasn't worth much for farming. West Texas dirt was so poor it'd take three people to raise a fuss on it.

Cayenne pulled the harness off the mule, hitched up her dress, and swung up on its bony bare back with nothing but a lead rope looped around its muzzle. *Hank, you get everyone gathered up and I'll ride to get Papa.*

Should we get help from the law, Miss Cayenne?

She snorted in disgust. *What law? The Yankee carpetbaggers have disbanded the Rangers and we don't even have a sheriff here. . . .*

Never needed one, the boy said.

Hank was right. The peaceful little community didn't even have a name and its residents were religious, non-violent farmers recently arrived from Europe or back east. In strange contrast, the community preacher, her papa, was one of the best rifle shots in Texas. She thought of the fancy One-in-a-Thousand Winchester rifle hanging with the little sawed-off shotgun over the fireplace.

She looked at her four little sisters who watched wide-eyed. *Lynnie, get everyone back in the house*, she ordered, *while Hank and I ride for help! And Angel,* she sighed, *quit sucking your thumb!*

"Ride for help," Cayenne whispered, twisting restlessly on the blanket. "Got to get help."

She had to ride for Papa so he could do something about the hostages and the Comanche war party. She tried to struggle to her feet so she could go get Papa, but someone held her down.

"Got to get help," she muttered, and when her eyes flickered open, she realized the war party had gotten her, too. She stared into the gray eyes of a rugged Indian who held her in his arms.

"Easy, baby," the half-breed said, "take it easy. I don't know where you think you're going, but you're gonna have to stay right here until that swollen leg goes down."

Gray eyes. Now why would a Comanche have gray eyes? But she remembered that Quanah Parker, the half-breed chief, had gray eyes. This man didn't look like Quanah. But he was a warrior. Had she been captured?

She looked up into his war-painted face, staring a long moment at the jagged white scar down his left cheek, and struggled again. "Got to get Papa," she whispered. "War party hit the church picnic. . . ."

"Sure, baby, sure." He kissed her forehead and she closed her eyes with a sigh, wondering how a member of the war party had captured her.

Funny, she remembered riding all the way on that old mule without getting caught by Indians, remembered getting the message to Papa. The men had assembled at the bank but no one had very much money. Everyone gave all they could raise, but it wasn't enough. Finally, Papa had mortgaged the ranch with that tight old banker to raise the ransom.

She remembered standing in the street, listening to the discussion. *Who was going to bell the cat?* Now that they had the money, who was going to be brave enough to ride into that Indian camp a few miles away?

Papa took off his hat and ran his hand through his thinning red hair. Joe McBride a was tall, handsome Scots-Irishman with eyes as bright green as Cayenne's own. He closed his eyes and seemed to pray a minute in the silence, and when he opened them, he said, *"I'll do it. I'll be the one to go.*

A sigh of relief swept through the crowd but Cayenne elbowed her way through. *Not you, Papa, not you! None of those hostages are related to you!*

Joe's green eyes regarded her thoughtfully. *Cee Cee, all mankind are brothers, and as minister to this little flock, it's my responsibility as much as anyone's.*

She caught his arm. *No, Papa,* she argued desperately. *What if you don't come back? If something happens to you, how can I raise the girls alone?*

He put his big work-hardened hand over her small one on his arm. *God takes care of his own,* he reminded her. *Where's your faith, daughter?*

And so big Joe McBride had carried the ransom. Even though he was one of the best shots in Texas, he went unarmed out to meet the Comanche so they would know they weren't being tricked. Cayenne had gone with the men who waited at a safe distance. Joe had thought he'd ride in, hand over the money, gather up the hostages, and leave. It hadn't worked out that way. The hostages were freed, but the war party kept Joe and tortured him. All afternoon the huddled little group of whites could hear him scream. And scream. And scream.

She could hear the screaming now. She had to help him! But as she struggled to get up, that gray-eyed Indian held her, put his hand over her mouth. "Hush, baby!" he whispered, clamping his hand over her mouth. "Hear me? For God's sake! Stop that screaming! If there's a war party within a mile, they'll hear you!"

No, that wasn't her screaming, that was Joe! Couldn't he hear it, too? She closed her eyes, too weak to fight the big half-breed who held her down. Her head pounded and echoed. *No, that wasn't the pain in her head, that was the drums.* The drums had beat a rhythm while the warriors danced and tortured her father. She remembered the echo of the drums and her father's screams. Finally, they had released him, sending him back more dead than alive. Quanah Parker himself had delivered her half-conscious, tortured father.

She remembered now the big gray-eyed half-breed, Quanah, and how he and a band of warriors had brought Joe back thrown unconscious across a pony. *This is not my doing,* he said. *One of the other clans did this! I stopped them from killing him, but I came too late to stop the torture. He is a very brave man, this big man with the fire-colored hair!*

Papa! Papa! Cayenne sobbed and rushed forward, horrified at his injuries. The small group of farmers looked at each other and at her helplessly as the well-armed, large group of Indian warriors wheeled their ponies and rode out.

They had done terrible things to him, and as she stared in shock, he moaned aloud.

I hate them, Cayenne wept. *I want revenge. An eye for an eye and a tooth for a tooth like the Bible says!*

Joe managed to whisper something and she bent over his burned, tortured body to hear him. *No,* he gasped.

Vengeance is mine, says the Lord, I shall repay . . .
Leave it to the Lord, Cayenne. . . .

Joe McBride was a hero after that and he deserved it. The settlers named the little settlement in his honor—McBride, Texas. The gentle farmers helped with the Lazy M ranch chores while Joe recovered as well as he ever would from his injuries. His faithful vaqueros stayed on for very little money. Life went on as usual . . . until that day three months ago when a letter came from her mother's cranky old aunt Ella, who was dying in Kansas.

Cayenne hadn't wanted to go, but Papa had insisted that even a grouchy old lady needed a little love and caring at the end, and besides, Cayenne could take that part-time teaching job there in Wichita.

Wichita. Cayenne remembered now standing in the street reading a letter. *She had to get back to Texas. The letter said there might be trouble, something about three men showing up at the ranch a few days before. Bill Slade, Trask, and a Mexican.*

Now where would she find a gunfighter who might help the McBride family against that trio if they turned out to be more than just saddle tramps?

The Red Garter Saloon. That's where cowboys and gunfighters hung out here in Wichita.

What was his name? Oh, yes, Maverick Durango; a tough half-breed Comanche with gray eyes. If she'd known he was Comanche, she wouldn't have asked.

She had nothing to lure him with to accompany her back to Texas but her innocence. She must make him want her. She had kissed him out there on the sidewalk in front of the Red Garter. *He had said, "No, Cee Cee, here's the way it's done."*

Then Maverick had kissed her; her very first kiss. She remembered the way he had lifted her up off her feet, kissed her expertly, thoroughly. She would never forget the heat of his mouth covering hers, the feel of him sweeping her up in his arms.

"I love you, Maverick," she whispered. And from somewhere, she heard a voice, felt a hand stroke her hair. "I love you, too, baby. By damn, I love you, too!"

She imagined the trio of men the letter had described. They had to be dangerous and they knew her papa. Joe McBride never talked about his past. When she was little, she remembered that often he went to the little community cemetery and stood for hours, staring at a grave.

Once she had asked whose grave it was.

Joe shrugged. "No one you would know, child." Tears came to his green eyes. "A part of my past. Let's just say my heart is buried here."

"But nobody can live without a heart, Papa," she said.

Joe sighed and swallowed hard. "Oh, yes, you can. You just learn to live with the pain where it was torn out."

And then when she was about nine years old, something had happened. Yes, it had been maybe ten years ago. She wasn't sure what it was. It had something to do with a boy who came to call on Papa. That night, there was a terrible fuss between her parents. They had awakened her with their shouting. After that, Papa visited that grave no more and the atmosphere seemed forever strained between her parents, even though Hannah suddenly began producing more children—four in the next seven years. The last one, little Angel, had cost Hannah Adams McBride her life. What made the girl Cayenne know that her mother feared to lose Joe, that she bound him to her with the host of children?

Cayenne was nine years old once more, listening to her parents fight. The loud words and screaming terrified her so that she hid under the covers of her little bed. Her name was being shouted—her name and the name "Annie." Cayenne had to stop her parents' terrible fight. She had to get up and tell them to stop screaming at each other. She struggled and mumbled, "No! No!"

"Cayenne, what is it?"

She opened her eyes at the voice and blinked at a rugged dark man leaning over her. The sun shone through the trees and she didn't know where she was. What was she doing lying on a blanket out under a cottonwood tree? And who was this virile man dressed like an Indian leaning over her? Cayenne tried to speak, couldn't. Her whole body seemed to throb like an exposed nerve and she whimpered. Immediately, the man bent over her, holding a cup to her lips, and she gulped the water gratefully.

"You've been unconscious for days now. Baby, I've been worried as hell about you." He smiled and the corners of the big gray eyes crinkled. He was especially handsome when he smiled.

She still couldn't sort out her thoughts, any more than she could remember who he was. But she sensed he was part of her memories, her recent past. When she closed her eyes, she remembered the taste and the feel of a man's arms around her, saw eagles soaring against the sun.

A spoon poked between her lips. *Canned peaches.* The juice was sweet and delicious in her fevered mouth. She swallowed automatically as he fed her, drifting back into unconsciousness. Later, she awakened enough to realize he bathed her perspiring, feverish body with cool water.

"Baby, it's okay. It's Maverick, remember? Don't

258

fight me. I won't hurt you." The voice was familiar, soothing. But when she opened her eyes, she saw a painted savage with gray eyes and wondered with horror how she'd been captured by the Comanche, how long she'd been here on this blanket. Why was her leg so swollen? Why did it hurt?

She drifted back into unconscious fever without asking who this "Maverick" was who never seemed to leave her side.

And finally, she half roused to noise, confusion, a blur of horses and blue uniforms. *Soldiers. What were they doing here? What was she doing here?*

She only half heard the shouts, the orders, didn't understand any of it.

"Grab the red bastard, Sergeant! Looks like we've caught Quanah Parker red-handed, not only with the colonel's gray horse, but with a white captive besides!"

Chapter Thirteen

Lynnie stood out in front of the Billings General Store, studying the envelope clutched against her faded calico dress. Cayenne had finally answered, although it'd been a long time coming. Mr. Billings said the Indian uprising had delayed the mail.

She looked up and down the dusty street. The tiny settlement of McBride, Texas lay asleep under the July sun. Trask must still be in the hardware store, and from here, she could see Papa sitting in the buggy at the hitching rail.

Pushing her wire-framed spectacles back up her freckled nose, little Lynnie stared at the envelope from Wichita.

She smiled now, looking at Papa sitting patiently in the old buggy then back at the letter in her hands. *Would he be angry that she'd written Cayenne for help?* No, Papa never got angry with anyone. She loved Papa, that big, red-haired handsome tower of strength and courage. *Well,* she thought sadly, *he had been handsome until the Comanche tortured him with fire.*

She stubbed her toe at a crack in the wooden sidewalk boards. Papa loved Cayenne more than he loved anyone, Lynnie had been smart enough to figure that out. He had seemed to love her even more than Mama.

Mama. Lynnie considered the subject for a moment as she walked slowly toward the buggy with the letter from Wichita. Hannah Adams had been a dumpy, homely woman; a distant stranger who seemed to be jealous of the affection her husband felt for his children, especially Cayenne. But even the children cared more for the big sister than they did for Mama. Cayenne and the old Mexican housekeeper, Rosita, gave them more love and caring than Mama did.

The big bay thoroughbred that young Hank Billings liked to race nickered from the hitching rail.

Nickering horses. That sorrel horse Slade rode had nickered, too, alerting her that three men were riding up the road to the front porch. Lynnie had been cleaning windows in the front parlor that day several weeks ago. She remembered now watching the back of Papa's head as he sat on the porch, whittling and rocking. Anyone else would have been vengeful and bitter against the Indians for what they had done to him, but not Papa. He was truly a religious man, accepting what had happened and going on with his life. Of course, he couldn't do all the things he used to do, but his burned, twisted fingers could still carve the little willow whistles that he always carried in his pockets to give away to the town's children.

When the trio of weather-beaten men rode up, the leader's sorrel gelding nickered and Lynnie had frozen motionless behind the curtains like a frightened quail "gone to ground" when danger threatened. She sensed that they were not ordinary cowboys looking for work. There was something sinister and dangerous about the way they wore their pistols strapped low and tied down.

Where could she get help? Everyone else on the ranch seemed to be taking an afternoon *siesta.*

Just who were those men? They looked rough and weary. Lynnie glanced at Papa's guns hanging low over the fireplace. By standing on her tiptoes, she might be able to reach the rifle, but she really didn't think she could hit anything with it. Now the sawed-off ten-gauge shotgun was different. Lynnie knew it laid down such a wide, deadly pattern that she could probably get all three even with her eyes shut. But then, Papa might catch some buckshot, too. Besides, suppose they turned out to be just cowboys, even though they looked like outlaws? She held her breath, watching and listening through the open window.

The leader might have been handsome if he hadn't had such a cruel mouth. "Well, Joe McBride! How in the hell have you been? Long time no see!"

Papa stopped rocking but it was a long moment before he spoke. "Hello, Slade. Figured you'd find my trail sooner or later, even after almost twenty-five years."

She wished she could see the expression on her father's face. But his tone didn't sound happy.

The second of the trio, the unshaven, heavier man riding the dun, leaned on his saddle horn. "Now is that a Texas way to greet old friends? Here we just happen to come into town and the storekeep tells us about this big hero who got tortured saving everyone from the Injuns."

Joe went back to whittling. "That'd be Billings. His wife and little girls were among the hostages. I'm no hero, though. Any decent man would have done the same."

Slade laughed. "Not me. I wouldn't let them do me like they done you. I'd rather be dead."

"I said any *decent* man. And I've learned to live with my disabilities; praise God anyway." He stroked his red beard.

"Well, I'll be damned!" The lean man grinned, but there was no mirth in his hard, handsome face. " 'Praise God'; now, that ain't the Joe McBride I used to know. I don't mind sayin' I'm impressed!" He addressed the other two. "Trask, Mex, ain't you impressed?"

His two partners muttered something but they didn't look impressed. They looked mean as polecats and bored. Slade slid from his gelding and sauntered over to lean against the porch railing, his big Mexican spurs jangling as he walked.

Papa shook his head. "Never learn, do you, Bill? Someday those spurs are gonna get you killed. Anyone lookin' to plug you could hear you comin' even in the dark."

Slade spat on the porch. "I ain't worried. There ain't many men who can outshoot me. But as I remember, you used to be one of them."

The unshaven, heavier one, Trask, dismounted. His lame foot dragged a little as he came up the creaking porch steps, sitting on the top one. "Ain't it something, though? Here we come into this sleepy burg on business, find out when we get here we got an old friend who's the town hero and owns a fine ranch besides." He looked over at the swarthy man on the buckskin horse. "Ain't that something, Mex?"

"Si, *amigo*. After St. Joe, I never thought to see this one again." He laughed loudly, tipping his hat back on his gray-streaked black hair. *None of them were younger than forty-five or almost fifty*, Lynnie thought as she watched from behind her curtain. *Where had they known her papa?*

"I don't have any money if that's what you're thinkin'," Joe said.

Slade lit a cigar. "Joe, you hurt my feelings! We come out to visit an old friend while we wait for our business deal to go through and you say mean things to us! We just want to stay and visit for a few weeks, Joe. Catch up on old times."

The light reflected off Papa's red hair as he shook his head. "I've closed the door on that part of my life, Bill. My life changed when my wife died, leaving me with five motherless children mor'n three years ago."

"You're breakin' my heart!" Trask sneered, scratching his unshaven face. "With a nice spread like this, you don't have plenty of money? How'd you get this ranch?"

Joe hesitated a long moment. "I married it," he said slowly, as if he were ashamed of his confession. "After St. Joe, I decided being poor was the worst thing in the world."

"Ain't it, though?" Slade laughed. "I thought you married Molly. She disappeared the same time you left us."

"Molly?" Joe mused, "Don't really know what happened to that poor girl."

"I shoulda killed you over her," Slade snarled through gritted teeth.

Papa's head turned toward the man. "Bill, I told you there was nothin' between us; never was, although I reckon she would have liked there to be. You didn't care two whoops in hell about that innocent, sad girl. You took advantage of her; let Mex and Trask have her whenever they felt the urge; forced her to use her charms to get information from that bank teller. . . ."

"I didn't say I cared nothin' about her," Bill Slade snapped. "But she was mine and I could loan her to my friends if I wanted just like I'd loan my horse. But I don't like anyone riding what's mine without askin'. . . ."

"You're lower than a snake's belly!" Papa's voice shook with fury. "No wonder Molly took off on her own!"

Slade snorted and went on smoking. "So you managed to rescue that wife who'd been carried off by the Comanche?"

For a long moment, Papa didn't answer. She heard the porch steps creak under Trask's weight, smelled the perfume of the pink roses and the stink of Slade's cigar when the hot breeze blew through the open window she stood by.

Papa sighed. "No. The wife I'm talkin' about was the child of a rich neighbor who owned half the land in the county near my poor little spread."

The Mexican swore in broken English, glaring down at Papa from his buckskin horse. "You just tell us you have no money, *hombre*. You got all your wife's inheritance?"

"It's a good enough spread, I reckon," Papa agreed in his soft Kentucky drawl. "I know you won't believe this, but I mortgaged it all, every inch of it, every bit of my bank account to help the town ransom hostages from the Indians a few months back."

The Mexican chewed the end of his mustache. "One of them hostages kin to you?"

"We are all brothers in the Lord," Joe said softly.

Trask sneered. "You sound like a preacher."

"Would you believe me if I said I was."

The three men hooted with laughter.

"Joe, if you don't beat all!" Slade wiped his eyes. "And then your red 'brothers' tortured you when you delivered that ransom?"

Papa nodded. "I think the others would have kept their word. But there was one called Little Fox who seemed crazy. He would have killed me if Quanah Parker hadn't ridden in at the last minute, forced him to set me free."

Inside the house, little Lynnie leaned against the wall, remembering that terrible day. Cayenne and Hank had ridden off to deal with the trouble, leaving Lynnie and the younger children in the care of old Rosita. The days of waiting were long for the family.

Papa had been more dead than alive when Quanah Parker returned him later. At first the doctor had not thought he would live but Joe had been determined. Cayenne said he feared to leave a houseful of young, orphaned daughters.

Outside, Trask belched loudly. "I'm tired of all this palaver. Who's on this ranch besides you, Joe?"

"Four of my five daughters. The oldest has gone to stay with an aunt in Wichita for a while because the old lady was sick and there was nobody to look after her."

"That all?"

"An old Mexican housekeeper and a few gentle Mexican hands."

"No foreman? No Texas cowhands?"

Joe shrugged. "Can't afford any extra help."

Slade smiled cruelly. "How good's the sheriff?"

Joe seemed almost hesitant as he answered grudgingly. "I don't suppose you ever lived in a place so peaceful we don't even have a lawman."

"What do you do about crime?"

"We don't have any. This is a quiet, religious bunch of immigrants in this area, Slade. If you're looking over our bank, you'll be disappointed. As banks go, it ain't much. Everyone in town spent all they had to ransom those hostages, except banker Ogle. He loaned his money at high rates."

"Naw," Slade shook his head, tossing away the cigar. "We got something better than that. We got a friend in the telegraph office. . . ."

"Here?" Joe said in surprise, "Why, old Mr.—"

"Naw, up in Kansas. He handles all the army telegraph messages. Something big's in the makin' with all those soldiers bein' moved in to deal with Injun troubles. But as far as you and the locals are concerned, let's just say we dropped in on this little burg to visit an old friend for a while."

"But you just said you didn't even know I was here until they mentioned me in town."

Slade threw his cigar into the pink seven sisters roses by the porch. "Did I say that? Why, when I tole everyone in town you was an old friend, they was all pumping our hands, clappin' us on the back. You're well-thought-of in this town, Joe."

Papa sighed. "That means a lot to me, Bill, being well-thought-of. My reputation's all I got now."

Trask belched again. "Wonder if over at St. Joe, they'd like to know where you are. . . ?"

"All right, all right." Joe stood up with difficulty. *The Comanches had held his feet over a slow fire, too.*

Lynnie hid behind the curtain and considered what to do. It was a big responsibility for a nine-year-old. She wished Cayenne were here. Cayenne always knew what to do. There was probably a marshal over at the county seat but that was several days ride and who would listen to a little girl? None of the poor farmers in the area could handle a gun well. She looked at the way the trio wore their pistols low and tied down, figured it would be murder to send any of the Lazy M's poor vaqueros up against them.

The trio seemed to have some secret they were using against her father. It was unbelievable to her that her father might have done anything that was not noble and brave. What should she do? In the end, she did nothing at all because she was little and afraid.

No, that wasn't true. She didn't tell the old Mexican cook or any of the vaqueros because they were as helpless as she was. But a few days after the trio came, one day when Lynnie was with old Rosita in town for supplies, she wrote a letter to her big sister and mailed it, asking Cayenne to help. Later, she wondered if she'd done the right thing. She'd heard the trio laughing about the girls in the town's one saloon. Lynnie didn't tell them that her big sister was much more beautiful than any of them. Such men would probably want to kiss Sister if she came home, and who knew what other things men did to pretty girls? Besides, there was a lot of trouble with

Indians right now and it might be dangerous for Cayenne to try to get back to Texas.

And suppose she'd been wrong? Suppose the trio weren't outlaws or gunslingers, just rough old trail *hombres* who were more tough talk than action?

Lynnie looked at the answer to that letter that she'd just picked up at Billings General Store. *Was Papa going to be angry because she had written Cayenne?* No, Papa never got angry. She smiled, watching two little boys stop by the buggy and strike up a conversation with Papa. He handed them each a willow whistle and showed them how to play it.

Maxwell's braes are bonnie, where early falls the dew, and that's where Annie Laurie . . .

Lynnie liked that song. Once, when she was very small, she had asked him if he had ever known a girl by that name and tears had come to his eyes. "Yes, I did," he whispered. "But it was a very long time ago, before I married your mother. . . ."

She waited for him to say more but he didn't, the green eyes staring into space as if remembering another time. The expression on his face told her that he had loved Annie very much, maybe even as much as he loved her big sister, Cayenne. She wondered if maybe it had been a little daughter who had died. When Lynnie mentioned it to her mother, Hannah had lost her temper and slapped her 'til her wire-rimmed spectacles fell off.

Don't ever mention that name again, Mama had shouted, and Lynnie never did. But when Papa saw the bruises on Lynnie's face, he cornered Mama and there was shouting and angry words.

Lynnie watched Trask come out of the hardware store, where he'd bought a new pair of spurs, and go into the town's one saloon. Banker Ogle owned that, too, even keeping it open on Sundays. He didn't go to church anyway.

Had Trask seen the letter in her hand? No, all he was doing was getting some whiskey. Slade would be mad if he knew Trask didn't stay with the McBrides like he had been told to do when they went into town. He always sneaked off to the saloon.

The two little boys sauntered away from the buggy, happily playing the willow whistles.

One of them turned back to yell at Papa. "Ma says come to dinner sometime, Reverend, and bring the girls. There'll be chicken-fried steak."

Chicken-fried steak. There were four things Texans liked to eat better than anything: barbecue, Mexican food, fried chicken, and chicken-fried steak, dipped in egg batter and fried all crusty brown and served with cream gravy.

There'd been chicken-fried steak for dinner that first night the trio sat down at the long family dining table. Old Rosita was proud to welcome Senor McBride's friends with a good dinner, pleased when Papa explained they'd be staying a few days to visit.

The three younger sisters, Stevie, Gracious, and Angel, stared down the long table, thrilled to have company at the isolated ranch.

Gracious twiddled with the untied ribbons of her sash. She never had learned to tie a bow. "Where do you know my daddy from?"

"Now, Gracie," Papa said. "It isn't polite to ask so many questions. Mr. Slade and the others were all friends in another place a long time ago."

Slade turned his most charming smile on the youngster. "That's right, kid. Too bad I never married. I'd have liked to have had a pretty kid like you."

Gracious turned brick-red with delight. Lynnie

sighed audibly.

Slade gave her a nod. "And you're the smart one, ain't you? Why, your dad tells me you're smart enough to go back east to school."

Primly, Lynnie pushed her wire-framed glasses back up her nose. "If we ever get any money by then."

Slade clucked sympathetically. "Be a shame if you didn't get to go. I'm expecting to come into an inheritance, maybe I might give you—"

"Papa wouldn't allow that," Steve pulled at her pigtails. "He wouldn't think it honest."

Trask paused in stuffing his face with buttered corn pone. "And your papa is right," he said. "But maybe we could loan the money and your papa could pay it back when he could."

Lynnie tried not to smile with delight. She dreamed of school, of buying all the books she wanted. If only it were true. . . .

The Mexican gestured down the table. "Now what about that pretty little *Senorita* there with the long pigtails? How old are you, *muchacha*?"

"Seven," she lisped. "I'm Stevie."

Trask belched. "A little girl named Steve?"

Joe answered sheepishly, embarrassed, "We were planning for a boy."

Slade leaned back in his chair, patting his full belly. "You got a nice family, Joe, beauties every one." He looked over at the toddler in the high chair. "If that little one keeps suckin' her thumb, she'll have crooked teeth, though."

Angel took her finger out of her mouth and looked around guiltily. "Will not!"

"Will, too!" Steve said. "Now, Angel, you know what Cayenne told you. . . ."

"Who's Cayenne?" The Mexican looked up from the hot peach pie he was shoveling in as fast as he could.

"Just the oldest of my daughters," Joe said quickly. "But as I told you before, she's in Kansas looking after a sick aunt. Afraid you'll never get to meet her."

Something in his tone let Lynnie know Joe didn't want the trio meeting his oldest child.

Slade smiled expansively at all the children, at old *Senora* Rosita who had just entered with more coffee. "You're a lucky man, Joe McBride," he smiled expansively. "You got the prettiest daughters in all Texas and probably the best cook this side of the Rio Grande."

Rosita paused and the Mexican caught her hand, kissing it. "*Senora*, my mother never made such food, I swear by all the saints!"

Rosita blushed like a school girl. "*Senor*, you flatter me! I've made better," she said, flustered, but she beamed at the Mexican.

It didn't take but a couple of days before the charming Slade had everyone but Papa and Lynnie wishing aloud the friendly trio would stay on the Lazy M forever. Papa said little but sat in his rocker on the squeaky porch for hours at a time, whittling. Sometimes he played a whistle as he finished it. He always played that same haunting folk tune. She thought about it now, wondering if it were the only one he could play or if he just loved it so.

She didn't tell him she'd overheard his conversation with Slade that first day. But when she tried gently to pry a little information out of Papa about the trio, he grew cool and distant. "You know what happened when Pandora opened the box and let loose a world of trouble because she was so curious? Don't open that box, Lynnie. If you love me, don't ask any more questions. They'll be gone in a few weeks and things will be as they were."

"But, Papa, who are they?"

"They're just old friends passing through, nothing more to it than that. I knew them a long time ago. . . ."

271

Hank Billings's thoroughbred nickered again and Lynnie decided she'd better let Papa know about the letter from Cayenne before Trask came out of the saloon. *Had she done the wrong thing in asking her big sister to take action?*

Lynnie readjusted her wire spectacles on her freckled nose, shook back her red hair, and walked purposely toward the buggy. Depending on what Cee Cee's letter said, Papa would have to make the decisions now. Lynnie had done all a nine-year-old girl could do about that trio!

Chapter Fourteen

Joe McBride sat in the buggy tied in front of Billings General Store and waited for Lynnie to return. The July sun beat hot on his bearded face and he shifted a little so he would be shaded by the buggy top.

He closed his eyes and yawned. The sounds and smells of the sleepy hamlet drifted to him and he smiled contentedly. Joe was not one to curse God for what had happened; what might have been. He said a silent prayer that he was alive and wondered if the Almighty intended to do anything about the trio of outlaws who had been staying at the Lazy M the past couple of weeks.

He wasn't sure just exactly what he could do about them himself. Even if he weren't so handicapped, a top gun would be loco to take on all three of those gunslingers. Besides, there was the safety of his beloved little girls, the gentle Mexicans on his ranch, and the harmless townspeople to consider. Maybe Slade's gang was just hiding out and would move on when things cooled down. That way, Joe wouldn't have to make any decisions about what to do. Yep, soon maybe, Slade's boys would head up to the old hideout in the Indian Territory known as Robber's Roost.

"Papa, there's a letter from Cee Cee." He jerked around as Lynnie's high-pitched voice brought him out of his musings. *Lynnie, so small and serious for her age, so bright. He had always hoped to send her away east to some fancy college but there was no money for that now.*

"A letter from Cee Cee? That's nice; I miss her. Did you see Trask?"

"He's gone over to the saloon." Lynnie climbed up next to him in the buggy and tore open the letter.

Slade always sent Trask with them when they went to town. What nobody told Slade was that Trask didn't watch them at all; he sat in Ogle's saloon and drank. Not that there was anything to worry about, Joe thought bitterly. Joe couldn't turn them in, get help, without revealing his own past. He was proud of his fine reputation here, and maybe saving his reputation meant even more to him than the possibility of going to prison or even being hanged over that poor teller who'd been killed in the St. Joe bank. Who then would look after his orphaned daughters?

Lynnie cleared her throat importantly. Joe knew she was proud of her new learning. "You want I should read you what Cee Cee says?"

Joe felt cold apprehension run up his back. "Oh, Lynnie, you didn't write and tell her about Slade, did you?"

She fidgeted a moment in the silence. "Well, yes, Papa, I did. I overheard you talking to those so-called friends of yours and didn't know what to do, so I wrote Sister and told her to come home."

"Lynnie, I wished you hadn't done that; no use worrying her. Besides, you're mistaken; these are old friends and they're welcome to stay and visit awhile." He prayed silently that God would overlook his lying since it was for a good cause. Lynnie might be in danger if she knew too much.

"Cee Cee always knows what to do, Papa," her voice was apologetic. "I know you *say* they're your friends, but I think they're up to something bad. I overheard them in the barn talkin' about an army payroll."

274

He put his arm around her thin shoulders. "Oh, Bill and the boys are just blowhards; don't mean anything. You know what Texans say, 'All hat and no cattle.' Probably nothin' to it."

His mouth went suddenly dry. *An army payroll. Now why would an army payroll come through a sleepy village like this one?* Town gossip at church on Sundays was full of all the troop movements and the Red River Uprising. "So read me your sister's letter," he said lightly.

Dear Lynnie: You'll be glad to know I've found the man I've been looking for. Yes, it's wedding bells for your big sister and Papa will have that son he always wanted. Isn't it exciting? My love's tall and dark with a scar down one cheek like a romantic dueling scar! And he rides a big gray stallion. I know you like horses so much! Must get this in the mail. Be home in a few weeks to make plans. Don't try to do anything 'til I get there. I intend to take care of everything. Love from me and my intended, Cee Cee.

Maverick Durango. Joe felt as if he'd suddenly been splashed with ice water. No, maybe he was jumpin' to conclusions. There was lots of tall, dark men out there for his daughter to meet. He tried to convince himself a long moment, but his inner voice said, *But how many of them have a scar down one cheek and ride a big gray horse?* No, his innocent daughter could only be describing Maverick.

Joe had met old Don Diego de Durango last year at the Cattleman's Association meeting when the old man had come over to congratulate him on his expert shooting, on winning the fine Winchester rifle. When he'd found out Joe's name, that aristocratic old man had hesitated a long moment and finally told him there was something they must discuss.

* * *

Lynnie twisted on the seat. "Is something the matter, Papa? You look sick. Are you all right?"

"Just a little too much sun, I reckon." He felt in his pocket with a trembling hand for a bandana and wiped his perspiring face. "Lynnie, I—I think I need to send a wire to Cee Cee."

"A wire!" Her voice was shocked. "Papa, that costs a lot of money!"

"I know, I know," he nodded. "But it's important that it get there fast."

It was probably already too late, he thought with a sinking heart. "What's the date on that letter?"

"No date, Papa."

Maybe there was just an outside chance Cee Cee hadn't yet left Wichita. "Lynnie, I'll sit right here so as not to arouse Trask's suspicions in case he comes out of the saloon. I'm the one they're watchin' anyhow."

He wondered if Lynnie realized how the three always kept some of the children as hostages just in case Joe wasn't afraid of blackmail? The blackmail was enough, Lord help him! His reputation in this town meant too much to Joe to have the outlaws tell his secret past.

He reached for some coins and held them out to her. "Mind you make sure Trask don't see you."

"What do you want me to do?"

How could he word it to warn Cee Cee but not alarm Lynnie? He could trust old Mr. Faine at the telegraph not to breathe a word or ask any questions. His wife had been one of those Joe had ransomed.

"Get Mr. Faine to send this wire fast as greased lightning: "Dear Daughter: Stay in Wichita until Indian troubles over. Stop. Don't bring that man here and tell him nothing. Stop. Will explain later. Stop. Love, Papa."

"Why don't you want him here? Why, Papa? It sounds like Cee Cee intends to marry him."

Marry him. How could his innocent daughter know

276

that Maverick Durango intended to kill Joe McBride? But he knew. The old Don had warned him. Annie Laurie's son was finally coming for his revenge.

"Why? Because it's dangerous with all those Indians on the warpath," he said truthfully. Joe thrust the silver into Lynnie's hands. "Now, go along and do as I ask, honey, and then let's not tell anyone about this letter." He reached out, took it from her hand, and stuffed it in his coat pocket.

"But, Papa, why—?"

"Just do it, Lynnie," he snapped, and was immediately sorry. He had never raised his voice to his precious daughters much less his hand as Hannah had done. But he was so afraid, not for himself but for his children. What would happen to them if Annie Laurie's vengeful son killed Joe and left his daughters orphaned?

"Let's say I favor another young man for your sister."

"Ohhh," Lynnie said with mature understanding. "That Jones boy at church, or—?"

"I'll discuss that with your sister when she finally gets home," he said. "Now take care of it for me before Trask comes out of that saloon."

Lynnie's little shoes fairly flew down the boardwalk. Joe sighed, rubbing his bearded face on his sleeve, listening to her footsteps fading toward the telegraph office. He could count on kindly old Mr. Faine to be discreet and not gossip about the wire he'd sent.

Joe felt suddenly like Job being tested by God with mounting troubles. Didn't he have enough problems trying to protect his family, this town, and his own spotless reputation without Maverick Durango suddenly showing up to extract his pound of flesh?

Annie Laurie. Joe's beloved first wife. Maverick Durango's mother by some savage Comanche warrior. It didn't seem quite fair that Joe hadn't sired Annie's son. They'd had such plans, such dreams together. And Joe had no son at all to pass that fancy rifle on down to. Ironic how things turned out. He shook his head, thinking. If things had been different, Maverick and Cee Cee might have been brother and sister, as it was, they were no kin at all. For a moment, he wondered what the angry young man looked like. Maverick probably had Annie's eyes. Did he also have that rare smile that lit up her face like a Texas sunrise?

His hand went to the crumpled letter in his pocket, remembering Don Durango's description. Half Comanche with eyes as gray as a gun barrel, riding a ghost gray stallion.

. . . and I looked up and beheld a pale horse and his name that sat upon him was Death and hell followed with him.

Revelations, chapter 6, verse 8, Joe remembered. His other hand went to another coat pocket and found the comfort of the worn Bible he always kept close at hand. He knew nearly every word of it by heart, even though he'd never been able to read well so he could still preach to his small congregation on Sundays. Well, nothing happened without a reason, and who was Joe McBride to question the Lord's mysterious ways?

Maybe he was apprehensive for nothing, Joe thought, still clutching the Bible. *Maybe the man Cee Cee had described and the description Don Durango had given him were not the same man.* No, it had to be. He felt it deep in his soul. If his wire reached his daughter in time, maybe she would lose the young man instead of leading the would-be killer to the Lazy M Ranch. It would be a while before he knew, and in the meantime, what was he going to do about his old outlaw partner, Bill Slade?

He buried his face in his hands. *Nothing. That's what he was going to do. Nothing.* Maybe the trio would just finally ride out and move on. It was obvious they were on the run from the law. If only the tiny town had a real sheriff. But the sleepy village had never needed one before. If Joe told anyone in town, there might be some shooting and some innocent townspeople would get killed. And he couldn't send for the marshal without his own outlaw past coming out. He was just human and weak enough to enjoy being a hero, enjoy the regard and respect this town held for him. And even after twenty-five years, wouldn't the law still want to hang someone for killing that bank clerk in St. Joe, even though Joe hadn't pulled the trigger?

The sound of feet running on the boardwalk made him jerk up, and Lynnie piled into the buggy, breathless. "I took care of it, Papa. Mr. Faine says the lines are down half the time because of the Indian troubles, but they're working right now and he'll get that message to Wichita."

"Good girl." He put the Bible back in his pocket and patted her thin shoulder. "Now, Lynnie, let's keep this quiet and everything you overheard, too. Obviously, Bill and the boys was just carryin' you high, you know, makin' jokes because they knew you was listenin'. They're just good ol' boys."

"If you say so, Papa." She sounded doubtful. But he knew his children trusted and believed in him just as this town did. Even in his prime, before he was tortured, Joe would have hesitated to try to go up against those three fast guns with his rifle, and now . . .

No, he wouldn't do anything to endanger his reputation, his family, or the gentle townspeople.

"Lynnie," he said, "do you think Papa would have friends that weren't fine, honest people?"

"Well, no, Papa, but they seem pretty rough."

She was a smart one for her age. He wished again he had the money to send her to some fancy school. Still, he didn't regret the fact that he had bankrupted himself to get the money to ransom the captives.

279

"You can't always tell about people from their looks, Lynnie. Deep in their hearts, Slade and the boys aren't all that bad."

No, they were worse. God forgive me for hiding the truth, Joe thought.

The seat creaked as Lynnie leaned out of the buggy. "Here comes Trask."

"Remember, don't discuss this," Joe cautioned.

"I won't, Papa."

Trask still had that bad leg from that St. Joe sheriff who had interrupted the robbery, Joe thought. He didn't turn his head, listening to the heavy man drag his foot a little as he crossed the boardwalk behind the buggy, came around, and got in. "Well, Joe, hope you didn't mind settin' in the sun while I had a few drinks," Trask laughed.

"From the smell of you, I'd say you had more'n a few," Joe said before he thought. *He needed to pray over his Scots-Irish temper*, he thought.

Trask belched and laughed good-naturedly. "Little girl, you get the supplies we came for?"

"I did," Lynnie said pointedly. "And if you didn't eat so much, we wouldn't keep running out of flour and stuff."

"Lynnie," Joe scolded, "that's not polite!"

"I'm sorry," the child said contritely. "Reckon I need to pray about my sharp tongue."

Trask laughed again as he snapped the reins over the old mule and the buggy moved down the dusty, uneven street. "This is the prayingest family I ever met! Sometime, Sis, remind me to tell you what your pappy was like afore he got religion."

"Don't, Trask," Joe said with a warning edge to his voice. *Would his little girls still idolize him if they knew he'd once been part of this gang for a brief time? That a bank teller had been killed in the escape when that sheriff showed up unexpectedly?*

Trask shrugged, brushing against him in the crowded buggy seat. "Suit yourself. We'll probably be moving on in a few more days, Sis, and old Rosita won't have to cook no more for us. Never thought old Joe'd end up as a part-time preacher with a houseful of little girls. Every man ought to have a son."

A son. What was it Annie Laurie had said to him? *A son, Joe. Every man ought to have a son. Someday, God willin', I'll give you mine.*

And now Annie's son by some savage warrior was on his trail. Well, that was in the hands of God, wasn't it? And nobody knew what the future held.

He and Annie sure hadn't known when they'd left Kentucky together, newly married, with big dreams about someday owning a big spread in Texas.

They'd thought they had the world by the tail back then, so young, so full of dreams and hope. Joe's mind went to the day he had seen her last, made love to her in the afternoon in that squalid little sod hut on the worthless few acres.

He rolled over and watched her, resting his chin on his hand. "I ought to be out plowin'," he said, but made no move to go.

"Plow later." She looked into his eyes and smiled. Why was it everyone thought the gentle girl so plain? When she smiled, she was beautiful the way her face lit up, the tiny crinkles around her wide gray eyes. "The crop's not doin' too good anyways."

He didn't want to think about how poor the land was, how they'd been cheated by banker Ogle as to how rich the soil was. When he'd sold them the spread, Ogle hadn't warned them the area was full of Comanche, either.

He kissed the tip of her nose. "Annie, girl, I haven't

done right by you. I had such big plans."

"Wherever you are, Joe, that's good enough for me." She reached to touch his face with her work-worn hands. "I'd like to see the Lazy M grow, became a big spread for our children and grandchildren. But if it doesn't, I don't regret marryin' you; I don't regret comin' to Texas one whit."

He loved her so much for her unselfish adoration that his heart filled up and for a moment he could not speak, so he stroked her soft brown hair. "I meant to build you a fine house with a long dinner table."

She smiled, entering into the spirit of the daydream. "And you'll sit at one end of the long table, and me at the other. And all up and down the table, our kids will sit, the kids I'm going to give you."

He imagined the scene and enjoyed it. "And we'll be prosperous, with lots of good things on the table and plenty left over for friends to come to dinner."

"And someday, our kids and grandkids will sit at that same table, so that even when we're dead and gone, why, we'll be there in spirit every time they gather 'round that long table. They'll sense our presence long after we're gone. We ought to have a lot of children, Joe, that's what life's all about."

He took one of her little work-worn hands in his and kissed the palm. "It don't matter to me if there's no kids, honey. But someday, you'll have help around the house and a nice buggy to drive to church on Sunday."

She laughed and kissed him. "Every man ought to have a son, Joe. Someday, God willin', I'll give you mine."

"I'd like that, Annie. A son who has your big gray eyes, your smile." And he began to sing softly to her in his fine tenor voice: *Like dew on the gowan lying, is the fa' o' her fairy feet, and like winds in summer sighing, her voice is low and sweet. Her voice is low and sweet, and she's a' the world to me, and for bonnie Annie Laurie, I'd lay me down and dee."*

Tears came to her eyes as he sang to her, and she reached up and patted his cheek. "You were my first man, Joe McBride, my only man, and I love you so! Your name will be the last on my lips the day I die, I promise you that."

"Such sad talk!" he scoffed. "We got years ahead of us, girl. We're gonna be two old people sittin' at that long table eatin' with all the generations, rockin' on the porch of that ranchhouse when I get it built and fixed up good and proper for you. Oh, it'll be fine watching our kids grow up, and then there'll be grandkids and great-grandkids. . . ."

"Oh, you make it sound so grand," she laughed, and pulled him down to her.

In her arms, he could forget the rough times, the land that would only grow sagebrush and cactus no matter how hard he tried. *Even the squalid little soddie became a mansion with her in his arms*, he thought as he kissed her and she smiled up at him again. How could he ever have thought her plain when that smile turned her small face into such glowing beauty?

She snuggled against him as he kissed her. "I'm lucky to have you, Joe. You was so handsome and all the girls wanting to marry you."

"No, I'm the lucky one," he protested, and he opened her blouse and kissed her breasts. He was a proud, vain man maybe, but he was pleased that his bride was a virgin, that no man had ever touched her but him. Somehow, that was terribly important to him. And they'd come to Texas because there was no future for almost illiterate, poor people in Kentucky unless they wanted to go into the mines as the generation before them had.

"Remember," she murmured as he undressed her,

"you got to get over to the Adams's ranch late this evening to get that new cow he's gonna let us have on credit."

"Plenty of time for that. I want to make love to my wife first." He kissed her.

"Don't think old Adams would have let us have it," Annie smiled, "but his homely daughter, Hannah, has taken such a shine to you!"

"How you talk, girl!" He tickled her and they rolled on the old straw-stuffed mattress in merriment. "Hannah Adams is so sour-faced her daddy'd have to hang a porkchop around her neck to get a hound to lick her face!"

"Well, her pa's big spread and money is better than a porkchop," Annie laughed. "She'd take you if she could get shet of me."

He caught her in his arms, kissing all the way down her neck. "Don't you worry about that," he whispered against her skin. "Annie Laurie McBride, you ain't never gonna get shet of this ol' Kentucky boy!"

He had made leisurely love to Annie, not realizing then that it was the very last time he would ever hold her in his arms. That after tonight, he would never see her again. If he had realized that those few hours were going to be their very last, he would have done things different, told her all the things he'd always meant to tell her about how much he loved her. But like too many people, he was awkward and shy with words, holding them in his heart until some future time. *Only there would never be a future time*.

He had wanted Annie to accompany him to the Adams spread, but she wanted to do some sewing and it was a long, hot ride. Besides, she said, winking at him, she thought with his handsome charm, Hannah would see they got a better deal on the milk cow if Annie didn't come.

The last time he ever saw her, she stood in the doorway in her blue homespun dress and waved as he drove away in the wagon.

He looked back. "Give me a smile, Annie Girl!"

And she smiled in a way that lit up her face, brightened his heart. "I still intend to give you a son someday; see if I don't!" she called, and laughed.

He waved back. "We'll start on that when I get back from the Adams place."

"Oh, you!"

He smiled, capturing her small form forever in his memory as she stood in that doorway. Then not realizing what the future held, he turned and drove away, whistling under his breath. *"Her brow is like the snowdrift, her throat is like the swan, her face it is the fairest that e'er the sun shone on. . . ."*

Joe cleared his throat, wiped his eyes.

"What's the matter?" Trask asked with annoyance.

"Nothing," Joe said. "Just a little dust from the road blowing in my eyes, that's all."

And now Annie's son was coming to kill him with all the cold-blooded premeditation twenty-four years of hate had built in the boy. An eye for an eye and a tooth for a tooth, that was what the boy wanted, and he couldn't blame him. Would this Maverick believe Joe if he told him he'd thought Annie dead? If the boy knew about the faceless body Hannah had identified as the missing Annie while Joe rode the outlaw trail with Slade, trying desperately to raise the ransom money?

He'd ask Mr. Adams to loan him the money, of course, but that old rich rancher had whined 'bout hard times, not looking Joe in the eye. . . .

He had married Hannah as that old man lay dying. He knew it was a mistake deep in his heart, but she loved

285

him so and he'd realized now the value of having plenty of money. Being poor was the worst thing in the world.

Joe soon discovered it wasn't. Being caught in a marriage with a woman he didn't, couldn't love, was even worse. His only happiness was the daughter Hannah had given him—Cayenne. It was only after Hannah's death that Joe found comfort in religion.

Now as the buggy bumped over the uneven road toward the ranch, Joe thought about Maverick again. *Revenge.* The scriptures said, "Vengeance is mine, says the Lord, I shall repay." But he was human and frail enough to want to live to see his daughters grown. Well, maybe Lynnie's wire would get there before Cayenne left Wichita. How was he to know? He wasn't even sure what he would do if Maverick ever confronted him. Even if his crippled hands could pull a trigger, could he really bring himself to do it?

Send me a sign, O, great Jehovah, he prayed as they drove toward the ranch. *Send me a sign so that I may know the outcome, that I may do Thy will. . . .*

A shadow passed between him and the hot sun, and he looked up, startled.

"Papa, what a beautiful pair of eagles flyin' overhead." Lynnie jumped up and down in her excitement, making the seat bounce. "They're circlin' the Lazy M ranch house, all free and soaring as high as a soul gone to heaven!"

Eagles. Joe smiled. He'd always liked eagles. But if it was any kind of sign from God, blamed if he could figure out what it meant. Would he even know the sign if God finally sent one?

Trask belched. "If I had me a rifle here, I'd shoot both them birds outa the sky," he growled. "Ain't got the range with a six-gun."

"Oh, shut up, Trask," Joe said with the sudden spirit and temper of the old days. "You always did begrudge any living creature a little happiness. The eagles aren't hurting anyone."

"I suppose you're right," Trask said. "The Injuns, now, they think eagles is powerful medicine, spirit animals."

Joe didn't want to think about Indians. He'd come home from the Adams's with the new cow that evening to find his place in flames, most of the livestock lying dead with arrows stuck in them.

Had it really been more than a quarter of a century ago? Of course it had. Not a day passed that he didn't remember those last moments, blame himself for not insisting Annie accompany him. He should never have left her alone. If he'd been there, the Comanche might have killed him but they'd never have carried her off while he had strength to pull a trigger.

Then the offer had come through a trader. Joe had no money to buy the weapons, the supplies the warriors offered to trade for his Annie. He had to get money, would do anything to obtain it. Maybe if he could raise the money quickly, the braves wouldn't rape her and pass her around as they so often did. He'd seen white women returned and turned away by their husbands. He'd seen others who'd gone insane from what they'd endured. He couldn't bear the thought of any man touching his innocent Annie Girl.

Neither old Adams nor Ogle would lend him the money. He was too distraught to even think at the time that Hannah might have had anything to do with that. Later, word seemed to get around quickly that there was a desperate young man armed with a Kentucky long rifle who could outshoot anybody on the frontier and would do anything for money.

Bill Slade and his partners had approached him in front of a backwoods saloon. "Are you as good with that rifle as everyone says you are?"

"Best shot in Kentucky," Joe said, and he was. When a man was poor and powder was dear, he learned to make every shot count.

Slade leaned against a post and studied him. "You interested in making quick money, lots of it?"

Joe's heart quickened. It had been a week since Annie'd been taken. He had to ransom her, had to. "Mister, I'll do anything if the money's right."

"There's a bank in St. Joe that's supposed to be full of money. . . ."

"Now, wait a minute, I didn't know you was talkin' about robbin' banks. . . ."

"My gal's been wheedling information out of the teller," Slade grinned. "It's a big bank that's handlin' all the settlers' money as they head for the Oregon Trail. Your cut'll be big," Slade promised. "More money than you ever seen in your whole life."

And in the end, Joe had gone with the three. Slade had a girl, a pretty girl named Molly, who'd come from a tumbledown shack on the outskirts of St. Joe. If he hadn't been so in love with Annie, Molly might have turned his head. The pretty girl-child was younger than his Annie, probably not more than fifteen or sixteen.

He remembered now as he rode along in the buggy that Molly's black hair had been cropped short and uneven when he'd met her at the hideout in St. Joe.

"What happened to your hair?" he asked.

The pretty brunette blushed, looking away. Obviously she had been very vain about her dark, thick hair. "My old lady. When she caught me out with Bill, she hacked my hair off, called me a Jezebel."

Slade laughed, tousling her hair with his hand. "Aw,

it'll grow, Molly. You got the prettiest hair I ever seen on a woman."

The girl looked Joe over. "Where'd you get the good-lookin' redheaded dude?" she asked archly.

"Now, Molly, you get your schemin' little eyes off him," Slade grinned, lighting a cigar. "He's in this strictly for the money, and he ain't plannin' on spendin' it on you."

"That's right, ma'am." Joe twisted his hat in his hands. "The Comanche carried off my wife, I need the money to ransom her."

"Oh." She looked crestfallen as she sauntered around him, looking him up and down. "Couldn't be tempted by no other woman, huh?"

Joe backed away uneasily. "No, ma'am. Not that you ain't a purty one, but you see, Annie's special. . . ."

"There's some thinks I'm special." She cut her eyes at him, winking back at Bill.

Slade slapped her familiarly on the bottom. "Just cause he's handsome, don't get any ideas, Molly. I don't want you wastin' your charm on him. There's a teller you need to cozy up to, find out more about money shipments and all."

"That old teller!" She made a face. "Didn't I do enough telling you how much money I've seen moving in and out of there?"

Slade pulled her to him roughly. "Do like I tell you, Molly, or you'll end up back at that shack hanging over a scrub board takin' in laundry for a livin' like your crazy ma."

She seemed to consider. "Good times and money is what matters to me, Bill, you know that. I never had much of either. My hair'll finally grow out and then I'll do it up with fancy combs and jewels."

Bill laughed. "Only if you play along with me, you little slut, do as I tell you."

Joe's hand doubled into a fist. "You shouldn't talk to a woman like that, call her names. . . ."

"She's mine," Slade said, "and she's used to it, aren't you, Molly?"

She shrugged, staring at Joe as if Sir Galahad had suddenly ridden onto the scene. "That don't mean I like it."

"You'll like it well enough when your lace stockings have money stuffed in the tops," Slade grinned. "Maybe I'll dress you up fancy, take you to St. Louie or San Francisco, where we can really have some good times."

Her pouty face brightened. "What do you want me to do?"

"Like I said, cozy up to that old teller, do whatever it takes to find out when the next gold shipment's coming in." He winked at her, "I ain't jealous."

Joe felt disgust and anger. He glanced around at Trask and the Mexican who lounged against the wall. Neither of them said anything. "This ain't right," Joe said. "I never figured on makin' some girl whore for us just to find out about the money."

"Then think about your woman layin' under some damned Injun buck and him pumping on her, passing her around. . . ."

Joe hit him then, catching Slade in the mouth and sending him flying. The image Slade had brought to his mind about his beloved Annie being violated was more than he could bear. "Don't you say that!" he shouted. "They won't touch her! They're waiting to see if I got the money!"

For a moment, he thought Slade would come up swinging, but the man was a cool one. "Reckon I deserved that," he shrugged. "Not the lowest-down white man who ever lived would want an Injun's leavin's, want to take a woman back who'd been raped by dirty savages."

290

Molly looked at Joe with warm, sympathetic eyes. "You got heart and guts, mister. Your Annie is a lucky woman, I'd say."

The Mexican yawned. "Enough of this, *amigos*. Let's make plans about the bank."

So Molly had been sent to seduce the old teller and find out when the money was coming in the next week. Then they'd hit the bank. Everything went wrong. A sheriff happened along and the teller tried to shout for help. In the confusion, Slade shot the man, but when Joe tried to stop and help him, Slade screamed at him. "Are you loco? This is a hangin' offense for the whole gang if they catch us!"

The noise attracted help for the sheriff and Joe took a slug in the arm. They couldn't get the safe open with the teller sprawled unconscious, so they didn't get away with a dime. Matter of fact, the gang just barely got away with their lives.

In a hideaway up in the Ozarks, Joe rested with his injured arm while Molly looked after him. The other three went out casing a small town to see if there was another bank they could hit soon.

Joe was inconsolable. "I should have known better!" he said. "I never stole a penny in my life! I didn't mean to hurt anyone! And we didn't get the money, either!"

Molly came over and sat on the edge of the bed. "You didn't shoot that teller. It was Slade's pistol. I can tell you wouldn't hurt anybody, Joe."

He shook his head. "You don't know anything about me, Molly."

She put her hand on his arm. "I've seen enough to like what I see. Good times and high livin' was always my dream, Joe, but for a man like you, I'd give it all up, live in a sod shack."

He looked at her. She was too young to know what she

knew about men. Just a girl, but her full breasts swelled above the low-cut dress like a full-grown woman's, and he looked away. Joe had been used to making love to Annie every night and his body wanted relief. But he was faithful to his Annie Girl. "You don't mean that, Molly. You're just grateful because I'm kind to you. A woman shouldn't have to put up with the way Slade treats you. I feel like killin' him for it."

"It was my choice," she shrugged, running her hand up and down his arm. "If I went home, my crazy old lady would beat me for my vanity, cut off my hair again so men wouldn't look at me."

Her hand felt warm moving up and down his arm. He could see the hollow between her breasts and wondered if her nipples were dark rosettes. "You're pretty, Molly, too pretty to waste your life the way you're doin', and I've got a woman already."

"You may never see her again." The girl leaned closer and he could smell the musky, womanly scent of her, the perfume she wore on her breasts. "I've loved you, Joe, from the first moment I saw you. I'd be your woman, go anywhere with you."

She unbuttoned the cheap yellow dress she wore, put his hand on her full, bare breast.

"No," he said, but he could feel his heart quicken as she leaned closer. Her nipple seemed to burn a circle against his palm. "No, Molly, this it ain't right. I love Annie. . . ."

The door flew open. Slade and his men stalked in.

"You slut!" Slade screamed, and he caught her as she tried to run, slapping her face.

Joe tried to stop him. "Don't touch her!"

The Mexican and Trask grabbed him, held him as he struggled. Slade threw the girl across the bed. "You little slut! Acting so hesitant when I want you to sleep with the teller and then diddling this bastard when I'm not around!'"

Joe struggled to break free. "It wasn't like that, Bill, I swear! I never touched her. . . ."

"You think I'm blind?" Slade roared. "You're pawin' her tits when I walk in and tell me that! My women are like my horses, Joe; I don't mind loaning one to a friend for a little ride, but you oughta ask first!"

"I—I never meant to even touch her," Joe protested, "don't know what came over me. . . ."

"I know what came over you," Slade grinned cruelly at the sobbing girl on the bed. "She's a hot one all right; no one man's enough for her. Sooner or later, she'll end up in some bawdy house. But I'll keep her until I tire of her."

The Mexican slowly let go of Joe's arms. "We have news," he said. "That bank teller died."

"Oh, my God!" Joe felt sick, weak.

Slade spat on the floor. "That's the breaks. There'll be a reward on our heads now; we'd better clear out!"

Joe thought about Annie. "I thought we were gonna hit another bank?"

Trask swore. "With a posse looking for us?"

"Trask is right," Slade said. "You might as well get back to Texas, McBride, see if you can find a bank on your own to rob. Maybe you can borrow the money you need." He glanced over at the tousled girl who sat on the bed wiping her eyes. "Get me a drink, Molly."

Joe watched the girl straighten her clothes and go over to pour Slade a whiskey. "I can't borrow any money. I got nothin'. I couldn't even give away that little patch of poor dirt I got."

The Mexican shook his head. "Tough luck, hombre. But at least back in Texas, if the Rangers rescue your wife, you'll hear about it."

So Joe went back to Texas. When he checked in with

the Rangers, the young Swede leader looked at him sympathetically. "We been looking for you."

How could they have heard so soon about the robbery clear up in Missouri? "You been looking for me?"

"Swen" Swenson nodded and pulled at his blond mustache. "Ain't you the one whose wife got carried off by the Comanche?"

Joe's heartbeat quickened. "You got news? You found my Annie?"

"Maybe." The man turned away as if he couldn't bear to look in Joe's face. "We'd like you to look at some clothes, see if you can identify them."

"Clothes? What do you mean, *clothes?*"

"You just look at them first, tell me if they belong to your wife." Young Swenson went into another part of the office, dug in a drawer, and came back. "You ever see these before?"

He spread a dirty, torn dress out on the cluttered desk—cheap blue homespun.

In his mind, Joe saw his Annie waving to him that last time from the doorway. This is what she'd had on. Hope made his heart pounded hard. He jumped up. "Yes, these are Annie's." He grabbed the fabric, clutching it between his big hands as if by doing so, his beloved would be in his embrace again. "Where'd you get these? Is she okay? Is she—"

"Mr. McBride, are you a drinking man?" The Ranger looked at him sympathetically.

"No, not much," he stammered. "Annie didn't like it." And suddenly, he was angry, realizing the man was holding back. "Tell me, for God's sake, tell me!"

The Ranger opened his desk drawer, taking out a bottle and two glasses. "Sit down," he gestured to a chair. "You're gonna need this."

And now he didn't want to hear, realizing the news wasn't good. Joe spread the clothes on the desk, stroking them gently as he had often stroked his Annie Girl. The hand that accepted the whiskey trembled so badly he spilled a little of it getting it to his lips. It was cheap and raw, burning all the way down his throat to his empty stomach. Then he collapsed in the chair. "Tell me."

"Oh, God," muttered the Ranger, draining his glass. "Why does it always have to be me who gets the bad ones?"

Joe didn't answer, just watched the man drink. A big clock on the wall ticked loudly in the silence.

The Ranger took a deep breath and squared his shoulders. "We were already sure. Your neighbor's daughter, Hannah, was kind enough to help make the identification."

"Identification?" He stared stupidly at the man.

"Mr. McBride, we took these off a body found over at the edge of the county."

"No!" Joe stood up, upsetting his chair. "No, it can't be my Annie!"

"I know how you feel. But Hannah Adams identified her: light brown hair, small build, and she was wearing these clothes. . . ."

He wouldn't believe it. "Did the woman have gray eyes and a small face?" he asked. "I want to see that body for myself and—"

"McBride," he hesitated, pouring himself another drink, "the shape that body was in—well, it's already been buried. You can't see her."

Joe's stomach turned queasy with the whiskey. "What—what do you mean?"

The other man fiddled with his glass, avoiding Joe's eyes. "What I'm trying to tell you is it'd been there for a while, didn't have no face. And the varmints had been chewin' it. . . ."

Joe screamed then, loud and long, stumbling over to pound his fists against the wall. "No!" he screamed.

"No! No! It ain't my Annie, I tell you! It can't be! They've still got her and I'll get her back when I can raise some money!"

And then his stomach revolted against the sight of the dirty, torn dress, the images the Ranger's words brought to mind, and the cheap whiskey. Joe stumbled outside and vomited off the porch. "No," he whispered. "Oh, God, no!"

But finally, he accepted the facts. The woman the kindly neighbors had buried had to be his Annie. Who else could have been wearing her clothes?

And he was grateful to the plump, homely Hannah for her comfort and sympathy, seeing a lot of her while her own rich Papa was dying. Finally, he had married her. He would find out fifteen years later that his Annie was still alive, but by then it was too late.

The buggy pulled up before the ranch house.

"Papa, are you sick?" Lynnie asked. "You haven't said a word all the way from town?"

Trask laughed. "Maybe he just ain't got much to say and he's sayin' it."

Joe didn't answer as Lynnie helped him from the buggy. It wasn't bad enough that his hands were so crippled; the Comanche had burned his feet, too. "Just help me up on the porch, honey," he said. "I want to sit a spell and think before supper."

He limped across the squeaky boards, flopping down in the old wicker rocker. The smell of seven sisters roses drifted in the hot summer air. Joe was tired, very tired.

"Papa, are you okay?"

"Just fine, Lynnie. Quit frettin' over me like a broody hen. Call me when old Rosita has supper ready."

"Me too," Trask yelled. "I'm going out to the barn."

Joe leaned back in his chair with a sigh, reaching into his pocket for the willow whistle he'd finished earlier this afternoon. He'd promised one to the little Edwards girl and he didn't want to disappoint her.

Unconsciously, he brought the whistle to his lips and played the old folk tune. Annie. Only one person meant as much to him as Annie had. His daughter, Cayenne. Because of his own miserable past as the town bastard, he'd hesitated a little while when that young man had brought him word ten years ago that Annie might still be alive. Had that made any difference in Annie's fate? Swenson had said he'd look into this new information, and every once in a while, in the ensuing years, Joe still checked with him. But long ago, he'd given up hope that Swenson's Rangers would ever find her. At least, now his beloved daughter would never be labeled a "bastard."

Maybe it was God's punishment or just pure irony that now, unknowingly, Cayenne might be on her way home with Joe's future killer unless she got his wire in time. Whatever happened, the Lord moved in mysterious ways.

Joe took out his Bible, turning it over and over in his hands. "Thy will be done," he whispered.

Then he bent his head and prayed for everyone, but especially for the soul of Annie's vengeful son.

Chapter Fifteen

Molly lugged her valise out the swinging doors of the Red Garter Saloon. Dusty Wichita lay asleep on this Sunday dawn in late July. She put the luggage on the wooden sidewalk and sat on it, looking up and down the street and listening for the stagecoach.

Wichita's loss was going to be Caldwell's gain, she thought. But somehow, she had a feeling it wouldn't be any different in that wild, wide-open town. Good times and fun seemed harder and harder to come by. Sometimes she wondered if she were merely going through the motions in a frantic search for excitement that was never quite enough.

She took a small mirror from her purse and looked at herself critically, searching for gray hairs. She found one in her soot-black locks, pulled it, and readjusted the expensive silver and pearl combs. *Tomorrow she would be forty years old. Forty.* Critically, she stared at her image, checking the fine lines around her mouth and eyes. Her mirror didn't lie. In another five years, her face would be wrinkled so that she would look like "five miles of bad road," as the cowboys said. *What would she do then?* What happened to saloon girls who grew too old and gradually lost their looks?

Well, she wouldn't worry about that now. She'd think about good times in Caldwell, that hell-raisin' settlement on the Kansas-Indian Territory border. Caldwell was the first town where Texas cowboys crossing the

298

Territory could legally get whiskey. That made it a wild, lawless stopping place on the Chisholm Trail. Oh, there'd be dancing and singing and lots of exciting times!

Molly sighed. Somehow, nothing was ever as much fun as she expected as she drifted from one town to the next, one bordello to the next. How many had she seen in a quarter of a century, always hoping the next one would provide the excitement, the fulfillment she craved and never seemed to find? Ten years ago, she'd been one of Miss Fancy's girls in San Antone. The years and the mileage were catching up with her. She wouldn't think about that now, she'd think about the thrill of Caldwell.

And after that . . . where would she go? That wasn't today's worry. She'd only think about the dancing, the parties, the kind of fun she'd never had living in a tumbledown shack on the edge of St. Joe.

Molly put the mirror away and looked at her hands critically. Pretty, long nails. Not for her the life of a washerwoman hanging over a scrub board like her ma. She thought about Ma now, wondering what had ever become of her. When Molly closed her eyes, she could see the kettle of boiling water on the fire out in the yard, smell the pungent, homemade lye soap, feel the steam on her face.

"I don't want to live like this, Ma," she complained, struggling with the kettle. Molly was fourteen, going on fifteen, the year she met Slade.

Ma brushed a wisp of gray hair from her eyes with a red, sore hand. "Be grateful you got food on the table and keep scrubbin'," Ma whined, reaching for another dirty shirt.

"I ain't grateful," Molly said with spirit, sorting through the clothes. "I'm too pretty to waste my life like this, I know it. The fellows in town tell me I am—"

299

Her ma came at her with the stirring stick from the wash pot and beat her about the head. "You stay away from those boys in town, you hear? They'll fill yore head with nonsense tryin' to get between yore legs!"

"Like Pa did yours?" She shouldn't have said it, knew better even as Ma beat her. But Molly Kelly, the washerwoman's daughter, had a rebellious streak.

"That's right!" Her head went up and down as she scrubbed a shirt collar. "And I been payin' for it ever since! I know what I'm tellin' you, girl, that's why you need to work hard and stop makin' eyes at men. We can have a good life if you'll just help with the washin'. . . ."

"A good life!" Molly scoffed. "You call bein' barely able to eat a good life?" She wiped blood from her lip and stared her mother down. "I never had me no fun in my whole life! I want fancy clothes and parties and men kissin' my hand and dancin' with me. . . ."

"Your vanity, your love of good times, will send you to an early death," Ma said direly, returning to her washboard.

Bill Slade, the town tough, had brought his shirts over for Ma to do. The way he looked the fourteen-year-old girl over let her know what he thought of her. He promised her fun and excitement if he could ever come by when Ma wasn't home. But when Molly planned it that way, his idea was to throw her down on the shack's floor and mount her in a frenzy. When she cried, he slapped her 'til her head rang. Then he gave her money to stop her weeping.

She looked at the silver in her hand as she wiped the blood from her thighs, deciding it was easier than doing laundry. She hadn't realized men would pay for that. Slade kept coming by, filling her head with stories about parties and fine dresses, about faraway places like San Francisco. It went on for months before Ma walked in unexpectedly one day while Molly was washing herself off. There was a terrible scene with Ma screaming "Jezebel" and taking a pair of shears to Molly's magnificent, long hair, leaving it cropped and ragged.

At that point, Molly threw a sadiron at her and fled the shack forever, moving in with Bill Slade.

It had been exciting—except when he beat her. Bill Slade was as mean as a riled porcupine. He had two partners, saloon toughs called Trask and the Mexican. The three of them sat around drinking and making plans about how to get rich without working for it. When Molly tired of the cramped hotel room, reminding Bill Slade that this wasn't what he had promised her, he beat her up again, letting his friends rape her while he watched and laughed.

Word must have gotten around that Slade needed a fourth man, a man extra good with a rifle. A handsome red-haired fella named Joe McBride showed up, desperate for money, saying he didn't care how he got it. . . .

Molly looked up and down Wichita's deserted street, wondering if the stage was going to be late. Joe McBride. She thought of Joe fondly, wondering whatever had happened to him. In all her life, there'd been only two men Molly really gave her heart to—and neither one of them loved her back. The first had been that big, handsome Kentuckian, Joe McBride. The other man was Maverick Durango. But she was a lot older than Maverick, almost old enough to be his mother, and she knew that she had no chance there, either.

If Joe hadn't spurned her, she might have had a son of her own; as it was, she had no one who really cared about her. She thought jealously of the woman he had spurned her for, wondering if he ever got his Annie back. Twenty-five years. Had it really been twenty-five years since she'd seen Joe that last time? *My, how time flies!*

The thought so depressed her that she got out her little mirror again, reassuring herself that she didn't look almost forty, touching the expensive combs smugly. Long ago, Molly's hair had grown out and never been cut since Ma had taken the shears to it, chopping it off around her ears. Men told Molly she had the most beautiful hair of any woman they'd ever met. They all seemed to like to tangle their fingers in it when they made love to her.

Joe McBride. She'd done her best to seduce him. There was something about his green eyes, his gentle ways, that reached out to her. A decent man like that should never have gotten mixed up with Slade, but he needed money bad. Wherever he was, he might think he was still wanted for murder. Molly smiled to herself with satisfaction. After all these years, the time limit on the robbery charge had surely run out. And Molly had contacted the sheriff in St. Joe, letting him know McBride didn't kill that bank teller.

Molly sighed now, looking up and down the Wichita street, wondering where that damned stage was. There wasn't a soul on the street except Wilbur, the telegraph operator. *Lord, he'd seen her!* She'd hoped to get out of town without having to say good-bye to him.

His Adam's apple bobbed in his thin neck. He saw her, changed directions, and came toward her, a scrap of paper clasped in his bony hand. *Did he ever go anywhere without that damned green eyeshade?*

"Molly, what's this? You goin' somewhere? You didn't say nothing about leavin'. . . ."

"Just decided to go last night after hearin' some of the cowboys talk about what a good-time town Caldwell was."

"But I'd thought maybe someday, you and me—well, you know. . . ."

She frowned at him and brushed a wisp of hair back

up into the fancy combs. "Just cause you give me a gift don't think it means you own me. You think I could live on a telegraph operator's salary?"

His Adam's apple bobbed. "Molly, them fancy hair combs cost me a whole month's salary," he gestured toward her. "I ain't always gonna be poor. I got big plans. . . ."

"Everybody's got big plans. Had me some myself before I had to face reality." She thought about Joe.

Molly stood up and shook the wrinkles out of her dark red traveling dress. "You ain't never gonna amount to much!"

"No, I got friends! And they're gonna cut me in on something." He stood looking at her hungrily, the forgotten paper clutched in his thin hands. "Gunmen! Real gunmen! All I got to do is let them know when the army payroll's gonna be transferred onto the Austin stage. It's secret! The army don't want to let anyone know about that payroll for all them soldiers in the Red River campaign, afraid the Indians'll attack in force."

She looked at him skeptically. "If there was a payroll, they'd send soldiers to guard it."

"Naw," he adjusted the eyeshade excitedly. "All them soldiers is busy fightin' Injuns! I think the army thinks if they ship it like a regular trunk, nobody'll notice, be any the wiser. . . ."

"Oh, Wilbur, you're just big talk," she scoffed.

"No, Molly, listen! I'm to wire them when the army decides the date, when the payroll box is goin' on the Austin stage, and my friends is gonna rob it as it goes through some little jerkwater town somewhere west of Austin, I don't know where just yet. But they'll cut me in for helpin' them!" He grabbed her arm, "I'll be able to buy you a lot of nice things besides just pearl combs. . . ."

She brushed his hand off in annoyance. "Is that what

that message is about?"

He glanced down in confusion at the obviously forgotten, crumpled piece of paper. "This? No, this is a message that finally got through for that little school teacher. The wire's back up again. Injuns keep cutting it. No telling how long it'll be back up this time."

That snippy little school teacher. Her lip curled in anger as she remembered the sassy little redhead sloshing water all over Molly and Maverick. "What happened to that little tart, anyway?"

Wilbur grinned, obviously delighted to be the bearer of bad news. "Why, she left town a week or so ago with that trail boss from the Triple D right behind her."

Molly felt a surge of jealous fury. "Maverick?"

"That's the one," he nodded with malicious delight. "Ain't he the one you broke a date with me over when he hit town? Everyone's says you was sweet on him."

"So what if I was?" She shrugged. "If they left town separately, that don't mean they met anywheres."

Wilbur adjusted his eyeshade against the early dawn light. "I figure they left separately so nobody would suspect nothin', figuring to meet up out on the prairie someplace. They rode off the same direction."

"Which way?"

"Southwest." He pointed off toward the flat, desolate prairie outside Wichita.

"There ain't nothing out there but buffalo grass and rampaging Indians." Molly peered that direction, remembering the redhead's words about Maverick accompanying her back to Texas. Jealously, she imagined them traveling together, sharing a blanket at night. . . .

"I don't know what to do with this message since she's gone. . . ."

"Message?" Molly looked from his thin face to the crumpled paper in his hand. "Who's it from?"

"Her daddy. I ain't supposed to discuss the wires that come through; that's confidential. . . ."

"Wilbur, don't get highfaultin on me." She held her hand out. "Everybody knows you gossip about all the messages you handle worse than some old ladies' sewing circle. Let me see it."

He hesitated only a moment before handing it over.

Molly stared at it. She reread it twice, then threw back her head and laughed. Tears came to her eyes as she stared at the paper. "Well, if that don't beat all! No wonder she looked so familiar to me! I kept thinkin' I'd met her someplace else! Joe's daughter! Joe's daughter!"

Wilbur stared at her. "Are you all right, Molly? What's this all about, anyway? If you know these folks, do you want to maybe send the daddy a wire, tell him he missed his daughter? It might be important to him. . . ."

"No, I'm not gonna send him no damned wire tellin' him they're on their way." Jealous fury made her hand shake as she crumpled the message, throwing it down in the dirt of the street.

She had lost Joe McBride to Annie, and now his and Annie's daughter had stolen Maverick from her. Hell, no, she wouldn't do anything to stop whatever was going to happen when they all came together. She was only sorry she wouldn't be there to see it. Maybe it was serious enough that the two men would shoot it out; maybe they would kill each other. Well, it was good enough for them!

Wilbur peered at her anxiously. "Are you all right, Molly? You don't look so good. Are you sure you don't want to do nothin' about this message?"

She thought about it a long moment. She could warn Joe with a quick wire that the pair was on their way; that might help him some. He'd managed to rescue that

305

Annie girl and had a daughter by her. Annie, the girl he'd spurned Molly for. Hell hath no fury like a woman scorned, Molly smiled slowly, watching the breeze blow the scrap of paper along the street toward the stagecoach that had just rounded the corner, rattling across the bridge.

"No," she said. "Forget it, Wilbur, it ain't important." She leaned over and picked up her valise.

The little telegraph operator caught her arm. "Don't go, Molly!" he whined. "These three guys is gonna cut me in on a big thing. I'll have money to buy you nice things. . . ."

"If they've got any kind of brains at all, they'll double-cross you, Wilbur, and you won't get a dime, maybe end up in jail—or dead."

He looked toward the stage rolling up, harness jingling, wheels creaking. The driver pulled back on the reins. "At least wait a while and think it over. Caldwell's no place to go right now. There's Indian war parties everywhere and the country between here and Territory is isolated and dangerous."

The driver of the stage stepped down. "You for Caldwell, ma'am?"

She nodded, handing him her valise. "Sure am, mister. They tell me the fun and the good times never stop in Caldwell. And fun and good times is what I'm after!"

The driver took the valise, shaking his head doubtfully. "Well, they do say it's a wide open, hell-raisin' town."

Molly let him help her up the step into the coach. "My ma always said I was bound for hell if I didn't change my ways," she laughed archly, flirting with him a little. "She said I'd never live to grow old, but I fooled her!"

The driver climbed back up on the stage beside the silent guard. She was the only passenger. Somewhere in the hot July Sunday morning, a church bell tolled the

306

faithful to rise and come to services. But her area of town, the street of saloons and sinners, slept peacefully on.

Wilbur gripped the door, looking up at her. "Don't go, Molly! Listen, we'll get married, go off somewheres when I come into my cut of that deal. . . ."

She yawned, weary of the little man who actually had tears in his eyes. "You make me sick," she smiled cruelly. "I hated it when you touched me. I only let you make love to me cause they was such nice combs." Molly reached up to touch the pearl ornaments. Then she leaned back in the seat as the stage pulled away, leaving Wilbur standing in the middle of the dusty street staring after her.

When she looked out the window, she saw the scrap of paper she had crumpled and thrown down, blowing along in the dust. *Damn men, anyway!* She hoped Maverick and Joe did have a go at each other, whatever their disagreement was. She was only sorry she wasn't going to be there to see it.

Hours passed as the stage headed south across the flat plains from Wichita. *They were making good time, probably ten or maybe even twelve miles an hour,* she thought with satisfaction. Maybe she should have gone to Dodge or Newton instead. She could take a train to those towns. But no, she wanted to be where the action was and she'd heard it was at Caldwell on the Chisholm Trail. Tonight, she'd be singing and dancing in a new saloon, someplace where the fun never ended. Molly smiled grimly, remembering her ma. *She'd show her. She'd show her.*

Molly leaned back against the seat, smiling in smug satisfaction. Yes, she'd made the right decision about leaving Wichita, about the message. All that talk about Indians was just that—talk.

The gunshot, as well as the sudden shout of the guard on top, made her jump. "Injuns! Injuns!"

She heard the driver crack his whip and the stage lurched forward as it picked up speed.

Alarmed, she leaned out the window, looking around as the coach swung forward crazily.

"Comanche!" the driver shouted, cracking his whip. "Comanches!"

Molly's heart beat in her throat. She looked off to the west and saw the mounted riders coming. Maybe it was just cowboys; maybe . . .

Their savage shrieks rent the air, echoing across the midday stillness. The pinto ponies galloped, gradually catching up to the moving stage. They were close enough to see the paint on their dark faces now. *Fiends straight out of hell,* she thought as the guard fired at them, firing again while the driver fought to control the team and keep the stage on the rutted trail.

As she gripped the window with white knuckles, looking around, she saw the war party gradually gaining on the running stage. She had a sudden memory of the things she'd heard of people committing suicide to avoid being taken alive, of men shooting their women to save them from being captured by the Indians.

Molly waved frantically at the guard as she hung out the window. "A pistol! Give me a pistol!"

He nodded, leaned off the swaying coach, and tried to hand a Colt through the window. But the coach jerked even as she reached for it with trembling hands. In that split second, she missed grabbing the pistol by inches and it fell, tumbling into the dust of the trail. The stage careened onward and the horror on the guard's face as he stared back at her reinforced the terrible danger of it all.

The lathered horses plunged forward as the driver shouted, cracking his whip again and again. But still the war party gained on them. The stage bounced again and her hairpins loosened so that the velvet black locks cascaded down her neck to her waist. Dust rose off the trail in clouds, choking her and settling on her lips, on the scarlet traveling costume she'd been so vain about.

The midday heat seemed to engulf her, suffocate her. She felt dampness under her armpits, perspiration running between her breasts, down her back. She smelled her own sweat of terror as she clung to the window ledge, watching the Indians moving up relentlessly, shouting and screaming.

The guard fired again and a brave shrieked, clutched at the sudden splash of red on his chest, and tumbled from his running paint horse.

The wind caught her long hair, blowing it around her shoulders in a wild, black cloud. The warriors seemed to realize for the first time that she was on board and she saw their faces light up with lust and anticipation.

She shouted up to the guard. "Oh, God! Don't let them take me! Don't let them take me!"

He hesitated, looking down at her hanging from the window, and as she looked up at him, she read his thoughts. A shotgun was all he had. But she was a vain woman, though a brave one. She didn't want her body mutilated even to protect herself from torture. She imagined a cavalry patrol finding her body with its face blown away.

Oh, no, dear God, she couldn't bear the thought of that! Shaking her head at the guard, she retreated back into the coach and lay back against the cushions, panting and trembling. No, she'd take her chances with the Indians rather than have her beauty marred! Ma always had scolded her about vanity!

The braves rode at a gallop along each side of the stage. Now she could see their grinning, painted faces. She cringed against the cushions, hoping to avoid their

309

stares, but the ugly one with the small, foxlike features gestured and fired arrows at the running stage horses.

The guard fired again, taking another brave from the saddle. The fox-faced one loosed an arrow from his bow toward the top of the stage, and then the guard screamed in agony, tumbled past her window, and hit the ground with a thud.

Horrified, she leaned out the window, looking at the prone form on the road behind them. Already, braves were dismounting running ponies, shrieking in triumph as they brandished skinning knives.

Even a shotgun blast in the face might beat what was waiting for her, she thought as she cringed against the seat, trying not to look at the grinning, triumphant faces riding alongside. But she'd passed up that chance and now it was too late.

A galloping brave aimed an antique rifle upward and fired. The shot echoed and reechoed. The driver screamed, falling from the coach as the horses, given their head, galloped madly through the churning dust of the hot July afternoon.

And then she felt the coach hit a rock, careening on two wheels for a moment before it broke free of the running team, spinning crazily as she bounced around inside. She wasn't going to survive the crash, she thought with giddy hysteria. She tried to hang on but she lost her grip as the stage rolled over and over.

But she wasn't dead. Her eyes flickered open. Maybe it was all a nightmare. Maybe she'd wake up back at her room in the Red Garter; maybe . . . She looked up, trying to focus her eyes. It finally came to her that she was lying on the ceiling of the stage staring up at the floor. She moved her arms and looked down at her legs in the confused swirl of red taffeta and petticoats. She wasn't hurt.

The door jerked open and the war-painted, foxlike

face peered in, laughing in triumph as she screamed. Roughly, he reached in and dragged her kicking and screaming out of the overturned stage toward a waiting circle of warriors.

The warriors laughed, speaking to each other in their own language. They looked just like the painted demons from hell that Ma used to describe would get her someday.

It suddenly occurred to her that they were just men after all, and wasn't she used to charming men? She stood up, smiled at them archly, and shook the wrinkles out of her clothes. "Any of you speak English?"

The sharp-featured one leered at her. "Me, Little Fox, I speak," he tapped his chest.

For the first time, she noticed he wore a stained Turkey-red shirt and a little beaded necklace around his dirty throat. Now why did those things look familiar to her? One of the others wore yellow satin sleeve garters on his bare, dark arms. She almost laughed at the way he looked.

Did she have the courage? "I—I know what men want," and she tried to smile at him. "Keep me for your woman. I'll make you very happy."

She paraded herself brazenly to the silent circle, shaking the magnificent long hair back. "Or let the soldiers ransom me for much food and guns."

Ransom. She thought of Annie Laurie and Joe's frantic attempts to save her. Maybe if Wilbur did get rich, he'd ransom her. . . .

Little Fox advanced on her, fingering the beaded necklace he wore. "You saloon girl? You sleep with buffalo hunters?"

"I sleep with any man who wants me." Was that what this brave wanted to hear? He came so close she could smell the dirt and sweat of his dark skin, the rancid bear grease smeared on his swarthy body. He smelled of the smoke of a thousand campfires.

"Buffalo hunters rape my sister, kill her." He fingered the necklace again with long arms. "We get them"—he patted the front of his red shirt—"make them beg and beg to die!"

Someone in the band translated and the warriors laughed, moving in closer. She realized abruptly that Little Fox stared at her silver and pearl hair combs.

She took them off and held them out. "You like? You can have!"

He took them with a sneer, putting them in his soot-black braided hair. The hot sun gleamed on them.

She tried to smile invitingly. After all, a man was a man, and if she pleased him, he would let her live, maybe let Wilbur ransom her.

He said something in his language, reached out suddenly, and caught the bodice of her dress. He ripped it to the waist so that her full breasts were visible. The other laughed and shouted encouragement.

Molly had to force herself not to cringe, not to show fear as his dirty hand caught her breast, squeezing cruelly.

"Buffalo hunter's woman!" He spat it at her, and she saw the anger, the livid hate in his dark eyes.

He struck her with his fist so that she stumbled backward and fell. Her mouth filled with her own blood, lying on her back as he jerked aside his loincloth and stood looking down at her, scorn and hate in his eyes.

With his big knife, he cut her dress, stroking his hard, erect manhood as he looked at her. "I treat buffalo hunter's woman like they treat my sister!" And he fell on her as the others watched like a pack of silent, hungry wolves.

He bit her breasts, raped her brutally while she lay there sobbing, choking on the blood from her torn lip. He stank of old grease and smeared her with his sweat.

312

His breath reeked of rotten raw liver.

This can't be happening, she thought wildly as he finished with her, but she didn't fight him. Bill Slade had treated her this way, too. And for money, she'd taken on white drunken hunters and brutal cowboys. The only gentle man she had ever known was Joe McBride and he'd never made love to her.

If she pleased him, maybe the brave would set her free. She didn't fight him, closing her eyes so she wouldn't have to look into his insane ones.

He rode her to a climax, grunting like any male animal in satisfaction. Then he stood up and gestured to one of the others. One by one, they fell on her, raping her savagely, biting her breasts and lips, bruising her with their hands. Several of them rolled her over and rode her from behind.

She tried not to think, to feel. She thought instead about how hot the dirt was beneath her bare body, about how the sun would darken her white skin she'd been so vain about.

When the last one of the dozen finished, Little Fox took her again as did most of the others, until her skin was smeared with the stink of their seed, the greasy sweat of their dark bodies.

All the time, her heart thumped with such fright that they grinned as they squeezed her breasts and made rude comments in their language.

Finally, Little Fox said, "I tire of this. It grows late. We must leave to go to the canyon to the south were we wait to meet Quanah."

She stood up, pulling her torn clothing around her, trying not to become hysterical. *She'd be forty years old tomorrow and she was going to live to be an old woman in spite of what Ma said.* "You can trade me to soldiers, to *Comanchero*," she stammered. "They'll pay good money. . . ."

313

He seemed to grin with relish at her terror. "Move fast," he gestured to the southwest. "Woman slow us down."

"Oh, but I won't!" She babbled, "I ride fast. And I'll warm your blankets at night!"

He smiled slowly as he advanced on her, and she remembered thinking how ridiculous he looked in a buffalo hunter's Turkey-red shirt, her pearl and silver combs in his black hair. He took out his knife and one of the warriors laughed, gesturing with a lance that had hair hanging from it.

Molly stared at the hair, stared and stared as Little Fox advanced on her. She turned to run but she was surrounded by the ring of silent predators.

"No!" she shrieked. "No!"

"For my dead sister!" She saw the sunlight reflect off the blade as it came down toward her eyes. *He's going to stab me!*

She tried to twist away from the sudden pain as the knife struck twice. The sudden darkness was agony and she screamed and screamed as she fought him.

She felt his hand grab her magnificent mane of hair, the sharp blade of the knife cutting along her hairline as he scalped her.

The he cut her throat with one swift move and threw her down to choke and struggle in the dirt, her scarlet blood soaking into the torn red tafetta, into the dust of the trial to Caldwell.

Little Fox threw back his head and laughed in triumph. "For my sister!" He held the long black hair aloft.

Now the war party mounted up, the fine ebony locks streaming from his Comanche lance as the braves turned and galloped off to their rendezvous.

Chapter Sixteen

Maverick had seen the soldiers coming for a long distance as he sat patiently at Cayenne's side, listening to her mumble, watching her thrash in her delirium.

Because of her snake bite, they had been stranded here for days. Food was beginning to run low and Maverick had been afraid to shoot passing buffalo or deer, not knowing whose keen ears might hear the sound of the echoing shots. For the last two days, he'd been catching long-eared jackrabbits in snares to make a rich broth for the semiconscious girl. But it worried him that they'd been in the same spot too long. Sooner or later, a war party would cross their trail and maybe follow it right into the small campsite by the spring.

And yet she couldn't ride, so they couldn't move on. It occurred to him once, as he thought bitterly of Joe McBride, that Maverick didn't need her any more. Maverick had gleaned enough information from the innocent Cayenne to find the man he'd sworn to kill.

The Comanche in him said, *Leave her here and follow your quest. She may die anyway, and what is she to you, this whelp of the wolf you hunt?*

But in his heart, he was as white as his mother's Kentucky ancestors; Annie had seen to that. It had been her final vengeance on her tormentors, her torturers.

The boy called Eagle's Flight could think like a warrior, track like a warrior, and if need be, kill without mercy like a Comanche brave. Against the tribe, there was no one so deadly as one who had been raised by them, knew all their tricks, all their hiding places. He looked at the sick girl as the boy, Eagle's Flight, would have and he thought of deserting her. But the man called Maverick Durango knew he could not do that; he loved her too much. She would not love him when he killed Joe, and he had sworn on Annie's dying body the night he escaped forever from his father's people. Soon Maverick could finally say after all these years, *Suvate; it is finished.*

It occurred to him now as the day lengthened into hot orange and yellow heat that the approaching cavalry patrol might shoot first and ask questions later. Quickly, Maverick changed from the warrior garb to pants and boots, stuffing the warrior things in his saddlebags. He was still attempting to wash all the war paint from his features when the small patrol rode their lathered horses into the little oasis.

Maverick raised his hand in greeting, but before he could speak, the captain shouted, "Grab the red bastard, Sergeant! Looks like we've caught Quanah Parker red-handed, not only with the colonel's gray horse, but with a white captive besides!"

"Now wait a minute," Maverick gestured. "I can explain—"

But the white officer and the black troops he led weren't going to give him a chance, Maverick realized in sudden horror, looking into their grim faces. He made a dive for his holster that lay near the unconscious girl, but a soldier reined his heaving mount in between Maverick and the weapon.

The captain leaned on his saddle horn, picking at a pustule on his scarred face as he grinned down at Maverick. *He was old for a captain*, Maverick thought; gray streaked his hair. "Christ! How lucky can I get! Maybe there'll be a promotion back to New York in this for me! You heard me, grab him, men!"

"Yes, Suh, Captain Baker!" Two of the black cavalry men dismounted and moved toward Maverick.

Maverick hesitated, looking from the middle-aged officer to the black troopers. "Now, wait just a minute," he shook his head, backing away. "You got this all wrong. . . ."

"Injun, you're the one who's wrong, gettin' caught red-handed like this!" The officer sneered. "Every soldier on the plains is on the lookout for Quanah, knowing he's leading this uprising. . . ."

"I'm not Quanah," Maverick backed away. "My name's Maverick Durango, and if you'll get in touch with the Triple D Ranch over in the Hill Country—"

"Christ! Don't try to fool me!" Baker picked at his face. "We all heard what Quanah looks like—big half-breed Comanche, eyes gray as a gun barrel."

Maverick hesitated. What should he do now? If he managed to escape, what would happen to the unconscious Cayenne? Could he depend on the cavalry officer to get her to safety in the supply wagon they had with them?

One of the black soldiers turned toward the mounted officer. "Suh, you want us to—?"

"Yes!" Baker swore under his breath as the two big blacks grabbed Maverick and he fought them. The officer dismounted and came around to face Maverick. "Stupid nigger troops I got! Seventeen years I been in this man's army and I don't get no promotions; they stick me in the Territory and give me nigger troops!"

Maverick stopped struggling, realizing he would have to talk his way out of this. The black soldiers frowned as they looked at the white officer. Obviously they didn't think much of him, either.

Maverick said, "Look, Captain, I'm a half-breed all right and I ride a gray horse, but that doesn't mean I'm Quanah Parker."

The officer studied the big gray. "You ain't no warrior? Ain't that a scalp I see dangling from that Injun bridle?"

He should have known that would get him in trouble. "I can explain about that. That gray's from the Triple D . . . ."

Baker motioned to his black sergeant. "O'Bannion, check the brand on that horse."

Maverick shook himself free of the two black soldiers. He watched the sergeant walk over and inspect Dust Devil's rump. The sergeant was a giant of a man with a lighter coffee-colored skin that betrayed white blood.

Sergeant O'Bannion pushed his hat back, rocking on his heels as he studied the horse. "It's shore 'nuff carryin' a Triple D brand, Suh."

The officer frowned, obviously not willing to admit he might be wrong. "That don't mean nothin'!" he snapped, taking out a handkerchief and wiping the sweat from his bumpy face. "I don't know where Colonel Mackenzie got his gray pacer to begin with and I need a promotion to get out of this hellish state! I can do that by bringing in Quanah, the colonel's horse." He gestured. "So tie up that half-breed and we'll take him along with us; sort the whole thing out when we get back to Fort Sill."

Maverick whirled, knocking down the first trooper that grabbed him, but now the rest of the soldiers ran to overpower him, tie his hands behind his back. "You're making a big mistake!" Maverick shouted and cursed. "By damn! You pus-faced bastard, I'll have your neck when the old Don Durango finds out what you've done to me!"

318

Captain Baker strode over, slugging Maverick now that he was safely tied up. Maverick tried to lunge at him anyway, half groggy from the blow, the sweet coppery taste of his own blood running in his mouth, down his lip.

"Shut up, Injun!" Baker shouted. "I never had a promotion all those years! First I got stuck at Fort Smith before the war, then almost court-martialed 'cause I made a mistake in a battle judgment. For that, they sent me to this hellhole to lead nigger cavalry!" He spat disdainfully as he pushed Maverick so that he stumbled and fell to the ground.

The man grinned down at him. "Christ! This may be my one chance to get out of this hellhole and it's certainly a good enough reason to turn back from this patrol!"

The giant black sergeant looked at Baker anxiously. "Beggin' yore pardon, Suh, but we ain't gonna continue searchin' for my big brother?"

"No." The Yankee officer went over to the spring and splashed his face. "I don't know why he deserted, he wasn't treated no worse than any of the rest of you niggers! We'd have hung him anyway if we caught him!" He filled his canteen, taking a long drink while the troops watched him thirstily.

"Suh," O'Bannion hesitated. "If you've had all you want, can the men get a little water?"

Baker yawned. "Yeah. I just wanted to get mine before they got their dirty mouths in it. I don't drink after horses, neither." He grinned at his little joke and Maverick saw the hatred for the officer reflected in the other men's eyes.

Cayenne moaned aloud and Maverick looked toward her anxiously, struggling against his bonds. "She's used to having me right by her side," he said. "She's been snake bit."

"Stay right where you are, Injun!" The man picked at his face as he went over, knelt by the prone girl, and stared down at her. "Christ! What a beauty! Haven't seen such a pretty gal since '58 when that blonde from Boston, Summer Van Schuyler, got carried off by the Cheyenne!"

Cayenne moaned again, thrashing restlessly on her blanket. Maverick tried to struggle to his feet to go to her, but the big sergeant reached out and grabbed him.

The captain laughed. "That's right, Sergeant, keep Quanah under control."

"I'm not Quanah," Maverick snarled, struggling in the big black's hands. Bound as he was, Maverick had no chance of breaking free and getting to Cayenne.

She moaned again and the Yankee leaned over, stroking her face. "She's beautiful, she—"

"Get your hands off her!" Maverick went loco at the sight of the other touching her pale, lovely face. "Get your dirty hands off my woman!"

It took three troopers to hold him while the officer laughed. "Your woman! I'll just bet you been mounting this poor, unconscious girl three or four times a day, you filthy savage! Why, I ought to—" He swaggered over to Maverick, unsheathing his knife while the troopers held the half-breed.

Baker grinned. "I ought to cut you, Injun, for rapin' that white girl. We ought to geld every Injun on the plains to protect decent women!"

Maverick froze, staring into Baker's eyes as the man turned the knife over in his hands. Should he try to talk his way out of it, fight his way toward his horse?

The black sergeant stepped halfway between the two men. "Suh," he ducked his head humbly, "I ain't exactly interfering, but you don't have no orders to do nothin' to Quanah if you catch him."

"Nigger, don't tell me what to do!" Baker brandished

320

his knife and Maverick held his breath. It occurred to him that they were a long way from civilization. If Baker decided to kill Maverick and leave him for the buzzards, the blacks might be afraid to report it. "Christ! I suppose you've got a point, O'Bannion! This heat is gettin' to me! It was crazy to send us out looking for one lousy black bugler even if he did play the best of any of 'em."

Black bugler. Deserter. The pieces fell neatly into place. Maverick suddenly remembered the dark man at Adobe Walls playing charges for the warriors.

The New Yorker went back to stare down at Cayenne. "We'll wait 'til dark, then start moving toward the fort."

Maverick swore with fury. "You can't move her! She's sick! You can see that!"

Captain Baker leaned over, put his hand on the girl's shoulder and she smiled in her sleep. "Maverick," she whispered. "Maverick."

Baker leered up at him maliciously. "You're rotten, you known that? Even with her unconscious and helpless, you've been climbin' her, ain't ya? Well, I might try a little myself some night as we move back to the fort. She won't know the difference and my troopers won't tell."

"By damn, I'll kill you if you try that!" Maverick snarled and struggled to reach the grinning man. "I'll tell them at the fort and you'll end up in the stockade . . ."

"The stockade'd beat riding around looking for nigger deserters and takin' a chance on losin' my hair to Injuns." Baker stood up. "If she'd let an Injun touch her, she's just a slut and don't deserve no respect. Besides, nobody at the fort would take niggers' or Injuns' word against a white officer's."

Maverick glared at him then with eyes as cold as winter's ice. "You touch her," he whispered, "and I'll hunt you down, let you die slowly as only Comanche

321

know how!"

The officer looked at him a long moment, then shivered and stood up. "Big talk," he scoffed, "and it's a long way to Fort Sill. You may not make it, Injun."

"You may not, either," Maverick reminded him. "You know how many Indians you may have to ride through to get back to the Indian Territory?"

The other man swore. "I know better than you what my chances of gettin' grabbed by a war party are! This is a full-fledged Uprising and the biggest bunch of troops ever thrown into an Indian campaign—some three thousand, I hear."

Maverick whistled low and leaned against a tree. "Even the combined tribes won't stand a chance against a force like that even if the Kiowa decide to join them."

Baker laughed. "Don't play innocent with me, Quanah," he tipped his hat back. "You know as well as anyone the Kiowa hit the warpath a couple of weeks ago when those supplies they'd been promised never arrived."

Maverick frowned. "What about Pat Hennessy? He was trying to get there in plenty of time with food. . . ."

"Aha!" The officer's eyes gleamed in triumph. "So you admit you were there!"

Maverick shrugged. "I don't know what the hell you're talking about! Yes, we ran across Pat Hennessy and—"

"And tortured all those poor devils, turned the wagons upside down, stole or wasted all those supplies!"

"No," Maverick shook his head. "You ask Pat about—"

"A dispatch finally got through. Hennessy's dead and you admit you were there!" The officer crowed. "This ought to get me a promotion, a permanent assignment back east!"

"Dead? Pat Hennessy's dead? When did it happen?"

Maverick felt dread and horror deep in his soul. Now the Kiowa would take the war trail, too, and there would be even more death and destruction.

"As if you didn't know," the other sneered. "You red devils must have caught him sometime between July 2 and 4; the bodies were in too bad a shape to know for sure. Poor Hennessy'd been tied upside down to one of his own wagon wheels, roasted alive over a fire."

Maverick cringed, remembering the big, good-natured man. If he and Cayenne had ridden along with the teamsters, they would have been caught by the raiders, too.

The New Yorker leaned back against a rock, lighting a cigar as the troopers scurried around, setting up camp and tying horses to a picket line. "The army intends to surround you red bastards. Mackenzie's coming up from the South, Major Price from New Mexico to the West, Colonel Miles down from Fort Dodge, and the nigger troops from Fort Sill, Indian Territory and Fort Richardson in Texas are moving in to help close the trap."

Maverick could almost pity the Indians. "If the army had kept all those damned buffalo hunters off the tribes' hunting grounds, this Uprising wouldn't have happened."

The smaller man took a deep pull of his cigar. "Don't give me that 'bleeding heart stuff' about breakin' treaties, Quanah. Sooner or later, the whites are gonna take all this land, no matter what kind of treaties we sign! The buffalo hunters are doin' America a favor by killing off all the game so we can starve the tribes back onto the reservations."

Maverick gave him a long look. "And you call us savages?"

That night, the troopers loaded the unconscious Cayenne in the wagon, forced the resisting and still bound

323

Maverick onto his gray stallion, and started east. The fact he had to mount the gray from the right side only seemed to further convince Baker that Maverick was really an uncivilized Indian. Maverick watched closely every time the officer rode close to the wagon and stared down at the helpless girl. The expression on the pitted face gave away his emotions. Sooner or later, Baker might try to take advantage of her unconscious condition.

Maverick noticed the big black, O'Bannion, watching with sympathetic eyes. Here might be someone who would help him. But that first night, he never got a chance to visit with the sergeant.

They found a spring to camp near at dawn and spent the day there. Cayenne seemed to be feeling much better, Maverick noted with relief. She never became completely conscious, but she did rouse enough for Maverick to feed her and take care of her needs. The captain let him, seeming amused by the sick girl's dependence on the half-breed. *She didn't seem aware that the soldiers existed or that anything was wrong*, Maverick thought as he sponged her face.

Well, there was no use in alarming her. The passage of time was to her advantage, since she seemed to be getting stronger and Maverick had not yet come up with a plan to escape from the patrol. When she finally did rouse enough the second night to ask about the soldiers, Maverick lied, telling her they had picked up an army patrol escort all the way through west Texas. He didn't tell her they were really headed southeast toward Fort Sill in the Indian Territory.

And Baker couldn't have been more charming, more solicitous to Cayenne as she drifted in and out of consciousness. But the New Yorker seemed preoccupied with being deep into hostile Indian country. Maverick figured it was only a matter of time until that officer felt

324

secure enough to halt the patrol and enjoy the sick girl while the black troops looked on helplessly. Maverick struggled with the ropes that bound his hands behind him until his wrists were raw and bleeding, but he couldn't escape. He had a feeling that when the swaggering, pimply-faced man finally raped the helpless, half-conscious Cayenne, he'd enjoy making Maverick watch. And of course he'd deny it if Cayenne told on him when they got back to the fort. What white man would listen to or care about any woman who'd been sleeping with an Indian or a 'breed? He thought of Annie again and gritted his teeth.

The third night, the horses were exhausted from being pushed too hard by the inexperienced officer. He made the decision to let the patrol sleep a few hours and move on in the middle of the night. The big sergeant, O'Bannion, stood guard duty that evening. When the camp was quiet, Maverick jerked his head at him.

The coffee-colored man crossed through the sleeping forms around the small fire, coming over to where Maverick lay trussed on the outside edge of the circle. "What you want, Renegade?"

"Can't you loosen these ropes a little?" Maverick whispered. His arms ached from being tied behind his back and he could feel dried blood from the rope cutting into his wrists.

The sergeant squatted down and made a clicking sound of sympathy. "That Baker is a sonovabitch," he whispered, and he untied the ropes and offered Maverick a small sack of tobacco, and a paper.

Maverick took them, nodded his thanks, and rubbed the circulation back into his raw wrists before rolling a cigarette. "You're okay, O'Bannion. You know I'm not Quanah, don't you?"

The black man nodded. "It don't make no sense even

if you are a gray-eyed half-breed riding a gray horse. Why would a chief be out in the middle of nowhere lookin' after a snake bit white girl?"

Maverick smoked and studied the young man. "Where you from?"

"Tennessee. A big plantation called Shannon Place on the Mississippi."

"Your daddy a white slave owner?"

O'Bannion's round face broke into an amused grin. "My Daddy's half white, but he wasn't sired by Mr. Shawn, no Suh! My daddy's mama was raped by some big cracker back in Georgia and Mr. Shawn O'Bannion bought her when she was sold down the river. Finest man who ever drew breath, Mr. Shawn is; got rich in the California gold strike." The quadroon paused. "My older brother's just a little crazed, you know, like maybe he inherited a streak of loco meanness from that white man. If I can find him and have a chance to straighten him out, take him back home—"

Maverick smoked a long moment. Should he tell? End the black's quest? It seemed a merciful thing to do. "O'Bannion, you been kind to me, so I'm gonna tell you something so you won't spend the rest of your life worryin' about your brother."

The strong dark features studied his a long moment. "You got bad news, don't you? The Indians get him, torture him to death? He was always talkin' about oppressed people, how we ought to join together, rise up against the whites."

Maverick smoked, remembering the black bugler sounding the charges at Adobe Walls. "Your brother was a brave man, a very brave man. He did join the Indians."

O'Bannion didn't say anything for a long moment. "I was hopin' he finally found the freedom he was looking for, a little happiness."

"He did," Maverick said softly. "I think those weeks

326

he spent with the Indians must have been happy ones if he was willing to fight on their side. They at least accepted him, treated him like an equal."

"You're telling me he's dead?"

Maverick tried to think of something comforting to say. His heart went out to the young black man. Finally, he nodded. "Yes, he's dead. Killed in a charge. Never knew what hit him. To die bravely and quickly is all a real man, black, white, or red, can aspire to."

The other ducked his head so Maverick couldn't see his brown face, made a choking sound for a long moment. A slight breeze blew the scent of campfire smoke toward them, a cricket chirped somewhere, a horse snorted and stamped its feet. The heat of the night enveloped Maverick as he waited and smoked, the tobacco abruptly bitter to his mouth. Without thinking, he reached over, put his hand on the big black's shoulder, and felt him shaking with sobs a long moment.

The sergeant finally seemed to get control of himself. "Thanks for telling me that. I can let Pa know now. We won't have to wait and wonder what happened to him. Did you bury him?"

Maverick nodded. He wouldn't tell him that the hunters had mutilated the bodies in a frenzy of revenge after they drove the Indians off, that the brother's head was even now impaled, rotting and stinking, on one of the posts of the fence in front of the settlement's store. "He died bravely and without pain," he murmured again.

"Thanks." He rubbed his face against his sleeve. "If you never had to wait to find out if someone you love is dead or alive, you don't know what real pain is."

Maverick wondered suddenly if Joe McBride had wondered and worried all those years over Annie. Of course not, otherwise he would have figured out a way to ransom her like he did those women and kids at the

327

church outing. But would the kind of man he thought Joe McBride was do something as brave as what Cayenne had described? The whole thing was becoming more and more confusing to him.

"There's a worse pain," he whispered, remembering, "and that's being the instrument of that loved one's death." He saw Annie's plain little face all twisted in agony, begging him, begging him. . . .

They smoked in silence. Finally, O'Bannion said, "You love that girl, don't you?" He nodded toward the wagon where Cayenne lay sleeping peacefully.

Did he? Maverick struggled with an agony of indecision. When he'd started out to kill her father, she had been part of his revenge. He had imagined throwing her down before her father, all dishonored and shamed, her belly swollen with Maverick's child. He had intended to gloat over it a few minutes before he tortured Joe to death. Then he would ride out, leaving her weeping and abandoned the way his mother had been abandoned. But now, as he thought about it, he realized he wanted the girl badly, wanted her by his side for all time, wanted to sire her children, raise them. *Eagles mate for life*, he remembered.

"I reckon I do," he answered grudgingly. "I've been afraid that damned captain of yours would rape her before we get to the fort."

"He might do it yet, the rotten bastard!" O'Bannion drawled. "I've been tryin' to figure what to do. . . ."

"Help us escape," Maverick said, tossing the cigarette away.

The black sergeant looked at him a long moment. "My brother hated the captain. I suppose that's why he run off and deserted. Tell you what," O'Bannion wiped his eyes. "I'll load up a packhorse with supplies and unhobble those two horses you rode in on."

Maverick looked toward the wagon. "She's in no

shape to ride. I'll have to hold her in my arms to get out of here."

The buffalo soldier nodded as he got up. "Baker sleeps like the dead. I'll give you a couple of hours' start, and along about dawn, I'll jump up like I've been layin' unconscious all night and shout that you've escaped."

Maverick gave him an admiring look. "There'll be the devil to pay."

The sergeant sighed. "I reckon I can be as brave as my older brother, and I'm much obliged for your kindness to him." He held out his big hand hesitantly and Maverick shook it.

"O'Bannion, you're as brave as any black lion hunter in your native Africa. I appreciate this. Maybe someday our paths will cross again. . . ."

O'Bannion waved his thanks aside. "We got things to do . . . friend."

"Sure . . . friend."

Moving stealthily, they saddled up the horses, got supplies. Two black troopers raised their heads and the sergeant motioned them to silence, so they put their heads down, pretending to sleep. "We're all loyal to the government," O'Bannion whispered, "even if it don't always treat the black troops right. But we wouldn't do a thing to help old Baker get his promotion even if it would get him outa our outfit!"

And so Maverick gathered up Cayenne, unconscious and feverish though she was, and placed her on the saddle before him. Leading her roan and the packhorse, he sneaked out of the dark camp and headed back southwest. Her body burned with fever as he held her close against him, but he knew they must escape before this white officer decided to rape her or maybe kill Maverick.

He walked the horse until he was safely away from the

sleeping camp, waving back at the black sergeant. Then he took off at a gallop, Strawberry and the packhorse struggling to keep up with the gray's powerful long legs. Her small body burned into his as he cradled her in his arms. Once she stirred as they galloped and the green eyes flickered open. "Maverick?"

"That's right, baby," he whispered, holding her fever-ish body close to his chest. "I'm here; I'll always be here. Everything's going to turn out all right."

He was lying, of course. How could it turn out all right when she found out too late that Maverick had used her to find Joe? She would hate him and curse him when she saw her father's dead body. The image of her tearful face upset him. To dispel it, he remembered another tearful face—Annie's face the night Pine da poi and the warriors had tortured her. . . .

A stiff wind blew sand like sharp needles as Maverick rode southwest. He tried to protect her small form with his body, only grateful that the shifting sand would cover their tracks so the patrol couldn't track them.

By dawn, he had found his way back to a small spring where they had rested yesterday. He dismounted, hid the horses in straggly brush, and carried Cayenne into the lea of the bushes for shelter. Her body still burned with fever. As the wind died to a feeble whisper, he decided that cool water would help. Maverick carried her into the small pool, staying there with her until his muscles were cramped and aching. But finally, her body seemed to cool and her eyes flickered open.

"Maverick? What happened? Oh, the snake—"

"I killed it, baby." He could only sigh with relief that she seemed to be conscious, clearheaded. He carried her, naked and wet, to lay her on a blanket, and got her some canned milk from the pack horse.

Away off to the north, he saw a faint smoke signal. There were war parties in the area. The blood froze in his

330

veins a little. Did he still speak enough Comanche to pass himself off as one? He'd better dress the part. Quickly, he stripped his clothes off, stuffing them in his saddlebags. In minutes, he was naked except for moccasins and a breechcloth, beads and war paint hastily applied to his face. If nothing else, he'd say he was Quanah's brother. The *Quahadis* were such an isolated band staying way out on the *Llano Estacado* that the chances were small any of the other bands would know what Quanah's brother looked like. And surely if he crossed the trail of the Comanche's allies, those tribes wouldn't have met Quanah's brother.

He thought about Pat Hennessy as he lay down next to Cayenne and watched her. It was ironic that the Kiowa would now take the war trail because Hennessy's wagons of food for them had been destroyed by some of the other rampaging tribes, the Kiowas' own allies who hadn't even realized where the food was bound for.

Cayenne opened her eyes and smiled up at him. "Have I been out long?"

"Long enough." He put his hand on her forehead. It was cool to the touch. "Thank goodness the fever's broken." She'd recover rapidly now and be able to ride again so they could move on toward their final destination. Suddenly he dreaded reaching that place. "We'll rest here through the heat of the day and ride out tonight. Remember, I'll be a Comanche warrior, and if we run across a war party, I'll pretend you're a captive and I'll try to talk our way out of it."

She reached out and put her arms around his neck. "I am a captive, Maverick," she said softly. "I love you."

Would she love him when he killed Joe McBride? He knew the answer. "Naw," he shook his head, trying to disengage himself. "You're just grateful, that's all."

She wouldn't let him pull away so he quit trying, enjoying the womanly scent of her, the velvet feel of her body against his. While she'd been sick, he'd missed the scent of vanilla on her skin again. He'd grown to love that perfume. "Sugar cookies," he said aloud without thinking.

Her small, freckled face was very close to his. "What?"

He felt himself flush, looking down at her. "When you wear vanilla, I always think of sugar cookies."

She laughed weakly, pulled him down, and kissed his lips. "Nibble on me a little, then."

"Are you loco? You've been sick. . . ."

"I'm not now." She reached up, kissing him again, thoroughly, expertly. He suddenly remembered her inept innocence out in front of the Red Garter Saloon. God, had she learned fast! He relaxed, letting her pull his face down to hers, kiss the corners of his mouth.

When this was all over, when they reached their destination, she was going to hate him, maybe try to kill him. He imagined not having her in his arms ever again, not having her nibble at the corners of his mouth. But he had sworn and he had a duty to a dead woman. He wouldn't think of that now. He would think of the way her hands caressed his dark nipples, the way her small pink tongue slipped between his lips.

"Stop it," he murmured. "We've got no business doing this. . . ."

But she didn't stop kissing him, and he found his hand traveling down her wet skin, stroking her small breasts into hard peaks of excitement, caressing her body all over.

"Baby," he muttered, "we shouldn't. . . . We shouldn't. . . ."

She opened her lips, sucking his tongue deep into her mouth as her hand went down to clasp his throbbing manhood.

He moaned aloud at the touch of her hand on his erect

332

hardness. "Baby, no."

"Baby, yes!" She whispered and pulled him on top of her, wrapping her thighs around his hard hips. His war paint smeared against her creamy skin as his lips went all over her body to kiss and caress. He winced as she dug her nails into his bare back when he sucked her nipples into twin mounds of erect pinkness, running his tongue down to the hollow of her navel. "Take me, dearest, take me!"

Then he took her very gently, in a slow symphony of lovemaking that rose to a crashing crescendo of desire and fulfillment. And he had never felt such happiness in any other woman's arms.

Later, as he lay next to her, propped up on one elbow, looking down at her sleeping face, a disturbing thought came to him. Suppose she had figured out that he was on a mission of revenge. Would she lure him with her body, try to tantalize him into changing his mind? Could this innocent-looking girl have some dire plot and plans of her own? Suppose she didn't really care about him? Suppose she was only trying to soften him, keep him from hunting down Joe McBride?

He didn't like that thought, but he suddenly realized it might possibly be true. Hadn't he used her to his own ends? Finally, he, too, slept, one arm thrown protectively across her small form. They rested there through the heat of the next day and made love again.

"Maverick," she whispered, "never leave me . . . never leave me."

He remembered his mother's words. "I'll be with you in spirit, always," he said softly, "even if I can't be there in body."

She blinked up at him. "What does that mean?"

He swallowed hard. "Nothing, I reckon. I don't mean nothing." He kissed her again to hush her and they slept

333

the afternoon away in each other's arms.

By dark, she was much stronger and he considered that they must ride on under cover of darkness. What was worrying him was that distant signal smoke he had seen on a far horizon the night before. Did the Comanche know exactly where the pair was?

Before he could carry his troubling thoughts any farther, he thought he saw a flicker of light on a far horizon and sat up. *Was that a signal fire far away on the bluff? Was a war party even now watching the couple?* Had they been watching all this time as Maverick had ridden through the darkness?

He stood up, a chill running down his back in the hot air as the sound of a bird call came to him, a bird he knew was not found in this area. A war party. Had he saved her from the army patrol only to lose her to a bunch of torturing Comanche?

Chapter Seventeen

He didn't tell her his fears as he awakened her. They rode out under a velvet black sky, a bright gold moon that Texans called a "Comanche" moon. Maverick shivered a little as he thought about it. Comanche were one of the tribes who liked to raid at night when the moon was big as a gold piece so they could see their way into the Texas settlements and the lonely ranches.

He had been on two raids himself against the *tah-bay-boh*, the whites. As a half-grown boy, he'd accompanied his dead father's younger brothers. But Annie had had her ultimate revenge. Although his skin was dark, the boy called Eagle's Flight had a heart that was as white as his mother's pale skin. On both raids, he had seen women hiding under hay in the barns, ignoring them so as to spare them while the warriors fired the houses, torturing the hapless cowboys who had fallen into their hands.

The couple rode southwest. The hot night breeze caressed his bare skin, for he rode dressed as a warrior would for battle, wearing only moccasins and a breechcloth, he and his horse painted for war.

He looked over at the proud, brave girl who rode

beside him, loving her, wanting her. It was bitter irony to him that she was Joe's daughter. For that reason, she was lost to him because of his duty, his vow. He looked up along the rim of low buttes, saw the signal fires, and knew they were being watched. Maverick would die to protect his woman but it might not be enough. No one could outride or outrun a Comanche war party if they took up the pursuit. His best weapon was deception, trickery.

"Cayenne," he said as they slowed the horses to a walk to rest them, "you're a very brave girl, but you're going to have to be braver."

He saw the puzzlement on her beautiful face as she looked at him. "Why?"

He memorized all the features of her face as he studied her so he could commit them to memory for all the lonely years that lay ahead of him without her. "I've got to tie you up. Don't look over at the horizon," he whispered, "just keep looking ahead."

She did as she was told, but he caught the sudden tension in her profile, her voice, as he leaned over, tying her hands behind her back with the rawhide thong from his gun belt. "What is it, Maverick? What in God's name are you trying to tell me?"

"There's a war party watching us from the ridge."

He heard her gasp but she recovered, kept staring straight ahead as they rode. "How—how long have they been there? What do we do?"

"I spotted them nearly an hour ago, but there's no point in trying to outrun them."

"Why haven't they attacked?"

He shrugged. "Still trying to figure out who we are, what we're doing riding through this desolate country that belongs to them."

Out of the corner of his eye, he saw them clearly

silhouetted against the Comanche moon on the ridge. Bile pushed up into his mouth as he remembered some of the things he had seen them do to captives.

"Maverick, I—I'm scared." But she kept riding, looking straight ahead.

"So am I, baby, so am I." His hands were wet with cold fear and it seemed to him he could smell his own terror along with the scent of wildflowers, sweating horses. The leather of his saddle creaked rhythmically as the gray picked its way across the barren, rough ground.

"Cayenne," he said, "they'll be coming down here to intercept us any minute. With any luck, they won't be from my old band, won't know me from the past." His hand went up to touch the jagged white scar on his dark war-painted face.

"And if we aren't lucky?" She looked over at him.

"We won't worry about that now." His hand went to the pistol on his hip. He would never let them take her alive, he vowed silently, trying not to think of the other woman whose torture he had ended. "If they don't recognize me, maybe I do look enough like Quanah to pass myself off as his brother, Pecos, and that's why I'm riding his gray horse."

"Suppose they're from Quanah's band?"

He looked over and saw the silhouettes start down a train off the rim of the world, riding silently as spectres in the darkness. "In that case, you better put that religion of yours to work, Cee Cee; start praying for some kind of miracle."

She didn't answer and he watched her. Her head had bowed and her lips moved silently. Funny, he had no religion, although the Durangos were Catholic and of course he no longer believed in the Gods of the Comanches. He glanced up at the big black bowl of a sky overhead; the stars blinking from millions of miles away. Was there really Anybody up there to hear her prayers? If so, would He listen? Then Maverick had no more time to think because the Comanche war party galloped toward them.

"Cayenne," he said softly as they rode near, "I'll pass you off as a captive, a gift for my brother Quanah."

The girl looked at him a long moment. He saw the fear in the green eyes, but she didn't panic. "You could revert to being an Indian again, couldn't you? Save your own life that way?"

He nodded, watching the warriors ride closer. So far he didn't recognize any of them. "I suppose I could. Either way, baby, your life is in my hands now. You got no choice but to trust me."

She tried to smile but he saw the tremble of her lips. "I'd trust you with my life, Maverick, I love you. There's something I've got to tell you about why—"

"No time," he muttered, "and stop calling me Maverick. You're a captive, remember?" *I love you, too,* he thought. *Why didn't I tell you while I still had time?*

The war party made its way down the crooked trail off the rim and galloped toward them. The bright moon cast giant, grotesque shadows of running horses and the men riding them along the rough terrain looked like spirit horses coming up out of hell.

"Maverick," she whispered, and he glanced over at her, saw the terror on her face. "I—I can't just sit here and wait; I'm going to run for it!"

"Shut up, captive," he snapped, reaching over and grabbing the roan's reins looped over her saddle horn. To try to run now would mean her death.

It was too late for anything as the war party thun-

338

dered up, surrounding them.

Maverick raised his hand in a traditional gesture of greeting and spoke in Comanche. "I am much relieved to see you." He leaned on the saddle horn easily, smiling even though his lips seemed too tense to bend into that curve. "I need a place to rest until I continue toward the camp of the *Quahadis.*"

The warriors visibly relaxed as they heard the familiar sound of their own language. "What band are you? Where do you go? Who is this white woman?"

Maverick looked them over, almost sighing with relief when he realized he knew none of them. There was even one Kiowa and a Cheyenne riding with the party.

"I am Pecos," he lied glibly, "brother to the great Quanah. He has loaned me his fine horse for my raid, and we are supposed to meet to the west."

Now he faced smiles, nodding heads. "Ah, yes, the great Quanah! We heard about the horse!"

The braves laughed and joked with Maverick and each other. All seemed to know the daring tale of the bold young half-breed stealing "Bad Hand" Mackenzie's favorite pacer.

The ugly leader had a hooked nose and red war stripes painted across his dark face. His pinto mustang was also painted for war. "I am Wind Runner and we welcome you, Pecos! I see you wear a *Tejanos'* pistol." He looked Cayenne up and down. "The Texan must have fought hard to keep her silence since she is indeed a prize!"

Maverick shrugged. "I killed him. Do you not see his hair hanging from my bridle? I took her on that raid and got separated from the others. The flame-haired one is a gift for my big brother."

The Comanche laughed. "Since it is a custom of

our people to let brothers share each other's women, have you enjoyed her?"

For a moment, he did not think he would be able to answer because of the horrible images that the man's words brought to his mind. He was a small, helpless boy again, covering his ears to her weeping while his dead father's four brothers enjoyed Annie. "Of course! Would I give my brother a gift I had not checked for quality?"

The men laughed and made rude jokes. Now the leader motioned, "Come with us. Many of our people along with the Cheyenne and some of the Kiowa are gathered in the great canyon a few miles ride to the south."

Palo Duro canyon, that great chasm on the west Texas plains that white men didn't seem to know existed. It should have occurred to Maverick that the warring Indians would gather there. It was also a good place to meet the *Comancheros* who brought the guns.

He nodded assent. They all wheeled their ponies and Maverick fell in beside the war party leader, visiting easily in the tongue he had not spoken in the ten years since he had escaped the Comanche as a boy of fourteen. He didn't look back at the trussed Cayenne while he held onto the roan's reins. To show any concern for her welfare might give the lie away.

Maverick looked at Wind Runner, then back at the Kiowa with his traditional hair style—braided but on the right side, cut short and hanging about the right ear. "The Kiowa ride with us now? I thought they were still discussing whether to take the peace trail."

The other made a noise of contempt. "You know the Kiowas! They talk a subject to death in council before they make a move, not like the Comanche who love to take action!"

340

Maverick grunted in agreement. "They have finished this season's sun dance then?" Any Indian would know the Kiowas were too superstitious to start any action until they had completed the strong medicine of the yearly sun dance.

"Yes, a few days ago. Were you there for our people's own first sun dance?"

Maverick snorted in disdain as they rode forward. He wanted to look back and give Cayenne some gesture of reassurance, knowing how frightened she must be, but he dared not. "Since when do Comanche copy the Kiowa and Cheyenne?"

Wind Runner shook his head. "The *Nerm* have become as frightened children, not knowing which way to turn now that all our medicine seems bad. We thought we would try the magic of that ceremony. The Cheyenne have joined this war and the Kiowa force is growing every day. Soon there will be thousands of us gathering in and we'll spread out, drive all the white men from our buffalo plains. Then things will be as they were before."

"Nothing can be as it was before," Maverick answered. "Somehow we must adjust to the changes or be destroyed."

The other warrior thought about it a minute as they rode through the cool night in silence. "No doubt you are right, but we do not know how to change so we must fight to keep things as they always were. No man worthy of the name stands by without taking action while his children starve. That is why the Kiowa have finally come."

"Oh?"

Wind Runner nodded. "They were promised food and supplies, but the wagons never arrived. More white men's lies!"

Maverick imagined Pat Hennessy tied upside down to his wagon wheel, screaming his life away while he was tortured. Unwittingly, the Cheyenne had taken the action that had finally brought the reluctant Kiowa into the plains war. "The Cheyennes to our north are coming to join us?"

"Yes. Many of their war parties are already raiding up through that area the whites call Kansas." He snorted in disgust. "They give it a name as if it belonged to them! The buffalo plains belong to us and we shall retake them! Isa-tai has foretold it! Many of the warriors of our band, led by Little Fox, are even now at that place the white hunters gather to buy supplies, and when that is destroyed, we will sweep out across the plains like a prairie fire of death!"

Adobe Walls, Maverick thought, but he said nothing. He could not reveal his presence at that place by telling that the Indians had lost that fight.

It took them the rest of the night and all the next day to ride to the Palo Duro. During that time, he was forced to treat Cayenne as any warrior might treat a captive, so as not to arouse suspicion. He handled her roughly, slapped her when she tried to object, fed her and watered her last of all at the small muddy sinkholes they came to, even after the horses had drunk. Her wide, accusing eyes studied him with such a betrayed expression that he felt shame and could not look at her. He dare not treat her better, show her any consideration. She would be safer anyway if she thought he had gone back over to his father's people, if she did not try to talk to him.

It was evening, with the sky all mauve and pink and purple as they rode to the bluff overlooking the giant

342

Palo Duro. The colorful canyon was more than a hundred miles long and eight hundred feet deep in places, Maverick remembered. The Prairie Dog Fork of the Red River had cut through the soft soil to gorge it out and the river still twisted a crooked path through the bottom like a long snake writhing in its death throes. *Probably no white man even knew it existed as a haven for the Indians here in the Texas Panhandle,* Maverick thought.

Below the war party stood hundreds of tepees along the small stream. As Maverick looked down, he saw the orderly circle of the Cheyenne lodges among the sagebrush, the stunted, twisted junipers that had given the canyon its name. *Palo Duro. Hard Wood, the Spanish had called it.* The Kiowa tepees stood strung out along the water since that tribe only circled its lodges during the ceremony of the Sun Dance. People moved like ants below him. From the rim, he saw at least a thousand Comanche, Cheyenne, Kiowa, maybe a few Arapahoe and renegade Kiowa-Apache gathered around campfires. Hundreds of horses munched contentedly on the rich grass.

Talk about riding into a hornet's nest, Maverick thought with alarm. He grunted, "The canyon is a good place for the tribes to gather during this war. The white men will never find it!"

The hook-nosed one nodded in satisfaction. "The *Comanchero,* old Pedro, whom we have dealt with for years, is due in a few weeks to bring more guns and powder. We have been hitting the settlements for booty to pay for weapons." He glanced back at the silent, weary Cayenne. "If your brother has no need of this gift," he said, "no doubt the fire-haired woman would bring much gold if sold for the *Comancheros'* pleasure or some Mexican whorehouse below the border. We have often done that in the past."

Maverick struggled to hold his temper, wanting to knock the brave from his paint horse for his suggestion. The thought of any man even caressing her arm, touching her face, almost drove him to a frenzy, but he must control his fury. "Maybe you are right," he shrugged as if bored. "If the great Quanah doesn't want her when I finally meet him out at the Staked Plains, I will try to get a high price for her from the *Comancheros*."

The only way into the canyon from where they looked over the rim was a narrow, twisting path wide enough for only one horse at a time. The war party took it single file.

Immediately, as the war party rode through the Comanche camp toward the big council fire, they collected a crowd of curious Indians who followed them to the big center council fire.

Maverick sat his big horse with the arrogant manner expected of a man of important family. "I am Pecos, brother to the great Quanah who leads this new uprising," he said, only glad that he saw none of his own clan among the faces. If his clan were here, they were camped at the far end of the canyon.

Important men of the tribe came out of their tepees as the word spread through the camp. Dogs barked and children laughed and played as the men came out to greet the returning war party. They surrounded Maverick, nodding in welcome. "Come sit. Eat. We know you must be weary."

Maverick dismounted. "I stay but a little while," he announced grandly. "I became separated from my group on a raid. I must meet the *Quahadis* far to the west, give my brother this gift." He went around, jerked Cayenne from her horse by her long hair, and

344

threw her down in the dirt by the fire.

The women laughed in delight, crowding around to stare and point at the captive.

Cayenne stumbled to her feet, her eyes glaring with defiance. *They don't call me Cayenne for nothing,* Maverick remembered, enjoying her show of fire and spirit. If he could have a woman of his own, there was none more suited to him than this one. The children she would produce would do any man proud. He thought suddenly of her sire, admiring Joe McBride a little in spite of himself. *Blood will tell,* Texans always said, and Cayenne had to get that brave pride from somewhere.

One fat old squaw pushed forward, looking Cayenne over critically. "Yes, this is a nice gift." She nodded, turning toward the other Comanche women who crowded around curiously. "I like to see men use their passion on captives; certainly the white men have treated ours badly enough!"

The other women nodded soberly at the old squaw's remarks. Many of them had lost loved ones to the white man's bullets and the old Comanche was obviously an honored woman of some importance. "My own daughter has been raped and killed by the buffalo hunters." Her sad expression changed to one of hatred as she glared at the helpless Cayenne who stood with her hands still tied behind her. "My son grieves much over his beloved sister's death and hunts the white men now as relentlessly as we might kill the great panther."

The old squaw reached out suddenly and caught the front of Cayenne's shirt, ripping it to the waist so that her beautiful, rounded breasts were visible to everyone.

Maverick had to control himself to keep from striking the old woman for her insolence. But Cayenne

345

shook her hair back, her chin high with defiance, ignoring the sudden hungry looks of the men in the crowd.

Maverick looked around at the men eyeing her fine, soft breasts, her pink nipples. He must not appear too possessive, too jealous of her. "Enough!" He made a signal of dismissal to the old woman. "You must not bruise or harm the girl in any way so that she is not a suitable gift to the great chief."

The woman nodded grudgingly, admitting the truth of his statement. "Perhaps the great chief will not want her, will turn her over to the women to torture. I could take that defiance out of her."

Maverick glanced at the angry Cayenne. *The only way anyone could break that feisty, proud little Texan would be to kill her,* he thought with great admiration, *and she'd go down rebellious and fighting. Rebel,* he thought. *Sweet little Rebel.*

Wind Runner pressed forward. "Hush, old woman. Even your son, Little Fox, would see the waste in that! Ask him when he rides into our camp if it is not so. If Quanah doesn't want her, his brother proposes to trade her to the *Comancheros.* With her beauty, we could get much gunpowder and weapons in exchange."

There was a murmur of agreement through the crowd and one of the old chiefs came forward. "You must be tired, Pecos. We are honored to have the brother of Quanah in our camps. Later, we will have welcoming ceremonies and feasting."

"I am very weary," Maverick nodded. "Tomorrow, I would enjoy visiting, hearing how the uprising goes from this quarter, but tonight I need only food and a blanket."

Wind Runner laughed. "We'll see you are given a

fine tepee, and of course, since your brother is not here, you can enjoy his woman as is the custom."

His words made Maverick flinch, remembering . . .

The other peered at him anxiously. "Is Pecos ill?"

Maverick recovered himself from the agony of memories. "I am tired, as I said. Show me this tepee where I may rest."

He grabbed Cayenne roughly by the shoulder, propelling the bound, half-naked girl ahead of him as the group followed curiously. When she stumbled and fell, he forced himself not to sweep her up in his arms. Instead, he put his moccasin on the back of her neck, pushing her face down into the dirt while the others laughed.

"Humiliation is a lesson captives are forced to learn," he said, remembering his Annie. But he hid his bitter anger as he reached down and jerked Cayenne roughly to her feet.

She looked at him as if he had betrayed her, and she said, "Maverick, why—?"

He hit her then, clipping her across the face so as to stop her words. It broke his heart to do it, but if she gave his disguise away, they would both end up being roasted over a slow fire and all the men would rape her and use her cruelly before they tortured her to death.

Cayenne's head snapped back and she stumbled from the force of his blow. When she looked at him again, blood ran from the corner of her soft, sweet mouth and a terrible fire of fury blazed in the bright green eyes.

Maverick yawned casually to the others. "I think I must break this captive as we do a wild mustang, so she'll be a dutiful slave for my brother's needs."

The fat old squaw laughed with delight, smiling

347

with admiration. "Even though you carry white blood, Pecos, you are a true Comanche at heart."

That he could never be, Maverick thought, remembering Annie. His mother had extracted her own vengeance on Blood Arrow's people by talking to her son endlessly about the white civilization she hoped someday would reclaim him. In his heart, in his soul, he was as white as Annie's Kentucky ancestors.

He grabbed Cayenne, roughly pushing her ahead of him as they walked to the fine tepee on the edge of the settlement. Wind Runner pulled back the flap, bowing Maverick inside. "This is my very own which I offer Pecos."

Maverick thanked him in Comanche, pushed Cayenne inside, and followed her. But even as he started to breathe a sigh of relief, the warrior followed him in, pointing out the nice features of the tepee, the small fire of scented mesquite crackling in the center. Because the man watched him, he threw Cayenne down on the ground, tying her hands above her head to one of the tepee poles. She lay there on her back, her fine globular breasts visible in the torn shirt.

"Maverick, why—?"

He put his moccasin across her mouth. "Shut up, slave!" he ordered. "It will do you no good to call for some white man who is dead in our raid!"

Wind Runner grunted with satisfaction. "She needs to be humiliated, raped into submission if she is to bear many sons for the great Quanah." He looked at Maverick quizzically.

This was a test, Maverick thought, *wondering if the brave suspected he was white in his heart after all.*

"You are right, Wind Runner. She needs to be humiliated, taught her place so she will be broken in spirit, serve a warrior's needs without fighting, without struggling." *As my poor mother did*, he thought.

He jerked off his loincloth and stood looking down at her. The first flicker of fear showed in her eyes, thinking she had been betrayed by a man she loved; a man she trusted with her life. Maverick fell on her, handling her fine breasts roughly. When she tried to protest, he hit her across the mouth, then kissed her to hush her, tasting her blood as he rammed his tongue between her lips.

While the other warrior watched, Maverick raped her brutally, bruising her soft white thighs as he took her, ramming into her velvet softness that any other time would have been wet with desire for him. But she was dry with fear and he forced himself inside her with difficulty, as a stallion takes an inexperienced filly.

I'm sorry, baby, he thought. *I must do this to you! I don't dare treat you well, rouse any suspicions.* Later he would beg her pardon, fall on his knees asking forgiveness for hurting her, humiliating her. But now it was only important that he save both their lives.

When he finished raping her, he wiped himself off on her torn shirt with a gesture of contempt, leaving her lying silent and frightened, staring up at him with her hands still tied above her head.

The other man stroked his own erection. "Would I had a brother with a woman like that to share!" He went to the tepee opening and turned. "You have food and a soft white woman to enjoy through this long night. Tomorrow, we will gather around the fires, discuss the war plans with the old chiefs. We are eager to hear of the great Quanah's plans, what he intends to do next!"

Maverick nodded curtly. "Of course, tomorrow," he said in Comanche. That gave him all night to think of

349

some logical words the Comanche might believe. At that time, his and Cayenne's lives would be on the line again. But he'd worry about that later.

Wind Runner left the tepee. Maverick waited, listening to the soft sound of the moccasins walking away before he moved swiftly to untie Cayenne and pull her into his embrace. "Oh, baby, I'm so sorry! I had to do all that! I was afraid they might suspect us if I treated you gently!"

He kissed her bruised face and she hesitated only a moment before she threw her arms around his neck, weeping warm, salty tears against his naked chest. "I—I didn't understand . . . thought you had decided to become a Comanche again!"

"Never!" he whispered. "I'd like to send every one of them into a wandering hell!" He took the rawhide and looped it over his gun belt. That was his own special vengeance against those who had hurt, humiliated, and tortured his mother.

He propped her up, gently washed her face, and fed her the roasted, crispy meat.

"Maverick," she said with a sigh as she lay back, "what will happen tomorrow?"

He leaned on his elbow, looking down at her in the flickering light of the little fire. "Don't you know tomorrow never comes?" He tried to sound light, bantering as he reached out and touched the tip of her freckled nose. "Let me do the worrying for both of us, okay? And trust me, baby, whatever happens, trust me. Whatever I do, go along with it without question."

She snuggled into the safety of his embrace. "I will, Maverick, I will. I guess I know now that you must love me, too; that you wouldn't do anything to hurt me."

350

Except kill your father, he thought, but he only kissed her closed eyes while she sighed with exhaustion. "Little Reb, it's been a long day. Go to sleep now and I'll keep watch. Nothing's going to happen."

"You promise, cross your heart and hope to die?" Her eyes flickered open sleepily and she suddenly looked very young, very innocent. He felt old, discouraged. He didn't have much faith in anything himself. His revenge was a flame that slowly consumed him, burning him out from the inside. But it didn't matter; nothing mattered but that he fulfill the vow.

Cross your heart and hope to die. How many, many times had Annie said that to her little boy as she taught him about the white civilization? She had promised Joe a son, she said, stroking Eagle's Flight's black hair. And she'd gotten him one. Joe wouldn't mind that he'd not fathered the son she'd promised. No, Joe would take Eagle's Flight as his very own and they'd all live happily ever after. Annie said that among the whites, the very best stories ended that way, just as they began, "Once upon a time . . ."

But Joe hadn't come for either of them, although they waited and waited. The years passed. The little boy grew tall and strong while his mother grew thinner and more bowed with cruelty and hard work. Perhaps things might have been different if his father, Blood Arrow, had not been killed on a raid before the boy's birth. As it was, he and his mother were mistreated and ridiculed by the aunts and jealous cousins, by his father's brothers.

"Just a little while longer," Annie would sigh as they crouched together, hiding when things got too bad. "Joe will come for both of us, you'll see. We'll go back to the white world and we'll fit in there."

"Tell me, Mother," he would beg, "tell me how it

351

will be. Tell me how it was."

Annie smiled and patted the top of his head. "Once upon a time there was a big redheaded man and he loved me so very, very much!"

"Will he love me, Mother? Will he really love me?" It was important to the fatherless boy.

Annie smiled. Her smile lit up her plain little face and made her big gray eyes crinkle at the corners. "Of course he will love you as I do, dear, because you are the son I promised him! We'll all sit down at a long dining table with lots of friends and relatives, and there'll be plates and knives and forks."

He considered a long moment. "What's a fork?"

She looked at him a little sadly. "I must teach you even more if you are going to be able to live in the white world, my son." She hugged him to her. "That's how white people eat. And on that long table, there'll be lots of food, chocolate cake like Joe likes and fried chicken."

Her own stomach rumbled and he thought how hungry they both were. Often in the cold winter, there was not enough food and babies died. White hunters were slowly killing off the game, pushing the Indians farther and farther out on to the desolate Staked Plains, the wilderness of west Texas.

He looked up at her. "And will you be at that table, Mother? Will you stay by my side forever?"

Annie hesitated a long moment. "Forever is a long time, Son, but if I'm not there in body, I'll be there in spirit. Do you understand?"

He didn't really, but he nodded because he knew it would please her and he loved her so.

"And Son, even if I'm not here, I'll live on forever because my blood flows through your veins as it will through your children's, through your children's children. As long as you don't forget me, I'll live forever in your heart."

He did not like the way she talked, the sadness in her eyes. "We'll get away, Mother," he said eagerly, "we'll run away and find this Joe McBride."

Annie shook her head. "They watch us too closely," she said, "and I don't have the strength for it anyway."

He hadn't noticed until she said that how thin and drawn she looked. After that, he took to saving some of his food for her, lying and saying he was not hungry so she would eat it.

The years passed and he grew tall while she grew more thin and sad every day. "Joe will come for us, you'll see," she said, but her voice no longer held any conviction. The boy had grown hard and bitter, hating the white man who did not want him, did not want his mother.

Once he said to her, "Maybe he does not know you're here, that you are alive."

She looked at him sadly and turned away. "He knows. A few months after I was captured, another woman was taken. But no warrior decided to take her as his woman and she was to be ransomed."

She paused a long moment, fingering the ragged old buckskin shift she wore. "She didn't want to be sent back dressed in buckskin, afraid her family wouldn't want her."

"And?" the boy prompted.

"She was about my size," Annie said, "even had hair the same chestnut color. I gave her the homespun dress I wore, traded with her so she wouldn't have to go back to the settlement in buckskin. She swore she'd find Joe, tell him I was still alive, tell him now that my warrior was dead, his brothers might sell me cheaply."

He knew without asking. There had been no answer. As Annie's body swelled with her half-Comanche child, she had waited for the help the other captive would send. No ransom came.

The years passed and the half-breed boy grew big and muscular. His heart turned hard and bitter against the man called Joe McBride who did not want him for a son, did not want his mother.

Annie made excuses. "He's trying hard to raise the money," she said lamely, "although I would have thought old Mr. Adams, our neighbor, or even banker Ogle might have made him a loan."

The boy said nothing.

"He'll come," Annie said as the months turned into years. "Maybe the girl had a hard time finding him, although I gave her good directions on how to get to our spread."

But the half-grown boy called Eagle's Flight no longer listened to her fairy tales about how the two of them would sit at the long table of the ranch house. He had long ago realized that the white man his mother loved would never come for either of them. The pair would spend the rest of their lives among the Indians, huddling together, hungry and cold while his mother taught him everything she thought he would need if he ever returned to civilization. She could read and write a little and she taught him as best she could, drawing in the dirt with a stick.

Sometimes when they were both miserable, she would tell him long stories about big white ranch houses with soft beds and great stone fireplaces with roaring logs. "Once upon a time . . ." she would begin, and he would ask, "Do all white stories begin that way, Mother?"

"Only the very best ones," Annie smiled, stroking

his dark hair. "And, of course, they always end
'. . . and they lived happily ever after.' "

Happily ever after. Maverick blinked in the darkness of the tepee now as he lay next to the sleeping Cayenne, remembering. But Annie's story had not ended that way. The man his mother loved never came to save them. So the son had made a vow on Annie's dying body. *I'll get Joe. I promise I'll get him, torture him slowly, cut his heart out and make him eat it as he dies for what has happened to you!*

He had been fourteen winter counts old that night as he stood there looking down at Annie's frail, workworn body, the scarlet blood smearing her still form, his hands, his knife. . . .

Maverick sighed, running his fingers thoughtfully along the jagged white scar on his face, thinking of Annie, of Cayenne. How he wished this story could have a happy ending, but of course, it could not. If he survived and made it to the Lazy M, he must kill his beloved Cayenne's father to fulfill the blood vow he had made ten years ago.

He cuddled the flame-haired girl close to him and listened to the drums echoing through the canyon as the celebrating continued long into the night. In all the world, only old Don Diego de Durango, the man who had adopted Maverick, knew of his past, his vow. He hadn't meant to tell even him, but one night in the Durango study, too much whiskey had made Maverick vulnerable and he'd told.

Maverick's forehead wrinkled with thought. And yet, Cayenne said that the old Don had met her father a year ago. Knowing that Maverick was searching for that man, why hadn't the old Don told him where to find Joe McBride? Why? If Joe McBride was as good a shot as everyone said, he had the advantage and the superior range with a rifle. He might even get Maverick before the half-breed could gun him down.

Cayenne sighed in her sleep, snuggling into his arms. Maverick kissed her hair gently. He could not have both love and vengeance, but he had sworn by duty first. A man cannot live without honor.

At least, Maverick decided now, he would not torture Joe McBride as he had always dreamed of. Out of love for the daughter, Joe would get a quick, merciful death, which was more than Annie Laurie had gotten. It was a long time before Maverick dropped off into a fitful sleep.

For the next several days, the couple rested in the Indian encampment that sprawled along the creek through the canyon. Maverick tried to make plans as he studied the sentries guarding the big horse herd, trying to figure out when the couple could possibly slip through the darkness, grab Dust Devil and Strawberry, and make a run for it. There were several trails out, none of them easy.

Well, he had a few days to rest up while he leisurely decided what to do, Maverick thought.

He was wrong. On the third day, shouts greeted riders approaching the camp down the narrow trail. As Maverick stood watching the war party approach, the fat, cruel squaw raised a glad cry and went running to meet them. "My son! My son!"

Maverick peered at them, Cayenne by his side. *Was one of those warriors really wearing yellow satin sleeve garters? Where had he seen those before?*

The long-armed leader wore a Turkey-red white man's shirt. The sunlight reflected off a beaded necklace, off some kind of hair ornaments in the leader's soot-black braids as the warriors rode in.

Cayenne laughed. "What's that in his hair? Looks almost like a woman's fancy combs!"

Maverick shook his head in puzzlement, staring at the leader, searching his memory as the group rode into the camp.

Wind Runner ran forward, yelling in Comanche, "Little Fox, how went the attack on the buffalo hunters?"

The man's small, foxlike features grinned as he waved his lance to show the new scalps dangling there, his long arms raised in triumph. "I have white scalps to pay for my sister's honor, for the slaughter of our buffalo!"

Maverick felt a chill go down his back as recognition slowly dawned on him. *Adobe Walls*. That warrior had been the one at Adobe Walls. Would the Comanche brave recognize him, too?

Chapter Eighteen

Maverick's blood almost congealed as he recognized the Comanche leader riding in ahead of his war party. What in God's name was going to happen if Little Fox recognized him from Adobe Walls? He and Cayenne couldn't possibly make a run for it through a thousand Indians.

He looked over at her and saw the frightened recognition in her face, too. *Many white women would have panicked*, he thought with admiration as he watched the little redhead. She was scared spitless, he could tell by her eyes, but she only stood there. Her gaze came to his, and she nodded ever so slightly, trusting him to deal with the situation, trusting him to look after her.

The hook-nosed Wind Runner pushed forward as the war party dismounted, and he raised a hand in greeting. "Hoa! Little Fox, how goes the war against the hated whites?"

Little Fox's face twisted in insane delight as he waved the lance. "You need ask?" He chortled in Comanche, "Do you not see the scalps I have brought back so that we might dance?"

Maverick stared at the various colored hair dangling from the staff, at the white man's shirt Little Fox wore, at the yellow satin sleeve garters on the other warrior.

Wind Runner motioned to Maverick. "Little Fox, I forget to tell you we are honored to have our great chief's brother, Pecos, ride into our camp. He is on his way to join Quanah on the Staked Plains."

Maverick took a deep breath and nodded a greeting. Any second, the other would sound the alarm and he and Cayenne would be tonight's entertainment as the pair were slowly tortured to death. "I'm sorry that I missed the fight," he said in Comanche to Little Fox. "But I have been raiding the *Tejanos* south of here." He pointed toward Cayenne. "Most of my warriors have been killed, but I captured a great prize to give as a gift to my brother."

Some of the warriors guffawed obscenely. Little Fox stared at Maverick a long moment and Maverick held his breath, awaiting the recognition. He hoped the braves could not see the pounding of his heart in his great naked chest.

But Little Fox only grunted and nodded a greeting. "Your own raid seems to be a success," he said in Comanche. "Your brother will no doubt be pleased to get such a prize." He glanced up at the setting sun. "And now, let us have feasting and dancing long into the night to celebrate my strong *puha*, my medicine!"

Maverick was so relieved the other did not recognize him that he almost collapsed, but he only said, "Of course! I am eager to sit and hear your tales of this war journey!"

He left Cayenne inside the tepee as night came on, dressed himself in all the stolen finery of the warrior he had killed, and went to sit in the big campfire circle to eat and smoke and listen to Little Fox brag about the raid on Adobe Walls.

"We killed many," Little Fox boasted. "We taught those hunters a lesson they will not soon forget!"

Maverick, sitting cross-legged in a place of honor,

looked around at Little Fox's men and saw them avert their eyes guiltily. It was not honorable for warriors to lie in such a manner. "Tell us the details of how it happened."

Little Fox told the story of Adobe Walls as if the Indians had overrun the place, killing every man. His warriors said nothing but their expression showed doubt in their own wisdom of having ridden with such a man.

The drums and the dancing began, the new scalps hanging in a place of honor near the fire. Maverick looked at them, especially the woman's hair that hung so long and black and magnificent. Why did it seem familiar to him?

Little Fox went on with his bragging. ". . . and then after we left this fortress of the hunters, we chanced on another party of buffalo hunters to the north. We surrounded them and held them there until they used up their ammunition."

One of the others laughed and nodded. "Some of them managed to kill themselves before we could take them prisoner, but not all." He stroked the yellow satin sleeve garters he wore.

Little Fox fingered his own Turkey-red shirt. "Not all," he grinned with satisfaction at the memory. "After we took these things from them, we staked them out naked in the hot sun, cut off their manhoods, and stuffed them into their mouths so they could not scream!"

Maverick had to control himself to keep from wincing in disgust.

The one with the yellow sleeve garters laughed. "Then we cut off their ears, drove wooden stakes through their bellies, and propped their heads up so the pair could watch themselves die. It takes a long, long time to die that way."

360

Little Fox fingered the beaded necklace he wore and Maverick searched his mind, wondering why that also looked familiar to him.

The leader said, "My sister's death is finally paid for." When he looked up, directly into Maverick's eyes, Maverick saw the insanity there. "These hunters were the ones who raped and killed my sister, so I wreaked terrible revenge, but I want even more!"

Buck. With sudden clarity, Maverick remembered the grizzled buffalo hunter in the Turkey-red shirt and beaded Indian necklace, his partner, Clint. *It was a horrible way to die, even though it was a just, terrible vengeance,* Maverick thought.

Little Fox seemed to be studying him thoughtfully. "And you say you are Pecos, our great leader's brother?"

What was it about the way he looked at Maverick? Could it be Maverick's imagination that there was hint of a smile in the other's dark, small features, as if he knew a secret joke?

Maverick nodded. "I go to join Quanah to the west, take him the white woman as a gift from my raid."

The others nodded and grunted in approval at the gift, but Little Fox smiled ever so slightly. "No need for that," he said. "The great warrior was with us on our raid and told us to meet him back here at the canyon in thirty sun's time." He looked up at the moon. "Quanah is now raiding across the great plains even as we have been doing."

Maverick gulped and recovered. "Yes, of course, I knew that. We planned to meet back at our camp to the west."

Little Fox grinned evilly. "By my calculations, the thirty suns are almost gone. You won't have to wait all those days to meet your brother clear to the west."

Maverick's heart pounded a warning but he only

361

looked calmly at the other. "What are you trying to tell me?"

Little Fox leered at him, reaching up absently to finger the pearl combs in his hair. "Quanah should be riding into this canyon probably tomorrow," he said, "and so you see, you won't have to ride clear to the west."

Quanah. Tomorrow. And when he arrived, Maverick and Cayenne would be unmasked as imposters. But Maverick only grunted in satisfaction, reaching for another piece of roasted meat. "That is very good news," he lied. "I am happy to hear my beloved brother will soon arrive."

The Indians danced before the flickering flames, the light throwing shadows across those eating around the great fire. The firelight glistened off the long, magnificent hair dangling from the lance stuck in the ground.

Wind Runner looked toward it. "I see, Little Fox, you have taken one of their women's lives in payment for your sister's."

Little Fox shrugged, reaching up to touch the pearl combs glistening in his black braids. "She was only one of their whores going from that place called Wichita on a stagecoach to one of their other settlements."

Molly. Oh, my God. Molly. Maverick sucked in a shuddering breath. No wonder the hair and the combs looked so familiar.

Maverick took another breath, fighting to keep from throwing himself at the other Comanche, wanting to throttle him with the rawhide thong he kept looped over his gun belt. His hands actually trembled as he held the roasted meat. For a moment, as he stared at the ebony hair hanging from the lance, he thought he might vomit and had to swallow hard to

362

control the sour bile welling up in his throat.

How many times had he made love to good-natured Molly, tangled his fingers in those magnificent locks that now hung before the fire? He saw her face before him, heard her voice telling him how much she loved him. And he felt suddenly guilty that he had never loved her, had only used her as men were wont to do a saloon whore, enjoying the relief her body could give him. *Molly. I'm sorry, Molly. So sorry. Forgive me.*

Little Fox looked at him. "You tremble, Pecos. What is the matter?"

Cayenne. If he lost his temper and attacked the grinning Comanche as he longed to do, Cayenne would have to pay for it. Maverick shrugged and continued eating. "I am only sorry I could not be there with you on your raids to share the triumph."

The other's face saddened and he fingered the necklace. "It does not pay for my sister," he said bitterly. "There are not enough deaths in the whole world to pay for what they did to her. I thought the revenge would make me feel better, but I feel empty, burned-out inside."

By damn, when he completed his own revenge, he wouldn't feel like that! No, he'd feel good! But Maverick only yawned and stretched. "It has been a long day and I am weary. Some of you may wish to dance and drink all night, but I think I will go to bed."

Wind Runner laughed knowingly. "If I had a woman like that fire-haired one waiting in my blankets, I would go to bed, too! After all, if Quanah rides in tomorrow, you will have to give him your gift and tomorrow night you will be sleeping alone!"

The other men laughed and nudged each other knowingly.

Maverick laughed. "What you say is true. But after all, she is nothing but a woman. I will steal another somewhere along the way." He stood up, looking down at the war leader sitting cross-legged on the ground. He had to fight a terrible urge to attack the man who wore Molly's fine combs in his hair. "Tomorrow we must make plans for our next attack on the white settlements."

Little Fox looked at the pistol he wore. "You have taken that from some dead *Tejano?*"

Maverick patted the gun arrogantly. "You think a live one would give it up?"

The warriors laughed uproariously.

Maverick turned away from the fire. "I learn to shoot it," he said, "so that I can fight them on their own terms."

Wind Runner grunted with satisfaction. "Quanah's brother is a very brave warrior."

Little Fox stared at Maverick a long moment. "I'm sure our leader will be happy to know his brother is alive and well."

There was some hidden meaning there but Maverick decided not to show that he sensed it. " 'Til tomorrow then," he said, and stalked away from the fire to his tepee.

Cayenne ran into his arms when he went inside. "My stars! When you were gone so long, I got nervous! Do you think that fox-faced one recognized us?"

"I—I don't know, Cee Cee." Maverick kissed the tip of her nose absently, his mind on other things. He would not tell her that the game was up, that tomorrow Quanah would ride into the canyon and then everyone would know that Maverick was not the brother but instead a white impostor. Cayenne would be so frightened if she knew and he must protect her. "Nothing to worry about right now," he lied. "Let's get a little sleep."

They snuggled up together in their blankets and he made very gentle love to her while the rhythmic beat of drums and dancing drowned out her soft whimpers of passion, her sighs of satisfaction as he took her, then held her close.

"Maverick, what are you thinking about? That was a close call today, wasn't it?"

"Nothing. I'm thinking about nothing," he lied, pulling her close against his chest so he could stroke her long hair. He thought about Molly, about Little Fox's dead sister, about Quanah riding in tomorrow, about his pistol.

He had only a few hours to come up with a plan, and if it didn't work, tomorrow night he'd be writhing and screaming over a slow fire, and a worse fate would await his darling. No, they'd never rape and torture her. If he couldn't save her, he'd do her the same mercy he'd done Annie Laurie, even though it would haunt his nightmares for the short time he had left until the avenging warriors killed him by inches. He flinched, remembering that long-ago time before he had fled the Comanches ten long years ago. . . .

Ten long years ago, the boy called Eagle's Flight had made a vow on Annie's dying body, sealed in her still-warm blood—a vow to kill her white husband. He had thrown the bloody knife from him with an anguished cry just as one of his uncles entered the tepee.

"What is this?" the hatchet-faced brave had confronted him. "We were not yet through enjoying torturing her, hearing her cries. . . ."

"Why have you done this terrible thing?" the boy screamed.

The other shrugged, yawning. "Because while you were gone hunting today, we captured a *Tejano* boy but this white bitch helped him escape before we could torture him. So she took his place!"

The boy called Eagle's Flight had lost control then, screaming with pain and rage as he threw himself at the big Comanche and they fought.

It was an unequal fight. The big Comanche laughed with delight, circling the boy warily with his knife. "So at last it comes to this, white whelp of my dead brother! You are no Comanche; you are her blood through and through!"

"I am white!" the boy screamed as he rushed bare-handed at the other. "I am white like my mother! White like her ancestors! I spit on my Comanche blood!" And he had spat in the brave's face, charging him bare-handed because his own bloody knife lay next to Annie's body.

The brave swore white man's curses that he had learned from white slaves as his knife jerked up with lightning speed, attempting to disembowel the boy.

Eagle's Flight managed to dodge, getting in two hard blows that sent the Comanche stumbling backward across the thin, limp body of Annie Laurie.

The warrior went down with a curse. His head hit the handle of the boy's knife, and he lay there groaning and semiconscious.

He would kill his uncle, torture him slowly! Outside, he heard Indians laughing drunkenly, calling for the brave to bring the white woman out for more torture. Eagle's Flight reached for a rawhide strip, catching the half-conscious man around the throat as the man recovered and fought him.

"I will trap your cursed spirit forever!" the boy vowed through clenched teeth, hanging onto the loop like a small badger finally sinking its sharp teeth into its tormentor. The Comanche tried to cry out but the boy's rawhide thong cut off his words, along with his breath, as Eagle's Flight throttled him.

His uncle struggled, trying to get his fingers under the thongs, terror widening his eyes so that the whites showed around the dark pupils as he fought the boy.

Eagle's Flight laughed deep in his throat. A Comanche feared death by choking or hanging as no other because it would leave a man's spirit trapped in his dead body forever. It was what Eagle's Flight wanted. Even if it cost him his life, the half-breed boy would have his vengeance for the agony they had inflicted on his mother.

Finally, the man gasped and died. Now the boy suddenly came to his senses, realizing he must get away! "I—I did it for you, Mother," he sobbed. "Oh, Mother! Mother . . ."

He went over, knelt by her still body, dipped his fingers in the cooling pool of blood she lay in, and touched the tips to his forehead. Then he put his hand on her thin form. "I swear by all that's in me, I won't rest until I kill them all, including that cursed white man who abandoned you, Mother! Yes, someday I'll find him, too, and I'll kill him slowest of all, as only one raised by the Comanche knows how! Nothing will stand in the way of this sacred vow; not money, not love, not even the loss of my own life will stop me from extracting the blood they owe me!"

He gathered up his knife and crept out of the tepee into the darkness, tears blinding his gray eyes that were so like hers. *He must live to fight another day*, he thought, *knowing what would happen when the drunken braves found the dead warrior.* He wished he could bury his mother with dignity before he fled but there was no way to accomplish this. And after all, Annie Laurie McBride was past all pain, past caring now.

He almost made it to the horse herd without running across another brave. But another of his uncles stood there in the darkness between him and the herd, swaying drunkenly on his feet as he urinated. Moving silent as a spirit of death, Eagle's Flight looped the rawhide over the man's head before the drunken brave knew what had happened.

"This is for Annie," he whispered fiercely as he pulled both ends tight. The Comanche was strong and he fought for his life, but the boy's anger gave him strength beyond his years. The man managed to make only one small cry, but it was enough. He squatted and watched his oldest uncle, Pine da poi, Whip Owner, look up from the circle of braves who laughed and shouted, passing a bottle of the white man's whiskey around.

Swaying drunkenly on his feet, Whip Owner grasped his cruel quirt with one hand, the hilt of his knife in the other as he walked out toward the pony herd to investigate. The other braves around the fire yelled coarse comments about going out to answer the call of nature, and they went back to singing and dancing around the drums that pounded out a rhythmic beat, drowning out everything as they shouted.

But the anger of the boy made him move prematurely in the brush, springing out from his crouch, and Whip Owner caught him across the face with the cruel quirt, leaving a trail of stinging fire. "You white whelp!" he snarled. "I should have killed you long ago but I kept thinking I could turn you into a Comanche warrior!"

"Never!" the boy shouted, and he dove in recklessly. Pine da poi pulled his knife. Moonlight reflected on its blade through the trees as he brought his arm back, but Eagle's Flight grabbed a stick and swung it hard, knocking the blade from the other's hand. They both reached for it in a silent struggle while the drunken warriors beat their drums and sang loudly over in the clearing, oblivious to the life-and-death battle being waged in the shadows of the trees.

His uncle smiled triumphantly as his big hand closed over the knife hilt. The boy threw up his hand to ward off the deadly blow and the blade glanced off, cutting a crooked slash to the bone across his left cheek.

His face felt on fire! Pine da poi laughed and staggered toward him drunkenly. "You have felt a wolf's sharp fangs," he said. "Now I finish the kill!"

But the boy tripped him and the man fell, struggling to get to his feet.

Those precious seconds had meant the difference between life and death to him, Maverick remembered now, listening to the drums outside, looking down at the fiery-haired girl nestled in the protection of his shoulder. He had wanted to stop to kill his uncle that night, count coup, but he could not spare the time as he fled for his life.

For weeks, the Comanche boy had starved and hung around the outskirts of white settlements, afraid to approach anyone, afraid they would not give him time to explain before they raised the alarm and shot him down.

Maverick smiled now, remembering. He had been a half-starved stray when the Triple D cowboys had cornered him in the Durango pasture. The hungry boy had killed a yearling steer, had cooked part of it, and was in the process of gobbling the meat ravenously when the roundup crew rode up, led by Trace Durango. That day the half-breed Comanche boy had closed the door on his past forever. Eagle's Flight had chosen his own new name, Maverick, and became a cowhand on the giant ranching empire.

A few weeks later, the Great Outbreak of 1864 had

come to a climax. Because of Maverick's heroism, old Don Durango had adopted him as his second son, giving him his own last name. Trace, an expert with a pistol, had taught the growing boy to handle a gun almost as well as he did himself. But as the years passed, Maverick never forgot his vow of vengeance. He tracked down a third Comanche uncle and killed him. And during the Great Outbreak, he had finally come face to face with his most hated uncle, Pine da poi.

Maverick lay looking up at the interior of Wind Runner's tepee, thinking with satisfaction of his uncle's scalp hanging from Dust Devil's bridle. The stallion had been Pine da poi's own horse.

Maverick started as he heard a soft footstep outside. "Yes, who is it?" he asked softly in Comanche.

Little Fox entered. "Ah, yes, Pecos, isn't it?"

Maverick nodded, motioning the warrior to a place by the fire. There was something sly and cunning in the insane eyes. The girl moved restlessly in her sleep, and without thinking, he reached out to stroke her as a woman does a frightened child, catching himself in time.

He looked at the other man. "You know that already," he said curtly. "What is it you want?"

Little Fox looked over at the sleeping girl. "Do you not know what I want?"

Maverick felt the hair raise on the back of his neck as he pretended careless indifference. "You know the fire-haired one is a gift for my brother. If the great Quanah does not desire her, perhaps he might trade her away for a rifle or a good pony."

Little Fox fingered the beaded necklace he wore. "White buffalo hunters raped and killed my little sister. And I live for nothing now but revenge."

370

Maverick nodded in understanding. Had he not lived the same way for ten years, thinking of nothing, thirsting for nothing but vengeance? Would his quest finally drive him as insane as this warrior appeared to be? "So? What do you ask of Pecos?"

Little Fox laughed. "Pecos? I do not know who you really are, half-breed, but Quanah himself told me he is the last of his family, that both his father and brother are dead!"

Maverick tensed, ready to attack the other man if he gave a sudden alarm, but Little Fox only smiled and gestured him back down. "I'll let the great chief deal with you as an imposter tomorrow when he rides in or maybe I could be persuaded to help you escape."

Maverick felt sweat gather under his armpits, on his face. "What do you demand for helping us escape?"

The brave ran his tongue along his lip, looking with lustful eyes toward the sleeping girl. "Not *us, you.*"

Maverick's gaze followed the Indian's hungry one, saw the way the warrior looked at the beauty snuggled down in the blanket. He didn't have to ask. He knew by the man's expression how he lusted after the flame-haired girl. Little Fox might help Maverick escape, but his words and expression made it clear what the price would be. *The girl.* Maverick took a deep breath, considering what to do next as he tried to appear disinterested.

What to do now. His goal after all had been to track down Joe McBride, to kill him, and he had enough information now that he could find the Lazy M Ranch without the girl's help. It would add to his revenge to be able to tell the rancher what had happened to Joe's beloved daughter just before he killed McBride. Yes, it would be a fitting retribution; McBride's darling Cayenne a slave of the Comanche, being raped and mistreated as Annie had been. *An eye for an eye and a tooth for a tooth. . . .*

Cayenne sighed and rolled over toward them in her sleep, exposing one of her beautiful breasts. Maverick had to grit his teeth to keep from slamming his fist in the Indian's face at the way the crazed savage looked at her. *She's mine,* he thought, *she's mine!*

He tried to remember that he should want to see her raped and hurt. But all he could think of was that he'd die before he'd let another man touch her.

Cayenne's eyes flickered open. Maverick saw the sudden fear in them as she looked at Little Fox, then she saw Maverick and smiled gently.

Little Fox chuckled. "The woman trusts you, cares for you," he said in Comanche.

Maverick nodded, realizing suddenly that it was true. "She is only a woman," he said in Comanche, pretending indifference, "and my slave. I think I will take your offer—my life in exchange for the woman." With his eyes, he tried to tell Cayenne what was happening, that she must trust him in this.

Little Fox stood up, running his hand over his swelling manhood. "I thought you would accept. So I've left your horses saddled in the big herd at the end of the canyon."

Maverick stood up too. "Why would you saddle two horses?"

Little Fox's gaze fastened on the frightened girl on the blanket as he stood towering over her. "It will need to look like you both planned to escape. If there is only the one saddled horse, someone might realize that a deal had been struck."

Silent as a shadow, Maverick's hand went to his gun belt, feeling for the rawhide thong there. He dared not fire a shot. To do so would alert the whole camp. He didn't trust Little Fox. Probably up in the rocks was one of the other's braves, waiting to pick Maverick off when he tried to ride out. That way, Little Fox not only got the girl but the big gray stallion as well, as war honors for having stopped the imposter's escape when Quanah rode in tomorrow and Maverick's deception was uncovered.

Cayenne was going to have to help him on this. He knew Little Fox spoke a little English, so there was no way to warn her except hope she trusted him enough to play along. "Woman," he said in English, "my ruse is uncovered and Little Fox offers me a chance to escape with my life."

The emerald-green eyes widened. "What must we do?"

Maverick laughed, "I am lucky that he hungers for you, white squaw! He'll take you in exchange for my escape!"

Cayenne gasped, looking from one to the other. For a long moment, Maverick was afraid her fiery temper would jeopardize his whole plan. "Why, you yellow Yankee! You're gonna ride out and leave me?"

Little Fox slowly uncovered his turgid manhood. "I'll see that you don't miss him, white bitch! I've thought of nothing else but mounting you since I rode into camp and saw you! And if you please me enough, I won't add your hair to my war lance!" He moved slowly toward her while she cowered against the blanket.

Maverick caught her gaze. *Trust me*, he tried to tell her with his gray eyes. *Trust me, Cee Cee, I'll look out for you.*

She hesitated, staring back at him across the other man's shoulder. And then she seemed to believe what he was trying to tell her with his eyes. "Well, if the great Little Fox wants me, perhaps I should be flattered. . . ." She opened her shirt so that her fine, white breasts showed, ran her hands down her rose-tipped nipples.

Maverick watched her smile invitingly at the brave, shaking her flame-colored hair back. He had to fight to stop himself from grabbing the warrior as he dropped to his knees before the girl, reached out, and ran one dark hand across her soft breasts.

Little Fox laughed as he pawed her creamy skin. "I'll enjoy you night after night," he muttered thickly, licking his lips. "And I'll see if I can hurt you enough to make you scream and beg as my sister must have screamed and begged, as that black-haired white woman cried and begged as I tortured her."

Molly. He was talking about Molly. Maverick fought to control himself as he stood quietly behind the warrior, who had eyes only for the beautiful, half-naked girl cringing before him.

Maverick's gaze caught Cayenne's and she seemed to understand. *Trust me, baby*, he said with his eyes. *Trust me.*

Cayenne smiled invitingly at the warrior, though Maverick saw her lips tremble. "Perhaps I would enjoy being your woman," she said, slowly holding her arms out to him.

Little Fox's small features spread into a twisted grin as he grabbed the girl, ran his hands over her flesh. "I'll make you know you'd been mated by a stallion!" He breathed heavily, pawing at her as he threw her down, his hands running across her creamy skin, his attention on her as she smiled invitingly at him.

That was all Maverick needed. Soft as a sigh, he stepped behind the warrior, looped the rawhide over his head, and jerked both ends tight. The brave gasped, clawing at his throat, trying vainly to get his fingers under the thong. "Aaa-hey!" Maverick snarled in Comanche. *I claim this coup.* He reached for his scalping knife.

Cayenne jumped to her feet, watching the struggle. "Come on, Maverick, let's go!"

But Maverick's anger would not let him leave the scene until the man collapsed. "I want to make sure he's dead," Maverick snarled through clenched teeth, "after the way he put his dirty hands on you, after what he did to Molly. . . ."

Cayenne grabbed his arm, struggling with him. "We can't pay the price for your revenge, Maverick; we've got to get out of here now!"

Maverick stopped, realizing she was right, although he wasn't sure the warrior was dead. He dropped the limp body and put the thong back on his gun belt. "You always got to be right, don't you Rebel? I don't think he's dead. . . ."

Cayenne half dragged him out of the tepee into the darkness. "We don't have time to find out. What happened, anyway!"

Maverick looked around. The camp was silent now at this late hour. Even the dogs were asleep, the fires banked into small mounds of glowing glows. "He knows I'm not Quanah's brother," he gasped. "He was willing to let me get away if he could have you."

She looked at him a long moment. "A lot of men would have taken him up on it. Anything beats being tortured by Comanches."

"There's something worse," he whispered, looking around at the silhouette of the sleeping camp, "and that's thinking of you in any man's arms but mine."

"Maverick, I—" her voice quavered, "there's something I need to tell you about why I'm taking you to Texas. . . ."

"We don't have time," he snapped tersely. "Let's see if we can get the hell out of here! He said our horses were saddled and waiting."

He crept along with her behind him toward the

grazing pony herd. He wasn't going to tell her what he suspected about Little Fox laying a trap for him, probably having someone waiting in the shadows to finish him off. By damn, he should have made sure he'd killed that loco brave before he got out of that tepee!

In the moonlight, he saw the two horses standing saddled over by a big rock. He gestured toward them and Cayenne nodded to show she understood. He wasn't going to tell her their chances of getting away were almost nil. That rocky, steep trail up the canyon wall was a long ride and they were sure to be spotted by a sentry before they got safely to the top.

Was there a warrior waiting in those rocks with a deadly bow or lance?

"Cayenne," he whispered, "Little Fox may have laid a trap with those horses. If there's a warrior there, I need to draw him out, hold his attention. How brave are you?"

He saw her lip tremble but her head came up defiantly. "Braver than any damned Yankee," she smiled. "You want me to lure him out?"

Maverick hesitated. It would be dangerous. If there were a man in the rocks, he might shoot first before he realized he was dealing with a desirable, harmless woman. "No, I—I can't ask you—"

"Ask me? My stars!" she scoffed. "Just watch this Southern girl work!"

Before he could reach out and stop her, she slipped past him, walking with a tantalizing gait out along the path toward the horses.

Maverick held his breath, the sour taste of fear choking off his air. But he dare not run out to drag her to safety.

It was a hot night, he thought, *or was it only because he was so scared for her that he felt sweat beading and running down his war-painted dark skin?* Somewhere in the distance, a coyote howled and some of the horses in the herd snorted and moved restlessly. Maverick realized then that his fists were clinched so tightly his nails were cutting into his calloused palms.

A shadow stood up behind the rock, watching the girl for a moment as Maverick blended into the rock wall.

The man called out in Kiowa. "Who's there?"

Yes, it was the Kiowa from Little Fox's war party, all right, Maverick thought, watching the man scamper out of the rocks. His metal bracelets that the Kiowa favored reflected the light, and when he turned, Maverick saw the Kiowa hair style—long on one side, cut short on the other.

Cayenne pirouetted, putting her hands on her hips. In a mixture of sign language, border Spanish, a little English, and a smattering of Comanche she'd heard from Maverick, she let the warrior know that she'd seen him before, had a yen for him.

Maverick could see the sudden gleam of the man's teeth even from here as the Kiowa smiled. *That's it, baby, charm him like you do me; make him unable to think of anything else but you!*

Maverick moved now, as soft as dew upon the buffalo grass, putting one moccasined foot before the other as he crept around behind the man in the shadows. The Kiowa had his back to the rocks, looking down at Cayenne. She reached up and touched the bow, smiling at him. The Kiowa made an obscene gesture, indicating what he wanted.

She smiled at him, nodded, and reached up to stroke his bare arm.

Maverick crept up behind him and took a deep breath. If the man managed to scream, the whole camp would be alerted and then they'd find Little Fox

377

in the tepee. His hand went to his pistol for reassurance. He'd never let them take her alive. *One chance. That's all Maverick would get—one chance.* He gritted his teeth, took the rawhide loop in both hands, and crept forward. He could smell the rank sweat of the big Kiowa's body now as he crept up on him. *Now. Now!*

With a movement as quick as a scorpion stinging, Maverick slipped the loop over the man's head and jerked hard. The man gasped, tried to cry out, but Maverick jerked both ends, cutting off his scream.

The Kiowa was a big, powerful man and he struggled, trying to break free. The thong cut into Maverick's hands until they bled while he hung onto the cord, garroting the man. If he let go now, one cry would bring hundreds of Indians running.

Over the Kiowa's shoulder, he saw Cayenne's frightened face as she watched helplessly. The Kiowa struggled again and Maverick pulled hard on the thong, cutting into the man's neck. And then he smelled the stink of urine as the man's muscles relaxed and the Kiowa died.

Maverick was surprised to find he actually shook. He pulled Cayenne to him and found that she trembled, too.

"Maverick, I was so scared! So scared!"

"Naw! A Rebel scared! Naw!" He tried to soothe her, stroking her hair as he looked around, assessing their chances of getting out of here alive. "We've got an argument to continue about old Sam and that traitor, Jefferson Davis, remember?"

It had the desired effect. The redhead forgot about her fear as her eyes flashed. "When we get out of here, Yank—"

"Later," he whispered, "later!" He helped her swing up on Strawberry, mounted Dust Devil, and

378

rode out behind her on the narrow, dangerous trail. They might make it to the top in less time because he knew that trail from his childhood, but one false step and a horse could fall kicking and twisting in terror to the bottom of that canyon floor.

Cayenne looked down as they moved up the trail. "No, Cee Cee," he cautioned. "Stop looking back; look ahead. That's what's important, what's ahead of you not what's behind you."

She turned in her saddle, looking at him. "That's not a bad plan for life, Maverick."

If they had any kind of life ahead of them, he thought, looking down at the sleeping Indian village. Minutes had passed but it seemed like hours. Anytime, he expected a sentry to spot them, call out, alert the whole camp.

There were almost to the top now, he realized, looking up at the rocky edge. His heart began to pound with hope. They might just make it out of here after all! They might be miles away before the Indians found the dead Kiowa and Little Fox in tomorrow's daylight.

And then far below him, he saw Little Fox stagger out of the tepee into the light of a campfire and shout a warning, pointing up the side of the canyon.

Instantly, the camp began to come awake, dogs barking, people running, horses neighing.

"By damn!" Maverick swore. "I knew it was too good to be true!"

He glanced at Cayenne's pale face, saw her lips moving in silent prayer. "Baby, we've got to chance finishing this trail at a full gallop!"

"But if the horses slip and go over—"

"You rather die a quick death by falling or have the Comanche get you?" With that, he slashed out with his reins, caught the startled Strawberry across her

379

roan rump, and sent her galloping up the trail ahead of him. Then he dug his heels in the stallion's sides and bolted on up the trail behind her.

Dust Devil stumbled once in the rocks, and Maverick hung on, unsure for a moment if the stallion would fall and go over the edge. He heard a rock under the big stallion's hooves clatter down, strike an outcrop, and fall off into the canyon. He had a sudden vision of himself and the stallion falling end over end, the horse's mane and tail streaming out in the darkness as it fell eight hundred feet. But then the powerful mount regained its balance and galloped on up the path behind the little mare.

They were out and on top of the canyon rim. Maverick could hardly believe his good fortune as he reined in, looking back. Below him now, warriors were running, trying to catch up with their neighing, rearing horses.

Her face hone pale in the moonlight. "Maverick, now what? Can we outrun them?"

"No, but I've got a plan." He dismounted and reached into his saddlebags. Good! Everything was still there! He reached for the Lucifer matches. The wind came up suddenly, hot and dry as the Devil's breath on his half-naked body. He struck a match. It flickered and went out. Already below him, he saw mounted warriors starting up the crooked trail.

Maverick swore under his breath and struck another. The breeze caught it and blew it out as if the Devil were playing a joke. He turned and looked up at Cayenne. "If you believe in prayer, pray, baby! I only got one left!"

He saw her lips move silently and he was almost awestruck. The wind stopped for a brief moment as if God Himself had reached down to help them. In that split second, Maverick struck the last precious match, dropping it in the dry buffalo grass along the edge of the canyon.

Even as he remounted, slashing the stallion with the reins, the grass caught fire along the canyon rim and the rushing wind came up again, turning the area around the trail entrance into a sheer wall of flames.

"Come on, Cee Cee, we got to get to the Lazy M!" he shouted exultantly, and she dug her heels into the mare's flanks, galloping along with him. They took off south at a run while behind them the warriors, unable to get through the wall of flames, shouted in anger and frustration as Maverick and his woman rode away at a gallop from the Palo Duro canyon.

Chapter Nineteen

The old Don Diego de Durango sat enjoying the early morning sun near the fountain in the courtyard of the Triple D *hacienda*.

In another hour, the heat of this first day of August would turn the patio into a sweltering oven here in the Texas Hill country. But he would be seventy-five years old this September and the morning sun felt good on his arthritic old bones.

He tipped his flat black hat over his dark eyes and looked around, wishing some *vaquero* would happen along to talk about old times. All the household help seemed to be occupied, with no time for the old patriarch of the giant spread. He smiled, as cagey as an old gray fox. In that case, he could sneak a cigar without being scolded because the strong smokes he liked were bad for him.

He bit off the tip and spit it out. Then he lit the strong cigar, exhaling with a loud sigh as he readjusted his girth to the chair, listening to the musical splash of the fountain into the little pool.

A good cigar! He nodded agreeably to himself. After a while, he might go into the deserted study and have a good drink of whiskey. Pleasures were few and far between for the old, and even then, if his lovely daughter-in-law weren't upstairs with a new baby, she would gently lecture him about his health. He wished Trace were home. But he'd gone off to visit another ranch and discuss the price of some fine-blooded cattle he and the Don had agreed to buy. Then, too, Trace was so preoccupied with the responsibilities of this ranch, which covered most of two counties and had been in the family for three generations, that he would not often sit and discuss old times, old *compadres* with the Don.

Diego frowned, stroking his white mustache as he enjoyed the taste of the fine cigar. Most of his *compadres* were dead anyhow.

A small brown Chihuahua dog trotted through the open French doors of the house, its nails clicking across the paved courtyard of the sprawling *hacienda* as it came up to him, wagging its tail.

"Ah, Tequila, there doesn't seem to be much to occupy two old gentlemen like us today, is there?"

At the sound of its name, the old dog cocked its small head, wagging its tail, and hopped up into Diego's lap, where it settled with a satisfied yawn.

Diego stroked the tiny dog's gray muzzle and tasted his cigar. He wished Maverick and Sanchez would get back from the trail drive. They were long overdue, them and the whole crew. Probably they had gotten into a saloon brawl and ended up in jail again. He made a fist and took an imaginary swing, remembering the wilder days of his youth.

He petted the dog absently, thinking about Comanches and the snatches of news he'd heard about the Uprising. When he was around, everyone lowered their voices and he knew they wished not to worry him about the happenings in Texas.

By our Lady, he thought with annoyance. This old white-headed lion had fought Comanches, dealing with the loss of his wife, every kind of plague, prairie fire, and pestilence in the many years since he had inherited the Triple D from his father, who had carved

383

it out of wilderness. *Si*, Papa, too, had fought the Comanche to hold onto the ranch.

The dog in his lap stiffened suddenly and stood up, looking intently toward the northern horizon.

Diego craned his neck to see, too, but his eyes were not as good as they once were. "What is it, boy, Indians?"

He felt guilty that he almost half hoped a shrieking war party might come across the horizon so he could show everyone that Don Diego de Durango was still capable of action, that he was still a fair hand with a gun even though his eyes and hearing were not as good as they once were. No one really needed him anymore to do much of anything.

But the small dog's tail started to wag, slowly at first, then faster. Diego tipped his Spanish-style hat back and stared at the approaching riders.

The tiny pet bounced off his lap, barking excitedly as it took off at an arthritic run toward the riders trotting over the crest of the hill.

Diego stood up, shaking his cigar at the elderly pet as it limped out toward the riders. "You're too old for that, Tequila. Your rheumatism will give you fits tonight for trying to act like a young dog. You should wait and—"

His voice trailed off as he realized he lectured the elderly dog in the same manner that the humans around here lectured him.

The riders crested the hill and came closer to the *hacienda*. Diego's pulse beat faster. The trail crew was finally home! There'd be lots of good talk, lots of tales about past drives tonight!

Most of the riders split off to ride toward the bunkhouse, but a lone rider—a heavy, graying man—rode at a trot up to the courtyard where he reined in, the old Chihuahua bouncing excitedly while it barked and danced around the bay horse.

Diego limped forward with a glad cry. "Sanchez, old *compadre!* We've been worried about you! Where's Maverick?"

He caught the old *vaquero*'s arm, pulling him toward a seat on the patio. "Come, come, sit down, tell me everything."

Sanchez pulled at his gray mustache with his crippled hand, looking wistfully toward the house where his plump wife, the head housekeeper, would be. "Now, Diego? You want to talk now? I thought I might go in, have a plate of tamales and eggs. . . ."

"You can eat later." Diego waved him to a seat, offered him a cigar, and lit it for him. "No one has time for talk anymore. Why are you so late returning?"

"There was a small fight at the Red Garter." He grinned, accepting the cigar. "So we were forced to enjoy the hospitality of that Wyatt Earp's jail for a few days. Then there was news of war parties between here and there, so we hung around Wichita awhile." Sanchez took the cigar between his maimed fingers, leaned back with a tired sigh, and inhaled it. "I forgot how good one of your fine cigars taste, Diego. My wife sees me, I get a lecture."

Diego grinned with devilish delight. "You think I wasn't checking to see who that was coming so I could throw away my own if the rider was my son?"

Sanchez laughed, tipping his sombrero to the back of his graying head. "We are two conspirators, no?"

"*Si*," Diego winked and nodded. "Later we will go into the study and have a big drink of whiskey."

Sanchez crossed his legs with a smile. "I will get a big lecture if they smell whiskey on you later."

Diego muttered and smoked his cigar. "When those who lecture us were still dirtying their drawers, we were fighting Injuns, rounding up mustangs and breaking them to saddle. You are still young enough to be useful, *compadre*, but me? No one thinks Tequila and I are good for anything except to lay in the sun and warm our bones. Sometimes I wish I had a friend who had lots of time to sit and talk of the good old days."

Sanchez looked wistfully toward the house again, shrugged, and took another puff of his cigar.

Diego knew he kept his old friend from his wife, but he was lonely, eager for news. The two had been *compadres* since both were very young men, although Sanchez was not nearly as old as the Don was. He looked toward the bunkhouse. "Where's Maverick? Did I miss seeing him ride in?"

Sanchez rolled the cigar around in his mouth. "No, he didn't come."

"Didn't come?" Maverick of all people would give every glorious detail of the drive as if he sensed the lonely isolation of the old patriarch. And yet, even he who had raised the orphaned boy could not say he knew him well.

Sanchez winked at him in a knowing way. "A *Senorita*."

"Ah!" Diego leaned back, crossing his wrinkled old hands across his girth. "Oh, to be young and hot-blooded again!" He thought wistfully of his beautiful Cheyenne wife, so much younger than he. He had loved her so. "So you left him in Wichita?"

Sanchez shook his head. "No, *amigo*, he took off with her across the Indian Territory, across the Panhandle."

Diego felt alarm. He paused with the strong cigar halfway to his lips. "With the Indian trouble, our young stud did such a thing?"

Sanchez grinned. "The *Senorita* was very beautiful and very persuasive, I think."

Diego laughed, remembering his own young days.

"Maverick has always stayed so detached from women, always enjoyed and enticed them with his easy charms. I never thought one would come along that could make him think seriously."

Sanchez smoked, obviously remembering the girl as he smiled. "She had green eyes a man could get lost in," he sighed, "and hair the color of fire."

Diego leaned forward. "Ah, a redhead! A Texas girl, I hope!" He would miss Maverick if he went very far from the Triple D so that he could not visit him several times a year.

"*Si*, and what a firecracker! I think I have never seen such a fiery one! Her name's Cayenne!"

"Cayenne," Diego rolled it around on his tongue. "Now why does that sound familiar? Do we know the family?"

Sanchez shrugged. "The last name meant nothing to me. Oh, Maverick told me to give you a message." He stood up, yawned as he took one final puff, and threw the cigar down to grind out beneath his boot heel. "He said he'd be home in a few weeks. Our young Romeo's escorting the red-haired beauty back to west Texas. Maverick said you'd understand."

Diego didn't have the least idea what his old friend was talking about. He was a little annoyed and disappointed that Maverick was not here to enjoy a drink with, to tell him all the news when Sanchez was obviously so eager to go into the house. "Why did he think I'd understand?"

Sanchez's crippled fingers rubbed his swarthy face. "*Dios, compadre*, I don't know. He said to tell you the girl's father was McBride. Joe McBride. He said you'd understand."

For a long moment, Diego felt a pain grab his chest and he almost doubled over.

Sanchez stared at him anxiously. "Diego? Are you

387

all right? What in the name of our Lady is wrong?"

"*Nada,*" Diego managed to shrug. "It is nothing. I'm not even sure I ever met a McBride," he lied, averting his eyes. "*Compadre,* I am thoughtless, keeping you away from your lovely wife." He stood up, clapping the old *vaquero* on the back. "Here it is Saturday morning. She'll want you to take her into the village this afternoon shopping and visiting."

The other paused, looking wistfully toward the house. "Ah, old friend, I'm in no hurry if you want to talk some more. . . ."

But Diego wanted to be alone to think, to decide what to do. "No, you go on, I insist," He waved him away toward the house and stood looking after him. The small dog trotted at the *vaquero*'s heels as he crossed the patio to the French doors.

When he had disappeared inside, Diego collapsed limply in his chair, tossing the cigar away. *Joe McBride.* What was he to do about this terrible thing that was about to happen or might even have happened already?

Joe McBride. He had kept the information from the boy for a year now, lighting a few candles to the Virgin in hopes that Maverick's trail would never cross that of the big Kentuckian. It had been too much to hope for. Diego stared at the water bubbling in the fountain with unseeing eyes. *About one year,* he thought, *about one year ago I met him at the Cattleman's Association meeting in Austin.*

Maverick. He considered the strange, distant boy he had raised since the age of fourteen. There were more scars deep within him than just the one of his dark face. Now the half-Comanche was a grown man, as tough and rugged as the Texas Hill Country itself. No one knew Maverick well, although Diego and Trace had both tried. He seemed to keep people at arm's

388

length, as if he feared intimacy of any kind. Maverick could be kind and generous to a fault. But he had a dark side, this adopted son. The *vaqueros* whispered about Trace that while Maverick never forgot a friend, he never forgave an enemy. And he could carry a grudge longer than anyone the old Don had ever known.

He ran his tongue along his wrinkled lips, stared down at his arthritic hands. Once he'd been a good shot, as were Trace and Maverick. Last year, of course, his hands had shaken too badly to enter the shooting contests at the association meeting, even though the prize was a fine Winchester '73 rifle that had just been introduced. That was why he'd stopped by the table in the hotel to admire the gun and congratulate the man who had won it.

He remembered now holding out his hand. "*Senor*, my heartiest congratulations! Never have I seen such skill with a rifle!"

The red-haired man took his hand and shook it warmly. "You are too kind." His ruddy complexion colored with modesty. "Do sit down, *Senor*—?"

"Durango. Diego de Durango." He pulled up a chair, gesturing for a waiter.

"Ah, the Triple D in the Hill Country." The handsome stranger nodded, "Of course, your place is well-known."

Now it was the old man's turn to become embarrassed, flustered. The waiter came over. "Whiskey," he ordered, "since my son and old Sanchez are off looking at a display of new saddles and aren't here to lecture me." He looked into the other's wide green eyes, liking the honesty and the open friendliness he saw there. "*Amigo*, may I buy you a drink?"

"Thank you, no," Joe McBride gestured toward his

389

coffee cup and the waiter refilled it. "Enjoy your spirits, *Senor*, but I'm a man of the Lord and I find liquor causes me more trouble than it's worth."

Diego glanced around to make sure there was no one in the crowded dining room of cattlemen who would tattle on him before he lit a cigar, offered one to the other man who shook his head. "A minister who shoots so well? How can that be?"

The other man laughed good-naturedly. "I only felt the call three years ago after my wife died," he admitted. "But I'm from Kentucky and I was always able to knock a knothole from a tree when no one else could see it. Too poor to waste the powder, you know."

Diego nodded, although he did not know. His family was old Spanish aristocracy who had been in Texas since it had belonged to Mexico. "I don't believe I caught your name, *Senor.*"

The man paused, a forkful of steak halfway to his lips. "McBride. Joe McBride."

Diego went into a spasm of coughing. The waiter came just then and Diego grabbed the whiskey, gulping it.

McBride half rose from his chair. "Are you all right, sir? May I do something—?"

"No, no, I—I'm fine," he lied, waving the man back down. "Did you say Joe McBride?"

The other nodded, staring at him, concern in the honest face. "*Senor*, you have turned very pale. Should I call a doctor? Go find your son?"

Diego shook his head, signaling the waiter to bring him another drink. *It couldn't be the same man. It just couldn't be.* "Did you say you were from Kentucky, Mr. McBride?"

The other nodded, returned to his steak. "You know, I don't even have a son to pass this fine gun on to." He stroked the etched barrel. "Seems a shame now, don't it?"

"It surely does." Diego stared at him, accepting the whiskey from the waiter and sipping it thoughtfully while he watched the man eat his steak.

He liked Joe McBride instinctively. Everything about the man spoke of character, of honesty, of open friendliness. "You have daughters then, sir?"

Joe grinned and nodded, bringing out small photographs from his coat. "Sure do. Five of the reddest-haired girls you ever saw in your life!" He held the pictures out proudly and Diego took them, staring. Four of the girls were little, but there was a young woman of eighteen or so that showed a lot of fire in her beauty.

"That one will lead some man a merry chase some day," he laughed, handing the photos back. "Fine children, *Senor*."

The other man looked at the pictures fondly a long moment before returning them to his pocket. "That oldest is Cayenne; you know, like the pepper. I'm all the girls have," he said with a slight shadow crossing his face. "With my wife dead giving birth to the little one, there's nobody to look after them should something happen to me. Oh, my wife's Aunt Ella's in Wichita, but she's in pore health and doesn't much like kids anyway, so don't think she'd come to stay with us in west Texas."

He described the little community as Diego toyed with his whiskey glass, turning it around and around in his fingers as he considered. This couldn't be the same man, the unfeeling monster whom his adopted son hunted, intended to kill, and yet . . .

He must know. "*Senor*," Diego said hesitantly, "did you ever know a girl called Annie Laurie?"

The man's face paled, and his nerveless fingers dropped his fork so that it clattered to the floor. No one else seemed to pay the pair the slightest heed as they stared into each other's eyes in the midst of the noisy, crowded dining room.

The Don sighed. "I guess there's no reason to ask a second time. I'd hoped I might be wrong. . . ."

"What do you know of her?" the man demanded, half rising from his chair and reaching across to grab Diego's lapels. "What do you know of my Annie?"

The tragedy of his green eyes told the older man how very much Joe had loved the girl. Slowly, he reached up, disengaging the man's clenched fingers from his coat. "*Senor*," he whispered, "I think we need to talk."

The man stared into his eyes and his lips trembled. "You know of her? What—?"

"I think we'd better find a more private place to continue this discussion." Diego said. He stood up, threw money down on the table, and took the man's elbow that trembled in his grasp. "Isn't there a garden outside?"

The man stared at him, tears in his eyes, and nodded dumbly.

For a long moment, Don Diego feared the man would collapse, but he seemed to pull himself together. Joe picked up the prize rifle and let Diego lead him outside to a secluded bench under a live oak tree.

"She's dead, isn't she?" he whispered. "Otherwise, you would have told me. She's—"

"*Si.*" He could think of no way to soften it for the man. Joe McBride put his face in his big square hands and for a long moment his shoulders shook much as Maverick's had shaken when he'd finally told his adoptive father of the terrible night he had fled the Indian camp.

After a long moment, the man reached into his pocket for his Bible, clasping it in his hands as if drawing strength from it. Diego looked at it. The black volume was dog-eared and worn from much reading. "Your religion will give you strength."

Joe McBride nodded. "Yes, it has since the day my wife died." He looked off toward the horizon, where the sunset turned the sky golden and peach and orange as only a Texas sky can look. "He must have had you seek me out for a reason, *Senor* Durango. There's a time and season for all things. Why has He sent you to find me?"

The Don considered. *Had some Great Force caused him to be at this place in time at this moment to change the course of things?* He could only be grateful that Maverick was back at the Triple D and had no reason to go to west Texas. His trail might never cross that of Joe McBride's in his lifetime, and yet . . .

He sighed and pulled at his white mustache, trying to decide what to do. "McBride, you have five daughters and no wife?"

The big Scots-Irishman nodded. "I told you that."

Was he being disloyal to his ward? On the other hand, if he did not warn McBride, blood would be on his hands if Maverick should catch him unawares. "Annie's son is looking for you," he said softly, "and when he finds you, he intends to kill you."

"Annie's son . . ." The man stared into space, his green eyes seeing only a scene from the past. "She always told me she would give me a son."

Diego grabbed his arm, shook him. "Don't you understand what I'm telling you? He's out for blood and he won't give up until he finds you!"

The man looked down at the Bible in his hands. "Can't say I blame him," he said softly.

"I mean it, *Senor*, and he's a good shot; best with a pistol I ever saw. Trace trained him to shoot. I tell you this now because I can't stand by doing nothing while he orphans five children!"

"Well, I'll pray about it." Joe said, staring down at his Bible.

"Pray?" Diego almost shouted. "Pray?"

Joe shrugged. "What else would a preacher do? Do you expect me to go gunnin' for him?"

"Well, no," Don Diego muttered, rubbing his wrinkled face. "But if he comes after you, you should be at least prepared to defend yourself. . . ."

"I—I don't know if I could do that—kill Annie's boy, I mean." He stared off into the growing dusk. "I suppose I won't know whether I can pull the trigger on him until that time comes that, God forbid, he's standing there ready to kill me. That day, I'll find out what kind of man I am, what kind of stuff he's made of. I can't imagine Annie's boy as a cold-blooded killer. There'd be too much of Annie in his heart and soul."

The man had loved her, perhaps even more than Maverick had, Diego thought, *blinking away the sudden wetness that blurred his vision*. "If I thought it would do any good, I'd try to talk him out of it. All I can do is warn you, McBride, describe him to you in case he ever shows up in your area. That way, you at least got time to make your decision before he pulls the trigger."

McBride fingered the worn Bible in his hands. "He's got gray eyes, hasn't he?"

Diego looked at him sharply and nodded. "How do you know that?"

He smiled slightly as if remembering. "Because my Annie had gray eyes."

"But he's dark, with the blackest hair, like a Comanche warrior, and he's big, too. He's got a jagged scar down his left cheek."

Joe nodded. "I wonder if he has her smile? No one ever thought her pretty 'til she smiled."

Diego thought now how seldom he had seen the boy

394

smile. Maverick's mind seemed to be constantly on his grim revenge. It was his duty to warn this man who was being stalked so relentlessly. "Let me describe his horse, you'd spot that instantly: a giant of a gray stallion called Dust Devil."

"Revelations six, verse eight," Joe said softly. "Yes, it's a sign all right. I only wish I knew what the Almighty was plannin'."

"I don't understand, *Senor*."

"It's in the Bible." Joe turned and looked at him with those bright green eyes. ". . . and I looked and beheld a pale horse and his name that sat upon him was Death and Hell followed with him."

Diego shivered in spite of himself and crossed his chest quickly. "Are you sure it's a sign from God—or from the Devil?" he asked.

The other gave him a long, serene look. "Only time will tell, *Senor* Durango. Perhaps young Maverick will never find me."

"I pray it will be so." Diego said, and he stood up and walked away. . . .

The noise of laughter and talk drifted from the inside of the ranch to him out there by the fountain. He roused himself from his thoughts and looked around the patio. The sun felt hot on his stooped old shoulders now that it was late morning.

For a year, he thought, *for a year I have kept the secret, hoping that Maverick would either give up his search or never find the red-haired preacher*. Then, in the least likely place, Maverick had stumbled onto McBride's daughter and she was leading him innocently to kill her father. The chances of such a thing happening seemed infinitesimal to him and he looked up at the sky, wondering suddenly if God Himself were pulling the strings of the human puppets to bring these people, these events all together? No, of course He would not do anything that would create such tragedy, such horror.

Could anything be done to stop it? He remembered watching McBride shoot in the contest, wondered if Maverick realized the man he hunted was the top rifle in Texas? Despite McBride's hesitance to defend himself, Diego knew that men changed when under a loaded gun and life suddenly became very precious to them.

He stood, hobbled into the house, and found Sanchez in the kitchen finishing a big plate of chili pepper eggs and beef. "Is anyone else close by?"

"No." Sanchez wiped his mouth with his crippled hand. "All scattered through the house doing chores."

"*Muy bueno.*" Diego rubbed his hands together with relish. He had made his decision and he felt like a young man again. He was needed, he could make a difference. "*Amigo,* don't ask any questions, just gather up a few things for us and keep your mouth shut."

Sanchez paused with a tortilla halfway to his mouth. "What—?"

"No one can really stop us but Trace, and he's not home." Diego folded his arms. "Doesn't the Austin stage leave this afternoon for west Texas?"

"*Si,* but—"

Diego gestured impatiently. "Quit stuffing your face, *compadre,* and get a move on! We can be there by Monday night."

Sanchez blinked. "Be where?"

Diego grabbed his shoulder, pulling him to his feet. It was good to be needed again, to be able to make a difference. "West Texas," he said. "Now get some things and let's head for town before anyone suspects. . . ."

got back! I haven't even really gotten to take my boots off yet!"

Diego grabbed his arm, propelling him out of the kitchen. "We'll leave a note," he said as they went down the front hall toward the stairs. "They won't know until it's too late to stop us."

"Stop us from what?" The *caudillo* tried to dig his boot heels in but the other kept propelling him along.

"Stop Maverick from killing a man," he answered, then he had a sobering thought, "—or of getting killed himself. The best pistol in Texas is about to go up against the best rifleman in Texas—if it hasn't already happened."

Sanchez's weathered face registered horror. "What is this you say?"

"I say I am not too old to try to stop this tragedy!" He stared back at his old friend. "Don't you understand? There's going to be a killing! And we've got to get there to see if we can stop it! Now, pack our bags and let's make that stage!"

Chapter Twenty

Joe McBride got up out of the porch rocker with difficulty. Just how long did it take little girls to get dressed for services? He wished Cayenne were here to hurry them along.

In the distance, the bell at the weathered little church began to toll Sunday service.

"Girls," he shouted through the open front door, "come on, we're going to be late!"

Running feet pounded down the inside stairs. "Papa," Lynnie called, "I can't help it! Angel's wet her drawers again and I'll have to get her dry ones!"

"Besides," Stevie yelled, "they can't have services without the preacher!"

"Don't count on it," he called back. "They'll at least start the singing without us!"

Behind him, he heard the old buggy creak to a halt and he turned.

"Senor Joe," Juan said, "are you ready?"

"Spend half our life waitin' for women, don't we?" Joe grinned good-naturedly as the little girls pushed breathlessly through the creaky screen, fat old Rosita puffing along behind them.

"Here we are, Papa!"

Lynnie took his arm and helped him limp down the creaking steps into the buggy. The little girls piled in around them, along with Juan and the fat housekeeper.

"Angel," Lynnie scolded, "get your thumb out of your mouth and, Gracious, your sash is untied!"

Joe smiled to himself. The serious, smart one was stepping into Cayenne's spot.

Lynnie leaned over conspiratorially, whispering in his ear. "I just saw Trask mount up over at the barn."

Joe shrugged. "Doesn't he go everywhere we go?"

He didn't look back as the man rode up behind the buggy. Joe had other things to think about rather than whether Trask accompanied them everywhere they went. The trio knew he wouldn't alert the law. Besides his position, he had four little girls and his gentle Mexican help to protect. All night he had struggled with his conscience, trying to decide what to do. He'd heard Slade and his friends talking late last night, had sneaked down to listen to the conversation. He should have known they were up to no good. The Austin stage Monday evening would be carrying a secret strongbox with pay for all those troops up north of here. The message had come by wire from Wichita through some secret code they'd worked out. The trio planned to take the stage by surprise when it stopped to change horses in the sleepy little community, then escape up to their old hideout in the Indian Territory.

Sighing, he slipped both hands in his pockets. In one was his worn Bible, in the other a willow whistle he'd carved for that child at church. All these weeks he'd behaved himself, keeping his mouth shut to protect this town, his children, and maybe most of all his reputation.

But what was he going to do now? He thought about it as the buggy bumped along, the red-haired, freckle-faced little girls laughing and giggling while Juan drove the patient old mule. After all, it wasn't Joe's gold. If he kept his mouth shut, the robbery would go off as planned just before sundown tomorrow night and then

399

they'd ride out of his life and no one would be the wiser.

Decisions. You could tell a lot about a man's character by the decisions he made. Ten years ago, he'd made a wrong decision and now he might have to pay the consequences. Because of Hannah's threat, he'd wasted valuable time going to Swen for help in finding Annie. And now her son, like an avenging angel, was coming to get him. No, maybe not.

Joe ran his fingers through his red beard thoughtfully as the buggy moved along. Maybe the Lord had been with him and the wire had reached Cayenne. Maybe the man she described was not Maverick Durango. *No man wants to die, even the most religious,* he thought ruefully. But if it came to a showdown, what would Joe do?

Annie. Joe sighed, deep in thought. He knew the little girls paid him no mind as they laughed and chattered in the moving buggy. He always used the time driving to church for prayer and contemplation. Twenty-five years ago, his beloved Annie had been carried off. And for fifteen of them, he had thought her dead, mourning over a faceless body in a graveyard.

But ten years ago, a young man had come to the house, asking to see him and his wife.

Sensing this was something serious, Joe escorted the half-grown boy into the parlor. He chased Cayenne out to play, motioned Hannah to a seat on the Victorian horsehair sofa, and closed the door. "Now what is this all about, young man?"

What was that boy's name? Well, it didn't matter anyhow, Joe shook his head as the buggy bumped along. He'd left the area right after that; just a skinny, scared kid who'd been captured by the Comanche.

The boy looked from Hannah to Joe. "She—she sent me."

400

Joe looked into his face blankly. "Who?"

"The woman who helped me escape while the braves was gone huntin'."

Joe stared at the boy. "Who are you talking about?"

The boy ran his hand through his tousled hair, looking at Hannah a long moment. "Your wife," he said.

Hannah's homely face frowned. "You must be loco, young man. I never saw you before in my—"

"The other one," the boy blurted out, "the one with the pretty smile."

Joe felt his heart contract painfully in his chest and he stood up, giving a gesture of dismissal. "What a cruel thing to do! You're after money, right? You heard about that, think you can extract money from me somehow! Well, it won't work! She's buried in the little cemetery. . . ."

"No, she' ain't." The boy looked up at him, his eyes clear and honest. "No, she ain't, mister. She told me if I made it back to come to you, tell you she's wondering why you never ransomed her. . . ."

Joe swore suddenly and Hannah started, looking at him. Joe seldom swore. "Get out of my house, you rascal!" Joe said. "You'll not play on my feelings to get money. . . ."

"Her name's Annie Laurie," the boy said quickly, fumbling with his hat, obviously determined to finish his mission. "She has gray eyes and the sweetest smile I ever saw."

For a long moment, Joe thought he would faint. He swayed and grabbed at the stone fireplace for support. Of course there was nothing to it, couldn't be. Hannah had identified the body fifteen years ago while Joe was in St. Joe involved in a bank robbery to get money to ransom Annie. "Go on."

Hannah flounced to her feet. "Joe, don't encourage this—this scoundrel," she gestured, just a little too angry, a little too indignant. "He's heard the stories, that's all." She faced down the young man. "Let's get right to it: You know I inherited the Adams money, thought that we might pay you for bogus information."

"No, I—"

"Don't lie to me!" Hannah shrieked at him. "I'll give you money to get you to leave, but it's cruel of you to hurt my husband so!"

The boy stood up slowly, looking from one to the other. "I ain't after money," he said slowly, moving awkwardly toward the door. "And I'm leavin' Texas forever when I walk out of this place."

Joe still gripped the stone of the fireplace so hard his fingers hurt. His emotions were torn with indecisions, disbelief. "Wait, boy, tell me—"

"There ain't much more to tell, mister," the boy fumbled with his hat. "Annie helped me escape, even though I'll bet the Comanche might do something terrible to her for doin' it." He named a band of the tribe to the north. "I told her if I made it back, I'd bring you the message."

He looked from Joe to Hannah. "I guess she didn't know you'd remarried. By the way, she's got a half-breed son a little younger than I am."

Joe's guts twisted at the images that came to his mind of his Annie beneath some dark-skinned Comanche savage. *Someday, I'll give you my son,* she had said.

The boy paused a long moment in the doorway, looking from Hannah to Joe. "I can't do any more than I've done, mister. Now it's up to you."

The boy turned and went out the front door. Joe leaned against the fireplace with his eyes closed, listening to the horse trotting away from the ranch.

Hannah's skirts rustled as she came over to him. "Joe, there's bound to be a mistake. . . ."

"Is there?" He looked into her homely, plump face. "You identified that body, Hannah, buried it before I got back from St. Joe."

"I—I—" She twisted her short fingers together. "I thought it was her. . . ."

"Thought!" He confronted her, "Thought!"

Hannah bit her lip. "It . . . she was about the same size . . . brown hair. The body was in pretty bad shape by the time the Rangers brought it in, Joe, but I recognized that old faded dress she always wore."

"I always meant to buy her a new one," he said absently, going over to stare out the window as if he could see the grave from here. He wondered suddenly who the nameless woman in Annie's grave was, why she might have been wearing Annie's clothes. "Fifteen years," he muttered, "for fifteen years, Annie's been a captive, going through hell and me not even knowing she's alive."

Hannah caught his arm. "I—I thought it was her, honest! And all I could think of was that if she was dead, you might marry me! I did it because I loved you, Joe, always loved you!"

He looked down at her coldly and shook her arm off. "So you were only too eager to identify that body, even though you weren't sure, so you could step into her place."

"And what about you?" she screamed at him. "Weren't you eager to marry me, get your hands on my father's ranch, his money? Do you think I'm so stupid I didn't realize you wouldn't have looked at me twice without my inheritance?"

"You're right, of course." Joe ran his hand through his red hair. "God is not mocked," he said softly. "Someone told me that once and I guess we'll both pay the price for our sins."

Her face paled. "Joe, what do you intend to do? If

403

she's been with the Injuns for fifteen years, she's changed, might not even be sane. . . ."

"After fifteen years with the Comanche, she'd be lucky to even be alive, much less sane." He wrung his hands together with indecision, staring out the window. His beloved Cayenne swung in a big rope swing hanging from the limb of a chinaberry tree to the side of the house.

Hannah came over, looking out with him at the laughing red-haired child. "And what about her?" Her tone was bitter, jealous. "If you don't give a damn about me, what about her?"

"What do you mean?"

"If your first wife is still alive, Joe, we aren't married. That makes Cayenne a bastard."

He winced at the word, the cruel memories it brought back of children chasing him home from school, throwing stones and taunting him. *Bastard! Bastard! Joe carries his mama's name 'cause he ain't got no pa!*

He had a sudden image of the local children taunting and ostracizing his beloved daughter.

Hannah seemed to sense her advantage. "And there's that boy, too, a half-breed savage boy. What would you do about him?"

"I—I don't know." He watched his daughter swing higher and higher, singing that old folk tune he had taught her: *. . . and for darlin' Annie Laurie . . .*

"We'll go away somewhere," he babbled desperately. "I don't know how, but maybe we can work all this out. . . ."

"I ain't gonna raise no half-breed brat," Hannah crossed her arms contemptuously.

Joe turned, eyeing her coldly. "Then I'll take Annie and her boy, take Cayenne. The four of us will go away. . . ."

"Take my child! Likely chance!"

Joe looked at her. "You've never really cared about Cayenne, always been jealous of the love I have for her."

Hannah paced the floor. "I can't help it, Joe. I resent havin' to share you with anyone, even my own child."

"Then I could take her, and maybe Annie and her son, and we'll go away, start over. . . ."

"You think any Texas court would let you have her with all the Adams influence and money?"

He looked out the window again, struggling with the decision. I—I can't just not do anything."

"Why not?" Hannah shrugged. "As far as everyone's concerned, she's been dead fifteen years. Nobody but you, me, and that boy who's leavin' Texas knows about this. She may be dead by now anyway. The Injuns probably killed her for helpin' that boy escape!"

Joe McBride was a proud man and he had grieved for a dead wife all these long years. The innocent, laughing Annie he had known would not be the same person, might not even be sane. And what was he to do with a savage Comanche son?

The thought of the son brought to mind his Annie lying under some dark brute. She could have killed herself rather than submit. Lots of captured women did. Then he felt deep shame at his thoughts. Cayenne laughed again out in the swing, and tears came to his eyes as he watched his beloved child playing.

Hannah must have read his thoughts. "You can't keep Cayenne if you bring that Annie and her half-breed boy here, I'll see to that!"

He had a choice to make, and he let his pride, his love for his own child, make that choice. In this little nameless community, Joe was a rich and influential man. And that was very important to him. He had been a poor, nameless boy with others chasing him home, mistreating him because his pa was not legally married to his mother. They'd not do that to little Cayenne. Joe struggled with his decision for weeks before he finally went in to see "Swen" Swenson of the Rangers. The man was older, gray in the blond hair now, and he'd been promoted. Swen said he'd be on the lookout, but not to expect too much. Joe checked back with Swenson many times and the man always discouraged him, told him to forget about Annie. And finally, Joe quit asking.

After that, Hannah seemed to get pregnant often, as if trying to bind him to her with more children. As he never loved her before, he did not love her now. But there are many empty, bitter marriages that are held together by the love of little children.

And then three years ago, as her life slipped away after the birth of Angel, Hannah had motioned him to her side. "I—I was wrong, Joe," she whispered. "I've felt so guilty, but I loved you so. . . ."

"No, we was both wrong," Joe patted her short, plump hands. "It was me as much as you; my pride. I said it was love for the child but I think now it was purdee pride, thinking how people would whisper about Annie, how other men would laugh behind my back, what people would wonder about and say."

"May God forgive us," Hannah gasped. "May God forgive . . ."

Joe jerked out of his memories as the buggy bumped over the rutted road toward the church. Already, faint organ music floated to him on the breeze: *. . . Oh, come to the church in the wild wood, oh, come to the church in the dale . . .*

Juan whipped the old mule up a little. "We're late," Rosita scolded. "They've already started the first song!"

Trask laughed. "Well, now that I seen you to church like I was tole to do, I'm ridin' on down to the saloon for a drink! I'll be back about the time services is over!"

Lynnie snapped, "It wouldn't hurt you or old banker Ogle any to attend services, Mr. Trask!"

"Lynnie," Joe said, "that's not polite!"

But Trask just laughed and trotted off down the dusty road.

. . . No spot is so dear to my childhood as the little brown church in the vale . . .

Rosita said, "Tie the buggy to the rail, Juan, and let's hurry in. *Si*, that's right. Everybody's already in but us."

Joe let Lynnie help him from the buggy, holding her arm as he limped toward the weather-beaten little church with difficulty. "Go on in, everyone," he said. "I've got a very special sermon today and I'd like to pray over it a little first."

"But, Papa, you'll be late!" Lynnie protested.

He dismissed her with a wave of his hand. "They obviously aren't going to start the sermon without the preacher, and Brother Clemets always sings every single verse."

The sound of their feet going in could be heard over the singing of the small congregation.

. . . Oh, come, come, come, come to the church in the wild wood, oh, come to the church in the dale . . .

Joe held onto the stair rail to steady himself, bowing his head in prayer. He had made the decision last night, but weak as most humans, he was having second thoughts about the consequences, about what he had decided to do.

407

He heard the sound of a horse trotting into the church yard and raised his head.

"Mr. McBride," Hank Billings swung down from the big thoroughbred he rode, "what are you doing still outside?"

"Waiting for you," Joe said softly over the music drifting from inside the church. "I prayed you'd show up at just the right time."

"What?" the boy said.

"Hank, would you help me? It's something I can't do myself because I'm being watched. Would you do me a favor with no questions?"

"What a question, Mr. McBride! After what you done for my family, this town! Why, you just name it. . . ."

"Then don't ask any questions. First go to the telegraph and send a wire for the army to stop the Austin stage. . . ."

"Wires are down again, Papa says. Injuns, I guess. No messages going in or out."

Joe wondered if his message had reached Cayenne in time. With everything else, he didn't need to have to face up to Maverick's pistol right now. "Okay, then here's what you're to do. Get on that fast horse of yours, ride to the county seat. . . ."

"The county seat?" The boy whistled long and low. "That's a far piece—"

"I wouldn't ask you if it wasn't important," Joe said gently. "You get Captain Swenson and the Rangers, you hear? Get 'em back here by tomorrow night."

"The Rangers!" his voice was a gasp of awe. "You want me to bring Texas Rangers to this sleepy little burg? Why, what—?"

"Something's happenin' here about sundown tomorrow night," Joe said urgently over the hymn drifting from the church. "We got to have help, Hank! I'll tell

408

you everything when you get back!"

"I don't know if I can get them here by then," the boy said uncertaintly, "even with our thoroughbred."

"Oh, yes, you can," Joe said with conviction, " 'cause we're gonna have help." He turned his face up toward the hot sun. "Oh, yes, we're gonna have help!"

"My pa'll be askin'—"

"Go along with you, Hank!" Joe ordered. "I'll tell your pa about it so he won't worry! Now, go! And tell Swenson, if the wires are up to St. Joe, he'd better look into a bank robbery a quarter of a century ago!"

"Robbery?" Then he seemed to decide against asking any more questions. "For you, Joe McBride, anything!" And he turned, the saddle creaking as he swung up and galloped off.

Joe stood listening to the hoofbeats die even as the congregation finished the song.

He felt so helpless in the face of all this calamity. In the sudden silence as he stood there, a line from an appropriate poem came to his mind: . . . *He also serves who only stands and waits.*

Well, he'd done more than just stand. Through the open church windows, the organ music drifted as the congregation began another hymn. His favorite. It hadn't always been but it was now.

Lead kindly Light, amid encircling gloom, Lead Thou me on . . .

Joe mounted the steps with difficulty, opened the doors at the end of the church, and stood there a moment, listening.

The night is dark and I am far from home. Lead Thou me on. Keep Thou my feet, I do not ask to see the distant scene, one step enough for me.

Joe started down the aisle slowly while the small congregation sang: *I was not ever thus nor prayed that Thou shouldest lead me on. I loved to choose and see my path, but now lead Thou me on.*

It was a long walk so slowly up that aisle to the pulpit on crippled feet.

I loved the garish day and spite of fears, pride ruled my will, remember not past years.

He used the backs of pews to steady himself as he walked slowly toward the front, feeling the song had been chosen to speak directly to his heart.

So long Thy pow'r hath blest me, sure it still will lead me on o'er moon and fen, o'er crag and torrent, 'til the night is gone.

As he reached the rostrum, he listened to the final chords and thought of Annie.

And with the morn those angel faces smile, which I have loved long since and lost awhile.

He moved around behind the rostrum with difficulty, using it to balance his unsteady feet. Out of long habit, he took the worn Bible from his pocket, lying it before him, although he had memorized every word and did not need to see the print.

"Let us pray," he said softly, closing his eyes. He heard people shift in their pews. Someone coughed; a baby cried while its mother tried to shush it, finally taking it out with a rustle of her petticoats moving down the aisle.

"Heavenly Father, Great Jehovah," he said hesitantly, "forgive us for the sin of pride, for we have all been guilty of it, yes, every one."

He had prayed over his decision all night and now it was time to face the consequences of it. His voice grew stronger, louder with the strength of his convictions. "I, too, have been weak, glorying in the love and adoration of this town, yea, even encouraging them to idolize me."

He heard a murmur of protest from the audience, but he held up his hand to stay them without opening

410

his eyes. "I am guilty of the sin of pride of wanting men's good thoughts and good wishes for actions that any decent man would have done."

A murmur of protest went up again but he kept praying. Now that he had made his decision, he would not be stopped, no matter the consequences. "I have been a hero, an idol, and yet, idols have feet of clay if one looks too closely and one should give such adoration only to the Lord."

Now the buzz through the church was one of confusion, curiosity. "What'd he say? What's this all about?"

"Papa," Lynnie interrupted from the front row, "we don't understand. . . ."

"Lynnie, pray about your shortcomings in the field of impatience," he said gently. "I am trying to tell you, I have been so proud, so loathe to lose my reputation as resident saint, as it were, I have come very close to standing back and letting evil happen while I raised no hand to stop it."

A whisper went through the small crowd again and old Mrs Rumsley, the one who used the ear trumpet, said loudly, "What'd he say about raising his hand?"

Someone shushed her.

"Joe," Brother Edwards nasal voice began hesitantly, "we ain't quite sure what you're drivin' at. . . ."

"I'm saying no one should make such a hero of a man for doin' what's right and decent anyhow. But it was my fault for gloryin' in it, maybe encouragin' it when, if you knew the real Joe McBride, you might be shocked."

There was dead silence now and he bent his head, glad he didn't see their faces. If he could see their shocked eyes, he might not be able to to confess. "A long time ago," he said, "in another place and time, I was a thief, a robber."

411

He didn't look up, but he heard the sharp intake of breath from the small congregation, and Lynnie said, "Papa!"

He made a gesture to hush her. "It's true, it's true. I didn't steal anything, but I tried. At the time, I thought I had good reason to steal the money, I needed it so badly."

He didn't raise his head but he could feel the eyes of the group boring into him. The old church was so quiet that he heard a bumblebee buzz in through one window, out another. In the heat, ladies fanned themselves noisily with paper fans. "That was no excuse; I know that now and I guess the Lord knew it, too, because I didn't get away with a dime. Moreover, a man was killed in that robbery. I didn't shoot him but I'm responsible; I was there."

He waited a long moment but no one said anything. From the very back pew, the Harrison baby wailed fretfully. He felt sweat run down inside his collar in the August heat. "It was a long time ago," he said, "and I guess the sheriff in St. Joe is still lookin' for me. But I wanted to tell this congregation before I told Captain Swenson and turned myself in. That's all I got to say and I ask your prayers, hope you don't hate me too much for disappointing you." Tears came to his eyes, filled them. "One more thing," he said. "I request that at sundown tomorrow, you all gather in your homes and pray for the future of this church; this town, yes, even for me if you can find it in your hearts to do so. That's all I got to say."

With difficulty, he stumbled from the rostrum to a grip on the first pew. *It was a long way up that aisle,* he thought, *up the aisle and out to the buggy.* Somewhere in the crowd, a woman began to weep and he realized suddenly that it was old Rosita.

It was over and done with and he was glad he'd

412

confessed. Now he had no money, no reputation, no pride, but he'd done the right thing—finally.

He grasped the back of the pew to steady his crippled feet and started on up the aisle. He'd been protecting those outlaws, not so much because he feared for the townspeople or even his own family; he realized now he'd been protecting his own guilty past. Well, that was a club Slade couldn't hold over his head any more, and when the Rangers got here, they'd take care of that trio, maybe catch them red-handed robbing the stage. He wouldn't tell the people about that. The gentle farmers might try to stop the hardened outlaws and that was a job for the Rangers.

The part about Annie he couldn't tell without labeling his children "bastards" and they didn't deserve that, so he'd not tell it.

"Joe," Brother Clemets said, but Joe kept doggedly walking up the aisle toward the doors at the rear. If they were going to publicly condemn him, take his position as preacher from him, well, he expected no less.

"Yes?"

Brother Edwards walked across the creaking floor and caught Joe's arm. "It took more courage to do that, Brother, than it did to face the Indians."

"What? I—I don't understand. . . ."

And then the congregation seemed to break out of the spell of his confession, coming up off the wooden pews en masse and crowding around him. "We love you, Joe McBride! We'll pray for you, Brother, and you pray for us, too!"

A murmur first, then a roar of agreement went up from all of them as they crowded around him. "You got guts, Joe, I'll say that for you, to tell something none of us would ever have known if you hadn't told it!"

"That's right!" Billings said. "You're a braver man than I am, Joe McBride!"

413

Hands reached out to shake his in the press and confusion, and his little girl gathered around his legs.

"Papa," Lynnie said, "you were wonderful! Just like the heroes in my books! We're so proud!"

He started sobbing then, sobbing for all the years that he'd worried over this, all the weight that had been lifted from his back.

Mrs. Billings's high soprano began to sing: *In heav'nly love abiding, no change my heart shall fear . . .*

Mr. Harrison's deep bass picked it up: *. . . and safe is such confiding, for nothing changes here!*

One by one the congregation joined in and the music swelled as they sang with spirit and feeling until the rafters seemed to shake on the old weather-beaten building.

The storm may roar without me, my heart may low be laid, but God is round about me, and can I be dismayed?

Joe broke down and wept then as he joined the singing with fervor, hugging his little girls to him.

Later, before Trask rejoined them on their way home, he warned his family not to tell the trio about his confession; they wouldn't understand a man getting right with God anyway. But as they drove back to the ranch, Joe felt almost dizzy with it all. He hadn't been ostracized; instead, he was a bigger hero than ever. He hadn't told anyone about the bandits, not wanting to endanger them, but they'd all be in their homes tomorrow at sundown, praying for him, for the whole town and its future. If the Rangers would just do their job . . .

And when Swenson got here with the news from the Missouri law, Joe was ready to go back for trial, take his punishment like a man. But who would look after

414

his children? The congregation would help, of course, but he really would only feel confident about turning them over to Cayenne. If she only had a good, steady husband . . .

A shadow passed overhead and he jerked up.

"Papa!" Lynnie gasped, "the eagles are back! They're circling over our ranch!"

Was it a sign? He tried to think of an appropriate verse that had to do with eagles. Well, maybe just this once it might be a coincidence. . . .

Tomorrow at sundown, he thought. *Tomorrow night is the climax.* If the Rangers just get here in time. He thought suddenly about Maverick Durango. Was he coming for him? Was Annie's vengeful son even now on his way to kill Joe?

All he could do was wait and pray. Somehow, he knew that for good or evil, it would all come to a finish in the dusty little town of McBride, Texas tomorrow night!

Chapter Twenty-one

Cayenne studied Maverick as they reined up on the little bluff. In the distance to the south, she could barely make out the outline of the tiny hamlet of McBride. Should she finally confess? What would she do if he turned around, rode off, and left her without a word? But was it fair not to tell him until minutes before he ran smack-dab into the gunfighters?

"What day is it?" Maverick asked. "I've lost track."

Cayenne shrugged. "Must be Monday. I think I see wash hanging on lines like big white sails."

Maverick looked off toward the west. "The sun will be going down in another couple of hours. Is that McBride ahead of us?"

Cayenne nodded, her soul full of turmoil. *What was she going to do?* "We'll hit town just about dusk. Our ranch is on the far side of McBride. Maverick . . ."

"Yes?" His own face bore an expression of inner turmoil.

"I—let's sit down here a moment in the shade of this tree, rest the horses."

His brow wrinkled. "This close to home? Looks like you'd be in a big hurry if someone's sick after all you've gone through to get here."

"We've got to talk." She dismounted, tied Strawberry so she could munch grass, and went over to sit in the shade of a big mesquite. She'd made her decision.

Her heart was at peace now.

"About what?" He didn't meet her eyes and his finger went up to stroke the scar on his face over and over. Almost reluctantly, it seemed, he swung down, came over, and sat on the grass next to her.

How could she put it so he wouldn't hate her? Wouldn't be angry with her? She was going to tell him the truth even if he mounted up and rode off, leaving her on her own. Then she wasn't sure what she would do.

"Maverick"—she picked up a blade of grass, sticking it nervously in her mouth—"I—I've lied to you from the front end."

He looked at her sharply, then stared off in the distance as he rolled a cigarette. "Sometimes people have to lie."

"You're saying that the end justifies the means? That goes against everything I've been taught."

He didn't answer as he fumbled through his pockets before seeming to remember he'd used his last match to start the canyon fire. "People do what they must, I reckon."

She had expected curiosity, maybe anger, certainly not this evasive barricade of words he seemed to be throwing up between them.

"Aren't you curious about what I lied about?"

He looked at her, the unlit cigarillo in his mouth. "I take people as I find them, baby, at face value. Do you want to tell me?"

She stared at his remote, silent profile as he turned to stare off at the distant town. "I—I've got to tell you or my conscience would never let me rest. Maverick, there's nobody sick at my house."

"Then why the big rush to get home?"

She reached out and put a hand on his arm. "I—I needed a gunfighter, and you proved in that saloon you

417

could really handle yourself. . . ."

"I'm not a hired gun," he said coldly, not looking at her. "Why would you need one?"

"I got a letter in Wichita. Three men have come to my father's ranch and might be on the run—you know, outlaws."

Maverick looked at her. "So? Why doesn't your old man do something about it? Isn't he supposed to be such a good shot?"

"Against three men?" she asked. "My stars! Even if he weren't disabled because of the Indian torture, he wouldn't have a chance against three top guns. Besides, there's the children's safety and—"

"And?" He stared at her, his gray eyes as cold and remote as stone.

She looked away, not wanting to voice her suspicions but she must. "I don't know why Papa hasn't called in the Rangers. Maybe—maybe he's hiding something. Maybe a long time ago, he knew Bill Slade and the outlaws have something on him."

"Bill Slade?" He looked at her keenly. "Someone else mentioned him to me once; said he was mean as hell and a top gun."

Her face colored with shame. "So you see what I've lured you into," she said. "Without warning you, I've lured you into coming back with me to face him and his partners down."

She waited a long moment but he only stared at the town in the distance, chewing the end of the unlit cigarette. Whatever she had expected—anger, indignation—she had not expected him to simply stare into the late afternoon horizon. "Didn't you hear what I said?"

He tossed away the cigarette. "I heard. You didn't have to tell me, knowing I'd probably get on my horse and ride away. You could have let me ride into a showdown I'd have to fight my way out of. Why did

418

you bother?"

He turned and looked at her, and she shook her head helplessly. "Because I love you, Maverick, you surely must know that by now."

His hands came up, clasped her shoulders, and pulled her to him. "How much?" he whispered. "How much? Would you be willing to go off with me, be my woman, leave here without a backward glance?" His face was contorted with emotion and his hands trembled on her shoulders.

She slid her arms around his neck. "I—I can't imagine living anywhere but the Lazy M, leaving my family. But for you, Maverick Durango, I'd turn my back on it all, go anywhere with you, be your woman."

"Oh, Cayenne!" He pulled her to him, kissing her feverishly. "I'll ride out to your ranch, deal with your damned outlaws, and then I'm gonna take you away with me forever!"

She clung to him, loving him so deeply she would have sacrificed anything to stay by his side forever. "I love you, dearest; whatever you want I'll do even if it means living on the trail, maybe a shack somewhere."

He kissed her again and pulled her to her feet. For a long moment he stared down at her. She almost thought he would make a confession, too. He seemed to be caught in a turmoil of emotion. Finally, he said, "I've got something to do, but after that's over, we'll have each other and never look back! Now let's go to town!"

Out at the Lazy M, Joe heaved a sigh of relief as the little girls and old Rosita loaded into the buggy with much giggling and rustling petticoats. He leaned on the porch rail and admonished them. "Now, you enjoy your supper and prayer session at the Harrison's ranch, you hear? I'll see you tomorrow."

Lynnie said, "Why don't you go with us, Papa?"

"I got prayin' of my own to do right here." *Tonight,* he thought, *Monday evening.* In another hour, Slade's gang would try to move on that payroll coming in on the stage from Austin. He not only wanted the citizens safely in their homes, Joe wanted his beloved little girls safely away from this ranch. "I'm gonna do some praying all by myself," he said again. And to himself, he thought, *I got to pray that the Rangers get here in time.*

The buggy creaked as the lop-eared old mule pulled away with the children, Juan, and fat Rosita. Joe waved automatically as the little girls set up a shrill chorus of good-byes.

"And Angel," he said automatically, "please remember to keep your thumb out of your mouth."

He stood there a long moment, thinking as the noise of the creaking buggy moved farther and farther away. *What to do now?* Maybe he should do nothing at all. Let the Rangers deal with it. After all, he was in no danger if he kept quiet and let Slade's boys ride into town in a few minutes. If they did rob the stage without being stopped, they'd head up to the old hideout and he could tell the law where to find them later. At least, with the children gone and the townspeople all having the evening prayer session he'd requested, nobody would get hurt.

Could he possibly do anything to stop that trio all by himself? He limped inside, went into the parlor, and stood before the stone fireplace, thinking about the guns hanging there. Common sense told him to do nothing at all since, besides his physical problems, he was so outnumbered. Did he hear a horse leaving the barn at a gallop? No, maybe he was mistaken. When they got ready to go for the holdup, there'd be three horse leaving.

Bill Slade stood staring after Trask as he galloped out on his dun horse. He turned to the Mexican standing beside him in the barn door. "I told him to circle around, intercept that buggy, take it on to town."

The Mexican tipped his sombrero back and laughed. "*Si*, good thinking! That way, we'll have those little McBride girls and the servants to use as hostages or shields if anything goes wrong when we hold up the stage!"

Bill chewed his lip and looked across the landscape toward the rambling ranch house. "It'll be dark in about thirty minutes. You got our horses saddled so we can meet Trask in town when the stage rolls in?"

"*Si*, boss," he nodded over his shoulder. "Right here. What you gonna do about McBride?"

Slade snickered. "What you think I'm gonna do about him? You think I'd plan to ride out and leave him alive to tell where our old hideout is so we can be found later?"

"You got no qualms about shootin' a man in his shape?"

Slade spat on the ground and lit a cigar. "You know me better than that, Mex. Follow me on up to the house with the horses. After I kill him, I intend to take that fancy rifle hanging over the fireplace."

"*Si*, boss, I'll be right behind you." He scratched his swarthy face. "What do you intend to do about Wilbur?"

"I took care of that stupid little hick." Slade checked his pistol. "Now that we know the details of the gold shipment, we don't need him no more and one less means more for us to split."

The Mexican's white teeth gleamed. "What'd you do?"

"I sent him a secret coded message tellin' him to

meet us to get his share." He named the place he had indicated.

Mex snorted with laughter. "That place is a gathering spot for Indians!"

Slade shrugged. "Stupid little Wilbur doesn't know that. If the Injuns get him, not only do we not have to share with him, we don't have to worry about that stupid little hick in his green eyeshade leadin' the law to us. Which reminds me, I'd better go finish off McBride."

Slade strode on across the barnyard to the silent house, his big spurs jangling. *It wasn't too long 'til dark*, he thought as he blew smoke. He and Mex would finish up here and meet Trask in town just at the moment the stage pulled in. All he had to do now was walk in and shoot his unsuspecting old partner down.

Cayenne and Maverick reined in at the end of Main Street. "That's strange," she said, standing up in her stirrups, looking around. "Where is everybody?"

Maverick muttered. "This town always so deserted?"

Cayenne shrugged. "Not usually."

Loud music and laughter drifted to her. "Of course banker Ogle's saloon never closes." She frowned, staring. "I'd swear that's the Lazy M buggy tied up in front of the general store."

Maverick hesitated. "Comanches are like wolves sometime; we can almost smell a trap." He looked at her.

Her mouth fell open. "You don't think I'd set up an ambush for you? What reason could I possibly have? I love you, Maverick!"

He didn't answer, looking away as if he knew something he didn't want to share with her. "Well, if there's

422

no problem, I see redheaded kids in that buggy, maybe you better go see about them."

She nodded, dug her heels into Strawberry's sides, and started through the pale dusk of evening down Main Street. When she turned in her saddle and looked back at Maverick sitting like a dark, forbidding spectre on his ghost-gray horse, the scripture came to her again: . . . *and hell followed with him.*

The thought disturbed her and she waved at her little sisters, yelling as she approached them. When she glanced back, Maverick was gone.

What was he up to? Had he decided he wanted no part of facing those three gunfighters at her papa's ranch? Or had he already headed out there to deal with them? No, the Lazy M lay to the south of town. He'd have to ride past her to get there.

"Sis! Sis!" The little girls waved and she rode up, dismounting.

Only then did she notice the Mexican servants in the buggy. "Juan! Rosita!" She hugged them and reached to kiss all her little sisters. Automatically she straightened Stevie's pigtails, tied Gracie's sash, and pulled Angel's thumb from her mouth. "What are you doing here?"

Serious little Lynnie pushed her glasses back up on her freckled nose. "We were going to the Harrison's ranch for dinner, but Trask came riding after us, said there'd been a change in plans."

Old Rosita nodded, "That's right, Senorita. Trask say there is to be a surprise party here in town for your papa. We're to sit quietly until they bring him in, too. Then everyone who's in hiding in the stores and houses will jump out and yell, 'Surprise!' 'Surprise!' "

Cayenne looked around. The town looked pretty deserted to her. "So what happened to Mr. Trask?"

Rosita shrugged. "He went into the saloon, said he

needed to get wine for the celebration."

Cayenne's face furrowed. "Someone should tell him Papa doesn't drink."

Lynnie cocked her head seriously. "I think the idea of a surprise party is stupid! Doesn't this all sound strange to you, Cayenne?"

Cayenne had a sudden, strange intuition that Papa was in danger. Suppose this Trask had slipped out the back way and was on his way back to the ranch? The only way to find out was to see if his horse was tied around behind banker Ogle's saloon. She slipped quietly along the edge of the building into the alley. *Where was Maverick now that she needed him? He'd promised to help her; he'd promised.*

She rounded the corner, sighing with relief to see a dun horse tied there. She heard a slight sound like a man dragging a lame foot. But before she could turn around, a man stepped out of the dusk and stuck a gun in her back. "Evenin', miss. Just what are you up to?"

"Nothing," she blurted, feeling the barrel digging into her back. Whoever this man was, perhaps he thought she was looking at the horse to steal it. "You misunderstand," she stammered. "I'm Cayenne McBride and—"

"Old Joe's girl?"

She could only nod, suddenly frightened at the menace in his tone, the way he slipped his arm around her neck from behind as if to throttle her should she scream.

Somewhere in the distance, she heard the crack of a whip, the noise of the stage rattling along the road toward town.

The man with the gun in her back laughed under his breath. "Here it comes after all! I was beginnin' to think we'd been lied to. Is there anybody with you?"

"No." She must protect the children, must protect

424

Maverick. He'd been right after all about an ambush in the shadows.

She heard the stage rolling along at the edge of town now, the whip cracking, the driver yelling at the horses.

The man pulled her up against him so that she felt the heat of him all the way down her back and buttocks. "Honey, you feel real good to me," he whispered against her ear. "Now you just keep quiet, you hear? Slade and the Mex should be coming in from the Lazy M any time now. We'll catch this stage unawares as they stop to change teams, get away with the gold."

So this must be Trask, the third man in Lynnie's letter. *Robbery. They were going to rob the Austin stage.* Here she'd expected to have Maverick confront the trio out at the ranch, and instead, there was going to be a showdown on a deserted Main Street.

The man nuzzled the back of her neck. "Honey, I just love that scent you're wearin'. How'd you like to go with us when we ride out?"

She was so stiff with fright that her body couldn't bend to fit the contours of his as he pulled her up against him. She felt his maleness harden with desire as he rubbed it against her hips. "I . . . why don't we go now? I don't want to see the children get caught in any cross fire."

"Why do you think I got that buggy parked there?" He laughed, rubbing his unshaven face against her neck, and she winced from the sting of his whiskers against her delicate skin. "Now you must behave yourself until the stage pulls in. It's really lucky you happened along. We'll walk out there casuallike, as if we was going to board, and the guard won't be suspicious of a couple of sweethearts."

He glanced up at the setting sun. "The stage is a mite late and so are my pards. Slade and the Mex should be in place by now."

Maverick had sensed a trap and had ridden Dust Devil behind a building, out of harm's way. Now he tiptoed quiet as his Comanche ancestors through the alley. He wished there were some way he could move that buggy. If there was going to be trouble, he didn't want it caught in the cross fire. The black hair along his neck went up in a prickle of warning that had saved his life many times. *Now just where had Cayenne gone off to?*

She wasn't anywhere in sight. He heard a noise, looked off, and saw the Austin stage rolling in toward town. By damn, what was going on? He took a deep breath.

Maverick had spent the first half of his life among the Indians and all his senses were keener than white men's. He hesitated, took another breath. Vanilla. He almost smiled. She was somewhere close by, all right. He heard a sound he couldn't identify. It sounded almost like a man dragging a lame foot. Maverick crouched against the hardware store, listening to the stage roll down Main Street. It was strange as hell for the stage to be rolling in and only one man coming out the front door of the saloon to meet it.

He turned and crept quietly around the building. For a moment, he couldn't believe his eyes. Cayenne stood in a man's embrace, her back to him while he nuzzled along her neck. She had said she loved him, but what was going on here? He had the most terrible surge of jealousy, the likes of which he hadn't felt since the night Annie died in his arms. And then he saw the last dying rays of sunlight reflect off the gun barrel.

He stepped out, cocked his own. "Step away from her or you're a dead man!"

If she had been any other woman, she would probably have frozen in place, immobilized by fear, Maver-

426

ick thought with admiration. But as he watched, the peppery little redhead slammed her elbow into the man's soft middle. As he bent with a moan, stumbling backward, she hit the ground. "Now, Maverick! Now!"

Maverick fired at the same time Trask did. Trask's bullet went wild, hitting the man who had just left the saloon. But Maverick's bullet found its mark. The shot echoed and reechoed through the shadows of the empty streets as the man screamed, grabbed his chest, and stumbled backward.

When he went down on his back, Maverick holstered his pistol, strode over, and kicked the gun from the dead hand. A look of surprise froze forever on the dead face, the eyes staring straight into hell. Blood spread slowly across the dirty shirt.

"Maverick! Maverick!" She fell into his arms, weeping, and he held her against him, kissing her hair.

She looked up at him, tears in her eyes. "I was so scared! The kids'll be afraid! What happens now?"

"If the other gunfighters were in town, they would have showed themselves by now just as the citizens are." He nodded toward curious faces peeking out of surrounding buildings, upstairs windows. "That means they're out there with your dad. I'll have to corner them there."

"Oh, dearest, I'm so afraid for you!"

He kissed the tears off her face, and she turned to see the stage driver climbing off the seat, bending down to look at the fallen man.

"Who is this?" the driver shouted.

"Banker Ogle!" Someone said, "That wild shot got banker Ogle!"

"Baby," Maverick said, "you haven't changed your mind about leavin' with me; no lookin' back, no questions asked?"

"Oh, no! No!" She kissed him feverishly.

"Then wait here for me, baby, go look after those kids!" He thrust her away from him and mounted, trying not to look at the little red-haired girls staring up at him from the buggy as he rode right past them, setting out on the road south to the Lazy M. *He would take care of things, all right*, he thought grimly. Sure, he'd finish off those other two, but he still had a vow to fulfill to Annie, the one he'd made when he was fourteen years old . . . the night he killed her.

An eye for an eye, he thought with fury, trying not to hear the children talking excitedly to Cayenne. He was going to make orphans of them all, come back and carry off his woman; gamble that he could take her far enough away that she'd never hear what happened, never know Joe's blood stained Maverick's hands.

He urged Dust Devil into a lope and didn't look back at the curious people coming out into the street behind him as he rode toward the Lazy M to finish his quest.

Joe put his hand against the rough stone of the fireplace. Cicadas began their rhythmic hum outside as they always did as dusk settled in. He felt suddenly hungry, remembered he had forgotten about dinner. Rosita had said something about leaving a plate of cold chicken on the long oak table. He should leave the parlor, go into the dining room. . . .

He heard a sound, a man crossing the barnyard leading a horse. He had thought Slade's bunch had already left. Joe puzzled about it, listened without moving. He heard the creak of the squeaky porch, the jingle of spurs as if the owner moved stealthily. His heart started to pound faster as if it sensed danger. "Bill?"

"Sure, it's me." Joe didn't turn around as he heard

the man enter the room behind him. Why did he sound so tense, so nervous? "Just wanted to say good-bye to an old buddy," Slade said. "We're pullin' out now. Maybe we'll meet again some time."

"Sure." He wondered if Hank Billings had gotten the Rangers, if there'd be a showdown in town? But he dare not let on to anything.

There was a shout outside the window. "Hey, Bill," Mex yelled, "there's a rider comin'!"

Slade swore loudly and crossed to the window, his spurs jangling as he moved. "What the devil?"

Joe was careful to make no sudden movement as he heard Bill rustle the curtain back from the window.

"Mex," Slade yelled, "what's he looks like?"

"Dark," Mex called in a hoarse whisper from outside near the corral, "and ridin' the biggest gray horse you ever saw! I'll get him!"

Joe started but he didn't move. He knew who it was and why he was coming. His heart pumped rapidly but he didn't move as he heard Slade click back the trigger behind him.

A gunshot echoed and reechoed suddenly from the corral and Slade swore again, "Damned greaser! Shoulda waited! Now the stranger knows he's there!"

Joe stood stock still, listening. A pistol shot rang out and he heard Mex scream.

"Dammit!" Slade swore from the window. "Don't know who he is, but he's a damned good shot! He got Mex!" Then he laughed a little in his throat. "That's okay, though; one less to divvy up with. Maybe Trask can handle that stage 'til I get there! Almost dark, can't get a good shot from here, but looks like he's comin' to the house! I'll nail him when he comes up on the porch!"

Joe listened to him pull back the hammer, laughing a little under his breath. He almost felt a sense of relief.

Annie's boy had come to kill him but Slade was going to ambush the boy first. Then he felt ashamed to be so relieved. But oh, dear God, life was so sweet! If he did nothing at all, Slade would kill Maverick and Joe could quit worrying about having that vengeful ghost from the past continually stalking him.

All he had to do was stay very quiet while the unsuspecting boy walked up on the porch and Slade ambushed him through the open parlor window. And yet . . . this was Annie's boy. Could he stand by and let Slade kill him in cold blood without raising a hand to stop him, even if his own life were at stake?

His decision was the measure of the man. He listened to Slade grumbling softly under his breath, brushing against the curtains, heard the boy dismount outside. Very slowly, so that Slade wouldn't notice, Joe's crippled hands reached up for the ten-gauge double-barreled shotgun that hung low over the fireplace. And it was always kept loaded with deadly buckshot. His hands clenched on the weapon with difficulty, lifting it from its rack.

Disabled as he was, Joe couldn't stand by and let Slade kill the boy without making an attempt to stop him. He had the old, familiar gun in his hands now. He'd have to whirl and fire quickly. Once Slade realized what he was up to, Joe'd never get another chance.

His hands trembled as he clutched the shotgun, listening to the boy dismount, start up the creaking steps.

"Bill!" Joe shouted, and in one motion, he whirled and pulled the trigger.

The sound exploded in the darkness, the gun recoiling in his hands. Slade swore as the buckshot hit him, screaming in agony as he went down, twisting and kicking. *A hole big enough to put your fist in*, Joe thought, *the old double-barrel always blew a hole big*

430

enough to put your fist in.

". . . sonovabitch!" Slade groaned, "you tricky old sonovabitch! How'd you know I'd really come in here to kill you . . . steal that fancy rifle? Should never have underestimated you. . . ."

Joe stood there with the shotgun hot in his hands, smelling the fresh blood, the acrid powder. Uncertainly, he turned back toward the fireplace as he heard the clatter of boots on the porch, heard Maverick come through the squeaky screen. What did he do now? He still had one barrel. Could he let the boy kill him when Joe had the advantage of the wide pattern of that shotgun?

Cayenne ran out to meet the stage, her little sisters gathering around, people running from businesses and homes as the alarm was raised. "Thank God! There's been trouble!" She shouted to the driver, "They were going to rob you!"

The driver and the guard looked from banker Ogle's body to her. "What's going on here?"

She started to explain even as a dignified, white-haired old Spaniard thrust his head out the stage window. "*Senorita*, what's happened?"

"They were going to rob the stage," she yelled over the hubbub as the old man opened the door and stepped down, followed by the gray-haired Mexican with the crippled hand. She suddenly recognized Maverick's chief *vaquero*. "Sanchez, what are you doing here?"

"*Senorita* Cayenne!" he said, grasping her hands. "Have we come in time?"

She heard shouts off to the east and saw the Billings boy coming in at a gallop over the crest of a butte. *Were those Texas Rangers with him?*

Sanchez's words penetrated her consciousness as she

431

looked back at him. "In time for what? I don't think I understand. . . ."

"Are you Cayenne McBride?" The dignified old man faced her. "Thank God I'm in time! Where's Maverick? I'm *Senor* Durango!"

"*Senor* Durango?" *Why on earth would these two be so far from home?* "Why, he's gone out to the ranch," she gestured south in the growing twilight, "gone to see about my father!"

"*Dios!*" Sanchez groaned, pulling at his mustache.

The Don grabbed her arm and she was suddenly alarmed at the horror in his eyes. "How long ago did he ride out? We've got to overtake him!"

She felt a chill start at her feet, move slowly up her legs. "Why? He's about ten minutes ahead of us. There's a couple of gunfighters on my father's ranch he's gone out to deal with."

The Don barked orders. "No time to lose! We've got to get out there and hope we're not too late! You have a horse? Is there one for me? Sanchez, take charge of these children!"

Cayenne had a sudden growing apprehension. She could only point wordlessly to Strawberry and Trask's dun. "What's this all about?"

"No time to talk." The Don grabbed her arm, propelling her along with a brisk step that belied his age.

Sanchez yelled, "Diego, you're not supposed to ride—"

The old man swore in Spanish. "I'm still the Don of the Triple D and I'm tired of being treated like a sick baby! There's man's work to do!"

Cayenne mounted and watched him swing up on the dun. "*Senor*, can't you tell me—?"

"Did Maverick ever say anything about revenge? About hunting a man down and killing him?"

"My stars, yes," she stammered. "Something about

432

a low-down varmint who abandoned his mother to the Indians, but—"

"*Senorita*"—the old man looked at her a long moment—"the man Maverick's searched for all these years, the man he seeks vengeance against is your father! And I guess it's a toss-up as to who will die, since they're so evenly matched!"

For a long moment, she stared back at him in motionless horror. "No, not Papa!" But suddenly all the pieces began to fall into place and she realized in horror why the grim half-breed had ridden all this way with her. It wasn't for love, it was for revenge! She hated him then as she had never hated a man. Her deception had been nothing compared to his! Maverick had tricked her into leading him to kill her own father!

"*Senor* Durango, we'd better get out there as fast as these horses can gallop! It won't be an even match, it'll be cold-blooded murder!"

Unable to hold back her sobs, she slapped Strawberry with the reins, leading out at a dead run for the Lazy M.

Chapter Twenty-two

Maverick crouched against the side of the porch, listening to the echo of the shotgun fade away. Seconds passed and darkness deepened. No experienced Westerner would go up against the superior challenge of a shotgun at close range. Silence. Nothing. He had to go in that house and find out what had happened.

Moving silently as the Comanches who had raised him, he entered the hall, then stepped into the parlor. The scent of gunpowder and fresh blood made him gasp. Quickly, he glanced around. Darkness cast long shadows, but crumpled on the floor by the window, Maverick saw the form of a man, a ragged hole in his belly. *Shotgun*, Maverick thought with alarm. He tightened his grasp on the Colt in his hand. Opposite Maverick, a man stood with his back to him by the big stone fireplace. In the growing darkness, Maverick could barely make out the red hair but he knew by the size of him who that man must surely be. With his attention centered on the man, Maverick bumped into a table.

The man did not turn around. "Maverick Durango?"

Maverick cocked the pistol with a loud click. "That's right. Do you know why I'm here?" Even in the shadows of the twilight, he realized the man held a double-barreled shotgun, which put him at a distinct advantage . . . unless Maverick stood ready to shoot him in the back. He gritted his teeth. No, he couldn't do that; no honorable man would shoot another in the back.

The man nodded. "I knew you'd come someday; the old Don told me about you." He sighed. "In a way it's a relief, I reckon, to have it end, not to be listening for you, waitin' for you to walk in unexpectedly anymore."

Maverick looked at the crumpled man by the window. "Who'd you just kill and why?"

"His name's Bill Slade," Joe said softly without turning around. "He planned to ambush you as you walked up on the porch."

Maverick hesitated, reaching up to stroke the jagged scar on his cheek. "You killed him to save my life? By damn, that was a loco thing to do! Don't you know I've come to kill you?"

"I know."

"You yellow bastard!" Maverick growled, and passion and vengeance made the hand that held the pistol shake a little. "Before I kill you and ride out, I have to know. Why didn't you come for her?"

"I know you won't believe this," McBride said, not moving, "but I thought she was dead all those years, and—"

"Liar!" Maverick screamed, and it was all he could do to keep from pulling the trigger, pumping lead into the broad back. "You goddamned liar!" He tried to keep from sobbing but he was overwhelmed with emotion. "How could you have deserted her when she loved you so! The last name on her lips as she died wasn't mine, it was yours, you sonovabitch! Yours!"

Annie's face came to him now and he relived that final moment, holding the thin, tortured body in his arms, listening to his mother whisper, *Joe . . . I love you, Joe. . . .*

The man in the shadows of the fireplace seemed to shake too. "I loved her," he choked out. "You'll never know how much I loved her. I don't guess you ever loved a woman like I loved Annie."

"I love Cayenne that way," Maverick declared through gritted teeth, "and after I kill you, I'm going to take her away from here forever!"

"You'll go to my daughter with her father's blood on her hands? Do you think she'll love you then?"

Maverick swore an oath. "I'll take her away; she'll never find out!"

"Sooner or later," Joe said softly, still holding the deadly shotgun, "someone will tell her, and every day will be a hell for you, afraid this will be the day someone tells her and she leaves you."

Maverick hesitated and the pistol wavered in his hand. What Joe McBride said was true. Sooner or later, Cayenne would find out and he'd lose her. He could not kill the father and have the daughter. *But he had sworn, oh, God, he had sworn!*

Joe said, "And what of my other daughters? What about my orphaned little girls?"

"That's not my problem!" Maverick snapped, but in his troubled mind he saw all those freckled-faced children looking up at him from the buggy.

"Isn't it?" Joe said softly. "I think my Annie would have raised a son who cared, would have felt responsible. Funny how things turn out. She always promised me a son and now you've come to kill me."

"We waited and waited!" Maverick's voice rose with passion. "She said you'd come for us, that we'd all be together as a family, that you'd be the father I never had, but you never came! So now I've come for you, you rotten sonovabitch! An eye for an eye and a tooth

436

for a tooth like your Bible says!"

Away off down the road, he heard the sound of galloping horses. Maverick turned, glancing out the window. Two riders were coming at a fast pace. In the growing darkness, he saw only their silhouettes, but they weren't going to get here fast enough to stop him from killing Joe McBride. "I intended to put you through a Comanche torture," he said, "but now I'm just gonna kill you clean and leave."

"Vengeance is mine, says the Lord; I shall repay. But go ahead and shoot," the man said softly. "My back ought to be big enough for an easy target!"

"No!" Maverick swore, gesturing with the pistol. "Damn you! Turn around! You're better armed than I am! I'll give you a better than even chance! Cee Cee tells me you're a crack shot! Let's see if you can turn and fire, nail me with that shotgun before I get you first!"

The man shook his head slowly and the first rays of the rising moon glinted in the red hair. "No," he said, "I'm not going to ease your conscience. You'll just have to shoot me down in cold blood! Besides, even to save my own life, I don't think I could pull a trigger on Annie's son!"

The riders galloped closer now. Maverick could hear shouting but the words were carried away by the wind. He had to move fast or they'd get here in time to stop him. And yet, his emotions were in a turmoil. He'd expected to enjoy this moment when he finally had Joe McBride in his gun sights, had relished the image of the rotten villain on his knees begging for his life. But all he'd heard about this man told him Joe McBride was everything Annie had told her son he was. A man who would face Comanche torture for others was not going to beg for his life.

Tears ran down Maverick's face. "At the end, they

tortured her, hurt her too bad to travel! I couldn't take her out of there, but she was still alive! I couldn't take her but I couldn't leave her there alive!"

"Oh, my God," Joe said softly, "you poor, poor devil! You had to—?"

"Yes," Maverick lost control and sobbed, "she begged me to kill her! End her pain! I couldn't take her with me, she was hurt too bad! I—I cut her throat rather than leave her for them to torture! I held her in my arms as she died and the last name on her lips was yours! Yours! Now turn around, you sonovabitch, and use that shotgun! And when you try, I'm gonna blow your guts out!"

The two horses galloped into the barnyard now. He heard Cayenne's voice shouting. *She wouldn't get here in time*, Maverick thought, his gun hand trembling in indecision; she'd know he'd killed her father. But he'd lived the past ten years only for this moment when he could gun Joe McBride down for failing Annie, failing him.

"No," Joe said uncertainly, "I—I don't think I can kill you, even to save myself!"

Maverick heard the riders dismount and run for the house. "No, Maverick!" Cayenne screamed. "Oh, my God! Stop, Maverick!"

He had to finish quickly. "Turn around!" Maverick ordered. "You talk big, but when you turn, you'll take that shot rather than die! No man wants to die! Turn around and we'll see what kind of man you are!"

"And what kind of man you are," Joe said softly, and he turned around even as Cayenne's feet pounded up the creaking porch steps.

In that instant as the man turned, Maverick wavered, seeing faces in his mind: the plain, beloved face of Annie; the trusting face of Cayenne, who had led him innocently to her father; even the faces of four little

438

freckled-faced, red-haired girls looking up at him from the buggy.

But, too, in that split second, Maverick remembered all the years he had waited for his vengeance, how he had planned it with relish. His outstretched gun hand would kill the big man at point-blank range and he knew he was faster than the other. Then suddenly, he saw the insane eyes of Little Fox. Was he no better than that—a crazed animal, a burned-out shell of a man?

Maverick's hand trembled in that split second as Joe turned around. And in that heartbeat of a moment, he made his decision because of the man he was. Very slowly, his hand dropped limply to his side, the pistol useless.

He couldn't do it. After all these years, he couldn't pull the trigger on the man the two women in Maverick's life loved so. Even if Joe cut down on him with that shotgun as he turned, Maverick could not pull that trigger.

They both stood facing each other and Maverick winced, awaiting the loud explosion of the buckshot tearing a hole in his belly, awaiting the agony of slow death. He heard Cayenne's small feet running across the squeaky porch.

And only then did Maverick blink unbelievingly in the moonlit darkness, taking another look at the man's face as he realized that neither of them had pulled a trigger. "My, God! Your eyes! You're blind! Blind!"

Joe nodded, staring back at him with tortured, empty sockets. "You didn't know? A crazed Comanche did that with a burning stick when I went in to carry the ransom."

Wave after wave of tumultuous emotion swept over Maverick as he stared. He had almost murdered a blind man! "She forgave you," he whispered, tears running down his face, "but I never did. . . ."

"Maverick," Joe said softly, the shotgun hanging from his burned, twisted fingers, "your problem, the whip that drives you, is that you've never been able to live with what you did. Even though she begged you to do it, you can't forgive yourself! God has forgiven both of us, as has Annie. I'm sure of it, Son. Can't you find it in your heart to forgive me, to forgive yourself?"

Maverick gave a cry like a wounded animal as the truth of Joe's words knifed into his soul like a hot blade. With a curse and a sob, he brushed past Cayenne as she and the old Don entered the room, staggering outside to lean against an old chinaberry tree in the light of a Comanche moon.

Cayenne hardly glanced at him, her heart pounding in terror for her father as she ran into the dark parlor. "Papa, are you all right? He planned to—"

"Yes, but he didn't," Joe said calmly. He turned and hung the shotgun back up over the fireplace.

The old Don sighed loudly. "Thank the Holy Mother! *Senor*, are you sure—?"

"I'm fine, just fine." Joe turned around. "I guess I got Slade and Maverick got the Mexican."

For the first time, she noticed the crumpled body in the shadows by the window.

Quickly, she moved to a table to light a lamp. "Oh, Papa, it's been so terrible! Maverick got Trask, too! Those men must have intended to rob the Austin stage! *Senor* Durango came in on that stage to try to stop Maverick. . . ."

"Looks like there was no need," the old Don said.

Papa suddenly seemed exhausted and leaned against the fireplace. "It's Maverick I'm worried about. Cayenne, where did he go?"

Hurt filled her heart, threatened to choke her. She'd been betrayed, lied to by the man she loved. Cayenne

440

looked out the window. "He's leaning against the old chinaberry tree, Papa, the one with the swing. He—he's crying." She almost couldn't believe what she saw—the big, tough trail boss leaning against a tree trunk, his wide shoulders shaking with sobs.

"Daughter, do you love that man?"

Did she? "I—I thought I did, Papa." The tears came now, all hot and salty, though she tried to hold them back. "But he's lied and betrayed me, used me to lead him to you! He never cared about me; he only used me so he could kill you. . . ."

"But he didn't." Joe leaned against the fireplace and his voice was calm, full of faith. "When the chips were down, he was Annie's son after all, he just couldn't do it. I think his love for you played a big part, too."

She looked out the window, watching the man sobbing against the tree, and her very depths were in turmoil.

Joe said, "Cayenne, if you love that man, go out to him right now and tell him so, because any moment he'll mount up and ride out and none of us will ever see him again!"

The old Don's face furrowed in concern and agreement. "You're right, *Senor.* I've always known he had terrible scars I couldn't erase, that he needed more than the friendship we Durangos gave him. I'll go out to him. . . ."

But as he brushed past Joe, the big man caught his arm. "No, *Senor* Durango, only a woman's love can save him now. When he leaves here, he'll not look back. I can guarantee you that if she doesn't love him enough to go to him, when Maverick rides out, he'll be driven by such torment he may become the worst outlaw Texas ever saw!"

Cayenne stared out the window and saw Maverick turn away from the tree and start uncertainly toward the big gray horse. "He's leaving now, Papa! But how can I love him, ever trust him again after what he's done?"

"Love sets no restrictions, Cayenne," Joe said softly. "A girl named Annie Laurie taught me that. When you love someone, you love him! It doesn't matter if he's disappointed you or betrayed you, you can't help lovin', as I never really stopped lovin' Maverick's mother and she never stopped lovin' me!"

Cayenne looked out the window at the silhouette of Maverick walking toward Dust Devil, then looked back at Joe. "His mother?"

Joe nodded. "I got a lot of things to tell you, Cee Cee, but that's not important now. What is important is this? Do you love that man?"

And she had to answer with her heart. "Yes! Yes, I love him! I love him in spite of everything!" And she ran headlong out the door, screaming, "Maverick! Maverick! Wait!"

He was just about to mount as she ran across the porch, down the steps, out into the yard to face him.

Even in the darkness, she could see the tearstains on his bronzed face. He held up his hand to stop her words. "If you've come to tell me how much you hate me for using you like I did, for betraying your trust, I don't blame you." He checked his saddle girth. "I was rotten to do it, but I'd sworn to kill your father. Now I understand I really hate myself for what I've done!"

She looked at him. "You're riding out then? Where are you going?"

He shrugged, his shoulders slumped. "Who knows? Who cares? Become a saddle tramp, I reckon. I don't suppose the old Don would want me back on the Triple D after this. I'm good with a gun. There's lots of people who'd hire a man good with a pistol." He sighed. "Good-bye, Cee Cee. I'm sorry for what I've done; it was rotten. Forgive me."

She reached out and caught his arm. "Maverick, wait."

"Why?" He turned back to her, his expression sad, lost, as if wondering what she wanted.

How much did she love him? More than anything in this world!

"You asked me once if I was willing to turn my back on everything I care about, ride out with you. I'll still do that, Maverick."

He stared at her, unbelieving. "The life of a gunfighter is hard, baby, too hard for a girl like you. You belong on the Lazy M. I couldn't ask you to make a sacrifice like that; not for me."

"If you leave here, I'm going with you," she said stubbornly. And as she had done that very first time, she slipped her arms around his neck and kissed his lips.

For a moment, he stood as if startled, stiff in her embrace as she kissed him. She didn't take her arms from around his neck as she looked up into the surprised gray eyes. "Now you're supposed to say, 'No, Cayenne, here's how it's done,' and then you kiss me back!'"

For a long moment, he looked down at her as if he couldn't believe the way she was looking up at him, then he swept her up off her feet, kissing her over and over, "Cayenne! Oh, Cayenne!"

His tears streaked her face as he kissed her and her own eyes were not dry as she clung to him. "Maverick, I love you! You can't leave! You can't leave! We need you too much!"

"But your Papa—"

"He's the one who sent me out," she whispered, kissing him again.

Past his shoulder, she saw the buggy pulling into the

barnyard, and as they embraced, her little sisters tumbled over each other to get to her like a litter of playful puppies. "What's happening? Cee Cee, what's happening?"

Cayenne didn't take her eyes off his face as she clung to Maverick's still-trembling body. He had a lot of scars on his heart and soul to erase but she had all the time in the world to do it. Finally, she looked down into Lynnie's serious little face. "Nothing's happening, except I'm kissing my sweetheart."

Lynnie regarded them a long moment. Then she looked at Maverick. "Are you the one in the letter who's going to marry my sister?"

Cayenne flushed with embarrassment. "My stars, Lynnie, that wasn't a proper question. . . ."

"I damned sure am if she'll have me!" Maverick faced the little girls with a wide grin.

Stevie twiddled with an untidy pigtail. "You'd better stop sayin' *damn* if you intend to be part of this family," she admonished primly.

Cayenne's eyes filled again as she watched Maverick reach out and rumple the child's red hair. "I'll bet all you kids are just like your big sister—bossy and stubborn!"

Cayenne's mouth dropped open. "Why, you Yankee lover, you! Who's bossy and stubborn?"

He pulled her to him. "Hush up and let me kiss you again. I came so close to losin' you, baby; thought I was about to ride out and never see you again. . . ."

"I know, dearest," she whispered as she clung to him, awed by the scariness of how close they'd come to losing each other.

". . . and they lived happily ever after," Maverick whispered against her ear as his lips caressed there.

"What?"

He shrugged. "My mother told me all the best

444

stories of the white people begin with 'Once upon a time' and end with '. . . and they lived happily ever after.' "

"And so they do, Maverick," she murmured, kissing him again. "And so they do!"

Chapter Twenty-three

Captain "Swen" Swenson of the Texas Rangers swung back up on his horse and looked around at the citizens of McBride. "It's all over," he shouted. "You folks can go back to your homes and I'll go out to the Lazy M."

He glanced at the wire he'd just received from St. Joe, crumpled it, and stuffed it in his pocket. Joe McBride had been on his conscience a long time now and Swen might as well take care of it all at once.

As he rode out of town south into the purple haze of dusk, the undertaker's men were already picking up the bodies of that outlaw, Trask, and the banker, Ogle. Old Sanchez from the Triple D had volunteered to help Joe's cook and ranch hand get the buggy full of McBride children back to the ranch and they had already headed out ahead of Swen.

It was dark when Swen rode into the barnyard of the Lazy M and saw a swarthy man lying crumpled by the water trough as if he'd been waiting in ambush when he was killed. The Ranger's heart beat a little faster as he thought of the defenseless man he'd come to see.

"Joe? Joe McBride, are you here?" he called as he dismounted in front of the big, rambling ranch house.

Only then did he see the silhouette of a man and woman standing in the moonlight out under the old chinaberry tree with all the little McBride sisters watching them. But that pair was kissing and never looked up.

Joe McBride came out on the long porch with an older man as Swen went up the creaky steps. "That you, Swenson?"

Swen sighed with relief. "Thank God, you're okay, Joe! There's a dead man lying down by the corral and I was afraid—"

"There's one in the parlor, too," Joe sighed heavily, sitting down in his wicker rocker. "Swen, this is Don Diego de Durango from the Triple D."

"Evening, sir." Swen touched his hat brim respectfully as the white-haired old lion of a man settled himself in a chair. Everyone in Texas knew of the powerful and rich Durango family.

Joe turned his blind face toward him anxiously in the moonlight. "The Don's told me what happened in town. I hear my little girls laughing over there so I reckon they're all right."

Swen nodded, reaching for the crumpled wire in his pocket. "The Don's wrangler, Juan, and Rosita just drove in with the buggy. Everything's taken care of in town. Banker Ogle got killed by a stray bullet, but don't suppose anyone'll miss him. Maybe it's ironic that after the way he cheated you, you'll preach his funeral; preach the services for these three dead outlaws."

Joe nodded soberly. "That's what preachers are for. I'll try to think of something good to say; every man's got some good to him."

Swen bit off a chaw of tobacco, looking again at the young couple standing with the big gray horse out under the tree. "I don't know who that is embracing

447

yore daughter, Joe, but they're hangin' onto each other like they're afraid they might never see each other again."

"They came very, very close to just that," Joe smiled.

"We've already identified that one dead man as part of a trio that's wanted all over half of Texas for bank robbery." Swen nodded toward the corral and the parlor. "I suppose these are the other two?"

"Yes." Joe nodded, took out his knife, and began to whittle a willow whistle. "I got the one inside with a shotgun just as he was about to ambush young Maverick as he started up the porch."

At the sound of the name, the young man standing out under the tree linked his arm in the girl's and came toward the porch while the little sisters stayed to play in the old swing. Swen took a good look at him. *Were those tear streaks on that scarred dark face?* He couldn't be sure in the moonlight.

"Hello, sir," the young man said to the old Spaniard as he and the beautiful fiery-haired daughter came up on the porch. "Joe's right. Even though he knew I'd come gunnin' for him personally, Joe killed that gunfighter to save my life."

Joe paused, shaking his head modestly. "Annie always promised me a son," he said softly, "and God does move in mysterious ways his wonders to perform."

The old Don looked sad, pulling at his white mustache. "*Si*, it's true. I should have realized that Maverick had too much character to do what he'd sworn to do. I wasn't needed after all."

"That's not true, my friend," Joe protested, leaning forward in his rocker. "I had forgotten how much I enjoy your company! We must make arrangements to visit each other often now that we've found each other again."

"*Si!* We'll sit here on this porch and rock for hours,

or maybe out by my fountain, talking. And do bring all the children!" The old Don's dark eyes lit up eagerly. "The little ones can play with my own grandchildren, and that smart one, Lynnie, can use my library."

Maverick hugged Cayenne to him. "She'll need it," he said. "I'm going to see that one gets an education."

Swen thought about the telegram and pulled it out. "What I came about, also, was this wire I got from St. Joe."

The big man paused in his rocking. "So you've come to take me to jail? Now my conscience is clear and I'm willing to serve my time since Maverick's here." His blind gaze turned toward the younger man. "You are plannin' on marryin' my daughter, aren't you, son? You can take over this place. The Lazy M can stand for Maverick."

Swen spat a stream of tobacco juice over the porch railing. "Dagnab it, Joe, you didn't let me finish." He waved the paper. "The law in St. Joe ain't lookin' for you. Seems some gal named Molly Kelly wrote a letter, went to see the law years ago; cleared your name."

"Molly," Joe whispered with a gentle smile. "Dear Molly. Wonder whatever became of her? She always loved a good time!"

The handsome young half-breed cleared his throat as if he might say something, then the girl gave him a warning shake of her head. "Wherever she is, Joe, surely she's at peace now. She must have loved you very much to do that."

Joe chewed his lip. "I suppose she did," he answered softly. "But I was in love with Annie Laurie and no other woman could ever take her place in my heart."

Swen hesitated. This was going to be hard for a proud man like himself. "I—I came for something else, too, Joe. I—I owe you an apology."

"What?" Joe said.

"We both know everyone thought Annie was dead because Hannah was so eager to identify that body we found just because it wore Annie's clothes."

The young man made a sound of surprise and looked at Joe. "So all these years you really did think Annie was dead?"

Swenson scowled. "Let me finish while I still got the nerve to admit I'm wrong. I was too eager to close that case, didn't question the identification. Lord only knows who that pore dead woman was, why she was wearing Annie's dress."

The young man's face turned pale. "I—I know. Mother said the woman was to be returned to her people and was ashamed to go back dressed as a squaw. Annie gave her the dress."

"Probably they lied to that girl, was really taking her off to sell her to the *Comancheros*. When she realized it and tried to get away, they killed her, left her unburied, and never told anybody back at the Indian encampment. I shouldn't have been so eager to close the case." Swen looked from Maverick's pale face to Joe's.

The blind man shook his head. "We all make mistakes, all of us. We're only human after all."

Swen took off his hat, twisting it in his hands. "I—I got something else to tell you, Joe. Remember when you came to me ten years ago, told me some boy had escaped the Comanches, said Annie was still alive and in their camp?"

"I remember," Joe nodded. "Annie had helped him escape. You swore you'd put the Rangers to lookin' for my Annie."

Swen turned and spat off the porch. "I lied, Joe," he said softly. "Every time you came in to ask if there'd been any progress, I lied and told you we was still lookin' and would let you know when we learned something."

450

The young man stared at him a long moment. "By then it was too late anyway. Annie was dead and I was on the run, ended up on the Durango spread."

Joe folded the small penknife, dropped it in his pocket, and turned toward Swen. In the moonlight, his face mirrored great tragedy, sadness. "You mean, after you told me you'd look for her, you didn't?"

Swen leaned against the porch rail, the enormity of what he'd done washing over him. "I took it upon myself to play God," he said, "that's what I did; I stepped in and played God instead of leavin' the ending up to the Almighty!"

Senor Durango stared at him in the moonlight. "Why? Why did you do this thing, knowing how much he loved the woman, how badly he wanted her back?"

Swen ran his hand through his gray-streaked blond hair. "I was with Sul Ross that day in 1860 when the Rangers recaptured Cynthia Ann Parker. I saw what a terrible tragedy it was to bring her back to civilization. After all those years with the Indians, she was a white Comanche herself, never fitted back into the white family she had left." He paused, looking out across the horizon. "Maybe if we'd left her with the Indians, we wouldn't be havin' to fight her vengeful son, Quanah, now."

No one said anything. The children's laughter echoed from the swing and Swen took a deep breath, continuing. "I was afraid it would be the same with Annie Laurie after she'd spent fifteen years with the Comanche. I thought I was doing Joe a favor by not finding and returning her, don't you see?"

The old Don crossed himself. "May the Holy Virgin intercede for you," he whispered. "Your playing God almost cost Joe his life tonight!"

Cayenne began to sob softly and Maverick looked at him a long moment as he put a comforting arm around

451

the weeping girl. "Mister, I want you to know what misery Annie went through. I want you to understand how my mother waited and waited to be rescued. She never gave up hope, never quit trusting Joe to come for her."

Swen took out a handkerchief, blew his nose. "And I got to live with that, son. Every day for the rest of my life, I got to live with that."

Joe wiped his eyes. "I'll pray for you, Swen. I don't hold no grudge against you. Annie wouldn't have wanted that. She was the sweetest, most gentle person I ever knew."

Maverick looked at Swen. "You poor devil," he said softly, "now you'll get a taste of what I've gone through for ten years—the heartache, the bitter regret. . . ."

Cayenne put her arm around the young man, hugging him to her. And the look on her face in the moonlight told Swen how very much she loved the man. Swen had played God when he shouldn't have, and yet . . . if he had not, would this pair's paths have ever crossed? Maybe God had used him in some mysterious way to bring these lovers together who would never otherwise have met. The thought made his aching conscience feel a little better.

Swen sighed. "Every day, I'll think about what I did. Every single day, I'll regret it." He looked toward the northern horizon. "First week of August and the weather's sizzling! But already I see a cold autumn coming on in a few weeks time."

Quanah Parker pulled his buffalo robe around him as he sat the gray pacer and shivered. It was late in the month the whites called "September" and all signs pointed to an early winter. Already the winds were cold and now rain blew into the Palo Duro in contrast to the hot dry summer of this past year.

Little Fox rode up. "Oh, Great Chief, you are determined to leave this canyon? Why?"

Quanah nodded, looking back at his band gathering up children and horses. "Maybe it's my white blood," he muttered, "but I have a sense of impending *puha*, of coming disaster; bad medicine."

"But we have had some good engagements against the whites since our war against the buffalo hunters started," Little Fox argued, reaching up to touch the fine pearl combs in his black hair. "We have laid waste to white civilization, left dozens of their soldiers, their settlers dead and tortured. Our allies scatter out across the plains attacking and discouraging the *Tejanos*, the *Americanos*, from coming into our hunting grounds."

"And yet more will come," Quanah predicted direly, watching his people gathering up their things to ride out of the deep canyon. "We are few and they are many. In the end, my good sense tells me they will kill off all the buffalo and take this land for their own to farm and raise families."

Little Fox laughed and Quanah looked at him long and hard. The Plains tribes looked on the insane with a touch of awe. Certainly Little Fox had been touched by that spirit of the gods. Quanah had first realized it a few months ago when Little Fox had captured those harmless white women and children at the picnic. Then, while Quanah was riding hard to get there and set things right, Little Fox had broken the tribes' word, blinding that brave fire-haired man who had ridden in with the ransom for the white captives.

Quanah thought about that man now, wondered if he and that man could ever have been friends, lived peacefully side by side. They would never have a chance to find out.

Quanah signaled his followers and they began to ride single file out of the deep canyon of the Palo Duro.

"There will be more and more Bluecoats coming," he said to Little Fox. "The whites are very angry about the slaughter of that family by the Cheyenne several weeks ago. They will come looking for those four little girls Medicine Water took captive."

Little Fox laughed. "Females have always been prizes of war. Surely the white soldiers will not make such a fuss over four sisters."

Quanah thought of his own mother, returned by force to her white family, now dead if reports from *Comanchero* could be believed. "Since you have not experienced it yourself, you cannot understand what value *tahbay-boh* put on their women; how they will come after us like bears whose cubs have been stolen!" He shook his head. "I promise you that stealing those girls will send thousands of soldiers searching across the plains! And the soldiers will be not gentle with any Indians they capture because of it."

Little Fox sneered. "The Great Chief is afraid then?"

Quanah was too weary, too discouraged to react with anger, whereas only a short time ago, he would have knocked the man from his horse for his insults. "Even the most ignorant brave has heard that soldiers are riding at us from all directions to surround and kill us even as we used to do the great herds of buffalo before the white hunters began their slaughter. Only last spring, I let myself be lulled into thinking we had a chance of winning. But deep in my heart, I think I knew even then that it is only a matter of time until the buffalo are gone completely, that I will spend my old age on a white man's reservation."

Little Fox turned in his saddle to watch Quanah's people starting up the narrow, twisting path out of the canyon as the wet wind blew cold. "The *Comanchero*, Pedro, is due here any time. He will bring more guns, more powder to renew our fight. Stay only a few more days. . . ."

"No," Quanah said with determination. "Even if we get more guns, we haven't enough warriors to carry them against the thousands of Bluecoats coming toward us from all directions."

"But the soldiers will never find us in this canyon." Little Fox fingered the collar of the Turkey-red buffalo hunter's shirt he wore. "We can hide out here forever and keep raiding with the soldiers always wondering where we are going. This canyon is a haven to our people."

"The haven can easily become a trap." Quanah pulled the buffalo robe closer around his shoulders. "Sooner or later, the soldiers will track the braves here. . . ."

"Never!" Little Fox said.

Quanah shook his head. "My white blood tells me to leave this place, take my people out of this canyon."

"And what will you do then?"

"We will enjoy whatever time we have left out on the *Llano Estacado*." The great leader pulled his buffalo robe closer. "If our time of freedom is running out, we will enjoy whatever time we have left in our own land of the wild, bare plains. Those few days will be more precious to us because we know that soon it will end and we will be crowded onto reservations to be treated like beggars."

Little Fox looked to the north. "It is an early winter," he admitted. "You are riding out with a cold rain blowing in. If you must leave, better you should wait until the weather clears, and by then the *Comanchero*—"

"No." Quanah reined the gray around. "My white blood tells me this is just the kind of weather the great white soldier 'Bad Hand' Mackenzie would choose for

455

an attack, knowing Indians love to stay close to their camps in wet weather. Do not underestimate that soldier chief. I have fought him before and I know how clever, how relentless he is. Sooner or later, he will find this canyon."

And with that, he nudged the big gray with his moccasins and joined his people riding out of the Palo Duro in the cold, wet rain.

Colonel Ranald Mackenzie sat his mount in the cold mist and watched his men hold onto the struggling *Comanchero*. "Try again, boys; we need that information."

"No, *Senor*," the *Comanchero* gasped, "I—I know nothing."

"Pedro, you bastard," Mackenzie swore, looking down at the one-eyed bowlegged Mexican and the group by the wagon, "you damned *Comancheros* have supplied these Indians for a hundred years but you'll supply no more! I don't know how you sleep nights with all those tortured, scalped ghosts haunting you."

The red-faced sergeant looked up at Mackenzie. "Again, sir?"

The slight, spare officer fidgeted nervously, then nodded. He hated this part of it, but he had to know where those war parties were going when they so mysteriously disappeared after their bloody raids and he knew this man could tell them. "Again, Sergeant Murphy."

Pedro struggled and tried to protest as the soldiers looped a rope around his neck, tied the other end to a propped-up wagon tongue, and lifted him barely off the ground while he struggled and choked. Mackenzie knew that, like many mixed-blooded Comanches, Pedro was terrified of being hanged or choked to death so his soul might be trapped forever in his dead body.

Mackenzie watched a long moment before gesturing with his crippled hand. "That's enough, boys. Let him down and see if he's ready to talk yet."

Pedro was ready to talk now. As Mackenzie leaned on his saddle horn and listened, the *Comanchero* gasped out details of a great canyon lying a little to the north of the cavalry camp. That was all the officer needed. He had the information now to strike a mortal blow against the war parties.

It was still rainy and unseasonably cold as Mackenzie gave his orders. The troopers mounted up, ready to head north into the darkness.

"Sir, what'll we do with the *Comanchero?*" The sergeant gestured toward the man slumped despondently by the small campfire.

Mackenzie shrugged. "Let him go, Murphy. Sooner or later, the Comanche themselves will get him for giving away their location and it won't be a pretty death. He knows he's signed his own death sentence by telling us what we wanted to know." His lean body ached from the old wounds as he wheeled his horse north. "I hate it that I had to do that to get the information we needed, but there's lives at stake and we have a duty, Sergeant."

The sergeant nodded, falling in next to him as the horses rode out. "You did what you had to do, sir; all the men know that and respect you for it. None of us would ride under any other officer, you know that, sir."

Mackenzie nodded his thanks. He had seven war wounds from both the Civil War and the Indian campaigns, and sometimes they bothered him in bad weather. "I worry about those that ride with Custer. Sooner or later, he'll get them all killed."

"He find any gold on that trip into the Black Hills these past few months?"

Mackenzie shrugged, his slight body slumped in the saddle as they rode north. "I don't know," he grumbled, "but those Hills are sacred and protected by treaty. He'll have the Sioux and the northern Cheyenne coming into this Indian war if he doesn't watch out!"

"I suppose he was under orders," the red-faced old Irish sergeant said, "just like the rest of us; just doing his duty."

Duty. Doing his duty had cost Ranald's father, Commodore Mackenzie, his career. But that would not stop Ranald from doing his. "We'll try to take the Indians in that canyon by surprise," he said, straightening his aching shoulders. "And I'll send scouts on ahead, find out if it really exists, what the lay of the land is."

The sergeant looked back at him with frank admiration. "May I say, sir, I wouldn't trade havin' served with you for a general's stars."

Ranald smiled in spite of himself. "How long we been together, Murphy?"

The Irishman smiled. "You know that as well as I do, sir. The Civil War. I been with you longer than anyone. Remember last year when we went off down to Mexico looking for those renegade Kickapoos, Lipans, and Mescalero Apaches that was raiding back up into Texas?"

Mackenzie grinned in spite of himself, wiping the rain from his face. "I don't think I'll ever forget that pair we ran into when we tangled with the Indians."

Murphy laughed. "Ain't it the truth, now? She was such a rich, elegant beauty and he was just a tough Texas gunslinger. . . ."

"But handsome," Mackenzie reminded him, thinking about that unlikely pair. "They sure got themselves in a mess, didn't they?" He didn't expect an answer as he shifted his weight in the saddle, remembering how the Indians had carried off that fine Spanish lady. "Bandit from Bandera," he remembered, "what a lady's man he was!"

The column rode awhile through the wet darkness in silence. Then a scout galloped up. "Sir, we've found that canyon, all right. That *Comanchero* wasn't lying about it."

Mackenzie straightened his tired shoulders. "What's it like?"

The scout scratched his grizzled beard. "Like nothin' you ever saw, sir. Must be at least a hundred miles long, I reckon, and deep, like a raw wound through those red and pink canyons. You'd never know it was there if you was just lookin' for it."

Mackenzie felt the old excitement mount. "No wonder we've had such a time winning this Indian war! We'd chase those war parties and they'd just disappear into thin air. Guess they were riding to that canyon. Are there many?"

The scout took off his battered hat and scratched his head. "Only God knows and he ain't tellin'! Judgin' from the tepees, I'd say hundreds of every tribe and lots of horses, too. Maybe you'll want to wait 'til you can get reinforcements, sir. . . ."

"Reinforcements, hell!" Mackenzie said sharply. "That might be the safe thing to do, but in the meantime, we lose precious time! And if a war party spots this column, we'll lose the advantage of surprise!" He motioned for his officers to ride up.

The bluecoated men reined in, waiting.

Mackenzie considered all the possibilities as he wiped the cold rain from his face with his crippled hand. Command was an awesome duty, but like his father, he would not shirk his responsibility. "We'll ride all night," he decided, "try to get into that canyon before dawn; before the Indians discover we're here."

He saw the troubled looks his officers exchanged in the darkness. Only the old sergeant seemed to have any confidence in Mackenzie's decision. The others would rather do the safe thing, wait for reinforcements.

"We've got to strike while the iron is hot," he snapped. "This is our big chance to finish this war that those damned buffalo hunters started!" He shifted his weight in the saddle, wishing he rode as well as the reckless Custer. "Move the men out!" he ordered. "We're going to reach that canyon before morning and give those Indians a surprise for breakfast." He looked at the grizzled scout. "What's the name of this place we're riding to?"

"The Palo Duro," the scout said, "Palo Duro Canyon."

Mackenzie's old war wounds were bothering him again in this cold, wet rain. But he would not spare himself any more than he would his men. *Thirty-three years old*, he thought, *but in this biting cold he felt twice that.* "Make a note for history, men," he said to his officers. "Palo Duro will go down as the last great Indian battle in Texas!"

But later, as he rode near the canyon's rim, he wasn't so sure. In less than a hour, it would be dawn. There were hundred of tepees and grazing horses at the bottom, and it was a long way down. Were John German's four little daughters in this canyon? If so, did Mackenzie dare attack? All of the army was enraged over the slaughter of that luckless family found scalped by their wagon up in Kansas. The family Bible had let the troopers know there were four younger children who had been carried off.

The officer's horse stamped its feet and he took a breath of wet September grass, of steaming horsehide. *Horses.* He wondered for a moment if Quanah Parker and his own prized gray horse were down there? Then he shook his head. He had a grudging admiration for the big half-breed chief and he had a feeling Quanah was too smart to get trapped in that canyon.

The cold rain blew in his face as he turned back to his scout. "How do we get in?"

The scout looked troubled. "There may be other trails at the other end we don't know about. But what we've found at this end is a steep trail only wide enough for one horse at a time down the side of the canyon to the bottom."

Mackenzie rubbed his muttonchop sideburn nervously. "We'll take it."

"But, sir," a young captain protested, "it'll take an hour to reach the bottom and it'll be daylight by then! What happens if the Indians spot us? We'll be helpless strung out along that trail with them picking us off! A fall off that path is enough to kill a man or horse, even if the bullets and arrows don't get him!"

"I'm in command here, Captain!" he reminded the young man coldly. "Sometimes what they teach you at West Point doesn't apply out here fighting Indians. If this mission fails, if it's a disaster, like my father before me, I'll take the responsibility. Now let's move!"

But he had severe doubts as he rode down the crooked trail single file, a man riding ahead of him and behind him in the darkness. If they were discovered, the column would be trapped on the narrow ledge, and it must be six or eight hundred feet to the floor of the canyon that the Prairie Dog Fork of the Red River had cut through the high plains of the Texas Panhandle.

He shivered in the brisk wind of the early norther. If only the darkness would hold a little longer until he could get his column to the bottom. But even as he thought that, he saw the pale pink glow over the rocky

461

canyon walls to the east, realized sunrise was going to catch the troopers still strung out along the steep canyon wall.

There was nothing to do now but keep moving forward, even though he realized that the path was rockier, more dangerous than he had anticipated. His horse kicked a loose rock and it went over the edge. He listened and heard it clatter a long way down. The fall alone was enough to kill a man if his horse made a misstep.

Mackenzie shivered in the cold, shifting his slight body in the saddle. He couldn't remember when he'd had a good night's sleep or a hot meal. A horse whinnied at the bottom of the canyon and he held his breath, afraid the column's horses would whinny back, alert the sleeping Indians now that the first rays of dawn made the moving column faintly visible in the lavender haze of morning.

He thought about Quanah again. He wouldn't tell anyone how much he admired and respected the Indian leader. If things had been different, the two men might have been friends. *Duty*, Mackenzie thought grimly, *duty*.

The buffalo hunters had started this dirty war, and like all wars, innocent women and children on both sides lay dead because of it. And yet, because of last year's financial panic back east, some of those hunters had been desperate to do anything that would feed their own families. The whole thing was too complex to think about in black and white terms of who was right or wrong.

All he knew—and even Quanah must know—was that the Indians' way of life was doomed. The growing country would take by force, if necessary, the land it needed for all the immigrants crowding into the cities. Could the country afford the luxury of letting savages

462

roam thousands of unused, fertile acres when millions of hungry whites waited in the teeming slums, only hoping for a chance to turn the rich plains into producing farms to better their own lives? He'd let the politicians worry about the morality of this Indian war. Colonel Ranald Mackenzie would simply do his duty, follows his orders.

But had he made a mistake? Would he get his command killed? He looked around as he neared the bottom of the canyon, staring back up at the long line of troopers still on the steep canyon trail behind him. The canyon was breathtaking, walls hundreds of feet high, banded in pale pinks and mauves and purples. Who would have ever guessed that the gorge lay hidden through these flat plains? No wonder war parties could raid and disappear with such safety!

And then an Indian sentry spotted the column moving down the sheer rock wall and sounded the alarm. There was no more time to enjoy the beauty of the canyon. Shots rang out, echoing and reechoing as braves came awake, running out of tepees.

"Sergeant," Mackenzie brought his rearing, frightened horse under control, "we've got to provide a covering fire until we can get the rest of those men off that canyon trail!"

"Yes, sir!"

"And for God's sake," he signaled frantically to his officers, "keep those Indians away from that big horse herd! On foot, they're helpless! Mounted, they're the best light cavalry in the world!"

His ears ran with shouts and curses and echoing gunshots. Screams ran out as men were hit, went down. For a few minutes, Mackenzie didn't think the whole column would make it to the bottom with the warriors shooting at the helpless men on the trail. But then the soldiers were off that ledge and the Indians were scrambling up into the rocks, firing down at them.

The young captain panicked. "Look! They're up above us now! How'll we get out of here? We're trapped!"

Mackenzie dismounted, grabbed the boy, and slung him down behind the shelter of a boulder. "I got you in, soldier," he snapped with more assurance than he felt, "I'll get you out! Now get your fool head down!"

The tide began to turn slowly, Mackenzie realized as he fired. The Indians were intent on escaping, providing a covering fire for their women and children running away down the canyon. "Let them go!" he shouted. "Just stay between them and those horses, those supplies!"

The young captain protested. "I thought we came to kill Injuns! Let's ride after them and—"

"No!" Mackenzie snapped grimly. "We didn't come to kill Injuns, Captain, we came to do our duty! Our orders are to put them back on the reservation, that's all!" The acrid smell of gunpowder choked him as he turned to look for his trusted old sergeant. "Murphy, take some men, set fire to all those tepees and supplies. The tribes are helpless without them!"

The Indians were on the run now toward the other end of the canyon, maybe expecting Mackenzie's troops to chase them, to lead the cavalry into a trap somewhere along the twisting route. But Mackenzie signaled his men to let them go as he watched Murphy's troopers set the tepees and the tons of food and guns ablaze.

In only a few minutes it was over. On a rainy, cold morning in late September, hundreds of Indians were walking out of Palo Duro Canyon in defeat. It was a long way back to the reservations around Fort Sill on foot, with no food, no supplies.

Mackenzie swallowed, feeling the bitter taste of pity,

the sweetness of the victory, when only a few minutes before he'd thought he might be leading his troops into death and defeat. *The last great Indian battle of Texas*, he thought.

The young captain had recovered himself and now snapped his commander a smart salute. "Sir, as you can see, following your orders, most of the supplies the Indians left are going up in flames. But what are we to do with all these horses they left behind?"

Mackenzie abruptly felt weary and sad at the duty of command. Sometimes the decisions he was called to make seemed to prey upon his mind. He loved horses but he knew what he must do. He had learned a bitter, expensive lesson in a former campaign where he'd had the warriors on the run, having captured their big pony herd. But then the Indians had sneaked around in the night and stolen their horses back. A walking Indian was vulnerable. An Indian with a good horse under him was a dangerous, deadly fighting machine.

Duty. Mackenzie could not chance the possibility that, if he tried to drive the hundreds of horses back to his camp, the Indians might not raid him tonight and recapture the mounts.

He sighed, knowing what the decision must be. "Drive the head out of here, into that nearby little canyon we call the *Tule*. Inspect them there," he said. "Then pick out a couple of hundred to replace our own exhausted mounts, let our Indian scouts have a few as rewards for their help."

The captain looked at him a long moment. "That still leaves a huge herd, sir. What am I to do with them?"

Mackenzie ran his tongue over his lip, tasting the salt of his own sweat though the morning came on cool and rainy. He looked over at the red-faced sergeant who nodded understandingly at him. Murphy was an old

Indian fighter; he understood what must be done.

"Shoot them," Mackenzie said.

The captain stared back at him as if he hadn't understood. "Sir? Shoot fifteen hundred horses? I don't think—"

"It's not your duty to think, Captain!" Mackenzie snapped. "It's your duty to obey orders and it's my duty to put those Indians back on the reservation. Sometimes I don't like what I'm required to do but I never flinch from doing my duty!"

The old sergeant smiled. "Amen!" he said softly.

He gave Murphy a withering glance for his impudence. Because they had ridden together so long, he allowed the old Irishman liberties that no one else took. He must remember to speak to Murphy about things like that.

Mackenzie turned back to the captain. "Much as I hate it, my order is this: Take out a couple hundred of the best ones, then shoot the rest! We can't take a chance on the Indians recapturing them! That's our duty, Captain, to bring a fast, painless end to this Indian war!"

He went over by himself and sat down on a rock for a long time, not wanting to think about hungry, cold women and children walking the long distance back to Fort Sill. The black smoke from the burning food and tepees snaked upward into the overcast sky. From a long way off, he heard the echo of rifle fire as the troopers carried out his orders to destroy the luckless horses.

Quanah had made it out. Mackenzie smiled grimly, thinking of the big half-breed. Maybe he was a traitor, but he was glad that at least for a little while, the big half-breed chief and his people still rode wild and free.

Duty. Sometimes the weight of command seemed to cloud his mind, make him doubt his own sanity.

Mackenzie closed his eyes, accepting the cup of steaming coffee Murphy placed in his crippled fingers. Duty. He had done that and won a victory, yet it gave him no pleasure; he felt no pride in it. Probably, his West Point classmate, Custer, would be remembered forever and maybe he himself would be forgotten.

Mackenzie sipped the strong brew, warming his fingers around the tin cup. The stink of burning leather and dried meat choked him and he shivered in the damp mist. The echo of faraway gunfire came to his ears as the troops killed the hundreds of horses. *Maybe he would be lost in the pages of history,* he thought grimly, *but none would ever say that Colonel Ranald Slidell Mackenzie ever shirked his duty.*

Chapter Twenty-four

On the afternoon of that September day that Colonel Mackenzie rode into Palo Duro Canyon, Maverick Durango married Cayenne Carol McBride.

He would never forget standing at the front of that little weather-beaten church with the plump minister and handsome dark Trace at his side as best man. The weather had turned cool and rainy as the first norther of the season blew into west Texas, but in his heart the sun shone and birds sang.

He looked at the congregation as the organ played. "Isn't it a beautiful day?" he whispered.

For a moment, Trace's dark face mirrored disbelief, then seemed to understand. He looked out into the audience at his own wife as if remembering. "*Si*," he whispered with a nod, "there's no day so beautiful as the day your bride comes down the aisle and into your arms!"

The plump preacher cleared his throat as the music swelled and Maverick looked out at the congregation. Don Diego caught his eye and smiled.

Old Sanchez winked encouragingly. The church was full. Everyone from the Triple D Ranch had traveled here to attend the ceremony and the whole town had turned out for this wedding of their beloved preacher's child.

First down the aisle came little Angel, carrying her flower basket and throwing petals as she toddled toward him. Maverick smiled in spite of himself. At least she couldn't suck her thumb and throw flowers at the same time.

Next down the aisle came Steve, with her pigtails askew, and Gracious, both full of self-importance with their roles as bridesmaids. He didn't have to look to know that in spite of everything Cayenne could do, Gracie's sash would be untied. All three children took their places at the front of the church.

Maverick licked his lips nervously, whispering hoarsely to Trace. "I'd rather face a hanging than go through all this in front of all these people!"

His voice carried over the organ and the audience tittered good-naturedly. Even the minister's jowls nodded with understanding.

Now came the maid of honor, her little wire-rimmed spectacles sliding down her nose, but she pushed them back up and kept walking primly. As Cayenne had said, it might be unusual to have a nine-year-old maid of honor, but this was after all Cayenne's wedding and she'd do what her heart told her. If it hadn't been for Lynnie's letter, Cayenne wouldn't have met her future husband.

Now the music swelled again, the big doors at the back swung open, and Cayenne started down the aisle on Joe McBride's arm. She had to support and guide him gently as they started walking, but the pair smiled so happily that Maverick saw two ladies reach for handkerchiefs to wipe their eyes.

His bride. His heart filled so as the wheezy old organ played that he had to blink hard to keep the tears from coming. Who would have ever believed that instead of killing the man Maverick had hunted all these years, he would instead marry the man's daughter, become part of Joe McBride's family?

If only Annie could be here and know there'd been a happy ending just like the stories she always told him. A hand seemed to pat his shoulder reassuringly. He looked around. There was no one there . . . *at least, not that he could see.*

Never was there a more beautiful bride than his, he thought proudly, watching Cayenne walking slowly down the aisle, assisting her blind father. Her red hair swirled around the shoulders of the white lace dress. It was all he could do to keep from running down the aisle and gathering her into his arms.

Trace must have read his thoughts because he reached out, caught Maverick's arm, and gave him just the slightest shake of his head.

The church smelled of autumn wild flowers and something else. Maverick grinned as his bride moved closer. *Vanilla.* It would always be his favorite scent. Joe and Cayenne stood before them now, and Maverick looked around at the family as the organ stopped. *Red hair and freckles,* he thought with a grin. I'm destined to spend my life surrounded by red-haired, green-eyed freckled people.

"Dearly beloved," the minister said, and Maverick came back to the ceremony with a start.

He tried to listen to what the minister said, but he could only stare into the beautiful face of his bride.

". . . who giveth this woman?" the minister intoned.

Joe hesitated a moment, almost as if he couldn't bear to hand her over to another man's keeping. Then his sightless face smiled and he said, "Her family and I do."

His job done, Joe turned with difficulty as if to move to a front pew to sit down.

"Wait, Joe," Maverick said impulsively, reaching out to catch his sleeve, "if it's not too improper, I'd like you to stand up here with us through the ceremony."

Cayenne smiled at Maverick, her heart too full to speak as she watched him grasp her father's arm. She looked into Maverick's gray eyes. *I love you*, she told him silently. *Oh, I love you so!*

". . . and will you take this man to love and comfort until death do you part?"

She spoke in a spirited voice loud and strong with conviction. "I certainly will!"

"And will you, Maverick Durango, take this woman, Cayenne Carol McBride, to love and to cherish as long as you both shall live?"

Maverick looked deep into her eyes. "I sure as hell will!" he said. "And as a matter of fact, sir, if you don't mind, I'd like you to include the

471

whole family!"

The minister cleared his throat and a buzz of chatter ran through the little church.

Lynnie frowned up at him. "You mustn't swear!" she admonished.

Maverick grinned down at her. "I guess, little sis, you got a long time to teach me some manners!"

Someone in the crowd tittered with delight and old Mrs. Rumsley with her ear trumpet shrilled, "What'd he say? What's that about reaching for banners?"

The minister raised his eyebrows, giving it some thought. "A little unusual," he said, and his face broke into a smile. "But I like the thought behind it. Yes, indeedy, I do! All right then, all of you join hands in a circle."

Cayenne reached out and took one of Angel's little hands in hers, pretending not to notice the thumb was wet. Cayenne's other hand was held by Maverick and he took Joe's hand in his and Joe reached for Lynnie's, who reached for Gracie's, who grabbed Steve's and then Angel's little fist. They all stood holding hands in a big circle and she looked at Maverick, sent him a message with her eyes. *Thank you for accepting my family. Thank you, dearest.*

The minister seemed to be puzzling over what to say next. He cleared his throat. "A ring always seems to be part of every wedding and here we have a living ring, an unbroken circle more precious than gold. Now then, Maverick Durango, will you take this family to be your family forever

472

and ever, through sickness and health, through good times and adversity? Look after them and love them as I'm sure they will love you as their only son and brother?"

Maverick nodded solemnly, clasping her hand and Joe's. "I will, sir. I promise that 'long as I got a biscuit, they got half!"

Somewhere in the audience, Cayenne heard old Rosita begin to weep.

Mrs. Harrison's high voice carried in the silence. "Isn't that the sweetest, most sincere vow you ever heard?"

And Mr. Billings said out loud, "Looks like Joe finally got that son he always wanted!"

Little Angel turned toward the crowd and yelled in triumph. "And we got us a brother, too!"

Cayenne looked down at her, aghast. "Angel, hush! You aren't supposed to say anything!"

Even the minister joined the audience in laughter then. "This has been a very unusual wedding," he grinned, "but I wouldn't have missed being part of it for the world!"

Cayenne tried to follow the rest of the ceremony, but all she could do was stare into Maverick's eyes until she heard the words she had asked the minister to say: "I now pronounce you man and wife and expect you to live happily ever after just like in the fairy tales! Amen! Maverick, you may kiss your bride!"

Maverick did. He grabbed Cayenne and kissed her as if he would never let her go and she clung to him, thinking how close they had come to losing each other.

They kissed until the crowd whispered and tittered in good humor and Trace reached out, touching Maverick's shoulder with a chuckle. "Little brother, you got all the rest of your life to do that! Let's get to the food!"

Maverick looked around at the big crowd of townspeople who had crowded into the McBride ranch house to share the celebration. All around him people chatted and stuffed their faces with barbecue and cake, coming up to him to offer congratulations.

He caught Cayenne's eye across the crowded parlor and she winked at him, touched her lips, and blew him a kiss. How he longed to have her to himself, to hold her and kiss her. But he realized they must be polite to all the company. He watched the little sisters in the crowd, thinking how much they looked like Cayenne. Someday, those four would take four young men's hearts as their big sister had taken his. In the meantime, they were as untidy as usual, with pigtails askew, sashes untied. He was afraid to check and see if Angel might have wet her drawers.

Prim little Lynnie stood by Rosita, helping serve the stack cake. It was an old Texas custom that all the visitors bring a layer of cake and stack it up to show their love and approval of the bride. The higher the cake, the more popular she was. Maverick smiled. The cake had reached such a height that Cayenne feared it might tumble, so they'd made two stacks of it.

He watched Lynnie. She was a smart one, all

right. Maverick would have a sizable inheritance from the old Don. He'd send that one to college. She'd probably end up leading a bunch of those crazy suffragettes trying to get the right for women to vote!

The afternoon was a blur of people, of congratulations, of gifts, little old ladies kissing his cheek, men pumping his hand and commenting on the beauty of the bride.

And finally, it was evening and they'd all departed except the closest friends, the McBride family, and the visiting Durangos. Old Rosita called supper.

Maverick had never really noticed the dining room of this house, and how as he entered, he stopped and looked around. The long oak table. Just as Annie had promised.

Cayenne caught his arm. "What's the matter, dearest?"

He swallowed hard. "If Annie could only know . . ."

Joe paused next to him, patting his shoulder. "She does, Son, I assure you, she does."

And then it was just like he'd envisioned it a million times when he was a starved, lonely boy in a tepee. Joe took his arm, placed him at one end of the table, and sat down in a chair at one side.

Maverick protested, "But, Joe, this is your chair!"

He shook his head and smiled. "It's yours now, Maverick. I hand over both the reins and the welfare of this clan to your hands."

Maverick saw Cayenne blink back tears as she seated herself at the far end opposite him. All up and down the table were relatives, friends. Somehow, he suddenly felt Annie's presence. She would be with him always, in spirit and through his children. Without thinking, Maverick whispered, "God moves in mysterious ways . . ."

"Amen!" Joe nodded. "Amen! And now, I'll bless this food, this family."

Family. Maverick bent his head, struggling with the lump his throat. *His family.* The first of many meals at the long table Annie had talked about so many dreams ago. He looked up as old Rosita brought in steaming platters of fried chicken and chocolate cake. Yes, this was all the way the two of them had dreamed it would be.

He looked down the table at Cayenne and she smiled at him. A great peace came into his heart as he thought of Annie Laurie and the flame-haired girl he loved.

Later they all sat before the stone fireplace, the fire crackling merrily on scented mesquite wood, driving away the chill. He snuggled down next to his bride in a big chair, staring into the fire and remembering a cold, shivering kid who always hoped for and pictured a room like this.

Cayenne leaned closer. "What are you thinking about?" she whispered.

He thought of Annie but the memories weren't painful anymore. "Some time, I'll tell you," he said softly, patting her hand.

And finally, it was late enough for the bridal couple to excuse themselves and go up to the big bedroom at the top of the stairs, leaving the rest of the family and visitors still chatting before the roaring fireplace.

Cayenne put a dab of vanilla behind each ear after she had changed into a pale green nightdress. Then she brushed her hair until it shone like burnished copper and went into the big bedroom where her husband sat smoking, looking into the cozy fire. He had not undressed.

"Come here to me, baby," he said, pulling her down on his lap as he tossed the cigarette into the fireplace. She lay her face against his wide chest as he stroked her absently, both content for the moment to hold each other, hear the other's heartbeat.

After a while, Cayenne stood up, caught his hands, and pulled him to his feet. She looked up into his adoring eyes as his big, rough hands came down to cup her small face, turn it up to his, kiss the tip of her nose. "And to think I almost rode off without you!" he whispered.

"My stars! You don't think I would have let you do that!" She stared up into the wide gray eyes, and when he smiled, she realized how his face lit up, how handsome he was.

"You mean I didn't have any choice, you feisty little terrier?" His lips kissed her eyelids as she swayed in his embrace.

She grinned, winking at him. "They don't call me Cayenne for nothing!" she reminded him.

"By damn, I hope you can pass that kind of spirit on to children," he laughed under his breath, tangling his hands in her long hair. "I'd like little Sam to be as fiery, as peppery as his mama."

Her green eyes widened in shock. "Sam? Sam?" She pushed him away. "Why, it'll be a cold day in hell before I name one of my sons after that ornery old rumpot!"

"Now, Cayenne, I thought we agreed—"

"Agreed?" She backed away from him, gesturing in a fury. "I don't remember agreeing to no such thing! I just took it for granted we'd name the first one Jefferson Davis like I said. . . ."

"Jefferson Davis!" He took a deep breath and his face turned red with anger. "Now, little Reb, you aren't gonna name no son of mine after that traitor to his country!"

"Traitor, is he?" She had been tricked by this blasted, hardheaded Texan! She looked around frantically for something to fend him off with as he advanced on her.

"Come here, baby"—he held out both hands as if he were attempting to soothe a wild mustang— "now let's just cuddle up and talk about this a little. . . ."

"You're not going to change my mind, you ornery Yankee sympathizer! I've been tricked and I won't have it! You hear! We're going to get this straightened out before I get into bed with you!"

He kept advancing on her, and she grabbed up her hairbrush and threw it. It hit the wall behind him. She started backing away.

"Cee Cee," he admonished, unbuttoning his shirt

as he moved toward her, "everyone downstairs will hear you shouting!"

"Who's shouting, you—you—"

He started toward her, and she picked up her face powder jar off the dresser and threw it at him. It crashed with a shattering sound.

"Enough, baby," he said softly, and his gray eyes flashed sparks. "Stop that and come here to me!"

"Damned if I will!" And she took off around the room, running barefooted across the floor to keep the bed between them. He stalked her around the bed like a hunter after wild game. When she scampered around the bed, he tried to intercept her. But she was quick and smart as well as angry. She couldn't help but smile at his frustration as he chased her around and around the big four-poster.

She picked up a flower vase. "Stay away from me until you promise I can name him Jefferson!"

He stopped, sighed, and stuck his thumbs in his belt. "If you don't let me catch you, there'll never be a child to name!"

She paused, putting the vase down slowly on the bedside table. She studied him across the bed, considering his words. And in that moment, he made a sudden dive across the middle of the bed, caught her in his arms, and kissed her 'til she was breathless. "Maverick, you're an untrustworthy rascal!" she gasped.

"That's why you love me, baby." He nibbled at the edge of her lips, running his hand down to cup the creamy globe of her breast. "We'll talk about it later," he muttered.

"Now," she demanded, "we'll talk now!"

479

He swung her up easily in his powerful arms and looked down into her face. "No, baby. I got better ideas for now."

She couldn't hold out any longer. Her arms slipped up around his neck and she kissed the strong line of his jaw. "Maybe you're right," she whispered as he carried her to the big four-poster feather bed. "We'll talk about that some other time. . . ."

The old Don held Angel on his expansive lap. He had paused in his storytelling at the sudden noise of angry shouts, of something thrown against a wall in the upstairs room. He grinned a little. "I believe the newlyweds are having a difference of opinion."

Joe coughed, an expression of embarrassment on his features. "Maybe I should have warned your son that my daughter is rather—ah, shall I say, she is sometimes a handful?"

Gracious put her hands over her mouth, giggling in delight. "What he means is, We don't call her 'Cayenne' for nothin'!"

The little girls all laughed with merriment while Joe coughed in confusion. "Gracie, you shouldn't have told him about Cee Cee's temper!"

From upstairs came the sound of glass crashing, the sound of running feet as if one of them might be chasing the other around the room.

Don Diego leaned back in his chair and smiled expansively, remembering his own younger days, his beautiful wife. "And we don't call our stubborn renegade 'Maverick' for nothing, young lady. I imagine they're about evenly matched!" And suddenly the upstairs grew very quiet.

Lynnie pushed her spectacles back up her freckled nose, looking at her little sisters and back to her father. "It's awfully quiet up there. Do you suppose some of us ought to go up there and find out what's happening—?"

Joe reached out and caught her arm. "I don't think that's necessary, honey. It'll be all right."

Lynnie looked at him and back to Don Diego. "But what are they doing? It's so quiet. . . ."

"Someday, when you're a big girl, you'll understand." The Don stroked his mustache, smiling reassuringly at her.

Joe nodded. "It's past your bedtime, girls; go on to bed."

The littlest one had gone to sleep on Don Diego's lap. His pants felt damp where she sat but he decided not to mention it as old Rosita came in and he handed the toddler over.

Steve's eyes half closed and she jerked awake. "I'm not sleepy yet."

"Girls," Joe said gently, "go to bed."

Diego smiled as he watched the weary, cake-smudged little girls stumble out of the room.

Trace and Sanchez were nowhere about, and he wondered if they were out in the bunkhouse playing poker with Juan and the *vaqueros*, but he didn't say anything. Joe looked like a good sport but he was, after all, a preacher. Trace's beautiful wife had taken her children to bed.

They sat in silence a long moment, enjoying each other's company, and then a thought struck

481

Diego. "In all the excitement, I forgot! *Senor,* I had a birthday this past week. I'm seventy-five years old!"

Joe had brought out his pocket knife but now he stopped and considered, dropping it back in his pocket. "I don't usually drink, *Senor,*" he said, "but I think we need to toast this happy ending, your birthday." He gestured toward the dining room. "If you'll look in the sideboard, I think you'll find some fine old brandy, a couple of glasses."

Diego got them each a drink, settling back down before the fire with a satisfied sigh. "I suppose we are both useless, Joe; you blind, me too old to do much."

Joe shook his head. "That's not true, Diego. If you hadn't taken the bull by the horns, come in on that stage, no telling what might have happened. Don't count us down and out yet. We're still useful. What is it that poet, Milton, wrote: 'He also serves who only stands and waits.'?"

Don Diego tasted his fine brandy, remembering the poem *Sonnet on His Blindness.* "Maybe you're right, Joe." He thought about generations passing into generations in a long, unbroken line. "You've got lovely daughters."

Joe sipped his brandy. "Aren't they, though? I've been so worried about how long I could keep this place running with me blind and not much money. I'm relieved to be able to hand it over to Maverick's capable hands. Remember the gun I won?"

The Don glanced up at the fine prize rifle hanging over the fireplace. "*Sí*, I remember. A one-in-a-thousand Winchester '73. That's a priceless weapon, Joe."

"I'm gonna give it to Maverick," Joe smiled, stroking his red beard. "Let's say it's a wedding gift."

"Do you mind if I smoke?"

Joe grinned. "When you're in my house, Diego, you smoke as many cigars as you want!"

"I think we're going to be great friends," Diego said, sipping the savory brandy and enjoying the strong taste of his cigar as he bit off the tip and lit it. "Of course Maverick has an inheritance from me and he'll be able to pay off your mortgage, fix this place up a little." He looked around at the threadbare furnishings.

Joe sipped his brandy. "The McBrides don't take charity," he said firmly.

"Charity?" the Don snorted. "He's family, man! To accept help from family is not charity, and besides, you'd offend him by refusing."

Joe stroked his beard. "Maybe you're right. And after all, I do intend to take him in as a full partner on the Lazy M since I don't have a son."

"Oh, but you do!" Don Diego smiled and nodded.

The other man's face lit up in a smile. "That's right, isn't it? I finally got a son." He fumbled in his pocket for a handkerchief and blew his nose. "I enjoy your company, Diego; I hope you'll come visit often."

Don Diego blew smoke, nodding happily. "I was just about to suggest that very thing! And, of course, you must come visit the Triple D!"

"I play the whistle, but not very well," Joe said, fumbling in his pocket.

"All the grandchildren would like that," Don Diego said. "And I've got a lot of stories from the old days I can't get anyone to stop and listen to anymore."

"Isn't it the truth?" Joe exclaimed. "Why, they're just all so busy I have a hard time even getting my little girls to sit very long while I tell them how it used to be when I first come to Texas. Why, one time I was rounding up mustangs on the Brazos—"

"You, too?" The Don leaned forward. "I did that years ago. And hot, *Dios!* Such weather!"

Joe leaned closer. "These kids don't know what real heat is! Do you remember that summer of? . . ."

Upstairs, Cayenne pulled Maverick down to her and offered him her breasts, gasping with pleasure and shivering as his lips kissed there.

"Mmm. You smell just like sugar cookies." Maverick sniffed along the hollow of her throat. "Don't ever stop wearing that vanilla perfume."

She shivered as he nibbled up to her ear, ran his tongue inside. "I won't," she said, "as long as that scent gets me attention like this!"

"It's nice snuggled down in this feather bed," Maverick whispered, running his hands over her warm skin. "This is the way to spend the winter, curled up making love to you."

She giggled, tousling his black hair, loving him

as she had never dreamed she could love a man. "We can't spend the whole winter in bed, silly!"

He pulled her to him, kissing the edges of her mouth. "I'd like to know why not?" he murmured.

"Well, I don't know why not," she shrugged, closing her eyes as his hands stroked her skin. *Comanche caress.* She shivered at the sensation. "No one ever has, that's all!"

He rolled over on his back, pulling her on top of him. Her breasts hung over his face and he reached up with his tongue, kissing the pink circles around her nipples. "At least we could try," he whispered.

She gasped as she slid down on the throbbing hardness of his staff, felt his hands grasp her small waist to hold her there. "I don't think even you could do this all winter, Maverick."

He chuckled, beginning to move rhythmically under her, pushing up deep into her body. "Try me, baby," he whispered, "just try me!"

Her mounting excitement took over as she rode his lean body, bringing them both to fulfillment. She had a sudden feeling of going over the edge as she opened her lips to moan, and he put his hot tongue deep in her mouth to muffle her cry of pleasure.

Eagles, she thought as the hot waves swept her under, sent her falling through space. She felt his virile seed surge deep into her womb and he gasped as he pulled her hard against him. She seemed to remember a day on a Kansas creek bank—giant, majestic eagles locked together, hurling through space as they meshed. *Eagles mate*

485

for life, she remembered. Oh, to spend the rest of hers in Maverick's arms! And in her mind and soul, she locked her wings about her love, joining him in eagles' flight. . . .

Chapter Twenty-five

Maverick finished his breakfast, enjoying the sound of birds singing in the June stillness of the ranch yard. Everyone else had left the long table where he now leisurely sipped a second cup of coffee and reread the headline in the *McBride Monthly Gazette: Uprising Finally Ends! Quanah Parker surrenders!*

He glanced at the date, June, 1875, before he took another sip of coffee and read the article:

At long last, the Red River Uprising ended this month as Quanah Parker led his hungry, defeated people into Fort Sill to surrender, the last of the warring bands to do so.

Colonel Ranald Mackenzie, hero of Palo Duro, now the new commander at Fort Sill, says Quanah will not be punished because since he signed no treaties, he is not guilty of breaking any. However, the other chiefs will not be so lucky. Seventy-two leaders of the Comanche, Kiowa, and Cheyenne renegades will be shipped off to prison at Fort Marion, Florida to make sure they start no more rebellions.

One prisoner wore yellow satin sleeve garters and a telegraph operator's green eyeshade as he boarded the train. We can only wonder what hapless white men died so he could own those. But on hearing his fate, one Comanche leader, Little Fox, committed suicide by slashing his wrists with a lady's silver and pearl comb he had evidently sharpened against the stone walls of his cell.

The four little German girls have all been found now and Colonel Miles has announced he will adopt these pitiful orphans. In the meantime, all the Indians have been forced back to their reservations and there are complaints there's not enough government food provided to keep them from starving and that the few supplies they do get are inferior. Charges of widespread graft and corruption among government contractors providing for the tribes are becoming a scandal.

"Poor devils," Maverick shook his head. He could feel pity for all the tribes now, even the Comanche. He had buried the scalp from his stallion's bridle along with the rawhide thong from his gun belt when he closed the door on his revenge. Love had softened his heart toward all mankind. He thought for a moment about Molly, Pat Hennessy, all the white and Indian victims of the Red River War.

Another item caught his eye: *New Invention Changing Ranching.*

That new invention, barbed wire, is coming to Texas as word of this cheap fencing spreads across the whole southwest. Farmer Joseph Glidden from Illinois patented the wire and some say it spell the end for the open range and the cattle drive. . . .

488

Maverick smiled as he turned to the *Local Happenings* column:

Congratulations to Mr. & Mrs. M. Durango on the new baby at the Lazy M Ranch. Joe McBride, well-loved local preacher, is busting his buttons over that first grandchild. . . .

The noise of giggling little girls running down the stairs interrupted his quiet morning coffee and Maverick looked up, smiling as the four came into the dining room.

"Hello, girls, all set for that trip to town?"

Gracie turned her back to him. "Tie my sash."

"Please," he corrected gently as he tied it. "Angel, quit sucking your thumb."

The red-haired toddler took her thumb from her mouth reluctantly.

Steve looked him over skeptically. "You're not getting to go to town? Have you been bad?"

Maverick pulled one of her pigtails. "Sis, let's just say I'd rather stay here with Cee Cee."

Serious Lynnie pushed her wire-framed spectacles back up her freckled nose. "We'll bring you a candy stick," she announced solemnly.

"You do that, Sis. Is Papa Joe ready?"

From the back of the house, he heard old Rosita scolding Joe for dawdling. Maverick got up and went to lean against the front door as Rosita led Joe carefully into the front hall.

Joe turned his scarred face toward the sound. "Son, can we bring you anything from town?"

Maverick straightened the man's collar. "No, Dad. Rosita, you all have a good time shopping and at the church social and don't hurry back."

Maverick went out onto the porch to watch them all pile in the buggy with Juan driving them into town. "See you all later this afternoon," he waved as the wagon pulled out. "And, Angel, take your thumb out of your mouth!"

With happy giggles and shouts, the little girls waved to him as the buggy pulled away. Maverick waved after them with a feeling of great contentment. *His family.*

He watched them until they drove under the big sign hanging over the gate. *Lazy M Ranch*, it read, *Maverick & McBride*. He had suggested the McBride name go first but Papa Joe wouldn't hear of it.

Only yesterday, the Durangos had departed after coming to visit a few days and see the newest member of the family. Maverick grinned. The old Don and Joe were wearing out the road between the two ranches visiting each other. Now Maverick had two families. He was a very lucky *hombre.*

He stood there until the buggy faded into a small dot in the distance. Then he surveyed the surrounding pastures critically, looking at the fine-blooded cattle and horses he'd bought this past year. Dust Devil whinnied a welcome to him, then went back to grazing near the mare, Strawberry. The roan's new foal gamboled about the pasture, its little red tail straight out behind it like a flag as it ran.

Maverick leaned against the porch rail and grinned, watching the speckled baby play near its dam. *Red mane and tail*, he thought. Even the horses on this spread have red hair. He'd let the little sisters name the foal.

He thought about it, laughing out loud. "Freckles." Of course a bunch of freckled little redheaded girls would pick that name for Strawberry's foal.

He looked around the landscape. The next item on the agenda was a big new barn. He'd already remodeled the house, bought new furnishings. But he hadn't replaced the long table. It was part of his dream. *His family. His ranch.* Just like he and his mother always imagined it would be. He could think of her now without hurting, remembering only the good memories. His wife's love had erased the terrible scars of his mind.

Pink Seven Sisters roses by the porch scented the late June day and he broke off one, sniffed it. His favorite scent would always be vanilla. Then he smiled, thinking they had the whole day, the whole house to themselves. A small wail drifted from the open upstairs window and he grinned again, picked some of the roses, and went back inside. The most important people in his world were waiting for him in the big room at the head of the stairs. He climbed those stairs, two at a time.

The high sweet voice drifted through the closed door along with the rhythmic sound of a rocking chair. "*. . . gave me her promise true that ne'er forgot will be, and for darling Annie Laurie . . .*"

He opened the door, "Cee Cee?"

She smiled at him from her rocker, motioning him in.

He thought she had never been so beautiful as she was at that moment in a delicate pink dressing gown, her hair like soft swirls of flame on her small shoulders. And in her arms, she held the baby who nursed contentedly. *His woman. His child.* His heart seemed to fill to bursting and he stood there, drinking in the sight of the two of them a long time before he put the roses in a vase on a table and went over to her.

"You look like the angel on a Christmas tree," he whispered. With a hesitant finger, he touched the baby's delicate hair. "Red like Mama's," he smiled.

Cayenne looked up at him and her eyes told him how very much she loved him. The baby's eyes flickered open at his touch.

Cayenne smiled. "Gray like Daddy's."

The baby looked at him and seemed to smile, and the smile was familiar, too. *If your grandmother could only know about you. Well, maybe she does. . . .*

For a moment as he stood looking down at them, he could not trust himself to speak. When he finally could, he said, "You don't know how much it meant to me for you to choose that name."

Cayenne reached out and caught his hand. "I knew there could be no other name for this baby."

At the sound of her mother's voice, little Annie Laurie Durango opened her eyes sleepily, milk running down her chin, then dropped back off to sleep.

Cayenne stood up, handing the tiny, precious bundle to him, and he marveled again at how perfect the child was. Maybe Papa Joe was right.

Who could hold a child and not believe in miracles? Very gently, he kissed her tiny fist, carrying baby Annie to tuck her in her crib.

Cayenne studied him. "Are they all gone for the day?"

Maverick sighed with relief. "Yes, I didn't think they would ever get things together and out the door! There's times when my family is a real handful!"

"Families are like that." She came over and slipped her arms around his neck. "Do you know what today is?"

He kissed the tip of her freckled nose. "Saturday."

She looked annoyed, then coquettish. "No, I mean besides Saturday."

He pretended he didn't. "It's the week before we finish branding all that new stock?"

"No, silly! It's our anniversary." She nuzzled his neck and he took a deep breath of vanilla, of the clean scent of her fiery hair.

"Can't be." He kissed the top of her head, enjoying the warm feel of her against him. "We got married in September."

"You've forgotten!" She looked stricken and he only smiled. *There was a dainty necklace in his pocket for her but he wouldn't give it to her just yet; a delicate gold necklace with a graceful winged eagle charm.*

"You've forgotten," she said again as if she couldn't quite believe he would do such a thing. "It was just a year ago today that I walked into the Red Garter Saloon. . . ."

493

"Oh, yes"—he pretended to search his memory—"and I rescued you from a drunk. . . ."

"Then we ended up out on the sidewalk and I threw myself at you. . . ."

"Somehow, I don't recall. . . ."

"You've forgotten how I grabbed you and kissed you?" And she kissed him.

"Oh, I seem to remember now," he teased. "Then I think I picked you up off the ground and said, "No, Cayenne, here's the way it's done." And he kissed her now as he had kissed her that long-ago day, thoroughly, expertly.

When he stopped, she clung to him breathlessly. "Am I any better than I was?"

He pretended to consider. "I think you need about fifty years more practice to get it right!"

"Oh, you!" She ran her hand through his black hair, tousling it.

He swung her up in his arms, carried her over to the big bed, and lay down next to her. It was enough for now to be able to hold her close, feel her heart beat against him. *Where she was, there he would always be.*

"Do you love me, Maverick?" She snuggled against him, her flame-colored hair falling across his big chest.

He had to swallow hard before he could answer. "I'm just a cowboy, baby, I don't have much of a way with words." He kissed her eyes, her lips.

"Oh, Maverick, I wish everyone in the world could find such happiness, such love! There are so many, many lonely people out there!"

"Like I was," he murmured, kissing her again.

494

"But if they keep hoping, when they least expect it, love will happen along and the wait will have been worth it."

He stroked her hair and she lay her face against his chest. "Maverick, dearest, I've been thinking about the names for the next baby and I've come up with three."

Maverick looked askance. "Don't get any ideas; all you get today are kisses!"

"You think I'm just desperate for your body?"

"Aren't you?" he teased.

She laughed. "My stars! You're trying to get me off the subject! I've given it a lot of thought, and since we're going to give Annie a bunch of brothers—"

"We are? Reb, you do intend to give me enough time out of bed to run this ranch, don't you?"

"Just barely," she murmured, snuggling against him. "I'm serious, Maverick, I've come up with three boys' names we can agree on."

He looked at her suspiciously. "And those names are?"

"Any Texan would be proud to name his sons for the fallen heros of the Alamo," she said. "What about Travis, Crockett, and Bowie?"

"Amen! Those are true Texas names!" *You little Rebel*, he thought as he kissed her again, thinking he had a long, long time to persuade her. *We'll name that fourth one Sam Houston Durango.*

She smiled smugly, curling up in his arms. *You ornery Yankee sympathizer*, she thought as she kissed the corners of his mouth and held him close. *I know exactly what you're thinking. A woman who loves a man as much as I love you can see through him like clear spring water.* Besides, she had a long, long time ahead of her to sway him about the fourth son's name. With enough kisses, she knew the big man was as soft and pliable as homemade taffy in her hands.

"What're you smiling about?" he demanded. "You look like a kitten that's dipped its paws in a saucer of cream."

"Nothing except how much I love you, dearest." She put her face against his chest, listening to his heartbeat. *Where he was, there she would always be.*

And with them, she thought, *would be their children: Annie, Travis, Crockett, Bowie—and little Jefferson Davis Durango.*

He kissed her deeply and she shuddered at the feelings that swept over her, impatient that she had to wait for his lovemaking.

His warm tongue slipped between her lips to tease and torment, and his hand stroked her thighs. "Just wanted to remind you what we've both been missing," he whispered.

His teeth nipped her lips ever so gently. She realized suddenly she was as soft and pliable as taffy when he made love to her.

"Joe," he murmured, "we'll call that fourth one Joe. But the fifth one . . ."

"We'll argue that one when we get there." She laid her face against his wide chest. "We've got time. That's a lot of lovin' from now."

"I'm looking forward to it," he murmured, blow-

496

ng in her ear until she shivered. "And by the way, 've a little something for this anniversary."

When she saw what it was—the tiny charm dangling on the delicate gold chain—her vision blurred with tears. "Oh, Maverick! You didn't forget! You didn't!"

"Never, baby. Come here to me."

He placed the chain around her neck and turned her small face up to him with his big hands. "Cayenne Carol McBride Durango, I think it would take years just to tell you how much I love you!"

"I've got time," she whispered, snuggling contentedly against his chest. "Now tell me how much," she teased.

"Well," he began as he kissed the tip of her nose, held her very close. "Once upon a time, there was this tough old trail boss who saw a sassy redhead in a green dress and he loved her from the very first moment he saw her. . . ."

To My Readers

Everyone's heard of Custer's Last Stand, but only historians show interest in the Red River Indian Uprising of 1874 despite the fact that it was the greatest army expedition against the Plains Indians ever undertaken and involved famous people such as Quanah Parker, Bat Masterson, and the most competent Indian fighter of them all, Colonel Ranald Mackenzie.

It is a fact that the wagons carrying food to the Kiowa were ambushed and the drivers tortured to death sometime between July 2 and July 4. It was hard to tell from the condition of the bodies. Pat Hennessy himself had been tied upside down to one of his big wagon wheels and slowly roasted alive. There's some who say it wasn't Indians at all, but white men masquerading as Indians so they could rob him. The massacre site is about fifty-eight miles northwest of my home here in the Cross Timbers section of central Oklahoma. There's a small town on the massacre site now named for Pat. The town's name has been misspelled as Hennessey.

Many of Oklahoma's rivers are notorious for quicksand. The Cimarron is one of the worst.

know it well since it's only twenty-six miles from my front door. Just a short distance from where I had Cayenne and Maverick trapped by the quicksand was once the scene of Oklahoma's worst railroad disaster. Early on a rainy morning, September 8, 1906, a trestle gave way near the town of Dover, dropping a Rock Island train into the rushing flood waters of the Cimarron. No one knows for sure how many died that night, probably less than a dozen. But you might be interested to know the giant locomotive from that wreck, old #628, is still there, sunk deep in the quicksand of the Cimarron.

Some of you may laugh at the use of vanilla as perfume. But I can tell you it was common on the frontier. One of my earliest memories is that of my Texas grandmother, born the year of the Red River Uprising, dabbing vanilla behind her ears. She told me many times that "strong scent" was for "hussies."

The vanilla plant, a member of the orchid family, seems to have been discovered by the conquistadors deep in Mexico. By the way, Mexico doesn't produce enough vanilla for its own use and its labeling laws are not as strict as ours. Look with skepticism at those giant bottles of "pure vanilla" being sold cheap to tourists. Not only is it possible that you aren't getting pure, undiluted vanilla, but it may contain coumarin. Coumarin has a medical component, Dicumarol, which is closely related to the anticoagulant, warfarin, used in rat poison. The U.S. Food and Drug Administration banned the use of coumarin in our food back in 1955.

499

An interesting legend that has never been unraveled completely is that of the black man who played cavalry charges on a bugle, fighting on the Indians' side at Adobe Walls. The black cavalry served heroically in the old west. Although the legend says that the dead black was a soldier who had gone over to the warriors, there's also the possibility that he was a dark mixed-blood who had been adopted and raised by the Indians.

Speaking of the soldiers who participated in the Red River Uprising, between them, these men were awarded some thirty or so Congressional Medals of Honor during this campaign. This medal is our country's highest award for bravery and gallantry above and beyond the call of duty. That so many were awarded tells you something about the soldiers who served. There were, of course, no medals for the brave Indian warriors except for scalps, many of them taken from innocent settlers who paid for the greed of the buffalo hunters with their lives.

A few buffalo hunters did get their just deserts. The horrible torture inflicted on Buck and his pa in Chapter Eighteen came straight from my research books.

Some of you will be curious as to what happened to the major players of the Red River Uprising. The four little German sisters were indeed adopted by Colonel Miles. The four grew up, married, and reared families. The last of the four Julia, died in California in 1959, at the age of ninety-two.

Billy Dixon, the buffalo hunter who actually fired the famous shot at the battle of Adobe Walls

ecame an army scout. During September, he was
ne of the heroes of the battle of Buffalo Wallow
nd won one of those Congressional Medals of
Ionor. Finally, he became a rancher and lived to
e an old man, dying in his bed of pneumonia in
913. His final resting place is the Adobe Walls
attle ground.

I have walked that Panhandle site while re-
earching this book. Adobe Walls is a little more
han a hundred miles northeast of Amarillo and is
ard to find unless you're very determined. There's
ot much to see except for granite markers com-
nemorating the battle and the burial sites of some
f those killed there.

Bat Masterson and his friend, Wyatt Earp, went
n to their destinies as colorful legends of the west.
Eventually, Bat became a writer on the *New York
Morning Telegraph*. He died at his desk there on
October 25, 1921.

Quanah Parker became something of a celebrity
fter the Uprising. He was not punished because
e had never signed any peace treaties with the
whites, so he was not guilty of breaking away. He
pent the rest of his life leading his people down
he peace road and entertaining famous celebrities
uch as Teddy Roosevelt, for whom he arranged a
volf hunt in 1905. After seeing the stars on cavalry
fficers' insignia, he decided he deserved stars, too,
nd painted giant ones on the roof of his home
ear Cache, Oklahoma. The town of Quanah, the
ounty seat of Hardeman County, Texas, is named
n his honor. His war bonnet and lance are on
display at the excellent Panhandle-Plains Historical

Museum in the town of Canyon, Texas.

Finally, Quanah was buried in full chief's finery next to his famous mother, Cynthia Ann Parker, and little sister, Topsanah (Prairie Flower). You may visit the graves situated on Chief's Knoll in Fort Sill's old cemetery. His monument reads:

Resting here until day breaks and shadows fall and darkness disappears is Quanah Parker, last chief of the Comanche. Born—1852. Died—February 23, 1911.

The other leaders of the Uprising were not so lucky. Seventy-two of them were gathered up and shipped to prison at Fort Marion, St. Augustine, Florida, where many died from the unaccustomed humid environment. The prisoners became tourist attractions for curious whites, but finally the survivors were allowed to return to their families.

Colonel Ranald Mackenzie never did get his prized gray pacer back that the daring Quanah had stolen. After the great chief surrendered in 1875, he offered to return the horse but Mackenzie, perhaps in deference to the chief's courage and pride, declined to accept it.

Mackenzie had perhaps the most tragic ending of them all. He came from an illustrious family, won many honors in the Civil War, and would be wounded seven times in his long military career. His father, naval Commander Alexander Slidell Mackenzie, is remembered because of a controversial incident aboard his ship, the *U.S. Somers*, during which Slidell hanged three young sailors accused of mutiny. One of the three was Philip Spencer, son of our nation's Secretary of War. No ne would ever accuse a Mackenzie of wavering in he face of command! Herman Melville, author of *Moby Dick*, wrote a book about the Spencer mu- iny called *Billy Budd*.

Ranald Mackenzie would be commanding officer t Fort Sill after the Red River Uprising for two ears, then he would be sent to help corral the ndians who had killed Custer. By now, both he nd Nelson Miles were generals. In 1883, Macken- ie went insane and was confined to an asylum. He lied, forgotten, on January 19, 1889, at his sister's ome on Staten Island, New York and was buried t West Point.

Also buried at West Point earlier had been Ronald's reckless fellow officer, George Armstrong Custer. As Ranald Mackenzie rode across Texas in 874 to keep his date with destiny at the Palo Duro Canyon, Custer was leading an expedition earching for gold in the forbidden Black Hills. Less than two years later, the outraged Sioux and Cheyenne ended his career on June 25, 1876, at he Little Big Horn.

The Palo Duro is the largest state park in Texas nd it is worth a trip to that site about twenty niles southeast of Amarillo. When you stand at he bottom as I have done and look up at those teep walls, you can only marvel at the bravery of oth red and white men who were willing to risk heir lives on those crooked trails. Palo Duro was, ndeed, the last big Indian battle in Texas.

Two inventions would finally close down the pen ranges and change the west forever: barbed wire (we call it bob warh here in Oklahoma), patented in November of 1874, and the proliferation of the windmill, which would pump water and make arid stretches of land usable.

The giant herds of millions of buffalo would be wiped out in only a few short years. By 1889, a census found only 1,091 American buffalo left alive. The last wild buffalo in Oklahoma Territory, a "lonely old bull," was killed near Cold Spring, in Cimarron County, in October, 1890. It is ironic that when Teddy Roosevelt authorized the Wichita Wildlife Refuge in the Kiowas' old hunting grounds, buffalo had to be imported for it from the New York Zoological Society. Their descendents roam freely on the Refuge, which is near old Fort Sill and is a popular tourist attraction.

I've received many letters, curious about how I started writing. A fellow Oklahoman, the famous romance writer, Sara Orwig, discovered me in a graduate class she taught at Central State University in Edmond, Oklahoma. When I told her I was one of the few white people in the world who knew the whereabouts of the Cheyenne Sacred Medicine Arrows, she encouraged me to write about that subject and it became my best-seller, *Cheyenne Captive*. Some of the characters mentioned in the book you just finished—Captain Baker, the blond socialite, Summer Van Schuyler, and Shawn O'Bannion—were characters in that book.

That was followed by a sequel, *Cheyenne Princess*, about the rich and powerful Durango ranching family in the Texas Hill Country during the

Great Indian Outbreak of 1864. If you read that one, you may remember that I told you the true story of little Millie Durgan, the white child who was carried off during the Elm Creek Raid and adopted by the Kiowas. According to her grandchildren, little Millie was in the Palo Duro Canyon ten years later when Mackenzie made his famous raid and was one of those who walked all the way back to Fort Sill in the cold.

If you've read those two novels, you know how much research I do, even to the small details. It is a fact, according to old-timers, that longhorns always milled to the right, that Kiowas took one ear when they scalped a man, and yes, there was a terrible plague of grasshoppers on the plains during the summer of 1874.

Would you like to drive along the old Chisholm Trail? Start down in San Antonio, Texas on U.S. Highway 81, which roughly follows the Chisholm Trail, and drive it up across my state and on up into Kansas.

I love the Lone Star State second only to Oklahoma. It was down around Bandera, Texas that I heard the tale that became the basis for my next book.

It seems once upon a time, there was a blond wisecracking, arrogant gunslinger everyone called the Bandit. Now Bandit got into trouble one night in 1873 because he shot the Oklahoma Kid for cheating at cards in a tough Bandera saloon. He was forced to escape from the Kid's vengeful gang on a stolen horse.

Down below the border, he crossed the path of

505

an elegant Spanish *Senorita*, whose mother had been an American. This rich beauty, a distant cousin to the Texas Durangos, was on the run herself for personal reasons. Bandit, who had always lived by his wits and his gun, didn't expect to be mistaken for a missing wealthy heir. And she didn't expect to get carried off by the Indians. Neither one meant to get mixed up with Colonel Mackenzie's cavalry, who had sneaked across the Rio Grande without written orders to clean out the raiding Kickapoo, Mescalero Apache, and Lipan warriors.

This sheltered lady's name was Amethyst and she wore that jewel because it was just the color of her smoky lavender eyes. She'd never met a rough, tough-talking American gunslinger and he'd never met a real lady before. And in the magic of the Mescalero moonlight, they clashed like fire and gunpowder! First Bandit stole the lady's jewelry, then he stole her innocence.

And then *she* stole *his* heart!

Come along for romance, heart-stopping adventure, and Indians as the Bandit from Bandera meets the elegant lady in my next western tale. . . .

For further reading, here's just six of the forty-four reference books I used:

Bat Masterson, The Man & the Legend, by Robert K. DeArment

The Buffalo Soldiers, a Narrative of Negro Cavalry

in the West, by William H. Leckie

The Buffalo War, the History of the Red River Indian Uprising of 1874, by James L. Haley

The Comanches, the Destruction of a People, by T. R. Fehrenbach
Life of "Billy" Dixon, by Olive K. Dixon

Wild, Wooley and Wicked, the History of the Kansas Cow Towns and the Texas Cattle Trade, by Harry Sinclair Drago

And to all you readers who share my love for the old west . . .
    'long as I got a biscuit . . .

    Georgina Gentry

ROMANCE FROM GEORGINA GENTRY

COMANCHE COWBOY　　(0-8217-6211-7, $5.99/$7.50)
Cayenne McBride knows that Maverick Durango is the perfect guide to lead her back home to her father's Texas ranch. And when the fearless half-breed demands that she give up her innocence in exchange for his protection, Cayenne agrees, convinced she can keep her virtue intact . . . until she falls in love with him.

WARRIOR'S PRIZE　　(0-8217-5565-X, $5.99/$7.50)
After spending years in Boston at a ladies' academy, the Arapaho maiden Singing Wind returns to Colorado. Ahead of her lies a dangerous trek into the Rocky Mountains . . . where a magnificent warrior dares to battle for her body, her heart, and her precious love.

CHEYENNE SONG　　(0-8217-5844-6, $5.99/$7.50)
Kidnapped by the Cheyenne warrior Two Arrows, Glory Halstead faces her captor with the same pride and courage that have seen her through hardship and bitter scandal. But as they make the brutal journey through the harsh wilderness, Glory and Two Arrows discover passion as primal and unyielding as the land they are destined to tame. . . .

ROMANCE FROM FERN MICHAELS